Praise for Lorelei James's
Cowboy Take Me Away

"This is an amazing series, and *Cowboy Take Me Away* is spot-on in wrapping it up."
~ *USA TODAY*

"This is where it all started, where all of our sexy cowboys came from, and it's fascinating to see the similarities that the characters themselves see only too late."
~ *The Good, The Bad and The Unread*

"Lorelei James has single-handedly made cowboys a public sex figure with the Rough Riders series so I am sad to see the series come to an end. *Cowboy Take Me Away* marks the last book of the series and what a better way to end it with the couple that started it all."
~ *Fresh Fiction*

"I loved this book, it was an emotional read that had me laughing, crying and panting for more..."
~ *Under the Covers*

"I laughed, I cried, I got angry, I was sad. But through it all I couldn't help but fall even further in love with every single character in the series. Such a perfect ending to such a wonderful family saga."
~ *The Book Pushers*

D0920747

Look for these titles by
Lorelei James

Now Available:

Cowboy Take Me Away

Lorelei James

SAMHAIN
PUBLISHING

Samhain Publishing, Ltd.
11821 Mason Montgomery Road, 4B
Cincinnati, OH 45249
www.samhainpublishing.com

Cowboy Take Me Away
Copyright © 2014 by Lorelei James
Print ISBN: 978-1-61922-552-7
Digital ISBN: 978-1-61922-397-4

Cover by Scott Carpenter

First Samhain Publishing, Ltd. electronic publication: June 2014
First Samhain Publishing, Ltd. print publication: February 2015

Dedication

Thank you to my readers who've stuck with the Rough Riders series for the past seven years...it's been a journey I'll never forget and I'm so glad I got to share the McKay family with all of you.

Now sit back and enjoy this story of young love that grew and matured during life's joys, triumphs and sorrows, a love that stayed the course and is still going strong after fifty years...

Chapter One

Carson McKay ambled across the yard, his pace measured as he surveyed his western kingdom on the high plains of Wyoming. Everywhere he looked he saw proof that he'd poured a lifetime of blood and sweat into this ranching operation. His slow gait wasn't due to taking time to smell the freshly mown hay, but mostly from his hip replacement surgery two months ago.

According to his doctor, the years he'd spent in the saddle contributed to the problem.

But the hours he'd spent on horseback defined him. To him the only thing better than a good horse was a good woman—although his wife would argue that point.

Speak of the devil.

Carson squinted at the image on the horizon moving closer. Since his doctor had ordered him not to ride for six months, his wife had taken over exercising his mare, Sheridan. Although Sheridan was getting up there in years, the old gal still had a spark of feistiness. But her attempts to show Carolyn who was boss had ended when Caro started carrying a riding crop. Just the threat of it kept Sheridan in line.

He kept his gaze on the horse and rider burning up the pasture. As always, Carolyn was a sight to behold astride a horse. Despite the woman not being born to the saddle, she'd learned to ride after they'd married. She defined beauty and grace no matter what she did.

And he was a lucky, lucky man.

He raised his arm to greet her but she didn't acknowledge him. That's when he noticed Sheridan was tearing across the field at a full gallop like the hounds of hell nipped at her hooves.

Why the hell wasn't Caro reining her in? Carson shouted, "Pull back!" but they kept coming in hard and fast.

Carolyn angled forward, desperately reaching for...?

Shit. Looked like the bridle had broken and Carolyn had lost the reins. Sheridan's Achilles heel was if she got spooked, she wouldn't stop until she'd reached the safety of the barn.

Just then Sheridan's ass end skidded out and she came to an abrupt stop.

Everything happened in slow motion.

Somehow Carolyn managed to hang on...until Sheridan reared

up, throwing Carolyn off with the force of a bucking horse. In a blink of an eye, Carolyn hit the ground.

Despite the shooting pain in his hip, Carson started to run.

The panicked voice in his head screamed, *why the fuck wasn't she moving?* Even as logic dictated she'd probably gotten the wind knocked out of her.

Carolyn hadn't stirred by the time he'd reached the gate. Or by the time he'd closed it behind him.

His silent plea, *please let her be okay, please let her be okay,* repeated on a continual loop until he got close enough to see that she wasn't okay. Not at fucking all.

Carson fell to his knees in the dirt beside her. In shock, he couldn't do anything but stare.

Her eyes were closed, her face was slack, her arms and legs were akimbo. At least her neck didn't look broken.

It wasn't, was it? She was breathing, wasn't she?

Carolyn's phantom voice, urging him to stop gawking and do something, prompted him to press his fingers into the side of her throat, checking for a pulse.

Faint, but there.

Thank God.

He placed his hand on her chest. Shallow breaths, but he could feel her lungs laboring.

"Caro? Sugar, can you hear me?"

No response.

He pulled his phone out of the leather case hooked to his belt and dialed 911.

"Crook County dispatch. What's your emergency?"

"This is Carson McKay. My wife got thrown from her horse and she's not movin'." Dispatch asked a few more questions, which annoyed him and he cut the dispatcher off with, "Just send the goddamned ambulance." He rattled off his address by rote as he stroked Carolyn's cheek. Somehow he kept it together when he saw the blood seeping out from underneath her head. "And hurry." He ended the call.

Then he picked up her hand, pressing her palm to his face. When he heard Sheridan's distressed whinny, he forced himself to leave Carolyn's side.

Sheridan came right over when he whistled. He unsaddled her first and then removed the bridle. He didn't bother to check the bridle's malfunction; he just threw it beside the saddle and returned to his wife. She still hadn't moved.

"Stay with me, sugar." Needing to assure himself she was still alive, he rested his lips against the pulse point in her wrist, praying help arrived soon.

The ambulance took them straight to the Spearfish hospital.

Carson filled out the pages of paperwork—without complaint. But he did it by her bedside while the doctors assessed her. He observed from across the room when they shaved the back and top portion of her head. He kept one hand wrapped around the metal rail of her hospital bed when they wheeled her to X-ray. He reclaimed his chair when they returned to her room. He never said a word. He listened. He observed. He prayed.

A lot.

Then the medical personnel gently but firmly removed him from her room. He paced in the waiting room for family members of trauma patients.

Trauma.

One hour stretched into two, into three, into four. When the nurses asked if he wanted to speak with his family members gathered in the main waiting area, he said no.

At hour six, two young doctors, Dr. Vincent and Dr. McMillan, the neurologist from Rapid City, scooted two chairs in the waiting room across from him.

"Mr. McKay. As you're aware, your wife hadn't regained consciousness since the injury. We know from the X-rays that the blunt force trauma of impact with the ground has caused her brain to swell. We've taken no course of action yet simply because we needed to observe her these past few hours. Sometimes patients come out of these incidents on their own. That is not the case with Mrs. McKay. During our observation the swelling in her brain has increased considerably."

Considerably. Jesus. "Does she have brain damage?"

"Too soon to tell."

"So, what now? I just sit here and hope she opens her damn eyes?"

"No. With what we've observed we can detail our proposed treatment."

"Which is what?"

The doctors exchanged a look. Neither man seemed old enough to practice medicine and that didn't set Carson's mind at ease.

The dark-haired doctor spoke first. "We'd like to place your wife in a medically induced coma."

Carson opened his mouth to say *the fuck that is happening.*

"Hear us out. We've already given your wife an IV of Mannitol that reduces cranial pressure from swelling via drainage. But it hasn't worked as well as we expected. So Dr. Vincent—" he gestured to his red-haired colleague, "—your wife's anesthesiologist, has proposed using a sedative called Propofol, normally used during surgical procedures, to put Mrs. McKay into a temporary coma."

"Ain't she already in a coma?"

11

"Technically, yes. But putting her in a medically induced coma gives *us* control—not her body—and with the drugs we can bring her out of it at our discretion. It also allows time for the brain swelling to decrease, which hopefully will limit the amount of permanent damage to the brain tissue."

"This isn't an experimental procedure? You do this all the time?"

Dr. Vincent nodded. "It's the best possible way to deal with the altered metabolism in the brain that's caused by injury. With pharmaceuticals we can keep the brain from shutting down and maintain other important body functions. But that also means your wife will be on medication to keep her heart pumping and medication to keep her blood pressure steady. Plus we'll put her on a respirator to mechanically control her respiration rate."

Dr. McMillan rested his elbows on his knees and leaned closer. "We'll keep her chemically sedated only as long as we have to. There are other risk factors with this treatment. Pneumonia and blood clots being at the top of the list—muscle paralysis is a possibility too."

Carson's head spun. He had to remind himself they were talking about *Carolyn*, the woman he loved, being hooked up to all sorts of nasty machines with chemicals being pumped into her body.

"We've conferred with our colleagues at the neurosciences department at Denver General Hospital—getting a second and third opinion—and they've agreed our proposed treatment has the best chance of success. If you agree we'll need to get this underway immediately."

"Is there another option?"

"If we do nothing there's a chance—albeit an infinitesimal one—that her body will spontaneously heal."

"Or she might never..." Recover. Carson closed his eyes. No fucking way. He couldn't—he *wouldn't*—accept that.

"Is there someone else you need to discuss this with before making a decision?"

He thought of his kids. Carolyn was their mother, but she was his wife—his entire damn life—so this decision rested solely on his shoulders. "No. Go ahead and treat her." He swallowed hard, trying to dislodge the lump in his throat. "How long will she be...?"

"A minimum of five days. Most likely a week to ten days. Since she has an open wound on the back of her head and the brain used it as a conduit to try and dump excess fluid, the risk of infection is extremely high—much higher than normal. As soon as we have your consent, we'll dress the wound and put her in a sterile environment."

The docs exchanged another look.

"What aren't you tellin' me?"

"After she's hooked up to the respirator and EEG, we'll move her to ICU. Visitation will be limited."

His eyes narrowed. "How limited?"

"We'll allow...five minutes an hour."

"That time is allotted for other family members. Not for me, right?"

Dr. McMillan shook his head. "That includes you. To be completely honest, we're mandating no visitors for the first twenty-four hours as we're adjusting her medication levels and when the risk of infection is highest. I cannot emphasize this enough. Your wife is highly susceptible to infection."

"Make no mistake; I ain't leavin' her side even in the twenty-four hours she don't know I'm here. I may only get five minutes an hour with her, but the other fifty-five minutes of the day I will be right outside her door."

"Mr. McKay, I'm not sure—"

"I am one hundred percent sure that I will *not* leave my wife alone in this state. If that's gonna be a problem for you, say so now."

"As long as you know the only reason we're putting these restrictions on visitation is to protect her."

Carson nodded. Then he sighed and rubbed the back of his neck.

"Other questions?"

"Not right now, I'm still tryin' to get a handle on all this."

"Understood. It's a lot to process. We have work to do, to get the treatment started."

And he had nothing to do but sit around and wait.

"Mr. McKay?"

Carson glanced up at the nurse. "Yes?"

"Your wife has been moved to ICU."

He pushed to his feet. "Any change in her?"

"I don't know. I'm only passing along the information about the room change."

"Thank you."

The young nurse—her nametag read Lissa—waited for him by the door. "I'll take you to where your family is waiting."

Any time before when he'd had to deal with hospital visits or waiting around for any kind of news, he'd had Carolyn as his buffer. As his rock. When it'd been a prolonged wait, like when they were holed up waiting to hear word on Cam when he'd gone missing, they'd taken turns bolstering each other. Always in private. Not because he'd been ashamed of his fear and grief, but because he'd never had to explain it to her. Or she to him. They just understood each other on a level that defied logic.

Carson said, "It'd be a huge favor if you were there as I explain the situation because they ain't gonna like it."

"Of course."

They rode the elevator from the second floor to the main level.

How was he supposed to deal with his kids' upset over the

13

situation when he hadn't figured out a way to deal with his own yet? Especially when in doing the only thing he could to protect her, he'd piss off his kids and Carolyn's sister by enforcing the "no visitation" rule.

She'd do it for you. If your life was on the line you can bet your ass she'd bar the damn door without apology.

But his sweet, wonderful Carolyn could get away with that. His kids would just think he was being an asshole, because he'd been that man more than a few times over the years.

Carson paused outside the waiting room, taking stock of his family.

Cord paced. Colby sat in the corner with his head resting against the wall. Colt stared out the window. Cam studied the carpet. Carter twisted and untwisted a magazine between his hands. Keely prowled the perimeter. Carson's brother Charlie watched TV, his wife Vi by his side. Carolyn's sister Kimi sat beside his brother Cal.

Keely's head snapped up. Then she was throwing herself into his arms. "Daddy! What happened? No one will tell us anything besides Mama's been admitted. Please tell me she's okay. Please."

Carter pried Keely away from him. "Keels. We talked about this. Back off and let Dad talk."

A million expectant eyes bored into him.

Just spit it out.

"Carolyn was exercising Sheridan. Near as I can tell, something broke in the bridle. Then it spooked the horse and she reared, throwing your mother off. I saw it happen so I was able to get to her immediately. She was instantly knocked unconscious. I called an ambulance and we've been here ever since."

"Has she regained consciousness?" Cam asked.

"No. She's had X-rays and tests and they've been observing her. Her brain swelling increased to the critical stage." He paused. "She's in a medically induced coma. In doc speak that means they've taken control of her body with drugs and machines, tryin' to reduce swelling and circumvent permanent brain damage."

"For how long?"

"Five days to a week. Or longer."

He waited as that sunk in. And he could tell by the way they were gaping at him it'd take them time to process it—not that he had a handle on the situation. He was a mess.

Couldn't they see that?

No. They'd see him as they wanted to and he braced himself for the upcoming fight because guaranteed it'd be a doozie.

"You're sure that was the best choice? Or was that the only choice the doctors gave you?" Keely demanded. "Who did you have advising you on the medical procedure? Did you even call Doc Monroe?"

He loved his daughter, but it took every ounce of restraint not to snap at her. "Doc Monroe is not a neurologist. Dr. McMillan is. I agreed with their proposed treatment plan because it has the greatest chance of success."

"But I think—"

"I do not give a good goddamn what you think, Keely. I made the decision for my wife. And if you think I made that fuckin' decision lightly, think again."

Silence.

Carson inhaled a slow breath and tried to keep his tone even. "As long as you're all here, listen up because I'm gonna say it one time and there will be no arguin'. Carolyn has an open wound on the back of her head from the fall which was oozing brain fluid. The risk of infection is very high, especially in the comatose state she's in with all her primary body functions bein' maintained by chemicals or a machine. She's in ICU and there's no visitation for the first twenty-four hours."

"Then after that?"

"Extremely limited."

"For anyone?" Keely asked.

"For anyone."

"Even you?" Kimi asked.

"They're allotting me five minutes an hour. That's it. And since she's my wife, those five minutes are mine and mine alone."

He steeled himself against Kimi and Keely's recriminations, because the looks on their faces indicated they were about to let fly.

"That's not fair. You should give the rest of us a chance to—"

"If you say to say goodbye to her, Keely, so help me God I will have you goddamned banned from this hospital, do you understand? There will be no sayin' goodbye, no thinkin' this is the end for her because it is not." So much for keeping calm. "Carolyn needs positive thoughts. No cryin' or carryin' on. Which is why the two of you—" he pointed to Keely and Kimi, "—ain't getting anywhere near her when she's in this state."

"Dad. You are being completely unreasonable. If you'll just let us talk to the doctors—"

"No. I've already handled that."

"Without input from any of us," Cord said.

"Wasn't your decision to make." His gaze swept over his children. "Any of yours."

"We are here for you—for both of you. Don't shut us out."

Carson briefly closed his eyes. This had to be said—no matter how much it hurt them, or hurt him—so they understood he needed their obedience.

"I am shutting you out for a very good reason." He looked at Keely. "How often have your kids been sick in the last two months? Six, seven times?" He gestured to his sons. "Same with all of you. You have no idea what your kids have been exposed to. When you come here after

15

bein' around them, you'd be exposin' her to all of them germs and infections your kids have been exposed to. A simple infection could kill her. Kill her, do you understand me? I will not take that chance with her life."

"The doctor actually said that?" Kimi asked skeptically. "Because I want to hear that for myself."

Nurse Lissa stepped forward. "Legally the only person the doctor has to explain the seriousness of the risks to is Carson, Carolyn's husband. Just because you don't like what he's telling you doesn't mean he's making it up."

"So none of us can see her," Cord stated flatly.

"And it sounds like we won't be welcome in the ICU waiting room either, since we have contact with our germ-ridden kids," Colby added hotly.

Carson opened his mouth to tell them that wasn't true, but Cam cut him off.

"So will we have to hear updates on her condition second hand? Third hand? Just like I had to hear on the goddamned *scanner* that my mother was in the fuckin' ambulance on the way to the hospital?"

"Cam," Colt said sharply. "Shut it."

"He didn't call *any* of us," Cam snapped. "We've all been on the receiving end of his ass-chewing for not informing the family of things going on in our households. And then he doesn't let any of us know that Ma has had a serious accident? Then we had to sit out here for eight fuckin' *hours* before he came out to even talk to us? That's wrong, Dad. That's why we're pissed off."

"Now you're just throwing down an edict without discussing it with us. She's our mother," Keely said.

"And she is my *wife*. She's been everything to me since the moment I met her. So I won't stand here and argue that you have rights when they directly conflict with mine."

"This is exactly what we're talkin' about," Cord said. "You're in shock, you ain't thinkin' clearly and you need one of us to help you navigate all of this."

And he lost it. "Because I'm an idiot rancher who don't understand plain English. How about this for plain English: get out. All of you."

Arguing erupted. Kimi with Cal, the kids with each other.

Nurse Lissa pulled him aside. "Are you okay?"

"No. I haven't been okay since I saw her hit the ground and..." His voice broke and he took a second to compose himself. "Carolyn is the backbone, the heart and soul of this family. It is unimaginable to them that she's in this state. I know they all want to see it—see her—for themselves; only then will it become real."

The noise escalated and Keely whistled to get everyone's attention. "So what's it gonna be, Dad?"

"He already told you how it's gonna be," Vi said, inserting herself between him and his children. "And this is how you support your father? By discounting everything he's told you? I'm appalled by the selfishness I'm hearing."

"Vi—"

She held her hand up to Charlie. "None of you have been in this position and I hope none of you ever have to be." Vi pointed at Carson. "His wife is fighting for her life and you're fighting with him. Think on that. You all need to take a break. Go home to your families."

Everyone stared—or rather glared—at Vi but no one contradicted her.

"Ma is our family," Cord said. "We have a right to be here. We have a right to see her."

"What is it you want from me, Cord? A fight?" Carson said wearily. "Fine, I'll give you one. Get out. I don't need this bullshit or guilt from you—any of you—for doin' what the doctor ordered."

"You ready to throw all of us out? It's the six of us against you. We can have you declared as incapable of making medical decisions."

Jesus. That gouged deep into the heart of him.

"Whoa, don't include me in your petty threats," Colt said. "Dad made a decision, it don't make me any less worried about Ma, but I will respect it. So suck it up and don't fuckin' argue with him for once, Cord."

"Who's sucking up now?" Colby snapped. "You're just hopin' by takin' his side that Dad will let you see her and that's a crock of shit, Colt."

Carter stepped forward. "Listen to yourselves. This is how you want it to be? We take sides for or against Dad? You're idiots if you think acting like this is gonna change his mind. He has every right to ban you, especially with your selfish attitudes about what *your* rights are. His rights, when it comes to Mom, trump ours. Always have, always will, and we've always known that."

"Carter sided with Dad, big fuckin' surprise. Like Colt, he's expectin' it'll get him to the front of the line when Dad comes to his senses and lets us see our mother," Cam said.

"I won't change my mind," Carson said. "This ain't a negotiation. You don't get a vote. I've said my piece. And I'm really glad your mother can't hear you right now."

"She can't hear us because we're not even on the same floor with her!" Keely said.

Enough. "I'm done here." He looked at Cal. Then Charlie. Then Vi. "I'll let one of you know if there's news or a change in Carolyn's condition and you can pass the news on to them. I can't..."

Vi moved in and patted his arm. "Say no more. You do what you have to and we'll take care of this."

"How are we supposed to get through the next week not knowin' nothin'?" Kimi demanded.

Carson looked at her. Then his children. "You can survive without her for a week. Better that than puttin' her at risk and tryin' to survive without her for the rest of your lives."

He walked out.

Upon returning to the empty ICU waiting room, he slumped against the concrete wall. Even if he closed his eyes he'd still see the anger, bewilderment and resentment aimed his way. His kids' reactions were much worse than he imagined. He might've relented and reminded them that although they couldn't see Carolyn, they could visit him in the ICU waiting room. But their sense of entitlement and anger toward him—not at the horrible situation Carolyn was in—guaranteed he didn't want them around. He had enough emotional upheaval right now.

Nurse Lissa's voice broke through his misery. "They'll get over it. I've seen this happen dozens of times. Actually it's more the norm than you'd think. These situations bring out the worst in people. And it sucks when people who love each other lash out at each other out of fear."

He'd gone beyond fear. He was straight up terrified.

"We have a tiny ICU here—two rooms. Right now the other room is empty, which means you are the sole occupant of the waiting room. If you're truly worried that your children will overstep their bounds and try to press the visitation issue, then you need to make a list and only those on the list will have access."

"Then they'll have to go through eye-recognition software, thumbprint scanners and all that fancy tech stuff?"

She smiled. "Not quite. But the regular rules state no kids under twelve, one person at a time, no one who's been in a foreign country for the previous six months, no one with an autoimmune disease...and anyone on your blacklist."

"Lemme think on it."

"Good idea."

"Am I allowed to leave?"

"Of course. But anytime you leave this environment you take a chance. I understand that people have jobs and lives. But if you can put it on hold for the duration, that'd be best. And it'll also...prove to your kids that you're not just paying lip service to the infection threat."

"Thank you. I..." Carson didn't know what else to say.

"It's my job. I'll get everything set up so you can spend a few minutes with her before the twenty-four hour isolation starts. I'll be back in half an hour."

Okay. He could keep himself occupied for thirty minutes.

His thoughts bounced all around the place. But after he'd calmed a bit, one memory jumped front and center. The first time he saw her at the dancehall...

Chapter Two

Fifty years earlier...

"See that sexy blonde over there? I'm gonna marry her."

Calvin McKay squinted at his twin brother Carson as if he'd grown horns. "What the hell, Carse? Who you eyeballin' now?"

Carson pointed with his beer bottle to the woman leaning against the bar, trying to look as if she was a regular at this honky-tonk—and failing miserably. His eyes moved over her, slowly, so he didn't miss an inch of her curves.

Sweet Jesus she was sweet.

With her long sweep of honey-blonde hair, heart-shaped face and full lips outlined with red lipstick, she commanded a lustful second, third and fourth look from every man in the room.

So why was she still alone?

Because she's waiting for you.

"Who is she?" Cal asked.

"No idea. Never seen her around here before." Women who looked like her were in short supply in Wyoming.

"Maybe she's just passin' through," Cal offered.

"Then I'd better make my move and convince her to stay permanently." Carson drained his beer and adjusted his hat. "How do I look?"

"How much you been drinkin'? You never give a shit about that."

"It's never mattered before."

Cal shook his head. "Right. You're so full of it."

"I'm serious."

"Fine. You look like you're already imagining her in the cab of your truck with her skirt pushed up and her panties pushed down, while you're pounding away between her thighs."

"I ain't that obvious."

"No, you're much smoother than that, but admit that we McKays have the fuck 'em and leave 'em reputation because of you, Carson."

"Bullshit. You and Casper and now even Charlie think you're so much more discreet, but you ain't."

"Don't get your hopes up that she hasn't already been warned about your wild ways."

"Guess we'll see, won't we?" Carson tossed his bottle in the trash.

He kept his gaze on her as he cut through the crowd. He must've looked like a man on a mission because no one got in his way.

When he stood behind her, close enough to catch a whiff of hair spray and her perfume, his heart knocked in his chest. Even his damn knees knocked. Why did this feel so important?

She sensed him and turned. Her eyes, the pale blue color of a summer Wyoming sky, widened slightly. Those tempting red lips parted and she unconsciously backed up.

Carson took advantage of the opening and stepped up to the bar so their bodies were mere inches apart. "You're the most beautiful woman I've ever seen. How about we skip all this dating bullshit and just head straight to the altar?"

Her confused eyes roamed his face. "Did you just ask me to marry you?"

"Yep. So what d'ya say?"

"Does that line usually work for you, cowboy?"

He tucked a section of silky blonde hair behind her ear. "It ain't a line. And trust me; I've never said those words to another woman in my life."

"You don't even know my name."

"I'm guessing...Angel?"

"Angel? Really?"

"That's a sight better than my first thought, which was...Cherry."

Her face flushed pink.

He followed the delicate curve of her ear with the tip of his finger to the start of her jawline. "What is your name?"

"Carolyn."

"Carolyn," he repeated, and continued to feather his thumb across that soft skin. "Pretty." Something primal overtook him and he leaned closer, almost desperate to feel the press of her lips against his. Desperate to make his claim. He lowered his head and brushed his lips over hers just one time.

Her plump lips were unyielding and her whole body stiffened.

Determined to get the reaction he needed, he let his lips linger, silently coaxing her to open her mouth in invitation and accept his kiss. To accept him.

Her exhale bounced off his lips as a sexy sigh.

Oh yeah. You're all mine now.

Feeling like he'd won a battle, he eased back.

That's when she slugged him in the jaw.

If he hadn't been paying better attention she might've done some damage beyond the blow to his pride.

Fire flashed in her eyes. "Don't ever do that again," she snapped. "Walk your smarmy cowboy self away from me right now."

"That ain't gonna happen." *Ever.*

"Do you always go around kissing women without their permission?"

Carson cocked his head. "Never. I am sorry for takin' advantage of your sweet nature, but damn, sugar, I wanted a taste of you. Bein's we're gonna be married and all."

Her shoulders snapped back. "Sweet nature? After I *hit* you?"

Funny that she didn't balk at his married comment but being called sweet got her back up. "Beneath that right uppercut you are sweet, aren't you?"

"You don't know anything about me."

"So tell me all about you. Every last little thing."

"You are unbelievable."

"So are you." Carson couldn't tear his gaze away from her and had to ball his hands into fists to keep from touching her. "How often do you hang out in dancehalls?"

She rallied against his intensive stare, lifting that stubborn chin. "None of your business."

"But it is. I'm offerin' to watch your back—and your front—" he winked, "—if you wanna cut loose."

"What makes you think I need your help ripping it up? Maybe I could teach *you* a thing or two about getting wild."

"Doubtful." Without breaking eye contact, Carson swiped the drink sitting on the bar in front of her. "You a whiskey and Coke girl? Or a rum and Coke girl?" He put the lowball glass to his lips and drank. "Just as I thought. You're a Coke straight up girl. That's *real* wild."

"There's no rule that says I have to drink alcohol when I come to these dances."

"True. So if you're not here to drink, then you must be here to dance." Carson reached for her hand and threaded their fingers together. "Would you please dance with me, Carolyn?"

She bit her lip. To keep from lashing out at him again?

"Come on, sugar," he cajoled with a smile. "I asked all nice and polite this time."

"Does that dimpled smile get you anything you want?"

"I'm hopin' it does this time."

"I don't even know your name."

"It's Carson."

"Carson? Of course it's Carson," she muttered.

He bristled. "What's wrong with the name Carson?"

Her skeptical gaze snared his. "Nothing. It just sounds like the name of a steely-eyed gunslinger hero who rides in, saves the western town and makes all the ladies swoon."

He flashed her another grin. "Only woman I wanna see swoon in my arms is you. So you gonna dance with me?"

"One dance. But keep your lips and hands to yourself."

Just to be ornery, Carson lifted their joined hands and kissed her knuckles. Twice. "No promises on that." Then before she hesitated, he

21

led her to the dance floor.

As soon as he'd clasped her hand in his to start two-stepping, the band switched to the slow song "Make the World Go Away."

"Where are you from?" he asked.

She tilted her head back and challenged, "How do you know I'm not a local?"

Carson's gaze roved over her beautiful face, drinking in every feature. "A girl that looks like you ain't ever gonna go unnoticed around here. Or anywhere else, for that matter. So if you lived anywhere nearby I'da heard about you, bein's I'm local."

Her cheeks bloomed pink and she looked away without comment.

"Carolyn?" he prompted.

"You're pushy. And arrogant. And I should be pushing you away."

"But yet...you're not."

"I know." She paused. "It's confusing. I never..."

"Me either."

"You didn't even know what I planned to say, Carson."

"Yes, I do. Because sugar, I feel it too. And I've never felt it before either."

She muttered something about a silver tongue. Her soft body and sweet scent had him pulling her closer as they moved together to the music.

After a bit he said, "I'm still waitin'."

"For what?"

"For you to tell me where you live."

She studied the buttons on his shirt. "My family lives outside of Gillette."

"The way you said that makes it sound like your family lives there but you don't."

"Very perceptive, cowboy."

When she didn't elaborate, he stopped dancing and said, "Look at me."

Her gaze met his. "What?"

"Whatcha hidin'?"

"Nothing. Really." She briefly closed her eyes. "Okay, that's... I know I'm being vague."

"Why?" Damn, he hoped she wasn't married.

"Because guys tend to run or make jokes when I tell them the truth."

"You escape from prison or something?"

She laughed softly. "Sort of."

Carson knew he'd do anything to hear that happy sound again. "Tell me."

"I was born in Gillette. When I turned twelve my parents sent me to Catholic boarding school in Montana. I lived in the dorm during the school year. Then I spent half the summer with my aunt in Billings and the other half down here."

"So you escaped from a convent?"

"That makes a better story than I graduated. Maybe that's what I'll start telling people."

"Your folks sent you to Catholic school in hopes you'd become a nun?"

"Possibly. But it didn't take."

"Thank God for that."

She offered him a sad smile. "Now they're pinning their hopes on my little sister, who is still at St. Mary's."

Her tone was relieved and melancholy and embarrassed.

Carson wanted to press his lips to her forehead—so he did just that. Then he murmured, "I'm glad you're here, Carolyn."

She didn't protest or try to pull away. If anything, she tucked herself more closely into him.

Before he got too comfortable holding her, the music stopped and the band announced it was taking a break.

"Let's get some fresh air." Then with a firm grip on her hand, he wove through the crowd and out the side door.

Those long legs of hers had no problem keeping up with his strides. He didn't stop until they reached his pickup. "Hang on a second." The driver's side door squeaked when he opened it.

"Carson. I don't know if I'm—"

"Just getting a blanket so you don't get that pretty dress dirty."

She crossed her arms over her chest and stood back, watching as he draped the wool blanket over the metal tailgate.

"Hop on up and take a load off."

When she scooted up, he caught a glimpse of the pale flesh of her inner thigh before she tugged her skirt down.

His dick stirred.

Needing a distraction from the lust-filled thoughts running through his head, Carson pulled a flask out of his back pocket. "Want a snort of whiskey?"

She shook her head and started to swing her legs on the tailgate.

He swallowed a mouthful of booze and rested his backside against the corner of the box. "How'd you find out about this dance? Bein's you're not local?"

"My friend Beverly. She's the only person I've stayed friends with after I changed schools. As soon as we arrived she took off with her boyfriend."

"That wasn't very nice."

"I'm used to it."

"Then why come here with her?"

"Because sitting alone at a dancehall is still better than sitting at home."

"Alone. Right. I'll bet as soon as you showed that beautiful face here the guys followed you like lovesick calves and wouldn't leave you be."

She shrugged. "A few did."

"Bet I was the only one who proposed to you."

"Bet I wasn't the only woman who's ever taken a swing at you." Her blonde hair cascaded over her shoulder when she tilted her head to look at him. "I can't believe I fell for that *let's get married* line."

"Like I said, sugar. That wasn't a line." Carson moved in front of her, creating space for himself between her knees.

"So if I called your bluff?"

"I'd have you in the cab of my truck drivin' like a bat outta hell to the closest justice of the peace."

"Why me?" Her eyes searched his. "Every woman in that place had eyes on you. And you know exactly how good you look, so it's not like you're unaware of your appeal."

Carson stroked her cheek. "Do I appeal to you? Or should I get nekkid so you can inspect me before you commit to me for the rest of your life?"

Sweet Carolyn blushed but didn't drop her gaze. "Don't you think we should get to know each other before you start planning the honeymoon?"

"You're right. Ask me anything."

"What do you do around these parts? Go to college?"

"Do I *look* like a college boy?"

Her gaze moved over him from his western shirt, to his jeans and boots and back up to his hat. "Maybe you're a rodeo cowboy?"

His lips twisted. "Not hardly. I'm a rancher."

"Isn't that the same as being a cowboy?"

"Not even fuckin' close."

"Don't snap at me," she cautioned, "and watch your language."

The woman had a spark. "Sorry. Just because I raise cattle don't mean I'm dumb enough to get on the back of a bull or a bronc. There are plenty of risks depending on Mother Nature to make or break you in the cattle business."

"Doesn't seem like you like it all that much."

"Some days are better than others. I'm a third-generation rancher so it wasn't like I had much choice."

"If you did have a choice and could do something different, what would it be?"

He steered the conversation back on track. "The better question is how would *you* feel about bein' married to a rancher?"

That startled her. "What?"

"I am what I am, Carolyn. That ain't ever gonna change. It ain't an easy life—physically, mentally or emotionally. Some years we're flush; some years we're broke. Takin' care of the cattle and the land is always my first priority."

"So any woman you marry will have to understand she'll come second to cows and crops?"

He watched her eyes, so wise and yet so curious, which was a damn potent combination when she focused it on him. "Yeah."

"No wonder you're having a hard time finding a woman to sign on for that life."

"That's the thing. I haven't been lookin'." He twisted a strand of blonde silk around his finger. "Then I saw you."

"And...what? You thought I looked like I'd be good with cattle? Or that I'd be a good cook? Or I wouldn't mind living hand to mouth? Or I had wide enough hips to birth a bunch of ranch hands? That makes no sense."

"Now you're getting it. It doesn't make a lick of sense that when I saw you standing up at the bar I imagined wakin' up to you every morning for the rest of my life."

Her jaw nearly hit the ground. Then she managed, "You did?"

"Umm-hmm." He tickled her lips with the end of her hair. "How old are you?"

"I'll be nineteen this summer. How old are you?" she asked.

Old enough to know better. "Twenty-four." He dropped his hand and retreated.

Carolyn snatched his forearm, holding him in place. "Don't."

"Don't what?"

"Don't look at me with regret."

"I wasn't."

"Yes, you were." Her fingers tightened on his arm. "Besides, I liked the way you were looking at me before you asked how old I was."

Definitely a spark there. "And how was that?"

"Like it didn't matter. Like you wanted to strip me bare and go wild on me."

"Is that what you want me to do?"

She bit her lip. "I don't know."

Carson angled his head closer to hers. "Ever been nekkid with a man, sugar?"

"No." She paused. "I've thought about it." Her wide blue eyes locked on his. "I've thought about it a lot more since I met you."

Holy hell this woman was killing him. She had no idea how sexy the combination of bold, innocent and honest was to a man like him. "Oh yeah?" He slid his hand up her arm and across her shoulder to cup her neck. "You gonna take another swing at me if I take this pretty mouth the way I want to?"

She lowered her lashes and stared at his lips.

Enough answer for him.

Carson tipped her head back and fused his mouth to hers.

This time she parted her lips and her breath exploded in his mouth. Her tongue sought his, boldly stroking and twining around his.

Giving him a complete taste of her. She used her teeth to nip, her tongue to explore. Her lips were soft and yielding, then firm and demanding.

The kiss blew his mind. While there was no denying their attraction, this immediate passion between them caught him off guard. As did her complete abandonment to it.

He lifted her off the tailgate and pressed her against the rear quarter panel, keeping one arm behind her back and the other hand curled at the nape of her neck.

Carolyn's hands clutched his shirt as she tried to pull him closer.

Finally, he had to take a breath that wasn't saturated with her taste and her scent. He moved his lips from the corner of her mouth down to the arch of her neck. "Damn," he panted against her throat.

"Are you okay?"

He dragged an openmouthed kiss up the smooth section of skin, stopping at her ear. "No, I'm not okay. I'm wantin' way more than a kiss, so I'm thinkin' we should just go ahead, hop in the truck and find us someone who'll marry us tonight."

She laughed softly. Then she planted kisses along his jaw, her breath whispering across his damp flesh, eliciting his shiver.

He spun them and leaned his back against the truck, wanting her soft curves pressing into him, wanting his hands on her luscious ass.

A wolf whistle rent the air. "Take it inside the truck, McKay," someone shouted.

Carson scowled at his drinking buddy. "Move along, Tucker."

"Looks like you're the one who's movin' pretty fast."

Assholes.

"McKay?" she repeated. "Your last name is McKay?"

"Yeah. Why?"

Carolyn stepped back. "I don't believe this."

"I don't know what you've heard, but I can explain—"

"You can't."

He followed her, hating the wariness that had replaced the heat in her eyes. "At least let me try."

"Ask me my last name."

Annoyed by the abrupt change in her, he said, "Fine, Carolyn, what's your last name?"

"West."

That stopped him. "What?"

"I'm Carolyn West."

"You're kiddin', right?"

She shook her head. "My dad is Elijah—Eli—West."

Carson had heard that name several times, always attached to a vile string of curses and a rant the likes of which he'd never heard from his closemouthed father. He'd warned his sons to stay far away from all members of the West family. He and his brothers tried to ask questions, but the old man had shut them down without explaining his reasons. Carson had put it out of his mind.

Then a few years ago he'd crossed paths with Harland West, proudly proclaiming himself Eli West's oldest son. The loud mouth started talking shit about the "mighty McKays" in the feed store in Moorcroft. Most of what the man shouted at him made zero sense—he'd blathered on about lies, bribes, blood money and theft—but Carson wasn't about to let it slide. They'd ended up in a knock-down, drag-out fight that left both of them bleeding and pissed off.

A year or so later, he'd run afoul of Darren West at Brass Tacks, a bar in the Wests' neck of the woods. Words were exchanged, fists went flying and they were both arrested for drunk and disorderly.

That hadn't gone over well with Jed McKay.

After the ass chewing on a whole new level, Carson became suspicious of why his father refused to talk about the past issues between the McKays and the Wests. He didn't give a damn if his grandfather—who he'd never met—had wronged the West patriarch or vice versa. He suspected even his father wasn't sure what'd gone down years ago, which made no sense as to why the man held a grudge.

But those West assholes held a grudge too.

Pissed him off that they used their family's history of bad blood as an excuse to come after the McKays now. That changed Carson's I-don't-give-a-damn attitude. He'd jumped into the fray with both boots. So mention of a younger West sister hadn't come up when Carson had been trying to beat the fuck out of Harland and Darren West.

Carolyn's brothers.

Fuck.

The fact Carson wanted Carolyn West with every breath in his body wouldn't go over well with his father either.

And he didn't give a damn.

Carolyn said, "I have to go."

His gaze flipped to her. "Don't leave. Let's talk about it."

"There's nothing to say—"

"You really runnin' away from me because my last name is McKay?"

"Why else would I..." That strong chin went up a notch and she crossed her arms over a pair of impressive breasts. "I'm not running away from you, Carson McKay."

"Prove it."

"How? By coming over there and kissing you?"

Carson grinned. "Not what I was gonna suggest, but sugar, I'll take more of them sweet and hot kisses anytime you wanna give them to me."

"What was your suggestion?"

"Meet me here tomorrow night."

"I can't."

"See? Runnin' from me."

"No, I have family obligations."

He raised an eyebrow. "On a Friday night?"

"Not everyone can go out and tear it up every night of the week like wild-living cowboys—excuse me—*ranchers*," she retorted.

Carson started toward her. "Whatcha gonna be doin' tomorrow night? Got a date?"

"None of your business."

The thought of some other guy picking her up, touching her, talking to her, tasting her sweet lips made him growl, "Tell me."

"Stop pestering me about this."

"Not a chance." By the time he reached her, she'd started studying her shoes. He tipped her chin up. "Talk to me. No bullshit."

"I'm afraid you'll laugh."

"Never."

"My dad gets paid on Fridays. He gives me money and I buy groceries for the week. So my Friday night is spent at the grocery store. Exciting, huh?"

"Your dad really is tryin' to turn you into a nun, isn't he?"

"Because I'm not out at the bars on a Friday night?"

"Because he's got you believin' that a beautiful, single woman shouldn't mind grocery shopping alone on a Friday night."

Carolyn closed her eyes. "You don't understand."

"I think I do. You're expected to take care of your family when you're home. No shame in steppin' up to your responsibilities and takin' pride in what you do. But the fact you're here tonight shows me you've carved out at least a little free time." He stroked her cheek. "And I want you to spend that free time with me."

"Carson—"

"Think on it. Please."

He didn't move until she gave him a grudging, "Okay."

Then he forced himself to walk away from her. He'd give her a week to make a decision. After that, he was going after her.

"Mr. McKay?"

He'd been so deep in the memory he hadn't heard Nurse Lissa approach. "Yes?"

"Let's get you suited up." As she helped him dress she detailed the protective outwear he'd have to put on every time, even for a five minute visit.

"You'll have a few minutes alone with your wife before the twenty-four-hour isolation begins."

Carson approached the bed, his stomach in knots, his heart so heavy he swore that it was what made his feet move so slowly and not this hazardous materials suit he wore.

He clasped her hand in both of his, hating how cold her skin was, hating the layer of latex between them. His gaze encompassed her beautiful face. He wanted to kiss her. Or at least put his lips on her forehead and bathe his lungs in her scent. Or press his mouth to the side of her throat, hoping to feel that familiar way her pulse leapt whenever he kissed her there—even after almost fifty years together.

But he settled for a light stroke on her cheek. "Sugar, don't leave me. I can't live without you—I ain't even gonna try." Emotion choked him so his words were barely above a whisper. But she needed to hear him, because he had no doubt she *could* hear him. The plastic face shield covering the lower half of his face required him to speak louder. "I'm here. Right here, right beside you where I've always been and where I'm always gonna be. I ain't goin' nowhere. I love you. Come back to me. Please."

He forced himself to move before his tears fell. Wouldn't want to give her an infection. He probably had rust in his tear ducts.

He couldn't remember the last time he'd cried.

Chapter Three
Carolyn

Come back to me. Please.
God. The man sounded so forlorn.
Why? Carson McKay never sounded like that.
Carson, honey, I'm right here.
Wait. Where was here? Where was she?
And why couldn't she see anything?
Wake up, wake up, wake up. You're in a dream.
But her eyes wouldn't open.
Come back to me. Please.
Come back...from this dream?
She listened but couldn't hear his voice.
Carson?
A loud click echoed.
Was that the sound of a door closing? Where was it coming from?
Carolyn followed the sound and floated down the pathways of her mind. Doors of all sizes loomed before her.
One of these doors had to lead back to her current reality. She shouldn't have retreated when they started jamming tubes in her nose and throat. But it was loud and painful—surely she wasn't dead if she could still feel pain?—and she'd hidden in the shadows of her mind.
But now, the deeper into her mind she traveled, the lighter it'd become.
So many doors.
Then she noticed one door was ajar.
Maybe it was the exit? Could she escape her subconscious?
The door made no noise when she opened it.
She found herself in her mother's bedroom, sucked back in time to early summer the year she'd graduated from high school.
The morning after the night she'd met Carson McKay...

"Don't hover in the doorway, child, come in." Her mother scooted over and patted the bed. "Sit. Tell me about the dance last night."
Carolyn settled on the twin bed and reached for her mother's

hand. The arthritis had gotten so bad in the last couple of years her fingers were claw-like and almost useless. It killed her to see her mother bedridden, to see the listlessness in her eyes from the amount of medicine she took to deal with the pain.

But her stoic mother wouldn't complain.

"*Liebchen,*" she said softly. "Talk to me."

Liebchen. Her mother had always called Carolyn her little sweetheart—it was one of the few German words her mother still used.

She forced a smile. "Beverly took off with Michael about half an hour after we got there."

Her mother clucked her tongue. "That girl is fast. Michael will get what he wants from her and move on."

"Oh, I don't know. He leaves for basic training at the end of the summer and as soon as he's done they're getting married."

"Ach. She's too young." She shifted on the bed. "Did Beverly introduce you to anyone?"

The image of Carson McKay's perfect face flashed in her mind and she felt her cheeks heat. His good looks aside, he was so much...more than the boys she'd gone to school with. The only trace of boyishness in him was in that dimpled smile and the devilry twinkling in his dark blue eyes. The rest of him was all man—wide shoulders, broad chest, strong arms, rough-skinned hands. An earthy mix of sun and soil and soap emanated from him; an irresistible musk that tempted her to rest her face in the crook of his neck and just breathe him in.

"You did meet someone."

Carolyn blushed.

"What's his name?"

"Carson. He's a little sure of himself, but that's probably because he's so good-looking."

"Did he ask to see you again?"

She finally met her mother's gaze. "Yes. But I kind of ran off after..."

Her mother's brown eyes sharpened. "Did he try something with you?"

"No. We were outside just talking—" *you'll go to hell for lying,* "—and someone shouted to get his attention. That's when I learned his last name is McKay."

Silence.

Carolyn looked down as she traced the frayed ends of the yarn ties holding the eyelet and satin quilt together.

The air seemed to stretch so thin she had a hard time breathing. Finally, she blurted, "But don't worry. I'll stay away from him."

"He knows...?"

"That my father is Elijah West? Yes."

"How were things between you before you learned each other's last names?"

She smiled, remembering the man's audacity. "Carson told me he was gonna marry me."

Her mother raised both eyebrows. "You mean he asked to marry you?"

"No. He said I was the most beautiful woman he'd ever seen and we oughta skip all the dating stuff and get married." She suspected he'd only been half kidding. Although Carson had seemed ready to run when she'd told him she was eighteen. But that kiss, that glorious kiss had changed his mind.

It'd changed everything.

She'd kissed a few boys over the years. Even if she'd made out with a hundred guys nothing could've prepared her for kissing a man like Carson McKay. Nothing. Carson was heat and passion. When he'd pressed his hard body against hers? She finally understood Beverly's claim about need overtaking reason.

"*Liebchen.*"

Carolyn's head snapped up guiltily. "Sorry. I know—"

"I think you'd like to get to know him better."

"I can't."

"Nonsense."

Shocked, she stammered, "B-but—"

"Whatever is between your father and Carson's father is their issue. Not yours. Not Carson's. You're an adult. You're allowed to make your own decisions. If you want to spend time with Carson? That is your business."

"And what happens when Dad finds out? He might kick me out."

"I won't let that happen. I promise."

Her mother had never stood up to her father. If Carolyn pursued something with Carson McKay she'd be totally on her own, with no support.

Like that'd be anything new.

Carolyn managed a fake smile. "I've found some patterns I'd like your opinion on."

"Clothes for you?"

"Yes."

"New clothes you can wear on your dates with Carson McKay?" her mom asked with a sly smile.

"Mom. Give it up."

"Never. Now show me what you're working with."

Late Saturday afternoon, Marshall, Stuart and Thomas, Carolyn's three brothers who still lived at home, traipsed into the kitchen.

"I love it when you're home for the summer," Thomas said, sniffing the air. "We get decent meals for a change."

Marshall and Stuart each punched him in the arm.

"Ouch! I'm only telling the truth."

"Truth is, you can't cook worth shit, Thomas, so it's worse for us when it's *your* night to cook." Marshall lifted the lid on the pot on the stove. "Sausage and cabbage smells good, sis."

"It's done. Wash up and we'll eat."

Stuart sidled up beside her. "Has Mom eaten yet?"

"She was hungry earlier so I sat with her while she ate. She's resting."

He squeezed her shoulders. "Thanks."

"Does she ever come to the table?"

"Nope. She eats in her room or she doesn't eat. That's her choice, not ours."

Marshall snatched two slices of bread off the cutting board. "Ma especially doesn't eat when Thomas cooks."

"I told you guys I'd rather be on dish duty every night. But that is another bonus of having our sister home. She cooks *and* cleans up."

None of them disputed Thomas's statement. As much as she loved her brothers, the instant she'd stepped foot in the house, they'd abandoned their regular duties and she'd become cook, cleaner, gardener, laundress and parental caretaker.

Carolyn took her usual seat at the table and looked at each of her brothers until they set down their utensils and bowed their heads in prayer. "Thank you, Lord, for the bounty you've given us. Amen."

After they crossed themselves and a chorus of *amens*, they dug in. She dished herself a plate. "Where is Dad, anyway?"

"At Harland's."

Their oldest brother and his wife Sonia lived on the small parcel of land that used to be the West Ranch. Since her father had no interest in ranching—he'd worked in the coal mine in Gillette her entire life—he'd passed the land on to his oldest son as soon as Harland was of age.

Supper was a fairly silent affair as her brothers were too busy stuffing their faces to bother with conversation.

Thomas pushed his plate away first. "Good meal, sis."

"You're welcome."

He grinned and said, "Thanks. So, got any plans for tonight?"

"Nothing after doing the dishes. Why?"

"There's a ballgame in Hulett. I'm meeting my buddy Randy there and then we talked about hitting Dusty's afterward. Guess there's a decent band tonight."

"Randy...is he your short friend with the big mouth?"

Thomas snorted. "That's Andy. Randy went to college on a partial baseball scholarship. He's home for the summer. He'd really like to meet you."

Since she'd lived in Montana the last six school years, she'd only stayed in contact with Beverly and she didn't know Thomas's friends.

"I'll go as long as you promise you won't ditch me."

"I almost wish I was goin' along tonight," Marshall said. "But I'll probably be heading to work about the time you two roll in."

"Sneak in," Stuart corrected. "Even when Dad will be pretty drunk after bein' with Harland, you don't want him to know what time you got home."

"Not a problem for me since I'm sleeping in the sun porch. I can climb through the window," Carolyn said. Sleeping in the sun porch didn't bother her. The small space had been tacked on the back of the house as an afterthought, and the poor insulation meant the room stayed cool at night.

"How long will it take you to get ready?" Thomas asked.

Her gaze swept the plates and pots and pans. "Half an hour to do the dishes and fifteen minutes to change."

"Leave the dishes tonight. I'll help you do them in the morning."

Carolyn snapped him with a dishtowel. "Now I know you're meeting a girl if you make that promise to get me moving."

Thomas blushed. "Just go get ready."

She styled her hair in long blonde waves. She slipped on a sleeveless plain white button-up blouse and added a snug-fitting baby blue cardigan. Feeling daring, she tugged on the pair of blue jeans her friend Cathy had given her. Cathy's wealthy grandparents lived in Chicago and owned a clothing company so Cathy had scads of fashionable clothing that she loved to share.

A quick brush of powder, thick black eyeliner and a couple of passes of mascara made her eyes look more dramatic. She finished off with a coat of red lipstick.

She tucked her money, lipstick and ID in her back pocket—how wonderful was it not to have to carry a purse?—before she slipped on her heels.

Thomas leaned against the Pontiac he'd inherited from Darren. His eyes went wide. "Jesus Christ, Carolyn, what the hell are you wearing?"

"Language," she snapped. Her brothers cursed like sailors. It drove her crazy.

"You can't wear pants. People will think you're a guy."

Carolyn tossed her hair and stuck out her chest. "Really? *I* look like a man? This Randy you're introducing me to is into guys?"

"Jes—jeez, that's disgusting and beside the point. Now go change."

"No. This is perfectly acceptable, completely fashionable attire to wear to a ballgame. And besides, I wore clothing like this all the time in Montana," she lied.

"Right. I can't see the nuns or the priests being onboard letting you prance around in that get-up, let alone Aunt Hulda." He shook his finger at her. "You get any shi—crap about that outfit? Don't come crying to me, wanting to go home. You're stuck." He climbed in the car and slammed the door.

As soon as they hit the paved road, Carolyn cranked up the radio. She was switching back and forth between the county station and the rock and roll station, singing along, when Thomas reached over and turned the music down.

"If you didn't like my singing you should've said so."

Thomas shook his head. "You were born with an angel's voice, sis. I turned it off because I need to talk to you about something."

"Okay." She had a warning flutter in her belly because Thomas was never serious.

"You've been back here for three weeks. Mom and Dad expect you to stay the summer but have you given any thought as to what you might do come September?"

She picked at the tiny balls of fuzz on her sweater and dropped them in the ashtray. "No. I mean yes, I've thought about it but I don't know what I'm supposed to do. Mom needs someone to take care of her; she has for years, so I'll probably—"

"No, Carolyn. I know you want to help, but you didn't go away to school just to come back here and become Mom's sole caretaker after you graduated."

She turned sideways in her seat and gaped at him. Then why did he—and her brothers—expect her to do everything for their mother? "But—"

"I've decided to go to college," Thomas blurted out. "I want a job where I don't have dirt on my collar and under my fingernails every damn day. So I'm moving to Denver with Randy at the end of the summer."

"How will you afford that?"

"I've been saving money since I scored that first job at Woolworth's. You still considering taking up your friend's offer to move to Chicago?"

She shouldn't have mentioned that to her nosy brother. Now he'd nag her even more. "I'm not sure if Cathy was serious or just being nice. And I don't know that I'm cut out for life in the big city."

"Do me a favor—don't tell Cathy no just yet. By the end of the summer you'll probably be more than ready to get out of Wyoming."

"Is that why you're leaving here?"

Thomas didn't speak until he'd parked in the lot behind the ball field. Even then he stared straight ahead instead of meeting her gaze. "There's no place for me here. Harland is trying to run a ranch. Darren is helping his father-in-law in his sheep business. Marshall has a great job with the railroad. Stuart is happy as a carpenter. I only took the job at the coal mine after I graduated from high school because I didn't have other options. Now I do."

As much as she hated the thought of Thomas not being around

every day to annoy her, she understood his need to set himself apart. "Have you said anything to anyone about your plans?"

He shook his head. "Not until I get the final application approval paperwork from the college."

"Well...I can probably keep that information to myself, but it'll cost you."

Thomas's soft gaze sharpened. "Cost me what?"

Carolyn poked him in the chest. "I don't want to be stuck doing all the dishes all summer. You help me and I'll keep quiet."

Thomas twisted her finger, like he did when they were kids. "Fine, you little extortionist. Let's watch the ballgame."

The baseball game was boring. So boring Carolyn found herself yawning a couple of times.

Thomas's friend Randy seemed decent, he was definitely nice looking and had the build of an athlete, but he stayed focused on the game as if it was the World Series. He sat next to her and every once in a while he'd pat her leg. His touch didn't cause that fluttery feeling in her stomach like when Carson McKay had gently stroked her face. A shiver rolled through her, thinking about Carson's rough-tipped fingers gliding across her skin.

"You cold?" Randy asked.

No. Just imagining another man's touch.

She shook her head.

"It'll be plenty hot at Dusty's tonight," Thomas said.

The game finally ended and all three of them crammed into the front seat of Thomas's car. Since she had to straddle the hump in the center, her right thigh pressed against Randy's left leg, and he considered that a sign she wanted to get closer. He stretched his arm across the back of the seat and curled his hand over her shoulder.

Randy said, "Who all are we meeting here?"

"Everyone that went to Buddy's last weekend."

"Including Millie?"

Thomas tensed beside her. "Probably."

Randy leaned in to whisper, "Your brother's got it bad for her. I imagine the two of them will sneak off somewhere to be alone, so I'm glad you're with me tonight."

Carolyn didn't like the way Randy assumed they were together. She definitely didn't like the way he placed his wet lips directly on her ear. She discreetly scooted closer to Thomas.

"We're here," Thomas announced.

The bar looked packed to capacity. She paid the cover charge—over Randy's objections—and immediately headed for the bar. She recognized a few people from the dancehall the other night. Several women gave her outfit a sneering once-over or laughed.

They're just a bunch of Wyoming hillbillies and wouldn't know trendy clothes if they bit them on the behind, she repeated to herself as she waited for her Coke. She decided to practice her wallflower impression when she heard a familiar shriek behind her.

"Carolyn West, I didn't know you'd be here!"

She faced Beverly. "It was a last-minute thing."

"Good Lord, what are you wearing?"

Carolyn cocked her hand on her hip. "Jeans. They're the height of fashion every place besides backwards Wyoming," she said very loudly.

Beverly hooked her arm through Carolyn's. "I gotta get me some of them. So who are you here with?"

"Thomas and a friend of his."

"Which friend?"

"Randy somebody."

"Randy Peeler?" she said with a gasp. "He is so dreamy."

Not as dreamy as Carson McKay.

Seemed she'd set him up as the gold standard.

"But watch Randy," Beverly warned. "Evidently he uses those fast hands for more than just pitching, if you know what I mean."

"I already figured that out. But thanks. Where's Mike?"

"Talking to some guys who are here on leave. I'm glad you showed up."

They gossiped for the next half hour. Mike returned and claimed Beverly for a dance. Just as Carolyn spied the perfect hiding spot, Randy loomed over her.

"There you are. Let's dance."

Carolyn barely had time to set her drink down before Randy was dragging her onto the dance floor. He pulled her flush to his body and would've tried to slip his knee between hers if she hadn't clamped her legs shut.

Randy laughed. "There it is."

"There what is?"

"The Catholic school upbringing. Loosen up."

Her brother actually liked this creep? She managed a fake smile. "I'd be a lot looser if you quit holding me so tightly."

She was ready to escape after one dance with Randy, but he kept blathering on. When the third song started, she begged to take a break. He kept his hand in the small of her back as he escorted her off the dance floor, acting like they were together.

"Would you like a drink?"

"Another Coke would be good."

He wrinkled his nose. "So you don't drink alcohol either?"

Either? Was he about to make another crack about her being raised in a convent? "No."

"Fine. I'll be back."

Randy situated himself so close to her she had to hold her drink in her left hand because she couldn't move her right arm.

She studied the crowd, hoping her brother or Beverly would rescue her from rambling Randy. When he said, "I like you, Caroline, you're a good listener," she'd had enough. The idiot didn't even know her name. "Will you excuse me?"

"The bathrooms are down the far hallway," he said helpfully.

But Carolyn left through the front door. Ignoring the lewd stares and drunken comments, she cut around the side of the building where it was dark and blessedly free of people.

She paced, wishing she hadn't come, wondering how long she'd be stuck with Randy while Thomas messed around with that Millie person, who he hadn't even bothered to introduce her to.

Maybe she should just go wait in the car.

Unsure what to do, she continued to pace.

"You'll wear out them pretty shoes if you keep doin' that, sugar."

Carolyn whirled around.

Carson McKay leaned against the side of the building, his white shirt a beacon in the darkness. As she walked toward him, she noticed the red glow of a cigarette in his hand as he brought it to his mouth and puffed.

"I didn't know you smoked."

He exhaled and dropped the butt to the ground, extinguishing it with his boot. "There's lots you don't know about me. So did your family fill you in on what bastards the McKays are?"

"No."

"Didja even tell them you were with me? Or did you keep that to yourself because you were embarrassed?"

"Did you tell your family that you asked a West to marry you?" she volleyed back.

Carson studied her. Or at least she thought he did; she couldn't read his eyes beneath the brim of his hat. He pulled his flask out of his pocket and drank. But he didn't say a word.

As much as she didn't like Randy's constant chatter, Carson's silence wasn't any better. She backed up. "See you around, Carson." She turned, intending to head back to the parking lot.

"Your butt looks good in pants."

She froze. Then she faced him. "Excuse me?"

"You heard me. So keep walkin' away from me real slow like, so I can enjoy the view."

Carolyn erased the distance between them in six angry steps. "I oughta hit you again."

"I don't recommend you try it." He lifted his head and met her gaze—the heat in his eyes should've sent her running. "I thought maybe I'd exaggerated how beautiful you are, especially after I learned your last name. But I'm standin' here, starin' at you like a fool because your beauty struck me dumb for the second time."

The thing was? The man was completely sincere. He watched her with a sort of awe she found very appealing. "That makes up for the butt comment."

He smiled that full out dimpled grin and her belly fluttered. "Oh, I meant every word of that, too."

Being this close to him...didn't seem close enough.

Hold on, sister. You don't know this man.

But I want to know him.

"Carson. What are we doing?"

"I don't know about you, but when I saw you talkin' with that guy and dancin' close with him, I wanted to break his face so I had to get the hell outta there."

That matter of fact, almost possessive tone sent a spike of heat through her. "If you want to hit him, aim for the jaw. Maybe that'll shut him up."

He smiled and reached for her hand. "That bad?"

"The worst. My brother Thomas invited me to hang out tonight and then ditched me with him."

"Getting ditched seems to be a habit of yours."

"But I'm the one doing the ditching now. He's inside. I'm not."

His fingers drifted across her knuckles. "Didn't seem like you wanted to ditch him during the two songs you danced together."

"You saw that?"

"Haven't been able to keep my eyes off you from the moment you walked in."

"I didn't know you'd be here."

"Had nothin' better to do. I was tryin' to take my mind off this beautiful blonde I met night before last."

"Were you looking for another woman to distract you?"

"Maybe." Carson brought her hand to his mouth and kissed it. "Would me bein' with another woman bother you?"

"Yes, it would bother me."

He tugged her and she fell against his body. "Then maybe *you* oughta be my woman and I'll only be with you."

Carolyn tilted her head back to say yes, and found Carson's mouth descending on hers. He tasted so good, so male. The trace of tobacco and whiskey just made the kiss more intoxicating.

Then his hands were sliding around her hips and down to her behind. She felt the imprint of every one of his fingers pressing into her flesh as he palmed her cheeks.

Carson changed the angle of the kiss, taking it even deeper. She followed his lead, letting her fingers curl into his hard pectoral and wrapping her other hand around the back of his strong neck.

His scent, his taste, his touch, if she lived to be a hundred she'd never forget this moment.

She made a small protest when he finally slowed the kiss. But he didn't let go of her. "Carson, I don't—"

"Ssh, just let yourself settle."

How did he know? Was he feeling just as untethered as she was?

Those strong hands slid back up to her hips. "You are the very definition of temptation."

"Sorry."

"Don't be." He rubbed his lips across her hairline at the top of her forehead. "So you really didn't tell your family about me?"

"It's none of their business."

"I like your feisty side."

"Did you say anything to your family?"

"Just to my brother Cal. He thinks I'm crazy."

She frowned.

He smooched her mouth. "Let's talk about something else."

"Like?"

Carson pushed her hair over her shoulder. "Like when are you comin' home with me."

Somehow she kept her jaw from hitting the ground. She'd told him about her life so he had to know she had zero experience...

Wait a second. Maybe that's why he was interested in her. He "collected cherries" as her friend Cathy called it. She stepped back. Way back. "I...I have to go." Then she turned and fled.

Carolyn didn't get far. A strong hand circled her arm and jerked her around.

Carson bent down until they were nose to nose. "Why the hell did you run again?"

"Because I'm not going home with you!"

"Sweet Christ, woman, don't you think I fuckin' know that?"

"Don't swear at me," she snapped.

He struggled for composure. "Caro. Sugar. I fu—screwed this up. I want you to come home with me, but you're not ready for that yet."

The *yet* part caused her to tremble.

"I was thinkin' out loud, getting ahead of myself as usual, okay? That's it. I promise."

She should've doubted his sincerity, but she believed him.

"I want to get to know you, but like you said, it ain't anyone's business what goes on between us."

"So you want to sneak around with me."

His eyes hardened. "No. But I thought you'd prefer that to me stakin' my claim on you in the middle of the damn bar on a Saturday night since your family don't know about us."

Us. Did he really consider them a couple? "You'd do that? For real?"

"In a fuckin' heartbeat. So what's it gonna be?"

"I don't know. I have no experience with any of this."

"Good." He snaked his arm around her waist, not-so-subtly

pressing their hips together. "I like that you're inexperienced."

"Why?"

"Because it'll force me to take my time and enjoy every moment of bein' with you." Carson dipped his head and tugged on her hair until she bared her throat to him.

Her entire body broke out in gooseflesh when his lips touched her skin. He nuzzled and licked the sensitive flesh until she had difficulty breathing and her body reacted in ways it never had before.

"You like this?" he murmured in her ear.

"Yes."

"I'll take it as slow as you want." He smiled against her neck. "Until you don't want me to go slow anymore."

"You sound so sure of yourself, McKay."

Carson lifted his head and looked into her eyes. "I am sure. Not because I've got experience but because of this." He curled his palm over her throat and rested his thumb at the spot where her pulse raced. "And this." Then he slid his hand down her chest and gently cupped her breast, sweeping his thumb over the hardened tip of her nipple. "And this." His hand slipped around her back, following her spine to the curve of her behind. Then he pressed her lower body against his and she could feel his erection digging into her belly.

Her gaze zoomed to his.

Taking her hand, he kissed her palm before placing her hand on his chest. "And because of this. My heart is damn near ready to beat out of my chest. My hands are shakin' at the thought that I might actually get to put them on you."

"Carson."

"Say yes."

"Yes to what?"

"Bein' with me."

"Yes." Carolyn framed his face in her hands and kissed him. Mimicking the way he'd kissed her. The soft wet glide of lips. The gentle rub and swirling tease of her tongue against his. She let all of the nuances of kissing him wash over her, not wanting to miss a single one. The smoothness of his cheeks, the strength in his jaw, the wonderful scent of his body heat drifting from beneath the collar of his shirt. The tightening and releasing of his fingers on her butt. How his big, strong body shook with need.

For her.

She slowed the kiss gradually, rather than just ripping her mouth free. She rested her forehead at the base of his throat and tried to figure out a way to calm the blood pumping, body tingling effect the man brought out in her.

Carson's lips connected with the top of her head and he stayed like that for several long minutes before he released her. "I want to see you tomorrow. Can you get away?"

"Probably. As long as it's right after church gets out."

"What time is that?"

"Around eleven."

"Which church?"

"Our Lady of Perpetual Help in Gillette. Do you know where that is?"

He ran the backs of his knuckles down her jaw line. "I'll find it. I'll try my best to be there by eleven, but I've gotta check cattle and do a bunch of other stuff before I can get on the road, so I might be a little late."

"I'll wait. But right now I have to find my brother and convince him to take me home."

Carson's eyes sharpened. "You make sure that jackass Randy doesn't volunteer to give you a ride."

"Carson—"

"I mean it. He touches you or comes on to you in any way, I will pay him a visit, because I know where he lives."

"Fine." She'd never had a guy show jealousy and it surprised her how much she liked it.

"Good girl. Until tomorrow." One last kiss and he headed toward the parking lot.

She watched him walk away, that cowboy swagger such an innate part of him she knew he'd been born walking that way.

Within ten minutes of returning inside the bar she found Thomas and pleaded a headache, asking him to take her home. She felt Randy's suspicious gaze on her but she didn't acknowledge him. When they reached the car, Carolyn crawled in the back seat. Thomas dropped Randy off at the ball fields.

He didn't say a word until they'd parked at home. "So is your headache from bein' in too tight a lip lock with Carson McKay?"

She scrambled upright from her prone position in the back seat.

"I saw you with him, Carolyn." Thomas whirled around and glared at her. "What the hell are you thinking, getting mixed up with him? The man has a bad reputation. He uses women and dumps them. He's reckless and rude; the typical McKay."

"So says you. I've not seen him act like that. He's different around me."

"Because he wants to get into your pants. Literally. If Dad finds out—"

"Thomas. Please. You can't tell him."

He sighed. "He'll find out. Trust me. There's bad blood between the Wests and the McKays and someone will tell him."

She leaned over the seat. "Do you know what happened between our families?"

"Dad refuses to talk about it. I've just heard him muttering about them bein' above the law, and bein' a bunch of liars and thieves."

Thomas pointed at her. "So if that McKay is sneaking around with you, it just proves the point. The McKays can't be trusted." He paused. "But I can. I'll keep your secret since you agreed to keep mine."

"But?"

"But I'm rescinding my offer of help with the dishes."

Chapter Four
Carson

"Why're you in such a damn hurry this mornin'?" Cal asked as they sped across the pasture to check the bulls.

"I've got plans so I wanna get this done." Carson scowled at his watch. If he took the shortcut on the back roads he might only be fifteen minutes late.

"What kinda plans?"

"None of your business kinda plans."

"It's her, ain't it?"

"Yeah."

"Why you even bothering with this, Carse? You know it can't go anywhere."

He downshifted and stopped so Cal could get the gate.

But Cal made no move to get out of the truck.

"What?"

"Answer the question."

"Why you pushing me on this?"

"Because I think you're getting involved with her for all the wrong reasons."

"As usual, you don't know shit." Carson threw open the door and stomped across the pasture to get the gate himself. Then he climbed back in the cab and drove through the opening.

This time Cal did get out and close the gate behind them.

They'd nearly reached the corner section where the bulls had gathered when Carson spoke. "I'm not pursuing her because I wanna piss Dad off or get her to sleep with me. It's different with her. From the moment I saw her I knew... Dammit, you were there." He scrubbed his hands over his face, realizing he had to shave before he left. "Makes me sound like a pussy, but I'll just say it straight out, okay? She's special."

"See? That wasn't so hard," Cal said with a grin.

"Jackass."

"You plannin' on bringin' her to the trailer?"

Carson shot his twin a look. "She's not ready for that. And why do you care?"

"A woman like that won't slide into filthy sheets with you in your pigsty of a bedroom. We both know getting her sweet ass into your bed is the final goal here. And if it's not?" Cal raised an eyebrow. "Then her wearin' pants last night wasn't just a fashion statement, was it? She gonna expect you to slip on a frilly apron?"

"Says the man who knows his way around a feather duster and a vacuum," Carson retorted.

"You're damn lucky I can't stand to live in filth 'cause it sure don't bother you."

"Fine. I'll fumigate my room." He'd rather live with Cal's nagging ways about the state of their trailer than spend a night living with their dad again. "But when she does agree to come over, you gotta give us some privacy."

Cal smirked. "No problem. I'm sure I can find a warm bed to sleep in."

"I'm sure you can." But his focus was already on a black bull, lying down away from the other bulls. "Was 729 acting sickly yesterday mornin'?"

"We didn't check yesterday; it's been two days. But no, he was fine."

"Don't look like he's fine now. Come on, let's go check it out."

The bull was dead. Which meant they needed to move the bulls out of that pasture now. Normally he and Cal would've just taken care of it, but Cal insisted he get cleaned up and head to Gillette.

Poor Cal was still arguing on the phone with Casper about getting his lazy ass out of bed and helping him deal with the dead animal when Carson took off.

Casper. His younger brother had had a vindictive streak since they were kids. Had a big damn chip on his shoulder too, where Carson and Cal were concerned, claiming they got preferential treatment from their father. Well, yeah, they did. Because they actually worked.

Thinking about Casper was sure to put him in a foul mood so he shoved it aside. He turned up the radio and hauled ass to Gillette.

He pulled into the church parking lot at twenty-five after eleven. His worry she'd be gone evaporated when she climbed out of a 1955 Oldsmobile 88. Seeing her in a slim skirt, a floral blouse, a tight short sweater and a pair of high heels that did amazing things for her calves, had him bailing out of the truck to meet her halfway.

She smiled at him. That beautiful I'm-happy-to-see-you smile that lit up her entire face. "Hi."

"Hey. Sorry I'm runnin' a little late." Rather than haul her into his arms and lay a big wet kiss on her, he reached for her hand and brought it to his mouth for a soft kiss. "Sugar, you are pretty as a

45

picture in your Sunday mornin' finery."

"Thank you."

Carson noticed she'd pulled her hair back and piled it up into some fancy hair-do. She wore just enough makeup to make her look polished, but not plastic. Instead of the vivid red lipstick she usually wore, her lips were a soft pink. Innocent looking but he knew the power of what that mouth could do to him.

"Umm, Carson?"

His eyes connected with hers. "Yeah?"

"Do you realize you made a...growling noise when you were staring at my lips?"

He grinned. "Nope. But it's only because your mouth looks so tasty and I can't wait to take a bite."

Carolyn stepped closer and placed her hand on his chest. "Maybe it'd be best if we left the church parking lot *before* you start chewing on my lips."

"That works for me. Are you hungry? The truck stop is a dive, but the food is good and I doubt you'll run into anyone you know."

She cocked her head. "The truck stop is fine. But I'll remind you that *you're* the local, not me, if you're concerned about anyone you know seeing us together."

"I could give a damn who sees us together, Caro."

"One of these days very soon, McKay, I'll expect you to prove that."

He stole one quick kiss. "And I'll be happy to." He opened the passenger door for her and helped her inside. The sleeve of her sweater snagged on a wire sticking out of the seat. "Hang on a second. You're caught." Carson gently pulled the metal free and smoothed the section of yarn back in place. He said, "All fixed," but kept running his fingertips over the back of her arm.

"Carson?"

His glanced up at her. "Did you buy this sweater because it's the exact shade of your beautiful eyes? Or because it's as soft as your skin?"

Something dark glittered in her eyes before she grabbed onto his chin. "Give me a taste of that silver tongue." She fit her mouth to his and kissed the holy hell out of him. Right there in the church parking lot.

And her lips formed a very sneaky, self-satisfied smile when she released him. "Drive, cowboy."

At the truck stop they chose a seat at the back of the restaurant.

"So what'd you tell your family you were doin' today after church?"

"They didn't ask. I put a roast in the oven and told them when it'd be done. As long as they're fed, they probably won't even notice I'm not there."

Carson reached for her hand. "I'm sad to hear that. I imagine bein' the oldest girl in a family of boys and your mama bein' sickly that most the household stuff fell on you."

Carolyn squirmed and sipped her Coke. Then she said, "It wasn't all bad."

But that didn't convince him. "How old were you when you started doin' all the cookin'?"

"Ten. But I didn't do it all. My brothers sort of helped and my mother supervised. She taught me how to do everything. I didn't look at it as a chore until a couple of years ago when I came home and my father expected me to do everything around the house." She disentangled her fingers from his. "What about you? How much work does your father do on the ranch?"

He pretended not to notice her physical retreat when his question hit too close to home. "He still runs everything. Me'n my brothers are just pups to him, as he reminds us every day. But he does listen to us. At least he did when two parcels of land came up for sale in the last year and he bought 'em up. With the extra grazing areas we added more cattle to our herd."

"I know I'm not supposed to ask a rancher how many heads he runs, but I'm asking you."

"Between us? Three hundred."

"Oh. That's a lot."

"Keeps us busy. We've had a couple of neighbors approach us about buyin' them out too, but we gotta wait to see how our finances are when we start selling cattle in October." He reached for her hand again. "I get plenty of ranch talk. I don't want that with you."

"Can I say something, and I hope you don't take it the wrong way?"

Hard not to bristle at that question. "I reckon."

"You seem a lot older than twenty-four. Not with the way you look, because heaven knows you've been blessed there, but how you act."

"My mother said God took an old soul and split it between me'n Cal in the womb. My dad..." Last week's conversation with his old man pushed front and center. *Jesus, son, what is wrong with you? You gonna be chasin' skirts, getting drunk, starting fights and driving that truck like an idiot until you kill yourself with your own stupidity? Grow up. And get your damn chores done. I swear lately you've been worse than Casper.*

"Your dad what?"

Carson refocused on her. "My dad and I don't see eye to eye on a lot of things."

"I know how that goes."

"And he's been a miserable jackass to everyone since Mom passed on."

She squeezed his hand. "How long ago was that?"

47

"Six years. Me'n Cal had just turned eighteen. She had a stroke. Standin' in the kitchen cookin' bacon and eggs one minute and layin' dead on the floor the next."

The waitress served their meals and he was grateful for the interruption. He'd ordered biscuits and gravy with a side of sausage and pancakes. Carolyn ordered chicken fried steak, mashed potatoes and gravy. He hid his smile. The woman could eat.

Probably because she's the last to eat in her household.

"How long do I have you today?"

"I should be home by four to start supper."

"Can I say something and hope you don't take it the wrong way?"

Her blue gaze narrowed. "What?"

Carson wanted to follow the edge of her stubborn jaw with his fingertips, but he refrained. He'd never been into that touchy feely stuff in public. "You seem older than eighteen. Not with the way you look, although, sugar, you are the prettiest woman I've ever seen, but because you inherited all these responsibilities and you just accept them without question and you're not bitter about it."

She delicately wiped her mouth with the napkin and set it aside. "Some people tell me that just accepting those responsibilities means I have no backbone."

"You're too kind and too Christian to tell those folks to fuck off, aren't you?"

She whapped his forearm. "Language."

He laughed. "Come on. Let's get outta here and blow off all responsibilities for a few hours."

Once they were in the truck, he said, "Where to?"

"Cut through town and head south on county road 19. I want to show you one of my favorite places."

The day wasn't too hot and the recent rain kept the dust on the gravel road down.

"Turn here."

Carson thought he knew all the nooks and crannies of Campbell County, but he'd never been here before. A wide meadow stretched to a line of trees. Given the healthy state of the trees he suspected a stream lay on the other side. "What is this place?"

"A picnic area."

"How'd you find it?"

"On accident. I took a wrong turn and ended up here. I've been here half a dozen times and never seen anyone else around."

He faced her. "You want to be alone with me, Caro?"

Her cheeks didn't flush like he'd expected. Her direct gaze and bold statement, "More than anything," burrowed right into the heart of him.

"Let's go."

"Grab the blanket," she said and hopped out of the truck on her own. She paused at the edge of the clearing and glanced down at her clothing and shoes. "I didn't think this through."

"Gimme a moment." Carson tromped out in the field, searching for a flat place with no rocks. He kicked a couple of small ones away and spread out the blanket. Then he returned to her and lifted her into his arms.

Carolyn didn't shriek a protest; she just curled her body into his and held on.

He gently lowered her onto the blanket. When he looked at her, she wore the oddest expression. "What?"

"That was the most romantic thing that's ever happened to me."

Carson McKay should've just handed his heart over right then.

Instead he leaned over and kissed her. When he finally released her mouth to take a breath, he stretched out beside her, his head propped on his elbow.

She'd slipped her shoes off and sat in a tight ball with her arms wrapped around her legs.

"Something wrong?"

"Do you think this is weird?"

"Us bein' together?"

"Us being together on a blanket in a field out in the middle of nowhere?"

"I don't know if it's weird, but I can say it's the first time I've ever done something like this."

Her head turned so fast he wondered if she'd given herself whiplash. "It is? I mean, which part of it?"

"All of it. After I've been working outside all day I tend to stay indoors if I have free time."

"So the last thing you'd ever want to do is lie on the hard ground, surrounded by weeds and bugs while the sun beats down on you?"

Carson pushed up and sat on his haunches. "No, the last thing I want is to see that pinched look on your pretty face. Tell me what you want from me, Carolyn. And don't be shy."

She blurted, "I want to roll around on the blanket with you and make out. But I have these stupid stockings on and I don't want to snag them and this sweater is scratchy, and it was really forward of me to ask—"

He put his fingers over her lips. "Problems that are easily fixed. Nothin' is gonna happen out here that you don't want to happen. Okay?"

"What if I don't know what I want? You have so much experience with this—"

"Whoa. Hold on. Is that why you're with me? Because you want me to give you some experience?"

"No, I'm here because I like being with you. When you kiss me...I feel things I never have before and I don't know what to do or how to act on those feelings."

Sweet Jesus she was killing him. *Killing* him. He'd never been interested in virgins. He preferred women with experience—that way there was no misunderstanding that a quick fuck wasn't a relationship.

But when he looked at her? Kissed her? Thought about touching her? He had the fierce need to be the only man who ever put his hands on her. The only man who'd put his mouth on her. The only cock that she'd ever know would be his. And he'd be the only man who'd ever hear the noises she made when she came.

"Carson? Say something."

He took her hands and removed her arms from around her knees. "Do you trust me?"

"I-I think so."

"Yes or no, sugar. No in between."

"You're so intense right now. The way you're looking at me..."

"Am I scaring you?"

"No. I like it."

Carson angled his head and brushed his mouth across hers. Just once.

She trembled.

He dragged his thumb across the base of her throat where her pulse pounded. "Do you trust me?"

"Yes."

"Take off your sweater."

He expected hesitation but got none. Carolyn kept her eyes on his as she slipped each button through the buttonhole. When she started to shrug out of the sweater, he shook his head.

"I do that." Carson slipped the material down her arms and kissed the curve of the shoulder he'd bared. "Now rest on your elbows and stretch out your legs."

Moving to the edge of the blanket, he circled her left ankle, bending her knee. Then using just the tips of his fingers, he slowly followed the curve of her calf until his hand disappeared beneath her skirt. He didn't need to watch what he was doing; he needed to watch her face as he touched her.

Her teeth dug into her bottom lip when he paused to stroke the crease behind her knee. He felt her tremble as his fingers continued up her inner thigh until they reached the band of her stockings where the tiny straps connected to the garter belt.

He bided his time unhooking the stockings, enjoying every brush of his fingertips on her amazingly soft bare skin. Once the stocking was free, he dragged it back down her leg, letting her feel the difference between the softness of the silk on her skin and the roughness of his hands.

After he tucked the stocking in the toe of her shoe, he reached for her other leg. He remained in the same position, catching his balance. Any more pressure on his cock and it was liable to turn blue and fall off.

Carolyn's gaze went a little unfocused when he traced the base of her toes and the top of her foot. Her chest rose and fell and her teeth were still digging in to her lower lip. She jumped when he drew circles around the inside of her anklebone.

"Easy."

"It's making me jittery."

"That's not a bad thing. Means you like what I'm doin'."

She nodded.

"Just imagine what it'll feel like when I do this with my mouth."

Her squirminess became a whole lot worse at that point.

Carson's fingers swept higher, caressing the sensitive skin of her inner thigh. Close enough he felt the heat drifting from her pussy.

Although he'd promised to take it slow, he had the overwhelming need to push her skirt up to her hips and fasten his mouth on that sweet, untouched flesh between her thighs.

"Carson," she said a little breathlessly.

"What, sugar?"

"You made that scary noise again."

His gaze snagged hers, then he grinned unrepentantly. "Better get used to it." Removing her stocking, he shoved it in the other shoe. "Now we're ready to roll around on the blanket and make out."

Her cheeks flushed that sweet shade of pink.

He rolled to his back and brought her body on top of his, swallowing her gasp as he kissed her.

Carolyn might be a virgin, but she didn't kiss like one. That seductively stroking tongue of hers could bring a man to his knees.

The passion between them knocked him for a loop. Being with her—fully clothed—was more intimate than being naked with other women. His hands were roaming down her back, cupping her ass, sliding around to grip her hips. When he couldn't run his fingers through her soft blonde locks, he broke the kiss, letting his lips skim her jawline to her ear. "Take it down."

She froze. "What?"

"Your hair. Take it down for me."

"Oh. Okay." She struggled to get upright, so Carson sat up and braced her butt against his legs as her knees straddled his waist.

She brought both arms up and started removing pins from her hair. Once the sections were all down, she combed through it with her fingers.

"Beautiful," he murmured and curled his hands around her face, sliding his fingers into her hair and taking her mouth in a deep kiss.

Carolyn pushed on his shoulders and he rolled back down without breaking their lip lock. The intensity of the kiss robbed him of air and he forced himself to ease off. Gliding his lips over hers, gifting her with soft smooches, nibbles and teasing licks.

"Carson," she said softly against his mouth.

"Mmm?"

"I want to touch you."

"You are touchin' me."

"Not your bare skin."

He pulled back and looked into her eyes—her eyes heated with desire. "Where do you want to touch me, sugar?"

"Your chest."

His cock twitched against his zipper in protest of not being her first choice.

Carson placed his hands behind his head and said, "Go ahead."

She tipped her face down, letting her hair cover her face. Starting at the top, she gently pulled the pearl button until it unsnapped.

Pop.

Pop.

Pop.

Pop.

When her fingers connected with his skin, his nipples hardened. She had to scoot back to reach the snap above his belt. Once she'd unsnapped it, she tugged the shirt from his jeans and pulled the edges apart, baring his upper body completely.

He didn't have anything close to a Mr. Universe physique, and he felt oddly exposed.

Carolyn spread her hands open on his lower abdomen and followed his torso up the center, her thumbs passing over his belly button, and then smoothing over the section between his navel and his sternum. Her finger span didn't come close to reaching the edge of his ribcage. She slowed her explorations when her palms reached his pectorals. Her thumbs traced the cut of muscle while her fingers sifted through the hair covering his upper chest.

Her thoroughness and fascination kept him from moving. The tips of her fingers traced his collarbones, then the hollow of his throat.

Finally she looked at him. No, the little innocent tease actually smirked at him. "I could get used to seeing your bare chest. It's so...strong. And hard. You've got so many muscles. I just want to..."

He propped himself up on an elbow and curled his fingers around her jaw, lifting her face. "You just want to what?"

She shook her head.

He held firm. "If you can't tell me, why don't you show me."

Immediately she lowered her face to the center of his chest, where his hair grew thickest, wrapping her hands around his shoulders for balance. She buried her mouth and nose in that spot, turning her head so his chest hair brushed her cheek. "You smell so good." Her tongue darted out and she licked his pectoral. "You taste good too."

Fuck. He'd never survive this. Never. Her soft hands. Her curious mouth. Her hot breath. The gentle swish of her hair across his skin.

When her wandering fingers started to track the thin line of dark hair that ended at his waistband, he snatched her hand. "Stop."

Carolyn's head snapped up. "Did I do something wrong?"

"No. But with the way you're touchin' me...I've only got so much willpower."

She scrambled off of him. Her focus zoomed to his crotch, where it was pretty fucking obvious how she affected him. "Carson. I'm so sor—"

He had her flipped on her back and his body on top of hers before she finished. "Don't ever apologize for makin' my dick hard."

She just blinked those baby blues at him.

"I wanna know what you're thinkin'."

"Next time I'm gonna ask to touch you there."

He rested his forehead to hers and groaned.

She twined her arms around his neck. "I like how it feels when you're on top of me."

"Seriously killin' me here, Caro."

"But I don't know what I'm doing."

Carson had no response for that so he snared her mouth and kissed her.

Her body started to move beneath his. Her hips arching, her thighs squeezing around his. She had one hand in his hair and the other snaked down to clamp onto his butt cheek.

Don't know what she's doin', my ass. The woman was turning him inside out.

Carolyn tore her mouth free and whispered, "Is this what it's like?"

"No, sugar, it's much better."

The crunch of tires drifted to them from up the road. Seemed their alone time was over. He quickly pushed up and straightened his clothes. He glanced down at her. Her clothing was still in place, but her hair... Anyone who saw her hair would know exactly what they'd been up to.

"What's that sneaky smile for, cowboy?"

"I realized I really liked havin' a picnic with you."

She attempted to straighten her hair. "This isn't a picnic. There's no food."

Carson bent forward and stole a kiss. "Then I guess next time I'll just have to make a feast of you."

Her cheeks flushed.

They spent the next two hours tooling around the back roads. Listening to the radio. Laughing and talking. He kept the vehicle moving because he knew if they stopped, and she got close to him again, he couldn't keep his hands to himself.

"Before we get back to your car, I want to know when I can see you again."

"This date isn't over and you already want another one?"

"Of course. What're you doin' tomorrow night?"

"I don't have any plans. Why?"

"You do now. Can you meet me at the rest area outside of Moorcroft at seven?"

"Sure. What are we gonna do?"

Carson kissed her nose. "It's a surprise."

Chapter Five
Carolyn

The day had been a scorcher.

By the time she'd hung all the clothes on the line, the first ones were already dry.

Her father and Thomas came home together. They set their lunch pails on the counter and each grabbed a beer out of the refrigerator. Even if her dad couldn't give her more than a grunt of acknowledgment, he did spend time with his wife every night.

"So what'd you do all day?" Thomas asked. "Bake cookies?"

"When it's nearly a hundred degrees? No. Which also means we're having cold-cut sandwiches for supper." She faced her brother. "I need to borrow your car tonight."

"Where you going?"

"Over to Beverly's."

His eyes turned suspicious. "Why can't she pick you up?"

"Because she always picks me up."

"Why can't you take Mom's car?"

"Because the left rear tire is almost flat."

He sighed. "I suppose you want me to fix that too?"

"You or someone else. I can't go to the store without a car, and if I don't get to the store, no one eats," she said sweetly.

"Good point." He swigged his beer. "Stu will be around tonight so we'll get it handled."

"Thank you."

"Leave the keys on the hook when you're done. I'm taking my car to work tomorrow instead of riding with Dad."

Carolyn sensed he wanted her to ask why, but Stuart wandered in. "I hope there's a good game on TV tonight. I'm beat."

"We gotta fix the tire on Mom's car first," Thomas said.

Stuart groaned.

"Supper is ready and on the counter. And somebody please remember to put away the leftovers." If there were any.

"Where are you goin'?" Stuart asked with suspicion that equaled Thomas's. "You've been gone a lot lately."

"As long as I feed you, wash your clothes and pick up after you, why does it matter?"

He patted her on the shoulder. "Have fun."

She never fixed herself up to go to her friend's house and doing so would cement her brothers' suspicions. So she shoved her makeup and change of clothing into the bottom of her big purse. Butterflies flapped in her belly, making it impossible to eat. As casually as possible, she strolled out of the sun porch toward the front door.

"Where do you think you're goin'?" her father asked, or rather, more like he shouted as an accusation.

"To Beverly's."

Lying about meeting a man? Next you'll be sneaking out of the house to meet him.

If she had to. She wanted to be with him. She'd do anything to see him again. Luckily, after talking to Beverly today, she'd agreed to cover for Carolyn—even as she warned her to watch her step with the notorious Carson McKay.

Her father said, "I don't think you need to be out tearing around on a Monday night."

Carolyn slowly turned around. "What will I do if I stay here? I've already cooked, cleaned, done the laundry and looked after Mom."

"You don't need to get smart with me, young lady."

"I'm not." She started toward the door again.

"Be home by ten. Not a minute later."

He'd be snoring away in his room by nine-thirty and wouldn't know what time she rolled in anyway—but the smartest thing to do would be to smile and nod her head.

But that rankled. She was an adult. Her brothers didn't have a curfew.

"Carolyn," her father said sharply. "Did you hear me?"

She started to retort but Thomas jumped in. "Geez, Dad, I don't think you have to worry about Carolyn. Now if it was me...?" He laughed. "I'd most likely roll in just as we were hopping in the car to go to work."

Thank you, Thomas.

It was hard to meander out the door when she wanted to run. When the wheels hit the pavement she let out a loud whoop—sweet freedom!—turned up the radio and rolled down the windows.

The heat of the day lingered even as twilight approached.

She pulled into a roadside rest area and dug her clothes from the bottom of her purse. Making sure the coast was clear, she switched her short-sleeved floral blouse for a sleeveless black western shirt with pink piping on the collar and placket, leaving the top two buttons undone. She ditched the drab gray skirt and slid a tight black knit skirt up her thighs and over her hips. She wished she could've stashed a pair of pink kitten heels in her bag, but she was stuck with the white canvas shoes she'd worn all day.

Her hair was a wild tangle after having the windows down in the car, but it'd look messier yet when Carson got a hold of it. She'd nearly screamed in shock yesterday after catching sight of herself in the mirror following their picnic. She'd scraped her hair into a ponytail, praying her brothers and father wouldn't notice her hairstyle change in the hours between when she left for church and when she'd returned home.

They'd been glued to some sporting event on TV and she'd breezed by them, no problem.

Lying and sneaking around didn't sit well with her. She'd happily introduce Carson to her family, if it weren't for the fact their families had bad blood. She'd try to remember to ask Carson specifics about it tonight.

Sure. It's a little hard to talk when his tongue is buried in your mouth, isn't it?

Yes. But good Lord could the man kiss. She could've happily kept her lips plastered to his all afternoon. And when he'd removed her stockings, his callused fingertips were a reminder that a man was touching her. A man who knew exactly how to elicit that shivery response from a woman.

Part of her wondered how much farther they might've gone if a car hadn't interrupted.

Because you would've eagerly shed your clothes and given your virginity to the smoldering cowboy right there on that blanket.

At the time she'd been too annoyed at the interruption to consider how it might've looked when Carson had swept her into his arms and carried her back to the truck, without stockings, or shoes, her hair a wreck, her mouth red from their intense kisses.

Her stomach flipped when she heard the rumble of his truck enter the parking area. She grabbed her things, expecting he'd want her to hop in when he pulled up.

But Carson threw the engine in park and jumped out, skirting the tailgate, making a beeline for her. He curled his hand behind her neck and yanked her against his body. His hat shadowed her face and then his mouth was on hers. Kissing her like it'd been weeks since he'd seen her, not just a single day.

She dropped her bag to the ground and wrapped herself around him, letting his heat and urgency consume her.

Just when she thought he'd break the seal of their mouths, he changed the angle and then tone of the kiss. Kissing her with such sweetness she ached. So many sides to this gruff cowboy. And he seemed determined to show her every one.

Lucky me.

Carolyn kept her eyes closed when his mouth finally migrated to her ear.

"I missed you, sugar."

That deep voice shot tingles down her arm, her spine, her neck. "The kiss proved that you missed me." She turned her head and kissed his jaw. "But it's nice to hear."

"Same goes."

She inhaled the soapy scent of his shaving cream and rubbed her lips across his jawbone. "I missed you too."

Carson stepped back. "Let's go."

"Where are we going?"

"I told you; it's a surprise." He helped her into the cab. His help meant his hands squeezing her butt as he hoisted her in. She arched an eyebrow at him. The man didn't even pretend it'd been an oversight. He merely grinned.

Before they took off, he said, "Why're you sittin' all the way by the door?" He patted the center seat. "Come here."

"You are so bossy, McKay." But she scooted closer anyway.

"Comes with bein' the oldest. Though I'm only older than Cal by a couple of minutes."

"What's it like having a twin?"

He shrugged. "Normal for me. We look enough alike some folks think we're identical, but we're not."

Her gaze traveled over his handsome face and she fought the urge to sigh with pure feminine appreciation. Hard to imagine another man looking as fine as him, with that midnight black hair, those compelling blue eyes, chiseled jawline, dimples in his lean cheeks, and the slight divot in his strong chin.

"Why you starin' at me?"

"Just trying to imagine if your twin is as good-looking as you. When will you introduce me to him?"

He scowled.

Laughing, she leaned over and kissed his cheek. "Honestly I was staring because I like looking at you. There's a whole lot to like about the way you look, McKay."

His hand crept higher on her knee and squeezed.

They turned off the highway into a pasture. Carolyn saw rutted tracks ahead of them, but it in no way resembled a real road. It was starting to get dark.

"You tensed up. What's wrong?"

"Wondering if we'll get shot for trespassing."

"Nah. Don't worry about it."

"You telling me you wouldn't be tearing after a trespasser on McKay land? Because that's not what I heard."

Carson stopped the vehicle. "Who's been talkin' shit about us?"

"No one."

"Bullshit, Carolyn. You wouldn't have said it if you hadn't heard something."

"Fine. Beverly and—" Darn. She snapped her mouth shut. She'd told him that her family didn't know about them, but both her mother and Thomas knew. Now her friend knew too. Somehow she didn't think that'd make him happy.

"Who the hell you been talkin' to?"

"I told you. Beverly saw you kissing me outside the bar Saturday night and she told me all sorts of stories about your family. How you all keep adding land, turning your ranch into a McKay kingdom." Then Beverly had detailed how many women Carson reportedly had on a string. Evidently the man had legendary moves between the sheets. Or in the barn. Or in his truck.

He scowled again. "I hate gossip."

How much of a simpering fool did it make her that she thought he looked fierce and sexy, not mean when his dark eyebrows knitted together and his eyes got squinty?

"You got questions about something, ask me."

"I did ask you. And you tossed off a smart aleck answer. I want to know why we're driving across someone's land."

"It's my buddy Alan's land. He gave me permission to take the shortcut to the lake."

"Lake?"

"Yeah, we're goin' to Keyhole."

Panic set in.

The truck stopped and then Carson's hands were on her face. "Sugar. What's wrong?"

"I don't swim."

"That's—"

"Ever. I don't even get near the water."

"You're afraid of water?"

"Yes!"

"Why?"

"Because I don't know how to swim!"

Warm lips pressed into her forehead. "Hey now. It's okay."

She closed her eyes. "I'm sorry to ruin your plans."

"They're not ruined. Because we're still goin' to the lake."

"What? No."

"Look at me." He stared into her eyes. "Caro, you're safe with me. I promise. Let's go down there and see how it goes."

"You won't make me get in the water?"

"We'll see, okay?"

She tried to shake free from him. "Doesn't matter because I don't have a bathing suit. There's no way I'm swimming in my clothes because the skirt could get tangled around my legs and pull me to the bottom—"

His mouth was on hers again.

And of course his distraction worked. After he kissed her senseless she burrowed her face into his neck as his fingers drew circles in the middle of her back.

"I'd never let anything happen to you," he said softly. "You mean too much to me."

That shocked her. "What? We've known each other five days."

His intense blue gaze never wavered. "I knew five seconds after I saw you that you were someone special who'd change my life forever." Then, seeming embarrassed by his answer, he retreated, put the truck in gear and they were on the move again.

They started up a small incline. At the crest, she could see and smell the water. He parked and came around to help her out. Holding her hand, he led her down the embankment.

She noticed the picnic table close to the water's edge and a couple of cottonwood trees creating a canopy above it. The air was cooler this close to the water.

"Careful. It's a little muddy."

So much for her white shoes.

After setting his hat brim side up on the table top, he dropped onto the bench and rested his forearms on the edge of the table behind him. She sat next to him, and took in their surroundings. This section seemed to be a small cove just off the main body of the lake.

He exhaled. "After the scorcher of a day this breeze feels nice."

"Did you work outside all day?"

"Pretty much. We shoulda fixed the section of fence last week, when it wasn't a hundred degrees in the shade. But my brothers overruled me. So it was on the list today. Dirty, damn, miserable work."

"Then why do it?"

"Because it needed done."

"Even when it's a hundred in the shade?"

"Even then. Stuff needs done even when it's fifty below with the wind-chill. Dealin' with the weather...hot and then cold." He snorted. "Kinda like dealin' with my dad. I'm used to that too. He doesn't have to do the shitty chores anymore. That's why he has us."

"That hardly seems fair."

He shrugged. "It is what it is. My dad won't just hand over the McKay Ranch to me or my brothers. We've gotta prove we're worthy."

"Worthy of what?" She didn't see Carson as the type who'd need validation even from his father; he oozed self-confidence.

"Worthy stewards of the land. He doesn't say too much unless one of us royally fu—screws up. But owning land isn't a right; it's a privilege. Guess that's something he learned from his dad when he and his brother came over here from Ireland."

"Speaking of our ancestors... Do you have any idea what happened between the Wests and McKays?"

"Nope, and I don't care. Water under the bridge." He faced her. "Besides, I've got a new appreciation for the West family."

Carolyn set her hand on his cheek. "Do you now?"

"Yep. C'mere. You're too far away." He plucked her up and settled her on his lap, facing him, with her legs dangling on the opposite side of his.

"Carson, I don't—"

"You don't want to be this close to me?" He pushed her hair over her shoulder. "Or you're feelin' it's wrong that you want to be this close to me?"

"Am I that easy to read?"

"Sugar, you're just that innocent. And I don't mean that in a bad way. With your background...there's part of you that feels what we're doin' is wrong." Carson kissed her chin. "But it's not. I believe you have more curiosity than guilt when I touch you."

"So I *am* very easy to read."

"I'll respect any boundaries you set. But I ain't gonna lie to you. If it was up to me there'd be no boundaries between us at all." He smoothed his hand down her hair. "It's different with you."

"Why?"

"I don't know. I just know I like bein' around you."

Carolyn studied his mouth.

"What?"

"Oh, I was so busy listening to your words that I missed flashes of that silver tongue."

He laughed. "Lemme show it to you up close."

This was yet another type of kiss, teasing, playful; still the passion between them simmered below the surface and that kicked her anticipation higher, knowing the kiss could change at any second.

In this position, she felt just how the kiss and their bodies being meshed together affected him.

Carson's hands slipped beneath her skirt. He stopped kissing her when his hands reached mid-thigh. "No stockings today."

"Too hot. But if I did have them on I'd let you take them off." There. That was bold.

His eyes glittered in the near dark. "You liked that?"

"You know I did. Your hands give me that shivery feeling. Inside and out."

He ran the tip of his finger from her chin down to the V of her blouse. "Did that do anything for ya?"

Her arms were a mass of gooseflesh. "Yes."

"How about if I do this?" He fastened his mouth to the skin below her ear and sucked.

"Oh. That..." Her ability to speak vanished when he placed soft kisses down the arch of her neck.

"I'm thinkin' you bein' speechless means you like it." He nuzzled the spot between her collarbone and her shoulder. "You smell so damn good."

"It's probably the powder I use."

"Or maybe it's just your skin." He kissed a path to the other side of her neck. "Makes me want to check if you have this same scent everywhere."

The entire time Carson's mouth was on her his hands weren't idle. He'd have one hand twisted in her hair while the other hand would roam; caressing her back, her behind, her hips, the outside of her thighs.

With every touch he wound her tighter. She had the urge to rub her thighs together to offer some relief to the ache she felt building there. She wanted to rock her pelvis forward to feel his hard bulge rubbing against her. She wanted his rough hands and his soft kisses on her breasts. She wanted to reacquaint herself with how warm and smooth and hard his chest felt beneath her hands and her mouth. And since she'd never wanted anything like this before she had no idea how to ask for what she wanted.

Then Carson's hand was on her jaw, forcing her attention to him. "Sugar, you still with me?"

She blinked at him.

"If you don't like what I'm doin', tell me."

"I like what you're doing. A lot. And I want more, but it... I don't know how..."

Keeping his gaze locked on hers, he feathered his thumb across the inside of her bottom lip. "I can't give you what you want if you don't tell me. You set the boundaries."

"I want to take your shirt completely off this time," she blurted.

He lifted an eyebrow. "Really? That's what you want?"

She nodded.

"All right. But here's the deal. If my shirt comes off, your shirt comes off too."

"You want me to take it off now?"

"No. I get to take it off you as soon as you've had your turn with me."

"Okay." Carolyn scooted back on his knees and dropped her feet to the ground before she stood.

"Whoa there. Where you goin'?"

"Nowhere. I thought it'd be easier if you sat on top of the picnic table."

His answering grin was very naughty.

But as soon as he'd moved, Carolyn had a moment of shyness.

Of course, Carson caught it and reached out to her. "I know I'm the first man you've been with." When she ducked her head, he tipped her chin back up. "I'm nervous too."

"Why?"

"I don't want you to be disappointed, thinkin' you're getting a guy built like Mr. Universe and end up with this."

Smiling, she leaned forward to kiss him. "I already had a little preview of you so I know getting *you* would be the better deal, cowboy." Her hands shook when she popped the first snap on his shirt. The second snap revealed a delicious glimpse of his chest hair. The third and fourth snaps even more. She experienced the urge to bury her lips in the dark curls and breathe him in like she'd done yesterday.

After she freed him of his shirt, she set her palms on his shoulders, marveling at how broad he was. Then she inched her hands down his upper arms, feeling every bump and bulge of his muscles. His forearms were thick, bunched with tendons and sprinkled with dark hair. As she let her fingers trail back up, she noticed the tan line in the middle of his biceps, separating the pale skin of his torso from the sun-kissed flesh on his forearms, neck and face.

She flattened her palms on his pectorals. His muscles were so firm. Hard, but not unyielding. His chest hair started below the hollow of his throat and spread out in a triangle across his upper chest, tapering to a thin line that disappeared beneath his waistband. Carolyn slid her hands down, her fingers ruffling through the springy hair. She could feel his heart beating and the flat disks of his nipples brushed the base of her hand. Her own heart raced and her mouth went dry in anticipation. She wanted... Oh how she wanted...

Take what you want. Do what you want.

Carolyn pressed her lips to the center of his chest, and immediately his musky, masculine scent surrounded her. Desire bombarded her from all sides. She rubbed her right cheek into that downy softness, then her left.

Hands landed on her head, pulling her away. For a second she panicked, worried she'd done something wrong. Then her eyes met Carson's and the molten heat in those blue depths stole her breath.

"Christ, woman. Do you realize you made a purring sound when you were rubbing on me?"

"I did? Does it bother you?"

He laughed. Then he took her hand and placed it over the bulge between his legs. "Hearin' you make that sexy noise gets me even more hot and bothered than you touchin' me."

Her cheeks went red hot and she slammed her eyes shut. She couldn't believe she had her hand on his... Why wasn't she pulling away? Why was she wishing she'd demanded to strip him out of his shirt *and* his pants?

"Much as I like how you're rubbing on me, if you keep doin' it something will come out of there but it won't be a genie."

Crude man. Just to be ornery, because he was teasing her, she locked her gaze to his and kept stroking her palm up over the hard length. "Maybe that's what I want to see."

Carson curled his hand around her face. "You will. But not tonight." He ran his thumb back and forth over her cheekbone.

"What?"

"You'd run if you could read my thoughts right now." He picked up her hand from his crotch and kissed her fingertips. Then he scooted aside and stood. "Now I really need to cool down." He unhooked his buckle and unzipped his pants.

"Carson. What are you doing?"

"Goin' swimmin'." *Thud, thud* went his boots.

When he yanked off his socks and dropped his pants, she got an eyeful of his erection. And she couldn't quite force her eyes away from it. She asked, "Do you have swimming trunks?" hoping he said no and that he swam naked.

"Don't need 'em." He grinned. "My boxers will do." He whooped and took off.

She watched him run straight for the water, splashing until he disappeared beneath the surface. And she caught herself counting the seconds until his head bobbed up again.

"Damn, this feels nice." He dove back under, then resurfaced, playing around like a kid.

Her friend Beverly had described Carson as gruff and quiet. A little cocky. Belligerent and prone to fighting if he'd been drinking. Beverly claimed the only time he smiled and turned on the cowboy charm was when he wanted sex.

That wasn't the man Carolyn saw at all. Not that they'd been with other people, so she could see if he was reserved in mixed company, but the man she knew was full of mischief and surprises, with a sweet intensity and blatant sexual confidence that drew her in like nothing she'd ever experienced.

"Sugar, you oughta come in. The water is beautiful."

"I don't swim, remember?"

He stood. "It's only up to my waist right here."

"A person can drown in an inch of bathwater."

"I'd never let you drown. No horsin' around or dunking you either. You wouldn't even have to get your hair wet."

"I don't have a swimsuit."

"The bra and panties you're wearin' would be just fine."

Strip? Right here? With him watching?

She wrapped her arms around herself. "I'm fine on shore."

"If I come back to shore and walk you in, step by step, will you consider it?"

"No."

"Oh. I see."

"What?"

"It's not the water you're afraid of as much as takin' your clothes off in front of me."

Her mouth dropped open. "That is *not* it."

"Prove it. Even if you don't get in the water. Show me that body

64

you're hidin', because I'll bet it's amazing."

"Did you hit your head on a rock when you dove in?"

Carson laughed. "Remember when I said if you took off my shirt, I'd expect the same from you? I'm thinkin' now's about as good as time as any. So take it off."

"Now?"

"Right now. Maybe do a little strip tease."

"If I could swim I'd run in there and dunk you."

"Try it." He flashed his teeth. "Show me whatcha got, 'cause sugar, you know I want it."

Would she really give in to his goading?

Looked like it.

As she popped the first snap, then the second, she realized he'd moved closer, but he hadn't taken his eyes off her. A tiny feminine thrill heated her blood. She wanted him to like her body, but she'd never been half naked in front of any man before.

"Keep goin'."

Once she had the buttons undone all the way down, she was surprised he couldn't hear the booming of her heart. Another moment of uncertainty had her facing the picnic table when she took the shirt off.

"Turn around."

She did but she couldn't meet his eyes.

"Huh-uh. No way am I lettin' you be ashamed of a body like that. Holy hell, woman. It's something."

That bolstered her confidence enough that she lowered the zipper on her skirt. She kicked off her shoes and shoved the clingy fabric down to her ankles. When she stepped out of it, she was tempted to hold it in front of her body as a shield.

"Caro, look at me...and don't you dare hide yourself behind that skirt."

How had he known? She lifted her head and heard Beverly's voice. *Throw your shoulders back. Be proud. If I had a bosom like that I'd be flaunting it.* So she did just that.

Carson had sunk so low into the water all she could see were his eyes and his nose. But his eyes were enormous and glittered in the darkness. Like an alligator. With the way he stared she felt like prey.

Finally he stood; the water rolled down his impressive chest. His arms were clenched at his sides.

"Do you care if you get wet?"

"What?"

He stalked toward her, the water no longer hiding his lower half. Didn't look like his dunk in the lake had cooled him off at all.

"Do you care if you get wet?" he repeated.

"No, as long as you're not hauling me into the lake."

"Good."

Then he was on her. Every hard, wet inch of his body plastered to hers. One hand held the back of her neck while he seized her mouth in a scorching kiss. His other hand clamped onto her butt.

Carolyn barely registered the wetness of his boxers against her underwear. Her entire focus was on that jutting piece of male flesh pressing against her.

In a state of shock, she didn't protest when Carson picked her up and carried her to the picnic table, carefully setting her on the end. He stepped between her thighs and broke the kiss. He nuzzled her ear. Some instinct had her arching slightly to offer him her throat.

"I swear by all that's holy, you are a work of art." He left a trail of kisses down her neck. "Let me touch you. Let me put my hands and mouth all over this beautiful body of yours."

"Yes."

A rumble vibrated against her neck. Then he kissed her so perfectly, so hungrily, so reassuringly, so sweetly, that he could've asked for anything in that moment and she would've given it to him.

Carson's hands were cool as he dragged his fingertips up and down her arms. He pushed her hair over her shoulder and guided her to set her palms on the picnic table, leaving enough space that he could grip her hips.

Her belly quivered when his thumbs traced the edge of her panties. Just a slow brush of his skin on hers and she felt like she couldn't breathe.

He kissed the corner of her mouth. "Easy."

"Sounds as if you're trying to gentle a skittish horse."

He chuckled. But he didn't dispute her statement.

Then she forgot about everything except more of that skillful mouth of his as he dragged kisses to the top of her breast. He nuzzled and kissed that section of skin while his thumbs kept up the caress between her hipbones.

His lips wandered to her other breast, treating it to the same teasing exploration. He followed the edge of her bra cup with his tongue. Even without touching her nipple it was already rigid, nearly poking through the lace insert.

The instant Carson's mouth enclosed around that hard tip, and he sucked it through the lace, she gasped. She gasped again when he suckled harder. He pulled the cup away and there was no barrier between his mouth and her bare flesh.

"Oh. I..." *Had no idea that would feel so good.*

Carson's magic mouth continued to tease and torment. Focusing on her breasts and then he'd kiss her neck in that deceptively lazy way that made her burn.

At some point his hands had migrated to the tops of her thighs and he was running the backs of his fingers from her knee to her inner thigh. Each stroke got bolder.

The first time his thumb connected with that bit of flesh at the top of her mound her entire leg twitched.

His hands returned to her face and his eyes searched hers. "Do you want me to stop? Yes or no."

"No. Please. Don't stop."

His lips met hers. "Lean back on your elbows."

Carson mired her in a maelstrom of need. His hands were never idle, worshipping her every curve from her shoulders to her hips. His mouth was in constant motion, kissing, licking, tasting her thoroughly.

Carolyn tingled from head to toe. Her head was muzzy. Coherent words were impossible. She'd just moan softly when Carson did something she liked. And she liked it all.

But she reached the point where she needed more. More body contact. Her hands on him, her mouth on him as he moved against her.

"Carson. Please. I want to feel it all tonight. Everything. I don't want you to stop."

He gently pulled her to a sitting position. "You talkin' about us havin' sex? Right here?"

She nodded.

"Just strip you bare and don't give a damn if you get bruises and bug bites when I'm on top of you? That's not...dammit, Carolyn, no."

Stung, she shrunk back away from him.

"Shit." He turned, took half a dozen steps and stopped with his back to her.

Retreat.

She quickly put on her blouse and had just zipped her skirt when he returned.

Without saying a word, he started to get dressed.

Rather than stand there suffering through his silent anger, she slipped on her shoes and picked her way through the vines covering the ground, stopping to lean against the big cottonwood tree. She gazed across the lake, now an ominous black. Although she wasn't a fan of the water, she liked the soothing sound of the waves hitting the shore. With the way her cheeks burned with humiliation, she welcomed the cool breeze.

Carson's boots crunched the vegetation and Carolyn automatically tensed up when he moved in behind her.

He set his hand on her shoulder and she jerked away. "Oh hell no. You ain't gonna ever cringe when I want to touch you."

"But it's okay for you to yell at me when I want to touch you? Wrong. I want to leave."

"You got more than a little sass in ya, doncha, sugar?"

"You'll see a whole lot more of it if you don't take me back to my car right now."

"Look me in the eye."

She shook her head.

"Turn around and look me in the eye when you let me have it."

Such a condescending... She whirled around and stood toe to toe with him. "Happy?"

"Not even fuckin' close to happy right now."

"Good."

He lifted the one eyebrow that managed to be both sexy and annoying. "Why's that good?"

"Let's just forget tonight ever happened." *Although I doubt I'll ever forget how mad you got when I threw myself at you.*

Then his hands circled her upper arms and he yanked her close enough to get in her face. "That's what you think? I got mad at you because you asked me to have sex with you tonight?"

She'd said that out loud?

"Well?" he demanded.

"Well, what else was I supposed to think when you yelled at me and stormed off? I don't have any experience with this, Carson."

"You think I don't know that? You think maybe I'm feelin' guilty for lettin' it get that far out of hand in the first place? When I said you could set the boundaries as to how far you were willin' to go with me? Then the second I put my hands on you I lost my goddamned head. The next thing I know, you're askin' me to fu—make love to you. And I see you—this perfect, beautiful angel, layin' there half-dressed, with love bites on her chest and I got pissed off at myself. Not at you—never at you."

Totally bewildered, she asked, "Why?"

"Because you deserve more for your first time than me rutting on you on top of a rickety picnic table and getting slivers in your ass."

"Oh."

He pulled her against his chest. "With the way I look at you and the way I was touchin' you tonight can you honestly tell me you thought I didn't want you?"

"I thought you did...then I wasn't sure."

"That's one thing you can be very sure about." He kissed the top of her head and smiled at her. "You ready to go?"

She nodded.

They walked back to the truck in silence. Carson held her hand but she could tell his mind was elsewhere.

The silence continued on the drive back to her car. After he parked, he kissed her—more chastely than she was used to from him. "I want to see you tomorrow night."

Her mouth opened before her brain engaged. "Where and when?"

"This same parking area around seven?"

How would her father react if she told him she was going out again?

Do you really care?

No.

Can he stop you?

No.

Carolyn wreathed her arms around Carson's neck and kissed him greedily. He had the skills to seduce her completely, but from this moment on she'd be a full participant in that seduction. He didn't get to call all the shots. She didn't relinquish his mouth until she'd had her fill of it.

For now.

She smiled and kissed that spot on his throat that made him groan. "See you here tomorrow night at seven. Don't be late."

Chapter Six
Carson

Carson leaned against his pickup, his elbow resting on the box, trying to look casual as he waited, even when everything inside him was wound tighter than a ball of baling twine.

Goddamn he had it bad for her. So bad he'd damn near sliced off his finger today. He'd been so lost in thought, remembering his hands roaming over the smooth expanse of Carolyn's belly, that he'd nipped his knuckle with the wire cutters and it'd bled like a sieve.

After he'd returned from the lake last night, he'd suffered through a lecture from Cal about slowing things down with Carolyn. Which Carson had taken to mean break it off with her. That hadn't gone over well; until Cal explained he'd meant slow as in proceed with caution, not as in come to a complete stop.

Which just proved how fucking antsy and touchy he was about her. How crazy in love he was with her.

After six fucking days.

Her car appeared on the horizon. He remained in place, watching as she parked, his pulse quickening when she climbed out.

Grinning, he held his arms open and she launched herself at him.

As soon as she'd wrapped herself around him, nestling her face in his neck with a soft sigh, Carson closed his eyes as he squeezed her tight. Yeah, this woman was his.

They remained locked together, not speaking, just...being.

His fingers twined in her hair and he tugged her head back to get at her mouth. He focused on tenderness with her. Brushing his lips over hers. Teasing and nibbling. Sucking her sweet breath into his lungs.

Impatient, Carolyn tried to wrest control. Framing his face in her hands and pulling him closer.

But Carson wrapped his fingers around her wrists and gently removed her hands. "Sugar, what's the rush?" he whispered against her lips. "All day I've been lookin' forward to takin' my time to enjoy this." He lightly licked the seam of her lips; his tongue followed the bottom of her teeth. She tasted like sweet sin.

When Carolyn released a shuddering sigh, he slowly kicked up the heat level of the kiss from warm to molten. By the time he broke the seal of their mouths, sweat dampened his skin and his cock pressed against his zipper.

Whoa. Her hands were on his ass, holding his pelvis to hers, forcing the teeth of his zipper to bite into his cock as her lips trilled over every hot spot in his throat.

"Uh, Caro?"

"You always smell so dang good."

"You wouldn't have said that earlier when I was covered in dust and sweat."

"Wrong. You'd still smell good. Like earth and man."

He groaned when her sassy tongue flicked his earlobe.

"I like that I can get you to make that noise," she said softly.

"You make some pretty sexy noises yourself when my mouth is on you."

She stilled. "Last night wasn't a dream, was it?"

"No." He grabbed her chin, forcing her to look at him. "You still all right with it? No regrets?"

"Just that you stopped."

Jesus. "I didn't wanna stop. You know that."

"I know you're worried we're going too fast. But I'll bet if I was any other woman, besides a virgin, you wouldn't have reined it in."

"You don't compare to other women and not just because you're a virgin."

"Then why?" she demanded.

Because you look at me like no other woman ever has. Like you see beneath the surface of a hell-raising cowboy to the man inside. The man I want to be.

"Carson?"

"Because you're you. From the moment I met you I've thought of nothin' but you. I can't explain it any better than that."

"I'll let it go...for now. But please don't treat me like I don't know my own mind, okay?"

"Okay." He fused his mouth to hers and the kiss soothed the restless parts of him. Parts he hadn't realized needed soothing. "Come on. Let's hit the road."

"Where are we going?"

"You'll see." He boosted her into his truck on the driver's side and slid next to her. She rested her head on his shoulder and her hand on his thigh.

"What did you do today, rancher McKay?"

"Besides check cattle? Fixed fence."

"Didn't you do that yesterday?"

"Yep."

"Do you do that every day?"

"We could. We should. But we don't. Just happened we did it two days in a row."

"What does fixing fence entail?"

"A fifth of Jack Daniels." He grinned at her. "Kiddin'. It's a tedious job that's never ending."

"Because the McKays have so much land?"

"Not that as much as there's a lot of fence. No matter how well the fence is installed, the elements and the cattle make a mess of it. Summer is slow until haying starts, so that's when we do the majority of the repairs."

"No wonder you wanted to cool off in the lake last night. But it didn't help much since you got us both all hot and bothered." She sighed. "That's all I thought about today. How it felt to be skin to skin with you. And how much I liked having your mouth all over me."

He hadn't even put his mouth where he most wanted it.

"I liked it when you bit on my neck almost as much as when you sucked on my—"

"Jesus, Carolyn. Stop."

"Language," she chided.

"Then you watch what you're sayin'."

"What?" she said innocently.

He snorted. "You know *what.*"

Her pause chilled the air in the cab despite the eighty-degree heat.

Aw hell, she hadn't been playing coy. She doesn't have enough experience to do that, remember?

"Oh. So that's how it is."

"How what is?"

"The virgin/whore thing. I'm a virgin so I couldn't possibly be thinking dirty thoughts about you and me naked, nor am I supposed to voice those thoughts."

"Not true."

"But you've said I'm different than other women, so do you separate them into the other category? What happens after my virginity isn't an issue? Then I'm a whore?"

Dangerous to have this conversation at sixty miles an hour. He kept his hands on the steering wheel and his eyes on the road. The woman would push and push and push... Yet he admired her for that trait. Just because she was innocent didn't mean she was a pushover. "How about we cross that bridge when we come to it."

"We crossed that bridge last night, Carson, when I was in my underwear spread out on a picnic table."

The image—the beautiful image of her writhing under him hit him hard. "What is it you want me to say?"

"The truth."

Don't do it.

But his mouth opened of its own accord. "Last night I wanted to fuck you. I *will* fuck you but it won't be on a whim on a hard goddamned picnic table. It'll be in a proper bed where I can take my time so your first time is special because God knows mine wasn't. It won't make you a whore. It'll just make you mine."

"Oh."

"And sugar, if you wanna talk dirty to me, I'm good with that. But I'd rather you didn't do it when I'm behind the wheel 'cause I'm liable to wreck my damn truck."

Silence.

After a minute or so of dead air, he chanced a quick look at her. The woman wore that I've-got-a-secret smile that spelled trouble. Shit. "Say something."

"Now that that's sorted out, where are we going?"

"I thought we could see a movie in Spearfish."

"Do you know what's playing?"

"Nope. But it'll be dark, you'll be next to me so I don't really care." Did that make him sound smarmy? He changed the subject. "So tell me about your day."

"My mom's friend Maxine Granger stopped by. She takes in mending and ironing, plus she does alterations and some custom tailoring. Maxine's daughter had a baby and she'll be gone to Kansas for at least a month. She's asked me to fulfill her sewing and alterations jobs during that time. Which will work out because I can do it from home."

"Won't that be a lot of work?"

She shrugged. "I'm used to it. I think my fingers are finally healed from last summer."

He frowned. "What'd you do last summer?"

"Same thing I've done every summer since I was twelve. Lived with my aunt and assisted her in the custom tailoring business she owns. It's a family thing on mother's side. My mom used to be an amazing seamstress and she started teaching me to sew when I was five. Then because of the arthritis…" She cleared her throat. "Aunt Hulda took over since she's a seamstress too. She paid for our private schooling and in exchange I worked in her shop on weekends and half the summer."

It'd be hypocritical if Carson said expecting a twelve-year-old girl to help out was child slavery; he'd been doing chores and learning the ways of the ranch since he was a boy. "Those sewing skills are obvious because you're always wearin' such nice clothes. Did you make 'em?"

Carolyn smoothed her hand down her skirt. "Yes. Do you like them?"

"Yes, I surely do like that you look like you stepped out of a magazine." *But I'd really like to see those pretty clothes in a pile on my bedroom floor. Or the floor of this truck.*

Pervert. Slowing things down, remember?

They parked in front of the movie theater. *Arabesque* didn't look all that interesting to him—he preferred a western—but with one theater in town there wasn't much choice. Unless... "Want to go to the drive-in? There's gotta be something better playing."

"I've never been to a drive-in. Sounds like fun."

They joined the line of cars waiting to get in to see *El Dorado*—a John Wayne picture he'd looked forward to seeing.

Once inside the lot, Carson chose a spot away from the high school partiers. "You want popcorn or a pop?"

"I'd take a Coke."

"Stay here. I'll get it."

She looked at him funny.

"What?"

"Embarrassed to be seen with me, McKay?"

"You caught me. It's such a chore to have a beautiful, classy blonde on my arm. Come on, then." He helped her out, keeping his hand on her lower back as they crossed the gravel parking lot to the concession stand.

Just after they'd cleared the line he ran into Jim Hagar, a guy he'd graduated from high school with. "Carson McKay at a drive-in? What, are all the local bars closed for some reason?"

Given his reputation, he probably deserved that. But also given his reputation, Jim oughta know Carson had no problem popping a loudmouth for a smart comment.

A boy of about two and girl of about four, both wearing pajamas, were running around, weaving between Jim's legs, yelling and hitting each other. He snapped, "Knock it off." Then he looked at Carson. "Bringing the kids to the drive-in gets me'n Barb outta the house without having to pay a sitter."

"I wouldn't know."

Jim's gaze landed on Carolyn. "This your wife?"

"No."

"I'm not surprised a wild man like you ain't married yet. What was it you used to say? You'd strap on that old ball and chain only when you were too old to keep running from the women trying to shackle you."

"Yeah, well, we all say shit at sixteen that makes us cringe now. If I recall you said you wanted Barb for one thing—her oral skills, and not the ones she used to become a Declam contest champion."

Jim blushed. Then he said, "Come on kids," and hustled away.

"Good friend of yours?" Carolyn asked dryly.

"How'd you guess? Livin' in the same area I'm forever branded by stuff I've done in the past."

She stopped and faced him. "Are you bothered by what he said?"

"No. That kinda shit always dribbles out of his mouth." He touched her cheek. "But that doesn't mean I wanted you to hear it."

"While he was saying that stuff about you, I watched his ankle biters throwing rocks at each other. I was hoping they'd miss and hit him."

Carson laughed.

Once they reached his pickup, he opened the passenger side and slid in next to her, then draped her across his lap. "What? You think I'd rather have a steering wheel in my lap than you?"

"No complaining if your legs fall asleep. Or if I fall asleep."

He swept her hair from her face. "Been thinkin' about how much I'd like to have you fallin' asleep in my arms."

She touched the brim of his hat. "Take this off. It bumps my face when you kiss me and it keeps me from running my fingers through your hair." As soon as he set it on the seat beside her, her hands were on his head, nails gliding over his scalp. "Your hair is like black silk. Not too long. Not too short. Why hide it under a hat?"

"I don't know how to answer that... Ah, damn. That feels good."

Carolyn tugged him closer by his hair and kissed him with sweet seductiveness.

His brain focused on the image of her using her mouth on his cock the same way. The thought of teaching her exactly how he liked it, of knowing she'd never done it to any other guy...

The speaker crackled and she jumped, breaking the kiss.

"Sounds like the movie is about to start."

She shifted sideways and he draped his arm behind her. "Now I wish I would've gotten popcorn. But it's annoying when one person is eating it and the other isn't."

"Mmm-hmm." He played with her hair and watched the previews.

"I can't remember the last movie I went to. Wait. Last year. My aunt wanted to see *The Sound of Music* which was pretty good. Did you see it?"

He lifted a brow.

"Right. Big, tough, hard-livin' cowboys ain't got time for that kinda musical nonsense."

Carson put his fingers over her lips. "You plan to talk through the whole movie?"

She opened her mouth to nip his fingers. "The movie hasn't started. And besides, I was hoping we wouldn't see *any* of the movie because we'd be doing other stuff."

"Carolyn."

"If you don't want to mess around with me, then why am I sitting on your lap?"

He shut her up with a kiss. "Behave. You might not want to watch the movie but I do."

She sighed dramatically but settled into him.

But forty-five minutes into the movie, she became restless. She started tracing the fingers on his right hand. From the tips to the knuckles. Then she turned his hand over and swept her thumb over the calluses at the base of each finger. After that she placed a kiss in the center of his palm and the inside of his wrist.

"Sugar. What're you doin'?"

"Exploring your hands. I love that they tell the story of what you do."

"That I toil outside in hot and cold weather and half the time I forget to wear my damn gloves?"

She ran his hand up and down her bare arm. "See? The way your rough skin feels on mine gives me goose bumps."

He placed her hand back in her lap. "Watch. The. Movie."

Five minutes later she said, "So what are we doing after this?"

Carson winced when two horses went down onscreen. Make believe or not he always reacted that way when animals got hurt.

"It's muggy enough that we could cool off at the lake." She fiddled with the buttons on his shirt, unsnapping the top two. "I'd even get in the water this time."

"Not a lake night. It's gonna rain."

"How do you know?"

"The way the sky looked earlier. How the air feels and smells now. Aw, hell. How come they never see an ambush comin'? It always happens."

"Because it's an ambush." Carolyn threw her leg over his thigh so she faced him, straddling him. "I'm thinking I need to ambush you."

Like he didn't see this coming.

But how was he supposed to resist taking it to the next level when she smelled so good. Or when he could feel the soft crush of her belly and her breasts against the hard wall of his chest. When he knew the sweet taste of her mouth and the no-holds-barred way she kissed. And the woman seemed especially determined tonight.

Why?

Why are you resisting her? You know where this is gonna end up anyway.

Not here, not like this. No way, no how.

"I love your chest. So strong and hard. So many muscles. Is it weird I like that you have a lot of chest hair? It's so manly. And you smell like you there. It's like the hair traps the scents of musk and salt and that outdoorsy scent, then it becomes you."

"I think we're missin' the gun fight."

She kissed the hollow of his throat. Then followed the tendons in his neck with her hot little tongue. "You still interested in watching the movie?"

He groaned. "You're makin' it damn hard."

"Isn't that what I'm supposed to do?"

Lord, she was insistent tonight. Maybe a little ornery.

You got ornery covered.

"My friend Laura lost her virginity at a drive-in."

"Not happening for you."

The light in her eyes disappeared. "Why don't I get a say? It's my virginity."

"We talked about this. There's a time and a place. This ain't it. Look, sugar. Can't we just have a normal date?"

"Is that why you're with me? Because I'm normal date material?"

"Yes. Now can we be done with this conversation and just watch the movie?"

But she wouldn't let it go. "It's starting to rain and you won't be able to see it anyway. And don't sidestep the question. What would you be doing if you were out on a date with someone else?"

This was a no-win situation and he oughta keep his damn mouth shut...but of course he just had to open up his trap. "I haven't been on a date since I was nineteen. I pick women up in bars, get what I want from them and walk away. I don't want that from you."

She looked affronted. "You don't want me?"

"I want you like fuckin' crazy." Carson snagged her wrist and pressed her palm against the fly of his jeans. "But that doesn't mean I'm gonna maul you at the drive-in."

"Even if I ask nicely?"

"Carolyn."

"You only have yourself to blame for how I'm acting. Since the night we met you've been showing me what desire is. What passion feels like. Is it any wonder I want more whenever I'm with you?" She traced his lower lip with her thumb, then she angled her head to make the same sweeping pass with her tongue. "Carson. Say something."

"It'd probably be best if you got off my lap."

"I thought you wanted me to sit on your lap."

"Not like this."

He felt her smile against his cheek. "You like this. I can tell."

The woman rocked her hips until her pubic bone bumped his erection.

He tried to stop her, but his hands gripping her ass had the exact opposite effect. The greedy male part of him wanted her to grind on him and show him how well she moved. Then he'd slip his fingers beneath her panties and see if it made her wet. Then he'd start sucking on her nipples...

"Carson. Touch me."

"No."

"Why not?" She dug her fingers into the back of his neck forcing his attention. "I see you looking at my chest all the time."

Do not look.

Dammit, why wouldn't his eyes listen?

"Don't you want your hands and mouth on me?"

"Of course I do. But that don't mean I'm gonna tear off your shirt, and take off your bra in a public place where anyone can walk past

77

and see your bare chest."

Her eyes widened as if that hadn't occurred to her.

So he took it a step farther to drive home his point. "If we get busy in my truck, everyone will know what we're doin' when it starts bouncing up and down. That'll draw an audience. That's what you want for your first time?"

"No. But—"

"Trust me. I'll know when you're ready. There's nothin' wrong with waitin' for it. Planning it."

"*You'll* know when I'm ready," she repeated.

"I ain't sayin' this to piss you off, but I do have more experience in these things than you do."

Carolyn pushed away from him and put distance between them.

The rain was really coming down and the movie was a total blur. But the voices coming from the speaker were rife with anger.

That's when he understood the anger in the air wasn't only from the movie effects or the humidity. She was mad.

Which meant she was really mad because he'd learned one thing about her in the times they'd spent together; she didn't have time for games. She wasn't playing at being mad.

"You gonna tell me what's got you huffing like an angry bull?"

Comparing her to livestock? Didn't think you were that dumb.

"Your expectations of how sex with me is going to play out— candlelight, flowers, chocolates and the release of beribboned doves at the moment of breaching my maidenhead—are not mine."

Christ. He hadn't thought she could be sarcastic either. Once she sank her teeth into something she wouldn't let it go.

"I thought you were different."

"Carolyn—"

"You look at me but you don't see me. You see what you want to see. You are like everyone else in my life who thinks it's their job to make decisions for me and what I want."

"Because I wouldn't fuck you, I'm an asshole?"

"No. I didn't ask you to have sex with me. But even if I had? You are dismissing what I want and how I feel."

Sadness filled her face and it hit him as hard as a punch in the nuts.

"Take me back to my car."

"We can talk—"

"No. It's not like we can watch the movie."

Fuck. Rather than try to climb over her into the driver's side, he jumped into the downpour and skirted the front end. Then getting in he almost sat on his hat. In trying to avoid that, he slammed his groin into the steering wheel.

"Motherfucking-cocksucking-son-of-a-fucking-bitch."

He breathed through the excruciating pain—he'd never racked

himself with a hard on before—and hoped he didn't pass out. He chanced a look at her.

She didn't even have that pursed set to her mouth when he cussed. She didn't snap, "Language," at him.

The windshield wipers slapped angrily as he pulled out of the parking lot onto the road. "This is not how I wanted the night to end."

"Just drive."

The air in the cab on the drive back to her car was hot and sticky—but that wasn't what made it uncomfortable.

Carolyn hadn't looked at him even one time. She'd just retreated. Hands folded in her lap, her gaze aimed out the window. Not that she could see anything through the fog on the inside and the driving rain surrounding them, but she pretended she could.

He hated dropping her off in the middle of nowhere, wishing instead he could pull up to her house, walk her to the door and give her a goodnight kiss. Yeah, like a normal date. Didn't most women want that?

So why the hell was this beautiful, sweet, pure woman so eager to give her virginity to a man like him?

Maybe for that reason.

Carson remembered from talking to the women who'd shared his bed that their initiation into sex left a lot to be desired. His first time at age fifteen hadn't lasted long at all. His partner, a twenty-year-old teacher's assistant, had lectured him on making sure the women he bedded had as much fun as he did. She'd taught him a lot.

And it wasn't as if he wasn't fucking dying to get his hands on her, his mouth on her and his dick in her. He just didn't want it to happen in a car or a truck. Carolyn deserved all that romancing stuff women loved.

He'd make it up to her. He'd take her out for supper tomorrow night. Then back to his place where he could get her completely nekkid and feast on her. Touch her, kiss her, taste her and show her how good it could be when he took his time.

Now that he had a plan, she couldn't argue he wasn't taking into consideration what she wanted.

Carson pulled alongside her car, put his truck in park and shut it off before he faced her. "Sorry that we ended up at cross purposes tonight."

Carolyn laughed cynically. "That's one way of putting it."

"How would you have put it?"

"You got your way. And whatever—" she gestured wildly, "—attraction you have for me is no match for your resolve to get your way."

"What the hell am I supposed to say to that, Caro?"

"Nothing. Goodbye." Carolyn bailed out of the truck.

Goodbye? Not goodnight? "Oh no. Oh *hell* no." Carson jumped out and caught her just as she started to unlock her car door. "You don't get to—"

Carolyn turned and shoved at him. "Leave me alone. I refuse to stand in the rain and argue with you."

She turned back and inserted the key, twisting hard. She did that twice more with no success.

Carson said, "Let me try."

"I don't want your help."

"I'm sure, but sugar, it looks like you need it." He curled himself around her, trying to block her from the downpour as he jimmied the lock.

And as he cranked and twisted, he was acutely aware of the soft cushion of her ass against his groin. The outer swell of her breast rubbing on the inside of his forearm. The way the rain released the flowery scent of her shampoo and the powdery sweet aroma of her perfume. The arm she'd braced against the window shook. He felt the heat rising from her neck and the press of her spine into his chest.

In that moment he needed her more than his next breath.

Then his mouth was on her ear. "Carolyn."

A shudder worked through her.

The keys dropped to the ground.

She tried to spin around but he held her in place. "Stay like this."

His hands moved to her hips and he followed the curve of her waist up to plant his hands on her breasts.

She arched against him hard, turning her head, baring her throat, reaching around to dig her nails into the base of his neck.

Carson tasted her skin, his lips gliding easily on the rain-slicked flesh. His teeth scraped along the tendon until his mouth connected with the spot where her pulse raged. He sucked hard.

Her moan as she gyrated her soft ass against his erection spurred him to take the next step.

Tugging her blouse free from her skirt, he worked the buttons until the back of his hand touched the bare skin of her belly. He trailed the fingers of his right hand to her left tit, and he slipped them beneath the satin cup, stroking before he lightly twisted the rigid tip while his mouth continued the onslaught of her throat. "Tell me what you want."

"Don't stop this time."

He bunched the sodden material of her skirt in his left hand and rolled it up, tucking it into the waistband.

The smooth skin of her thighs beckoned. While his right hand toyed with her hard nipple, his left hand delved between her legs. The heat and wetness soaking through her panties had nothing to do with the rain. A primitive growl rumbled free as he stroked her on the outside of her cleft, getting her used to his touch.

Carolyn bumped her hips forward, panting for more.

Pulling her panties aside, he hissed at that first slippery connection to the soft petals of her sex. He followed the wet slit, stopping at the top to finger her clit, loving that she nearly collapsed in his arms at his intimate touch. "Such a sweet, sweet pussy, sugar," he murmured beneath her jaw.

His fully erect cock protested the angle when he leaned forward to swirl his finger around her opening. His entire body was as rigid as his cock. Could Carolyn feel how hard his heart slammed in his chest as he pressed it against her back? Could she feel his blood pumping so fast and hot where her fingernails dug into the nape of his neck?

Carson's lips found hers. They kissed with desperation. He pushed his finger inside her, releasing another growl at the hot sheath that hugged it, knowing how fucking good it'd feel having his cock buried in the tight heat.

Once he started to thrust in and out, she canted her hips, trying to drive him in deeper. He added another finger, scissoring his fingers as well, even knowing the best way to stretch her fully was to use his dick.

"Carolyn." He nuzzled her cheek while he continued to drive his fingers into her. This wasn't how he wanted it to happen, but it was going to happen. "Stop me now if you don't—"

"Don't stop. Please."

At some point the rain had let up, changing into misty drops. Steam radiated from the pavement and he felt it rising off of him, out of him.

His head screamed with the need to have her. His hands left her body only long enough to turn her around and push her against the car. They were plastered together by the rain, and by need. Carson kissed her frantically as he unhooked his belt and dropped his jeans and boxers to his knees.

Carolyn's fingers were tugging on the buttons of his shirt. Then she raked her nails down his skin, stopping when the tips reached the head of his cock.

He moved her hand up, placing it around the back of his neck again. "Hold on." Grabbing the back of her left thigh, he wrapped it around his hip, bringing them groin to groin.

She buried her face in his neck and her hot breath sent goose bumps down his arms.

Carson bent down to align his cock, pausing at her opening. It was on the tip of his tongue to ask if she was ready or to tell her he'd go slow, but he hadn't done a play by play so far; no need to do it now.

Her hand on his chest tightened, her nails digging into his pectoral as he fed his cock into her.

He closed his eyes, tempted to grit his teeth as her sheath enveloped him. Jesus. She was so tight. Wet, but tight. And hot. An overwhelming need to move had him holding his breath.

Her softly whispered, "Yes, more," was the signal he needed.

He managed a couple of slow thrusts—pulling out fully and pushing back in to the root—keeping one hand braced on the car and the other hand on her knee, holding her steady.

When Carolyn started rocking into him, her hot tongue tracing his collarbone while her thumb scraped his nipple, he kicked up the pace.

It wasn't long before he rammed into that yielding channel harder every time, his balls no longer swinging forward, but tight. Ready to blow.

Without missing a stroke his lips traveled down her face, from her temple to her jaw and then over to fuse his mouth to hers. The burning passion between them flared higher. Hotter. She pulled his hair. Her kiss was ferocious. She canted her hips, matching his every hard thrust.

At that rate Carson knew he'd be spilling inside her soon. Not knowing how close she was, he reached between their straining bodies and spread open the upper section of her pussy. When he pushed back inside her, he kept his groin pressed into hers, keeping constant contact on her clit.

Carolyn started to shudder and he felt the rippling pulses of her pussy around his shaft. Instead of throwing her head back, she curled into him, pressing her mouth against the ball of his shoulder as she climaxed. With each rhythmic pulse her teeth sunk deeper into his flesh.

Who knew that sexy love bite as she came would do it for him?

Those glove-tight walls sucked every bit of seed from his balls. He didn't hammer into her as he started to come. Slowing down prolonged every hot burst and he couldn't stop the, "Fuckin' hell, woman," from tumbling out of his mouth before his brain functions ceased entirely.

At some point he'd tipped his head back. Rain spattering his face roused him out of that post-orgasmic void. He glanced down to see Carolyn staring up at him. Her hair was soaked; she had makeup smudged beneath her eyes. Her lips were curved in a very feminine smile; her eyes were half-lidded with sexual satisfaction.

She was the most beautiful thing he'd ever seen.

"Carolyn—"

She placed her fingers over his lips. "Don't say anything. This was everything I thought it'd be. Thank you." Then she kissed him with sweet reverence as she stared into his eyes. "This was perfect. You were perfect, Carson."

"Sugar." He framed her face in his hands and covered her mouth with his, their bodies still connected. They kissed until they each had their fill, balancing tenderness with lingering desire. "I wish I could take you home and tuck you in my bed."

"I do too. But I need to get going."

She only winced a little when he pulled out.

He lowered her leg and righted her panties and skirt before he fought with the wet, cold denim around his knees. Her hands shook as she buttoned her blouse. Carson didn't bother fastening his shirt; he was going straight home and Cal wouldn't care if he stumbled into the trailer naked.

He picked up her key ring and inserted the key into the lock. It popped on the first try. When he opened the door, she smiled at him.

"What?"

"For the first time ever I'm happy that lock sticks."

"Me too." He placed a kiss on the side of her neck and murmured, "Don't be alarmed if you think someone is followin' you home. It's just me."

"Carson. You don't have to. It's another thirty miles out of your way."

"It's late, it's raining, and you're alone, so yeah, I'm followin' you. Like it or not."

"Okay." She kissed his chin. "You're sweet."

He snorted. "First time I've heard that."

"Then I'm happy to be the first one to have noticed it."

"I wanna see you tomorrow, Caro." And the day after that, and the day after that.

"I don't know if I can swing it."

"The next night then." But he knew he couldn't stay away from her for even one day.

She planted another kiss on his lips. "Drive safe after you see me home, okay?"

"I will."

Chapter Seven
Carolyn

The house was so quiet.

It was strange being the only one home. Her father had taken her mother into Rapid City for doctor's appointments and they'd be gone until suppertime. Marshall was in Cheyenne overnight. Stuart and Thomas were both at work. For the next few hours she could do anything she wanted.

She could finish the pedal pushers she'd started last week. She could weed the garden. Or she could wander into the field behind the house, searching for wild parsnips and mushrooms, or pick a bouquet of wildflowers for her room.

Or she could sit here with the sun warming her face, reliving every moment of losing her virginity to Carson McKay.

Every single moment. Every word. Every touch. Especially his touch.

She'd really thought he'd hold out after lecturing her on sex in a "proper" bed, even after she'd made the smart remark about *his* expectations of candlelight, flowers, chocolates and the release of beribboned doves at the moment of breaching her maidenhead—were not hers.

But it turned out he'd been as powerless against the passion that exploded between them as she.

So she hadn't lost her virginity in any proper manner at all, rather one hot and bothered cowboy had pushed her up against her car and driven into her in the driving rain.

She sighed and closed her eyes. It'd been absolutely perfect. Water soaking their feverish skin. His hot mouth on her rain-cooled flesh. His hardness filling her softness, over and over. His rough-skinned hand clamped onto her behind. The sexy rumble of his voice in her ear when he wasn't kissing her. Kissing her like her mouth alone could sustain him.

And when she feared her body would simply fly apart from the bliss that beckoned, Carson took her to paradise, joining her, and everything in her life changed.

Dramatic? Maybe. But that physical connection was way more

than she'd ever expected.

Carolyn had just decided to quit lazing around and accomplish something, when she heard a vehicle turn up the drive. Probably just Harland or Darren coming to borrow tools or something, so she didn't bother to move from her comfy spot in the sun. Maybe she wouldn't do anything today but loaf.

Right. That's not your nature.

A door slammed. "Sugar, is this really how you're spendin' all your days?"

She sat up so fast her sunglasses went flying. Then she scrambled to her feet. "Carson? What are you doing here?"

He paused at the bottom of the steps. His left eyebrow winged up. "That's how you greet me after last night?"

Happiness nearly split her heart in two. She laughed and said, "Catch!" before she launched herself at him.

Carson caught her, his hands curling around her hips as his mouth found hers.

With the hungry way he kissed her and with her arms twined around his neck she felt like she was floating. The kiss went on for a blissfully long time. He broke the kiss slowly, treating her lips to little nibbles, a soft glide and then decisive smooches. "I probably oughtn't maul you on the front porch in case your mama is peeking out the window."

"She's not here. My dad took her to the doctor and they'll be gone all day."

"That right?"

"My brothers are gone too."

"So you're all alone?"

She kissed his chin. "Not anymore. Have you had lunch?"

"Nope."

"Come in." She tugged his hand. "I'll fix you something."

"In a second. Lemme grab something outta my truck."

Carolyn watched him amble to the driver's side door, enjoying the view of his tight buns and long legs encased in denim. Although it was fairly warm out today, he wore a long-sleeved shirt—not that the extra fabric could hide the broad set of shoulders. Shoulders she'd been clinging to last night as his body had moved in and out of hers.

She was still lost in heated memories of hands and mouths and bodies in motion when he stopped in front of her.

"Whatcha thinkin' about, Caro?"

Her eyes locked onto his. "Last night."

He dipped his head and kissed the side of her throat. "You ain't the only one." Then he looked at her and smiled. A sweet, slightly devious smile and Lord have mercy she was just gone for this man. "I brought you something."

That's when she noticed his hands were behind his back. "What?"

Carson handed her a box of candy. "Since I didn't give you the hearts and flowers romance you deserved last night, and since you were sarcastic about the doves at the moment of the official cherry popping, I thought I could at least bring you a sweet treat that'll remind you of me."

She laughed softly and studied the box of chocolate-covered cherries, hoping he didn't notice her damp eyes. This man was so sweet and he had a good sense of humor. "I love chocolate. Thank you."

"Hey." His fingers were under her chin, lifting her face to meet his gaze. "You okay today?"

"Very okay. I know last night wasn't...didn't play out how you'd hoped. But for me, it was everything I'd ever wanted it to be and more."

"Then that's all that matters."

"Was it okay for you?"

"No."

Her heart stopped. "It wasn't?"

"No," he said again as he brushed soft, seductive kisses across her mouth. "It was fuckin' amazing."

She smiled against his lips. "Oh. Good."

"Mmm-hmm." He started nibbling her jaw. "Sugar, are we really alone?"

She loved how his breath felt fanning her skin. "Yes."

"For how long?"

"For hours."

"That'll work." He lifted her into his arms.

"Carson!"

"Open the door."

She turned the handle and he strode inside the house and kicked the door shut behind them. "Which way?"

"To the kitchen for lunch?"

"No. To your bedroom. We can eat food after I've had a taste of you."

Her stomach cartwheeled so hard it kicked her heart into high gear.

"Caro?"

"Straight ahead. I sleep in the sun porch."

Once they were in her space, she tried to see it from his point of view. Half the room was packed with junk since it doubled as a storage room when she and Kimi weren't here. Her mother's sewing machine, dress maker dummy, ironing board, irons and sewing instruments were in the center of the room, along with stacks of material, thread, ribbons, notions, paper patterns, a box of buttons and other odds and ends.

In the corner, she'd pushed the twin beds together, making a decent-sized sleeping area for herself. A bed with pale peach sheets, lots of pillows, a bright reading lamp for the foldable flat board so she could hand sew pieces in bed if she chose. Her closet and dressing area was in the opposite corner behind two floral sheets. She'd hung her clothes on a dowel placed between two chains. Her underwear, slips and hosiery were in an old suitcase she'd cut in half and converted into dresser drawers.

The click of the lock brought her attention back to Carson. He wasn't looking at her surroundings. At all. His eyes were focused solely on her.

It dawned on her it was the middle of the day. There'd be no darkness, every part of her, every part of him would be completely visible. Every other time they'd been intimate had been at night. And she'd never completely bared herself to another person...well...ever.

"Don't," he said softly as he stalked closer.

"Don't what?"

"Don't think." He reached her and pushed her hair over her shoulder. "You're beautiful and I can't wait to get my hands on every inch of you. Last night was just the start. Trust me." He rested his forehead to hers. "You do trust me, right?"

"Yes."

"Good. First you gotta lose the clothes." He hooked his fingers in the hem of her baggy red peasant shirt and pulled it up until she raised her arms.

Her bra wasn't sheer, just plain white. She fought the urge to cross her arms over her chest.

His fingers slipped beneath the waistband of her skirt near her belly button, using her skin as a guide to find the button in the back. After unbuttoning her, Carson made short work of the zipper too. The navy blue cotton skirt fell to the floor.

Her panties matched her bra—bonus points for that, but her underwear wasn't sexy, just plain white cotton.

Then his mouth was on her neck and his hands started at her shoulders and moved down. Stroking and caressing her skin. His thumbs following the swell of her breasts while his palms curled around her ribcage.

At Carson's show of reverence, she relaxed even when every tender touch and nip of his teeth set her body on fire.

His hands stopped on her hips, those wickedly stroking thumbs of his brushed over the rise of her mound and the sensitive inner skin by her hipbone. And still he didn't say a word, he just explored. As his hands moved south so did his mouth. He palmed her behind in both hands as his tongue traced the edge of her bra, down one side and up the other.

Carolyn wasn't sure what to do with her hands. She wanted to run her fingers through his hair. Grip his shoulders. Or should she start to undress him too?

"Unhook your bra for me so I don't have to stop touchin' you."

She twisted her arms behind her back and tugged the clasp.

Carson's gaze met hers as he eased the straps down her arms. Only when the straps cleared her fingertips did he look at her chest.

"Perfect. Jesus, look at you." He held her breasts and rubbed his cheek and jaw from the top of the left side, down to her sternum and back up the right side.

Every kiss, every taste inched closer to her nipple and her body went rigid in anticipation. Then his mouth enclosed the hardened tip.

Wet. Hot. His tongue flicking, his mouth sucking. Her head fell back and she groaned as each determined suck sent chills racing down her body.

Carolyn was so lost in the way he worshipped her breasts that she didn't notice his hand had slid down the center of her torso until he was stroking her there. Right there.

"You like that."

"Yes."

"I can tell," he murmured against the side of her breast. "Your panties are getting wet." He nipped her breast with his teeth and stroked her faster. "Time to take them off."

She froze.

"Trust me, sugar, you want this." He captured her mouth in one of those kisses that made her mind fuzzy as his hand slipped inside her panties, his finger connecting with her bare flesh. "Take them off."

She tugged her underwear down, even while his finger kept up that long glide on her slit.

Carson broke the kiss to whisper, "Sit on the edge of the bed."

Somehow she managed it, despite the throbbing between her legs and her head floating in the clouds. She closed her eyes and started to lie back on the mattress but Carson's grip on her wrist stopped her.

"Huh-uh. I want you to watch."

Carolyn opened her eyes and immediately snapped out of the passion-filled stupor. Her gaze moved over him. He was still fully dressed. Was he going to strip for her? "Watch what?"

Carson dropped to his knees, right between hers. His hands landed on her thighs and he pushed them wider apart, his focus completely on her sex.

She felt her entire body turn the color of a ripe tomato as he stared at her *there*. Stared and made a growling noise as his fingers inched forward.

What was he doing? Her mouth went so dry she couldn't form a question.

Then those blue blue eyes hooked hers, sending a blast of heat through her. "Watch me put my mouth on you."

Wait. What?

Then Carson bent his head, moving closer and closer...surely he didn't mean to...? And a bolt of electricity shot through her at the first touch of his tongue.

The second and third licks were delicate, but no less powerful. She held herself stiff, waiting—hoping—for more.

"So goddamn sweet," he said roughly, but his lips were gentle as he brushed his mouth over the blonde curls at the top of her sex. He kept muttering.

"What?"

Again he looked at her. She blushed, thinking about the intimate position they were in. "Ever had a man's mouth down here?"

She shook her head. But something compelled her to say, "I didn't know that—this—was part of it. Of sex. I just thought it was...you know. What happened last night."

That surprised him. Then he grinned. "I love that you don't know nothin' about this and I'm the first to taste this sweet pussy."

Before she wanted to close her eyes; now she couldn't look away when he lowered his head.

He curled the tip of his tongue where the split in her sex started at the top of her pubic bone. He wiggled his tongue side to side, so it would hit that good spot and then he'd move it away. She wanted to force him to stay there and keep doing that flicking thing until the ache abated.

"That's my favorite spot, but I love it here, where all your sweet juice gathers." He swirled his tongue around her opening, keeping his eyes locked on hers. Then he plunged his tongue into her, like he'd plunged his hardness into her last night. He closed his eyes and groaned softly, his face lost in bliss as he tongued her deeply.

With each plunge and lick she felt the changes in her body. Getting wetter. Swelling and yet softening. Her thighs were quivering. Her spine tingled from the nape of her neck to her tailbone. She wanted that pulsing rush. "Carson."

He eased back, letting his hot breath wash over her tender tissues, and his tongue darted out to trace her inner folds. "Do you want me to make you come?"

"Yes."

"After that...you know we ain't done." He placed a soft kiss on the insides of her thighs. "I'm thinkin' I ain't ever gonna be done with you."

Before she could ask him what he meant, he fastened his mouth around that hot spot and began to suck.

Then he'd flutter his tongue over the swollen nub, pause and return to sucking.

Carolyn couldn't keep her eyes open. She threw her head back. She couldn't stop the pleading noises from coming out of her mouth. When he brought her to the edge of release and then backed off, she grabbed hold of his head, her fingers gripping his hair, holding him exactly where she needed him. "Don't move. Don't stop. Please."

And he didn't. The intensity of her climax...she'd never experienced anything like it. She cried out his name, she pulled his hair, she thrashed against the mattress and when he finally brought her down, she had the overwhelming urge to cry.

But Carson petted and stroked her. Planting sweet, soft, lingering kisses on her quaking legs and kissing the insides of her wrists. That's when she realized she still had a strong grip on his hair. Her hands fell away. "Sorry."

"Don't be. I loved that you didn't hold back even on your first time." He kissed her fingertips. "That seems to be the norm with you sugar, and I like it. A lot."

Carson stood. She noticed his hands shook as he began to unbutton his shirt.

He helped you get undressed; help him. Show him you want him.

Carolyn sat up and reached for his belt buckle.

"I got this," he said, staying her hand.

"I want to."

Uncertainty flickered in his eyes but he never missed a button. He tugged the arms free and the shirt fell to the floor.

By then Carolyn had already worked the belt buckle loose. She popped the button on the waistband of his jeans and noticed the zipper tab poked out. After she lowered the zipper to the base, she pulled apart the material and ran her fingers along the hard length.

He sucked in a swift breath.

So she did it again.

"Caro."

"I want to see it."

Immediately he bent over and shucked his pants and underwear. When he stood before her completely naked, her eyes widened. His manhood was bigger than she expected. Reddish purple at the tip. An angry-looking red. Veins stuck out clear to the base where it disappeared into thick black hair. She couldn't take her eyes off it.

"Can I touch it?"

"As much as you want."

She wrapped her fingers around the base. So hard. And hot. As she moved her hand up, she realized as hard as it was, the skin was also soft and smooth.

While Carolyn was touching him, Carson had his hand in her hair, pushing the damn strands away from her face, twisting tendrils around his finger.

"You're so quiet," he murmured.

"So are you." She followed the edge of the head with her thumb. When she reached the front, he hissed and it jerked in her hand. "Is that a good spot?"

"Yeah."

Okay. Now what?

His fingers were under her chin and he lifted her face up. "Talk to me. No time to be shy when your hand is on my dick."

"I don't know what I'm doing. I don't know what you want me to do."

Carson put her hand back down at the base and curled his hand around hers. Then he stroked upward, exerting more pressure than she would've dared to try. "Like this. The faster you do it the quicker I'll come. Usually."

The more she moved her hand, the more little beads of clear fluid appeared on the tip.

"Stop."

She tilted her head back to look at him. "Am I doing something wrong?"

"No. But I wanna be inside you when I come. Up you go on the bed."

Instead of trying to crawl backward, she rolled to her knees and crawled forward across the mattress.

Carson growled behind her.

She stopped and looked over her shoulder at him.

He was stroking himself. "I can't fuckin' wait to take you like that. Drivin' into you from behind. Feelin' your soft ass as a cushion for my hips."

Carolyn rolled onto her backside, propping herself up on her elbows to watch him.

"Why didn't that make you blush?"

"I don't know. I wish I didn't blush at all."

"It's sweet. And I plan to teach you all sorts of other fun stuff that'll really make you blush." Then he put his knees on the bed, lowering his head to kiss her ankle. He scattered kisses on her shin, knee and thigh as he moved up her body. He pushed her thighs apart and stopped to run his tongue down her slit to her opening and back up to lightly suck on her clit. "You're still wet. That means you liked touchin' me."

"I told you I did."

"Mmm-hmm." He pressed hot, soft kisses in a line up her belly and between her breasts. "Words lie, but sugar, your body don't." Carson's tongue zigzagged across her breasts, from one to the other. Teasing with fast flicks. Making her arch when he sucked her nipple deeply into his mouth.

But he didn't spend as much time there as before. Those soft, yet firm lips trailed kisses up her neck. Kisses that made her flesh tingle. And she loved having his chest pressed to hers, even when it made it harder to breathe.

Then Carson's face was above hers, his blue eyes glittering with an emotion she couldn't name.

"Reach between us and guide me in."

"But I—"

"I'm dyin' to be with you like this."

That's when she noticed his body was shaking. She arched up, smashing her mouth to his while her hands trailed down his sides and between their hips. After a couple of bobbles she aligned the head of his shaft at her opening.

He eased inside her just an inch.

"Look at me, beautiful."

Carolyn met his gaze and everything inside her went soft with the perfect and loving way this sexy man gazed at her in this moment.

"Ready?"

"Yes."

He slowly pushed inside her, keeping their eyes locked. They were so close they shared the same breath.

"You okay," he whispered against her lips.

"Very okay."

"You feel so damn good, Caro."

She slid her hands over his shoulders and his muscular back, loving the sensation of skin on skin. "So do you."

When he stopped she knew why he'd gone slowly; he filled her completely.

"Wrap your legs around me."

As soon as she shifted, her body seemed to open and he pushed in deeper. "Oh." Her hands found purchase on his butt cheeks. Whenever he angled his pelvis those powerful muscles flexed beneath her hands.

Carson kissed her, bringing her focus to the soft stroke of his tongue against hers.

During the kiss, she felt him start to move, pulling back and pushing forward. Her inner tissues were gripping him so tightly, trying to keep him buried inside.

His lips followed the line of her jaw to whisper, "You with me if I pick up the pace?"

"Yes."

Then Carson's mouth seemed to be everywhere, nuzzling her throat, leaving sucking kisses on the inner curve of her shoulder, his uneven breath in her ear proved he was as affected by this as she was.

He pushed his body up higher, but his gaze was glued to her face. "Look at you. I've imagined bein' with you like this, but my imagination didn't do it justice."

She opened her mouth, but closed it.

Carson stopped moving. "What?"

"We did this last night."

"Not like this, we didn't." He slid his lips back and forth over hers. "Last night was hard and fast and hot as fuckin' fire, but this? This is me makin' love to you, sugar."

And it felt like love; very overwhelming. The rough friction of his chest hair on her nipples, the weight of his body. The hot and sweet kisses that were perfectly matched to his steady surge and retreat rhythm.

She kissed his neck, loving the salty taste of his skin and the musk that smelled too good to come from a bottle.

His strokes became faster and he broke the kiss to stare into her eyes. "I can't hold back. Are you close?"

Carolyn wasn't sure; it all felt so good that she just nodded.

His thrusts came hard and fast. Then he threw his head back and groaned.

She watched him shamelessly; his eyes squeezed shut, his mouth slack.

He was even more powerful and stunning lost in passion.

Then he opened those amazing blue eyes—eyes still clouded with pleasure—and teased her with the languorous kisses of a satisfied man.

"What's the smirk for?" he asked.

"Are you happy now that we did this in a proper bed?"

"Very happy. I could get used to doin' that," Carson murmured against her throat. "A lot."

A dreamy smile creased her face as she trailed her fingers down his spine. "Me too. Though last night in the rain was fun."

"Mmm." Carson pushed up and watched her eyes as he pulled out slowly. "Sore?"

"A little."

"Maybe I'll have to kiss it and make it better later."

Her belly flipped. "Okay."

Carson grinned. "Liked that, didja?"

Even though she was naked just talking about that made her blush and she wanted to turn her head away to hide how much she'd loved that. Or if—when—he'd want her to do the same thing to him. Her gaze slid to his groin. He was still sort of hard. Which made her curious as to what it looked like when it wasn't hard.

His fingers slipped under her chin, forcing her attention on him. "Got a mighty interesting look on that beautiful face. Whatcha thinkin' about?"

She squirmed beneath his scrutiny.

"Tell me."

"Do you want me to do that to you?" she blurted out.

Carson's eyes widened and then turned fiery hot. "You tryin' to kill me, woman?"

"N-no, but I thought—"

"Yes, I can't wait to see these lips around my cock. But I ain't gonna push you. So how about you let me know when you're ready to try it."

"Okay."

"Get dressed before I crawl back in there with you."

Carolyn couldn't take her eyes off Carson as he put his clothes back on. It was just as intimate getting dressed together as it'd been getting undressed together.

As soon as they were fully clothed, Carson pulled her into his arms and just held her. No ravenous kisses, no roaming hands. His need for such simple contact with her sent her spiraling to the point of no return.

She knew then that she loved him. After less than a week.

It didn't feel wrong. Or impulsive. It felt like she'd found where she belonged.

He kissed her forehead. "I probably better go."

"I thought I was fixing you lunch?" Clasping his hand, she led him to the kitchen. "How about a sandwich? Ham salad on rye bread with pickles?"

"Sounds good. Way better than the bologna or peanut butter and jelly I usually have."

"There are days when that's all I want." Carolyn took everything out of the fridge and started assembling three sandwiches.

"Can I ask you something? Is it hard goin from livin' in a dorm and havin' all your meals prepared for you, to comin' back here and makin' three meals a day for your whole family?"

She shrugged. "It's what I'm used to. And without sounding flip, isn't that what all girls are expected to do? Learn to cook by our mother's side so we can take care of our own families? I'll bet your mom cooked for you."

"There was always food on the table when we were hungry and I didn't think much about it beyond that."

"That's how most men are."

"Do you like cookin'?"

Carolyn met his gaze. "I love it. There's something very satisfying about making an entirely new dish or hearing how much a meal is enjoyed." Feeling silly, she looked back down at her sandwich.

Carson's callused hand caressed hers. "Hey. You seem embarrassed by that. Why?"

"Some of my friends at school, they want to be nurses and teachers. A couple girls are going to beauty school to become hairdressers. My roommate, Mary Catherine, is attending college to become a lawyer. The wild girl in our class, Mary Claire, is moving to the east coast to become a stewardess. And then there's me."

"What about you?"

"I don't have those kinds of aspirations."

A pause. "And they all think you oughta be like them?"

She nodded and sliced a pickle in half. "I don't know what I'll be doing at the end of the summer. Everyone said it'd be a waste if I live at home and do all the household stuff for my family. My friend Cathy has asked me to move to Chicago. I could live with her and get a job as a seamstress or in a sewing factory."

"Do you want to live in the big city?"

"I don't know. My Aunt Hulda has offered me a fulltime job this fall. She pays me pretty well and I've learned so much from her."

"Wait. She pays you to work for her?"

Carolyn looked up at him with a scowl. "Of course she pays me. She didn't expect me to work for free." Even when her aunt footed the bill for Carolyn's Catholic education, she believed in "funding Carolyn's future", which would give her options.

"Sorry if you took offense to that." Carson blocked her against the counter. "The reason you don't complain about cookin' and cleanin', and havin' a garden is because you really like doin' that, don't you?"

"Yes. Everyone says it makes me naïve because if I don't expand my horizons, how will I know if I really like it or not? But I do like it."

"Don't listen to them people. They don't matter. They ain't livin' your life; you are." He caressed her face with the back of his hand and his eyes were so soft, but his face was so fierce with intent that she felt herself melting into him. "Don't take this the wrong way, but you are mature beyond your years. You've had no choice but to grow up fast and be responsible. There should be pride in that. There should be pride in all the things you do for your family—because you like doin' them. Anyone who tries to shame you for that ain't worth your time."

"Thank you."

"My pleasure." Carson peered over her shoulder. "That sandwich almost looks too pretty to eat."

She gently shunted him aside. "I'll get the plates."

They didn't talk much while they were eating.

After they finished, Carson said, "Best lunch I've ever had." He grinned. "The appetizer was tasty too."

She blushed.

"As much as I hate to eat and run, I gotta git." He snagged her hand. "Walk me out to the truck and make me all sorts of promises about when I can see you next, because if you don't, I'm afraid I ain't gonna leave."

Outside Carson leaned against the driver's side of his truck and pulled her close so she rested against him completely. Then he scrambled her brain with a kiss so steamy she felt him getting hard against her belly.

That's when he broke the kiss and rubbed his damp lips across her temple. "Thank you for today but when can I see you tomorrow?"

Ridiculously pleased, she said, "I could come to your place tomorrow night and cook you supper?"

"A hot woman and a hot meal? Gonna be another great day." He pecked her on the mouth and moved her aside. "I'll hafta draw you a map. My place is a little hard to find."

Carolyn waited as he dug around for a piece of paper and a pencil. He pressed the paper against the window and sketched out a very detailed map and handed it over.

"Easiest way to get there. I wrote my phone number on the bottom if you get lost, not that it'll help ya since you'll have to drive into Sundance to find a pay phone."

"I'll find you."

"Good."

She stayed in the driveway until he pulled onto the road, watching him go. After his truck was out of sight, she returned inside and wandered to the sun porch. She crawled onto her bed and sighed. The sheets smelled like him. She may never wash them again.

Chapter Eight
Carson

Exhausted, Carson sat on the tailgate, drinking beer number two and smoking his third cigarette when Cal pulled up.

His twin hopped out of his truck and ambled over. "That bad, huh?"

"Yep." Cal knew Carson only smoked when something weighed on him. Strange as it sounded, smoking always cleared his head.

And the shit going round and round in his brain wasn't making a bit of fucking sense.

His brother grabbed a bottle of Coors out of the paper sack, and sat opposite him on the old stump. "What's up? You've been awful damn secretive this week." He twisted the cap off the bottle and drank. "Speaking of...I covered for you with Dad today."

"What'd you tell him?"

"You were trackin' down parts."

Some piece of machinery was always busted so Carson wasn't surprised their dad hadn't asked specifics. "Thanks."

"I reckon what goes around, comes around."

"Yeah, yeah, I'll remember that." He took another drag and held it in his lungs before blowing it out.

"You gonna tell me what's goin' on with you?"

"Nope."

"Why not?"

"'Cause you'll laugh your ass off, then I'll hafta to beat on you and I don't feel like mixin' it up today."

Cal shook his head. "There's a first."

"Fuck off."

He laughed. "And you're touchy about it too. Gotta be a woman involved."

Carson ground out his smoke before helping himself to another beer.

"Come on. Gimme something. Quit actin' like a girl with the 'should I or shouldn't I?' bullshit and start talkin'. You tell me everything because you know you can tell me anything."

No lie there. Maybe it was some twin bond crap, or the fact they'd lived together and worked together, but he and Cal never kept secrets from each other.

But Carson couldn't force the words out.

When he heard the sarcastic voice cooing about those sweet and sentimental words being so tightly wrapped around his heart, he said screw that and blurted, "I'm in love with her, okay? Can't sleep, can't eat, can't fuckin' think without my thoughts turnin' to her."

"Who?"

He sent his brother a fiery look. "You know fuckin' who."

"Jesus, Carse, you can't be. It's the whole forbidden fruit shit that's convinced you it's love and not lust." He pointed with his beer bottle. "Take her to bed. That'll get her outta your system."

"Already did that and it's just made it worse. Or better. Fuck if I know."

"What's that mean?"

"Bein' with her...it's different. I feel different. It's like nothin' that happened to me or anything I did before I met her even matters anymore."

"Holy shit."

"Yeah."

They drank in silence.

After a bit, Cal said, "So what're you gonna do?"

"Drink until I pass out."

"Great plan. If you pass out, I ain't carryin' you inside."

"Then what good are you?"

Cal laughed. "No one else would put up with your shit, so you're stuck with me until I pass you off as someone else's problem."

"What the hell is that supposed to mean?"

"You really wanna know?"

"I asked, didn't I?" When Cal started picking at the label on his beer bottle instead of answering, Carson snapped, "Well?"

"That right there is what I mean. You are a hard man like Dad in so many ways. Always focused on getting the work done, makin' sure it's done right and movin' onto the next thing. But you've got a reckless streak a damn mile wide. It's your way of thumbing your nose at your responsibilities. During the week you're Carson McKay, heir apparent to the McKay ranch, driven to succeed. But on weekends, you're that wild McKay, always lookin' for a good fight or a fast fuck, and fuck anyone who stands in your way of havin' a good time."

Yeah. Not a whole lot he could say to that because it was dead on.

"How many times you been asked when you'll settle down and stop the fightin' and the drinkin'?"

"Asked by Dad? Or asked by the people I hang around with on the weekends?"

"Both."

"My drinkin' buddies are *worried* I'll settle down so they don't say nothin'. Every once in a while Dad will mention it ain't my job to answer every challenge with my fists, drink up all the alcohol in Crook County and sample every pussy in Wyoming."

Cal choked on his beer. "Jesus. Dad *said* that to you?"

"On more than one occasion."

"That shocks the hell out of me."

"Why? Dad ripped it up plenty in his day. He didn't marry Ma until he was thirty-one."

"You ain't gonna last until you're thirty-one, the way you're talkin'." Cal got a gleam in his eye. "What happens after you admit your undying love for Carolyn West and beg her to make an honest man outta you?"

Carson grinned. "First thing I do is kick your ass out. Then when my beloved and I can force ourselves to leave our bed, we'll hit the dancehall and the bars. Just 'cause we're married don't mean we gotta act like them old couples who stay at home and stare at the damn walls for fun."

Cal cocked his head. "So you do plan on getting hitched to her?"

"If she'll have me." As soon as Carson admitted that out loud, he believed it. He'd make it happen.

"Gimme another goddamned beer."

He handed it over. "Can you make yourself scarce tomorrow night? Carolyn's comin' over."

"Guess that means you ain't interested in hittin' Gentleman Jack's?"

"Nope."

"Maybe I'll pop Charlie's strip club cherry since I got a feelin' your strip club days are done."

"Good plan."

And that was that. End of discussion. Another thing he appreciated about Cal. He never wanted to talk things to fucking death, but he was always there whenever Carson needed to talk.

The following night Carolyn showed up on time, looking as tempting as strawberry ice cream in a pale pink dress, her hair swirled on top of her head.

He swept her into his arms, kissing her hungrily as he carried her into the trailer. So much for acting cool.

She sighed and placed a lingering kiss on his throat.

That simple, sweet gesture nearly did him in. But he'd sworn to himself he wasn't dragging her to his bed as soon as she waltzed in the door. He nuzzled her neck. "You smell good."

"Like pork chops and fried apples? That's what I cooked for them for supper and what I'm making us."

"No, like flowers and you. The scent of your skin drives me crazy."

Lorelei James

He dragged his lips across her ear. "Almost as crazy as how hot and sweet you taste between your thighs."

"Carson McKay. Stop dirty talking me right now. I promised I'd cook for you first."

He trapped her face in his hands. "Sugar, I'm not like—" *your family*, "—I don't expect you to cook for me if you don't want to."

"Which is exactly why I want to do it." She pecked him on the mouth. "I brought food with me, so if you'll show me where you keep your cooking utensils?"

"I'll warn ya, it's a pretty humble selection."

"I'll make do."

"Tell me whatcha need."

Carolyn rattled off—a cast iron pan, a sharp knife, a cutting board, butter, salt, pepper and flour. Luckily he had everything.

"Want a beer or something while you're workin'?"

"I'll take a Coke if you've got one."

Carson poured her soda on ice, grabbed a beer for himself and turned the radio on to the local country station.

He watched her work and they talked about their days while she fixed supper. It didn't feel forced as it had other times women had offered to make him a home-cooked meal. It seemed natural and he imagined how heavenly it'd be coming home to her—and this—every night.

"Carson?" she prompted.

"Sorry. Lost in thought. What did you say?"

"I asked if you're okay with me putting onions in this?"

He sipped his beer. "Depends on if the onions will keep you from kissin' me tonight."

She grinned. "Nope."

"Then put 'em in."

"Where's your brother? I thought maybe I'd meet him."

"He had plans."

"Do you guys have any problems working together all day and then living together?"

"Once in a while, but not really. I'd rather hang out with him than anyone else."

"So is it the same way with your other brothers?"

Carson shook his head. "My youngest brother Charlie is just outta high school and is finding his way." He realized that Carolyn and Charlie were the same age, which was just plain weird because she was ten times more mature than his baby brother. "My middle brother Casper is an ass. I hafta work with him for now, so I don't spend time with him outside of the ranch if I can help it. Although he is a mean son of a bitch so he's good to have backin' me in a fight if Cal ain't around."

Her eyes widened. "Is fighting a habit of yours?"

100

He could lie, but that'd come back on him the first time she saw him with a black eye or a busted lip. "I'd say it's more of a hobby."

She laughed, thinking he was joking and he let it go.

"I really miss my sister, Kimi. I saw her all the time during the school year."

"What's she doin' now?"

"She's with our Aunt Hulda. In years past I'd work with our aunt for six weeks of the summer and I'd be home six weeks. Kimi would be there and I'd be here, so we didn't spend our summers together." She turned off the stove. "Supper is done. You want to get the plates?"

"Be my pleasure."

First bite of the pork chop, Carson dropped his fork and grabbed her hand. "Forget about you bein' the sexiest, sweetest woman I've ever met, or the fact I'd like to keep you tied to my bed twenty-four hours a day, or that I never get tired of talkin' to you...this meal just proves that I was dead on with proposing marriage to you last week."

Carolyn blushed. "Silver-tongued devil, that's what you are."

He could tell he'd made her uncomfortable, so he dropped it, even when he wanted to convince her every word he'd said was the gospel truth.

After they finished the delicious meal, Carolyn popped up to do the dishes. Carson circled his arm around her waist and set her on his knee. When she opened her mouth to protest, he kissed her. Thoroughly. "Thank you for supper. Leave the dishes. I want you to ride along when I do the last cattle check."

"Really? Okay. Will I have to, umm...do cow stuff?"

He laughed. "No. But I'll show you how to open gates."

Carolyn asked a million questions as they bumped through the pastures, insightful questions so he knew she wasn't just being polite.

"In the next couple weeks, we'll turn out the bulls."

"Meaning what?"

Carson peered at her from beneath the brim of his hat. "You really need me to explain what happens when we put the bulls and the cows together?"

"Oh. Uh, no." Then a very female, very devious smirk tilted the corners of her lips. "But maybe you'd better show me what happens when a male and a female are alone together, to make sure I have a solid understanding of the process."

"Sugar, are you sure?"

"Very. You've been in my bed. Now I want to be in yours."

His dick went hard.

Instead of sitting on her side of the truck all prim and proper, Carolyn was all over him. Sucking on his neck. Nibbling his ear. Rubbing his chest. And those fingers kept sliding lower and lower.

"Caro. Slow down."

"I don't want to," she cooed in his ear. "I want to feel you. Every.

Hot. Inch. Of. You."

Holy shit. Her hand was on his cock. Rubbing on his cock. Damn...that felt good. He wondered how long before he convinced her to put her mouth there. He imagined those velvety soft lips dragging up and down the length and her wicked little tongue circling the tip.

"Carson," she whispered against his throat.

"What?"

"Are you going to open the gate?"

He blinked. He'd driven back to the trailer on autopilot, but some part of him had been conscious enough during his oral fantasy to not plow through it. He picked her hand up from his chest and kissed her fingertips before he bailed out.

Open the gate. Drive through the gate. Close the gate.

Now they were home free.

The instant they stopped in front of the trailer, Carolyn was on his lap. He didn't know how he managed to get them out of the truck and inside, while he was carrying her with her legs clamped around his waist, while their mouths were fused together. He just knew as he carried her down the hallway to his bedroom that her sexy little whimpers and moans made his dick harder yet.

His hat hit the floor when he dropped her on the bed. "Strip or I swear I'll rip off every stitch of clothes you're still wearing by the time I'm nekkid."

Carolyn stood and lifted the dress over her head. She unhooked her bra and tossed it at him, then shimmied her panties down her legs. She tilted her head and wore a cheeky grin. "Doesn't look like I'm the slow one getting nekkid, cowboy."

"Holy hell you are drivin' me crazy with that body made for sin and that fuck-me-now attitude."

"Prove it." She bounced on the bed and crooked her finger at him.

Carson lost a few buttons getting his shirt off. Lost a few brain cells when she parted her legs and showed him the hot, tight paradise awaiting him. He nearly fell on his ass when the big head reminded him he had to take off his boots before his jeans, while the little head strained to get out of his boxers.

Then, as naked as she was, he pounced on her.

She curled around him like a vine. Her mouth avid on his. One hand gripping his hair, the other hand scratching down his back to cup his ass. Her pelvis rocking. Her back arching, forcing more skin on skin contact.

He fought a grin. From chaste and curious to a hellcat between the sheets. Yeah, this woman was fucking perfect.

Slipping a hand between them, he touched her soft curls and wet center. He stroked that pretty pussy, circling her clit, then following her slit down to the tight entrance to her body. He pushed a finger into her, swallowing her moan. When she whispered, "Yes, please, more," against his lips, he added another finger, loving how ready her body was for his possession.

This time there'd be no foreplay.

But this time, he'd give her the reins.

Carson rolled, landing on his back with Carolyn astride him.

She broke the kiss on a gasp and pushed up. "What...? Why did you do that?"

"Because I want you to ride me." He cupped those perfect, perky tits, rubbing his thumbs over the pale peach tips. "You can go as fast or as slow as you want. And while you're doin' that, I'm gonna suck on you, and rub on you and enjoy the hell out of myself."

"But I don't know how to do this."

"You'll figure it out." He moved his hands up to palm her shoulders, urging her forward to kiss him.

Then as the kiss grew more heated, and his cock was weeping with want, he reached between them and poised the head at her opening. "Lower onto me when you're ready."

Carolyn immediately sank down to the root. She trailed her lips to the underside of his jaw. "I love how it feels when you're inside me."

"That feelin' is yours whenever you want it."

She remained like that, not moving, kissing his throat and nuzzling his ear.

He palmed her ass, squeezing the soft flesh. "Move on me. There's no wrong way. It'll all feel good."

"Help me."

Carson nudged her cheek so he could get at her mouth and kissed her with sweet heat.

She was tentative at first, but once she found a rhythm, she used her body like a weapon. Arching and rubbing her nipples on every upward glide, grinding her pubic bone against him on every backward push. All the while kissing him, only stopping to look into his eyes, their lips only a breath apart.

She owned him, this woman who gave him her all without question. The irony of a virgin teaching him what it really meant to make love wasn't lost on him.

"Carson," she whispered. "I need..."

"What? Sugar, just ask me."

"I need it harder. Faster."

He sat up so they were both upright. Keeping hold of her hips, he thrust up into her hard and deep.

"Oh. Yes. Just like that." Her head fell back.

Carson slid the elastic from her hair, shaking the strands loose so he could feel that blonde silk teasing his thighs as she rode him. "Rise up on your knees and then drop back down."

When she lowered down he powered up into her. The rhythm became frantic. He buried his face in her breasts, kissing the soft swells, bringing her nipples into his mouth and sucking hard.

She dug her nails into the back of his neck with enough force it stung.

He loved every fucking second of it.

Knowing he couldn't hold off much longer, he snaked his hand down her belly, finding her clit and stroking side to side until he felt her body tightening around him.

She cried out when the orgasm overtook her. Her lush body shaking as he rammed into her harder, his mouth at her throat, her clit throbbing beneath his thumb.

When the last spasm pulled at his cock, he slammed deep and stayed deep in those clenching pussy walls, each hot pulse sending an electric charge up his spine. Blood rushing in his head, racing through his veins, pounding in his balls.

Soft hands petting his hair roused him. He glanced down and saw he'd left a hickey on her breast. Shit. Were those...teeth marks?

Obviously he'd been lost in a fog. He opened his mouth to apologize, and Carolyn pressed her lips to his, the kiss intimate and powerful.

She rested her forehead to his after that soul-marking kiss. "I never knew it could be like this."

"I didn't either."

Those pleasure-hazed blue eyes bored into his. "Really?"

"Not a line, sugar. It's never been like this for me before."

Her entire face lit up. "Good."

"Cocky is a good look on you." He lightly slapped her ass. "Move off me slowly because we went at it pretty hard and you might be a little sore."

"It was worth it." Carolyn lifted up, only wincing slightly. But he realized it wasn't pain that caused her reaction but the long line of seed running down the inside of her thigh.

"Sex can get a little messy."

"Sex can get me more than a little pregnant too."

Carson froze. He'd forgotten to use a goddamned rubber. All three times. Unlike most guys, he almost always used one—he didn't want to knock up someone he had no intention of marrying.

But this was different. If he'd planted his seed in Carolyn, he'd happily marry her.

"We can use something, right? That'll keep me from getting pregnant?"

His eyes narrowed. "Thought Catholics were opposed to that."

"Catholics are also opposed to premarital sex, but that didn't seem to stop us. So as long as we're already sinning, let's just add another thing when I go to confession, okay?"

He laughed. "Okay." He brushed the hair back from her face. "Can you stay a little longer?"

"Another hour or so."

"I wish you could stay all night."

"Me too."

Around noon the next day, Carson was thinking about how he'd get a message to Carolyn that he wanted to see her, when a truck he didn't recognize pulled into the yard.

He wiped the sweat from his forehead with the back of his glove and waited for this person to get out of the vehicle.

The truck door slammed and a barrel-shaped guy stormed toward him. He didn't recognize the guy until he was on him, a meaty fist headed right for his face.

His last thought before he hit the dirt was he knew where Carolyn had learned to punch—from her brother Harland.

Chapter Nine
Carolyn

She hadn't seen or heard from Carson in two days. Not since she'd shown up at his place and he'd whisked her off to bed after she'd cooked him dinner.

Everything inside her tightened in remembrance of his fevered kisses. His reverent touches. How marvelous it felt to have his solid body beneath hers. His damp skin sliding against hers. The stretch and burn as their bodies connected so intimately. And how that discomfort had changed into pleasure as he taught her to trust her instincts on how to move with him.

Then Carson had been so sweet, yet fiercely possessive. The way he put his hands on her body as if every inch of flesh now belonged to him. The whispers in her ear that sounded like promises, even when her head had spun so much she couldn't process the words, just the intensity behind them.

After she'd left and had time to reflect that she'd had sex with him three days in a row, she expected guilt to weigh on her, because she'd been raised to believe that sex was to be saved for marriage. But an act so beautiful and loving between two people should be celebrated.

And she looked forward to celebrating with Carson many, many more times.

She was so lost in thoughts of heat and body friction that she almost passed the turnoff to Beverly's house. She knew Beverly would only be at the dance long enough to meet up with Mike and then sneak off to his place, and for the first time she understood why.

Beverly's mother and father were sitting on the front porch when Carolyn pulled up. She waved and waited for Beverly to tear herself away from what looked like a lecture. When she got in the car, she said, "I can't wait to be out of here."

"What's going on?"

"My parents think things are going too fast between me'n Mike. They'd really put up a fuss if they knew he intends to propose before he leaves."

"Beverly! That's great!"

"I know. I'm excited. Mike wants to get married as soon as he has a place for us to stay on base. Can you imagine? Me living in Georgia with all the other military wives?"

Happy as she was for her friend, Beverly was her only friend, and if she moved away, Carolyn would feel even more isolated.

Maybe you'll be spending all of your time with Carson anyway so it won't matter.

She could hope.

"...I've never wanted a big wedding anyway. I just want to be with him. I hope he gets stationed all over the world."

"You'll have to send me postcards from all of the exotic locations."

"I promise. Enough about me." Beverly turned in the seat and scrutinized her. "What's going on with you? Still a housewife in training?"

Carolyn scowled. Beverly constantly harped on how Carolyn was a "slave" for her family whenever she came home, and then she pointed out they managed just fine when Carolyn wasn't around. "Since you'll be a housewife long before I will, Bev, maybe *you'd* better pay more attention to what your mother does around the house."

"I already know how to do all that stuff. It's just my mother likes to do it so I let her."

I like to do it too.

Beverly poked Carolyn's leg. "We were talking about you. Anything new with wild man Carson McKay?"

She blushed.

"I knew it! Tell me!"

"We've spent some time together." She slid Beverly a sideways glance. "I told my family I went over to your house Monday night when I was with him."

"I can't believe you're sneaking around with Carson. I'm so happy for you."

"Really?"

"You deserve some fun. So what fun things did you two get up to?"

Carolyn blushed again.

"No," she breathed. "Did you really...?"

"Yes."

"All the way?"

"Yes." She bit her tongue to keep from adding—*and more than one time!*

"And?" Beverly demanded.

"And it was perfect."

Beverly squealed. "I told you!"

"Well, now I believe all the hype about it."

She laughed. "Are you meeting him here tonight?"

Her hands tightened on the steering wheel. "He's been busy the last couple days."

"He didn't call you and tell you his plans?"

"What would happen if my dad or one of my brothers answered the phone? Even if Carson didn't say who he was, there'd be questions about why a man is calling me and if I am seeing someone why I haven't introduced him to my family. And if they found out he's from the McKay family? I'd end up locked in my room for the rest of my life."

"Gotcha. I still don't understand about the West/McKay feud thing."

"Me neither. No one talks about it so Carson and I ignore it."

"Speaking of ignoring...I hope you're not mad that I'll be leaving with Mike for a while."

"I'll be fine. But I have to leave as soon as the dance ends so if you need a ride home, make sure you're waiting by the car."

"My folks didn't even notice Mike brought me home last time, so don't wait for me. Besides, maybe Carson has already made plans to get you away from the dance so you two can be alone."

Carolyn laughed when Beverly waggled her eyebrows suggestively.

The pasture next to the dancehall was filled with cars. Carolyn told herself she wasn't searching every vehicle they passed for Carson's truck.

Beverly grabbed her arm after she lost her footing beside a gopher hole. "I don't know why I bothered to wear heels to walk through a cow pasture."

"Because you're trying to impress your man."

"Nothing impressive about manure stains on satin pumps."

"And it's your unlucky night because I don't have a helpful household hint on how to remove those stubborn stains," Carolyn said wryly.

"That's what I love about you, Carolyn. Your ability to laugh at yourself and at me." Beverly wrapped her arm around Carolyn's waist. "As happy as I'll be to see Mike, I'd really like to just hang out with you tonight and talk. I thought we'd have the whole summer to catch up and now it looks like—"

"You'll be getting ready to become Mrs. Mike Flannery."

Beverly giggled. Then she groaned. "I don't know why I giggle every time I hear that."

"What time is Mike supposed to be here?"

"In half an hour. Let's go up to the bar and see if we can sweet talk the bartender into serving us."

The dancehall was owned by the community, so anyone of any age could be on the premises, but in order to drink, you had to show an ID that proved you were twenty-one. Or married to someone who was twenty-one. Or were a pretty girl who knew how to flirt with the male bartenders, as Beverly had learned.

But inside it was wall-to-wall people and the line to the bar was twenty people deep.

"Screw this. I don't need a rum and Coke that bad," Beverly complained. They exited out the opposite side near the front entrance and Carolyn scanned the area.

"If he's here, he'll find you." She tugged on Carolyn's blond hair. "You're hard to miss."

"We'll see."

Beverly fired up a cigarette. "So your folks don't suspect anything?"

"I told my mom I met Carson, but nothing more. My dad doesn't pay much attention to me unless I haven't cooked."

She rolled her eyes. Then she said, "Great. Just what I didn't need tonight."

"What?"

With her cigarette Beverly pointed to a group of women beside the stage. "See them? Catty little witches. The brunette is Edie, stay away from her. The skeletal-looking blonde is Tammy. If she sees me she'll try and pretend we're great friends and then she'll rip on me the second my back is turned. The chunky one in the middle? That's Missy. She's getting married in a couple of weeks."

"Did you go to school with them?"

"Yes. Unfortunately I have to be nice to them because they're customers. They were in the fabric store the other day looking for ribbon for their bridesmaids' dresses." She blew out a stream of smoke. "You haven't been in for anything new. What's keeping you away?"

"I'm doing some piece work and alterations for Maxine Granger for the next few weeks so you probably won't see me."

"Too bad. I love to see what you're creating." She blew out a stream of smoke. "Wait, you're working for Maxine?"

"Yeah. Why?"

"Because Maxine made Missy's wedding dress. And her bridesmaids' dresses. When they were in looking for add-ons for the dresses before the final fittings, they were complaining that they didn't know the seamstress that Maxine had pawned off on them. I'm assuming that's you?"

"Most likely. But they haven't scheduled an appointment yet."

"Maybe you'll get lucky and they've found someone else."

They talked clothes and fabric trends. Beverly was the only friend Carolyn had who cared about that kind of stuff.

Then her friend's face lit up. Mike must be here.

She scanned the crowd for signs of Carson, but with so many cowboy hats she'd never find him that way.

"Carolyn, we need a huge favor," Beverly said.

"Sure."

Mike draped his arm over Beverly's shoulder. "I had to hitch a ride here after working in Aladdin because I left my car in Spearfish. I'll pay you for gas if you could give us a ride."

"To Spearfish? Now?"

"Yeah."

She couldn't say no because Beverly had done tons of favors for her. "Of course I can take you."

Beverly grinned. "Thank you."

They loaded up in Carolyn's car and drove the forty-five miles to Spearfish. Mike filled her tank before she got back on the road. As the turnoff to the dancehall loomed, Carolyn debated on just driving home. Nearly two hours had passed and if Carson had gone there tonight looking for her, he probably thought she was a no-show.

But what if he's still there waiting for you?

She made the turn.

There were even more cars. She found a spot at the far back of the lot and started toward the building. When she noticed Carson's truck parked at the end of a row, her belly got all fluttery. She passed couples in various states of public displays of affection and in stages of undress. Guys were standing in groups drinking and laughing. She didn't stop walking when they whistled at her.

At the door she showed her hand stamp and weaved through the crowd, figuring she'd find Carson at the bar. A hand circled her waist and spun her around.

Her brother Thomas grinned at her. "Fancy meeting you here."

"Hey. I didn't think you were coming tonight."

"Nothing else to do around here." He tugged on her hand. "Let's dance."

"Thomas—"

"One song. Come on. I learned some new moves."

She laughed. "All right."

The dance floor was so crowded they could barely move. And Thomas was so determined to show off the swing dancing spins they ended up dancing to three songs. By that time she could hardly breathe and she walked out the open side door for some fresh air.

Large and small groups were scattered everywhere. Would she look stupid or desperate if she just wandered around by herself? Probably. But what choice did she have if she wanted to find Carson?

It didn't take her long to find him. He was in a group of four guys with his arm slung over the shoulder of one of the women Beverly had pointed out earlier. The nasty brunette.

Her stomach, her heart, her hopes—everything inside her crashed. She thought about all the things Carson had said to her. Had it all been a line?

How will you know if you don't ask?

What if she confronted him and he humiliated her in front of these people?

What if she did nothing?

Could she really look him in the eye and act like she hadn't seen his arm around the brunette the next time she saw him?

Did she scurry deeper into the shadows? Or step out of them entirely?

Her feet seemed to make the decision for her.

"...and you know that's all they want from you," said the cowboy to Carson's left.

"Don't matter," Carson said and took a swig of beer. "They know what they're getting into with me."

"I'll get into it with you," the brunette purred.

Carson turned his head and whispered something in her ear that made her laugh and snuggle closer.

As Carolyn stepped forward, she noticed she hadn't been in the shadows as much as she'd hoped because Carson was staring right at her—with no emotion whatsoever. He didn't bother to drop his arm away from the woman. Not an ounce of guilt crossed his face.

Say something.

"I wondered if you'd be here tonight."

He inclined his head to his posse. "We were hangin' out until I find something better."

Direct hit. He'd already found someone better.

"Hey darlin'," the cowboy on Carson's right drawled. "Come hang out with us."

"Yeah, Carson. Ain't ya gonna introduce us to your pretty friend here?"

A muscle in Carson's jaw moved. He slowly lifted his beer and drank before he said, "Nope."

"Aw, come on. You've already made your pick for tonight. I'm makin' this little gal my pick."

"No, you ain't. I'm guessing she came by to say she's gotta get on home."

Don't stand there looking pathetic.

But she, Carolyn West, was the very definition of the word pathetic right now. She didn't have the experience to deal with this type of rejection, so no matter what she said, Carson would be aware he'd crushed her hopes under his boot heel.

"Yes, I'm going home. Goodbye, Carson."

Grateful for the darkness, she walked away.

Chapter Ten
Carson

You are a total asshole.

Carson let his arm fall away from the brunette as soon as Carolyn disappeared from view, but his self-hatred remained.

"Who was she?" the woman cooed.

"Nobody."

The fuck she was. She was everything.

Let it go. Let her go. You planned to do this, remember?

That was the last fucking thing he wanted to do. Pissed off—mostly at himself and his goddamn cowardice—he took another long pull from his flask. Waited a minute for the booze to quell the burning inside him. No help. He still wanted to punch someone.

Good thing there was an abundance of drunken assholes who'd jump into a fight without much prompting.

The brunette's hand slithered up his torso from his belt buckle, stopping on his chest. "Where were we? You mentioned something about going back to your place."

The thought of having this woman in his bed—the bed he'd had Carolyn in just two nights ago—caused a sick churning in his gut. "Sorry. Not in the cards tonight."

"But you said..."

"I changed my mind." Carson walked off.

She shouted something at him but he didn't care.

He kept a spare bottle in his truck. After several mouthfuls of Windsor, he went looking for trouble.

Immediately he saw his target. Bob Delray. Big-mouth, know-it-all asshole. And he had a couple of his loser buddies backing him. Even better. With any luck, all four of them would jump in.

He'd barely reached the edge of the group when he heard "McKay" and then snide laughter. He marched up to Bob, who had an inch on Carson's six-foot-two frame. Bob outweighed him by a good fifty pounds, but all of that was fat.

"Heard my name," Carson said, getting right in Bob's business. "Got something to say to me?"

"Don't recall speaking directly to you, McKay, so just keep

walkin'."

"How about I don't. How about I stay right fuckin' here until you prove you can keep that fat trap of yours shut."

Bob stepped forward, his gut leading the way. "How about you make me."

Carson's answer was an uppercut to Bob's jaw. Before Bob recovered, Carson nailed him in the sternum.

Since Bob was still swinging as he went down, Carson connected with a right cross to Bob's ear and another one to his jaw.

That was the last punch he got in before Bob's buddies jumped him.

Fuckers had him pinned down so he couldn't fight back—but he sure as fuck wasn't letting these pussies get the best of him. He managed to crack one guy in the nose with his head and the guy dropped to his knees, yelling about his busted face.

He didn't know how many hits and kicks he'd sustained—his head had gone woozy from the booze and the pain—when the guys pounding on him went flying.

Someone hauled him upright to his feet by his biceps.

Carson wiped the blood from his eye and spit a mouthful of red goo on the ground. He swayed and someone tried to bolster him, but he jerked away. He was on his goddamn feet. He didn't need any help staying there.

A loud roar sounded. He glanced over to see Cal, Casper and Charlie doling out punishment to Bob's friends and a couple of other guys who'd stupidly tangled with them.

A crowd had gathered to watch the show.

Carson rested his hands on his knees, trying to breathe through the pain. Fuck. His ribs, his back, his head all throbbed. When he looked up, he saw three more guys rolling in the dirt and Cal and Charlie looming above them.

Then Casper took an elbow to the gut, which spurred him to tackle the guy and whale on him until Charlie tapped him on the shoulder.

"Anyone else?" Cal shouted, spinning in a circle.

"The McKays starting fights," someone yelled from the back. "Big surprise."

"And we always finish fights," Charlie snapped back. "Come up here and say it to our face, coward."

No one stepped forward.

"Anyone else wanna have a go at us? We're ready."

For a moment Carson thought the entire crowd might rush them. But then they slowly backed away.

"Not that it matters, but you wanna tell us what the fuck that was about?" Cal asked.

Carson bent down and picked up his hat. "I was walkin' by Bob and he made a crack about the McKays. Couldn't let it slide."

Charlie said, "Dad is gonna rip into us when he hears about this."

"Let him." Casper sneered. "Wasn't like we had a choice. He'd yell at us just as bad if he found out we let the number one son get a beatin' and we didn't step in to save him."

"Fuck you, Casper," Carson said. Even when Casper wasn't being an asshole, he somehow managed to turn into one.

"How bad you hurt this time?" Cal asked.

"I'm fine. I just need to walk it off." Sleep it off would be better. But even in his boozed and beaten state Carson knew the second he closed his eyes, he'd see Carolyn's face. The torment in her eyes when she noticed he had his arm around another woman. The way she seemed to shrink into herself when she believed he'd used her and was discarding her.

Rage roared inside him again. His fist might've connected with the metal hood of the car behind him if not for Cal lunging and knocking him sideways. "What the hell, Carse?"

"He's drunk," Casper said.

Not drunk enough. He didn't know if there was enough booze in the world to numb the pain.

"Leave him alone," Charlie said. "Let's go back into the dance. See if any of the ladies wanna get with us."

"Fine, but you ain't drinkin', pup."

They disappeared.

Cal positioned himself across from Carson as they leaned against the doors of somebody's cars. "You wanna tell me what's really goin' on?"

"I can help with that."

Carson faced the guy, recognizing him as another one of Carolyn's fuckin' brothers. "If you're gonna hit me, you'd better make sure you knock me the fuck out with the first shot. 'Cause I ain't goin' down easy." Especially not for a West again.

"Yeah. I saw that."

"Who're you? Cal demanded.

"Thomas West. Carolyn's brother."

Cal snarled, "What the fuck do you want, West?"

"To talk to Carson."

"You gonna talk to me like your brothers talked to me?"

Thomas stepped closer. "What'd they do?"

"Harland slammed me up against the barn and tried to choke me. Darren stopped by and said he'd drop a couple of diseased sheep into my cattle herd. Marshall said sparks from the railroad are known to start grass fires in prime grazin' land. Stuart was the least creative but the most to the point. He said he'd beat me to death with a hammer if I ever came near Carolyn again."

"Jesus."

"When the hell did this happen?" Cal asked, dumbfounded.

"Last two days." Carson reached for his flask, but remembering he'd left it in his truck, he dropped his hand. "Don't bother warnin' me off your sister. I'm done with her."

Thomas roared and grabbed the front of Carson's shirt. Then they were nose to nose. "Just like that? You walk—hell, you fucking *ran* away from my sister because *they* told you to?"

Carson pushed him back. "Shut up."

"I saw what you did to her tonight. Acting like you were with someone else. I just hope she made it home okay because she was crying so damn hard—"

"I said shut up." Carson stared at him, seething, thoughts of Carolyn driving into a ditch flashing in his brain.

"So it is true. What my dad has always said. The McKays are scared of the Wests."

Cal got in Thomas's face. "Bullshit."

"There's your proof." Thomas pointed to Carson. "Your brother is running scared. Being a jackass to my sister, breaking her heart because that's what my older brothers want. What about what you want?" He gave Carson a sneering once-over. "I saw you beat the crap out of five guys tonight, McKay. Because you thought some guy insulted you. But you're just gonna lay down like a whipped dog for my brothers after they gave you the ultimate insult? They told you that you aren't good enough for Carolyn? So you're going to prove it? You won't take them on and fight for my sister?"

"Why do you care? I thought you'd be happy. Ain't you the one tryin' to get her to move to Denver or Chicago instead of bein' stuck livin' here?"

"I never wanted to make that decision for her; I just made sure she knew she had options."

"So I'm an option?"

Thomas stared at him. "You were."

Fuck this "were" shit.

"You screwed up bad tonight," Thomas said. "You hurt her. I wanted to bust your balls for that alone. But I'm not like my brothers. Beating the crap out of you and threatening you...that's not what Carolyn would want. And I'm only doing this for her."

"Doin' what?"

"Helping you. And before you get that 'fuck you I don't need your help, you piece of shit West' look, listen up: you *do* need my help. You want to be with her, don't you?"

"Yeah."

"Prove it. You'll have to grovel, bare your heart and soul and all that embarrassing, romantic crap women love, and fucking *mean* it for her to even talk to you. Words can only go so far."

Probably not a good idea to say that getting her naked would be the best way to prove it.

Cal said, "So he's supposed to march up to your front door and say, 'Fuck you all, I don't give a shit what threats you made or what you think, I'm takin' Carolyn out on a date and you'd better get used to seein' me around'?"

"Yes."

"No way," Cal said hotly. "He'll have to show up armed with your brothers gunning for him."

"That's your solution? He walks into my goddamned house armed?" Thomas shot back.

"There's no other way I'm letting my brother walk into a roomful of Wests."

"I'll do it," Carson said softly.

"Carse—"

"Cal. I'm not walkin' away from her." He looked at his brother. "Thomas is right. I'm actin' like a pussy. I backed down because I thought..." He scrubbed his hands over his face. "That's the problem. I wasn't thinkin' straight. I am now." He locked his gaze to Thomas's. "Think your dad sent his sons after me instead of comin' for me himself?"

"No. I don't think my brothers have told our dad about you or I doubt Carolyn would've been allowed to leave the house tonight."

"She's an adult. She's been responsible for herself since she was twelve."

"It's screwed up, okay? Our mom sent her away because she wanted something more for her. Yet when Carolyn comes home, things go back to her doing everything for us. I guarantee our father won't be happy when a McKay shows up for his daughter." Thomas's eyes searched his. "Did you know that my dad and your dad crossed paths years ago?"

"No. What happened?"

"Words were exchanged, fists were involved and my dad put your dad in the hospital."

"Christ. I didn't know about that."

Thomas shrugged. "I wouldn't have known either if I hadn't asked my dad's friend Roscoe about it. My dad goes ballistic whenever the McKay name is mentioned."

"Any idea what prompted the fight between your old man and mine?"

"Word is it doesn't take much for the McKays to get pissed off and come out swinging. So I'm guessing, like father like sons—no offense."

"Fuck you. I am offended because I didn't start this one; your brothers did. Who's to say your dad didn't jump my dad back then?" Carson demanded.

"Seems like attack and retreat is the Wests' style," Cal said with a sneer.

"You wanna stand here and speculate about shit that happened before any of us were born?"

Carson shook his head. Motherfucker hurt.

"Good. I've got a couple of ideas on how to get back in Carolyn's good graces."

"What's your suggestion?

He zeroed in on Carson. Then he rattled off what he saw as the best course of action.

As Carson listened to Thomas's suggestions, the perfect way to prove his intent occurred to him. He was mired in thoughts on how to pull it off, when he realized Thomas was speaking to him again and he refocused.

"So I'm asking you, McKay. You gonna do right by my sister?"

"You can count on it."

Without another word Thomas walked off.

Cal broke the silence first. "Some night, huh?"

"I'll be feelin' it in the mornin', that's for damn sure."

"Maybe it's best if we head home. I'll follow you."

Carson pushed away from the car he'd been resting against.

"Is she worth it?" Cal asked. "You've known her for little over a week."

"Yeah. But it feels like I've been waitin' for her forever."

Chapter Eleven
Carolyn

Carolyn's red-rimmed eyes nearly kept her home from church.

At least her eyes weren't swollen shut like the last time she'd spent the night crying, after her cat had died.

But she'd never cried over a guy.

That's because you've never been in love before.

If this was love, who wanted it? At least her cat hadn't catted around on her.

Maybe she should head back to Montana and enroll in the convent.

During the miserable drive home she'd relived every awful moment: seeing him with that woman, witnessing the disinterested and dismissive expression on his handsome face.

Was it typical lovesick behavior to scroll back through all the times they'd spent together in the past week, searching for signs she'd missed that indicated he intended to use her for sex and then move on to the next conquest? She'd come up blank. Or maybe she was too naïve to recognize the warning signs.

Beverly had caught up with her as she'd dashed back to her car, tears already streaming down her face, the scream of pain and outrage stuck in her throat.

Her friend's look of pity made Carolyn want to crawl under the car. But with Beverly's gentle urging, Carolyn had told her what'd happened.

"Carolyn. Sweetie. He's got a bad reputation. He isn't interested in dating; he's interested in screwing as many women as he can. And I'm sorry it hurts, I wanna march over there and punch him in the nose, but that's why they call men like him heartbreakers."

"But I thought I was different. I was—"

"Special?" Beverly inserted. "I'm sure he probably told you that in such a way you believed it. He's very good at acting sincere because he's used that line on so many girls before and it always works for him."

"So I'm just a fool?"

"We all are. Heartbreak is a rite of passage."

Carolyn wiped her eyes. "Are you afraid Mike will break your heart?"

"Every day. But I love him every day anyway. Maybe Carson will come to his senses."

Maybe Martians will land on top of Devil's Tower.

She snapped out of the memory when she realized she'd started to drift to the center line of the road.

Much like she had last night.

The church service was packed. Several people her mother's age smiled at her as she slid into the fourth-to-last pew. She lifted out the hymnal and flipped to the first hymn. She loved these songs. It connected her to the past, imagining a church full of people across the world singing these same hymns of praise a century or two ago.

The organ played the processional as the altar boys lit the candles. A figure paused at the edge of the pew before sliding in next to her.

Carolyn looked over...right into Carson McKay's blue eyes.

Her mouth dropped open and she bobbled the hymnal.

Carson steadied the book and softly asked, "Can we share this?"

She nodded. Numbly. Dumbly. Her mind wasn't on the music or anticipating the inspirational bits she could take from this sermon to sustain her throughout her week, but got stuck on the cowboy sitting next to her. Out of the corner of her eye she saw Carson's black hair looked damp. She caught a whiff of his aftershave. He'd donned a dark brown western-cut suit. Polished dress boots adorned his feet. And she knew the man was turning heads, even in church.

The music crescendoed, signaling the start of the hymn. Carson adjusted the hymnal and she noticed his bruised and scabbed knuckles.

Her head snapped up and she caught sight of his handsome face. Her insides knotted, seeing his swollen and cut lip, the gash by his eyebrow. Another slice on his cheek. He had a serious shiner around his right eye, and bruises on his jawline.

What had happened to him last night?

When she realized she was staring and not singing, she tried to focus on the hymn. But Carson once again distracted her, his voice a deep rumble as he sang quietly beside her.

The hymn ended and the liturgy was recited. He didn't need to read along as he seemed to have it memorized. He had no problem knowing when to kneel. He knew the prayers. His motions were automatic, as if he'd done it a hundred times before.

Why hadn't she known that Carson had been raised Catholic?

She knew so many other things, hot and sweet and sexy things— *please Lord forgive me for letting my mind wander to such carnal thoughts during church service, amen.* But why hadn't she asked about his core beliefs? When her religious beliefs were such a large part of who she was?

Because you gave up your virginity to him within a week of meeting him. He probably thinks you don't have those core beliefs. Actions speak louder than words, remember?

Carson shifted to get to his billfold when the usher shoved the collection plate in front of him. She dropped a folded bill in the same time Carson did and their fingers brushed.

A jolt of awareness shot through her.

When Carolyn didn't jerk away, he considered that her approval to hold her hand.

How much of a pushover are you?

But she liked that he'd reached out to her—in more ways than one. Giving him the cold shoulder in church, where she'd learned to turn the other cheek, would make her a hypocrite.

The service ended and people started to get up.

She faced him.

His eyes were so somber.

"Carson, why are you here?"

"To ask for your forgiveness." He allowed a ghost of a smile before he winced in pain. "Figured I'd ask for God's too while I was at it."

"I didn't know you were Catholic."

"Baptized and confirmed in the Catholic Church in Sundance. Both my mom and Dad were Catholic. Mom made sure we went to church pretty near every week. After she died... Then we stopped goin'." His eyes searched hers. "We need to talk. You pick where that happens."

"Fine. It'll be somewhere isolated so I can yell at you without everyone thinking I'm a crazy person."

Another slight smile was there and gone. "I deserve every bit of whatever you dish out."

They waited to shake hands with the priest, a fairly young guy. Thoughtful and kind, he welcomed Carolyn as part of the congregation even when she only attended services a few times a year.

"Carolyn. I'm so happy to see you brought a guest today." He beamed at Carson and offered his hand. "I'm Father Dorian."

"Carson McKay."

"Are you from around here, Mr. McKay?"

"Sundance."

"Ah. I've filled in for Father Balough a few times at the St. Ignatius."

"I don't know him. Father Summerall was in charge last time I went."

"That's been a few years." He paused and Carson seemed to tense, as if waiting for Father Dorian's judgment on his poor church attendance. "Which means we're very happy to see you return to the fold. God's blessings on the day to both of you."

Carson kept his hand in the small of her back, steering her toward the door. He plucked his hat off the rack, settled it on his head and they stepped outside into the breezy summer morning.

"Father Dorian surprised me."

"Because he's so young?"

"No. Because he seems happy bein' a priest. I know from experience they're not all like that. Some of 'em are downright mean."

"I've had a few old-school priests at St. Mary's. But Father Dorian is just as wonderful as he appears to be. He comes out to the house to give my mother communion since she's unable to attend services."

He led her to his truck and opened the passenger door, assisting her up since her skirt restricted movement. Unlike last week, he didn't try and cop a feel or steal a kiss or make a suggestive comment.

He was acting very un-Carson like.

Then again, he hadn't acted like himself last night either, so it wasn't all bad.

They arrived at Founders Park, which hadn't been overrun with children yet. Again Carson was a gentleman, assisting her down the sidewalk to a picnic table beneath several large oak trees.

Her mother used to bring her here with Thomas and Kimi. She'd watch them from the car, letting them run wild on the playground. Kimi was so little Carolyn wondered if she remembered that their mother used to do...motherly type things with them before the arthritis rendered her incapable of everything.

"Whatcha thinkin' about, Caro?"

"Family stuff. What are you thinking about?"

Carson was by her side in an instant; his hands gently framed her face. "I'm thinkin' that I'm dyin' to kiss you. I'm thinkin' about what an ass I was to you last night. I'm thinkin' I don't even know where to start makin' this up to you." He paused. "Or if you even want me to try."

Somehow she kept her eyes locked on his and said, "Try the truth."

"I wasn't with that woman last night."

"You had your arm around her."

"I know. But that's all I did and only when you could see it. I dropped it as soon as you were gone."

"Why?"

"To make you think I was a bastard. That I'd just used you, I was done with you and I moved on to someone else."

Her stomach dropped to her toes and she tried to break free from his hold.

But he wouldn't let her go. "You need to hear me out. It's as hard for me to say as it is for you to hear."

"I doubt that."

Carson threaded their fingers together. "I'm sorry I hurt you.

Really fuckin' sorry. Afterward I punished myself by pickin' a fight, but the pain I received wasn't even close to the goddamn pain I saw in your eyes when I said the shit I did."

"Language," she murmured.

"See? You're too good to be true. But I want that goodness in my life. I need it. I need you. I know things went a little fast between us last week. I was so tied up in knots over you that I wasn't payin' attention to see if anyone else might've taken notice of us spendin' so much time together."

"Someone saw us?" They'd been so wrapped up in each other that they'd rolled around on a blanket at a picnic area. They'd practically skinny-dipped at Keyhole. They'd gone at it half-naked against Carson's truck—also just off the main road where anyone could've seen them. Then he'd come to her house. Specifically into her bedroom. And he'd parked in the front yard, bold as brass. "Who?"

"Your brother Harland."

Shock froze her vocal chords.

"Evidently he saw my truck from the road that day I stopped by and he saw our goodbye kiss. He followed me home. When he realized who I was... He returned when I was alone."

"Are any of these bruises from him?" she demanded.

"His marks are on my throat because he damn near strangled me before I knocked him on his ass."

She twined her arms around him and pressed her cheek into his chest. She thought she'd cried herself out, but not so. A few stray tears slipped free and soaked into his shirt. "Are you okay?"

"I'm getting there. Look. The short version is your brothers all showed up around my place and threatened me if I didn't break it off with you. Then they threw a buncha shit in my face I'd done in the past, which combined with them extolling your virtues, went a long way in convincing me to break it off with you because I didn't deserve a woman like you."

"All of my brothers did that?"

"Except Thomas. He watched me get my ass whipped last night at the dance after you left. So at first," a nervous laugh slipped out, "I thought maybe he was there to finish the job. Turns out he wasn't and he had some advice that pointed me in the right direction."

"Which direction was that?"

Carson tipped her head back and gazed into her eyes. "Straight back to you."'

Okay. So her knees went a little weak.

He caught her. "I'm done hidin', sugar. I'm with you. I don't want to be with anyone else. So I want everyone to know I'm with you—and that includes your family and mine."

Her jaw dropped.

He covered her mouth with his, gifting her with the sweetest, most romantic, most convincing kiss. Then he scattered kisses from the tip of her chin to her temple. "Please forgive me for hurtin' you. I'll do anything to make it right with you. Anything."

Carolyn clung to him, letting his soft kisses and promises bolster her courage. She'd never gotten into a fight with her brothers, besides the squabbling when they were kids. If she showed up at home with Carson McKay on her arm...what would happen?

"Caro?"

She turned and her forehead bumped into the cut on his cheek and he hissed. "Sorry."

"It's okay."

"No, it's not. How many guys did you take on last night?"

"A few."

She stood on tiptoe and placed her lips on the wound. Then the one by his eye. Then the bruise on his jaw. And finally his upper and lower lip.

Wrapped in his arms, she was surprised to feel his heart pounding so hard.

"Am I forgiven?"

Carolyn arched back, locking her gaze to his. "Yes. But if I see your hands or any other part of you on another woman? I'll do what needs to be done. To both of you."

"Won't happen again." He brought her hand to his mouth and kissed her knuckles. "What were your plans for after church?"

"I put a pork roast in the oven and told my family I'd be home to dish it up after church let out."

"Is there enough food for me?"

She looked at him, seeing the wariness mixed with hope. "You're serious."

"Very serious. I won't be throwin' any punches—unless I'm defending myself or you—but your family needs to know they ain't scarin' me off. We're done sneaking around, Carolyn. Let's do this. Meet each other's families and make it official that we're together."

Carson had on his brooding face as they drove to her house. But he kept contact with her, absentmindedly stroking his thumb over the inside of her wrist in a way that soothed her, yet awakened every nerve ending beneath that section of skin.

When they pulled into the driveway, she noticed her brother Harland's vehicle was there, as well as Darren's. Strange. They never showed up for Sunday dinner.

"Looks like the gang's all here," Carson said dryly. "You think Thomas might've tipped 'em off that I didn't give a damn about their threats?"

"Maybe. More likely is someone saw us together at church and called my mother."

"Sugar. You all right?"

She looked at him. Really looked at him, this handsome man, who'd changed her from the moment he'd entered her life ten short days ago. Here he was, battered and bruised, but still willing to stand beside her. She kissed him very gently. "This won't be easy."

"Nothin' worthwhile ever is."

The front door slammed and her brothers filed out and spread out, arms crossed, poses belligerent. Her dad eased down the steps and waited in the center of his line of sons.

"Stay put. I'll come around and help you out."

Both hers and Carson's palms were sweaty when they met, but Carson kept a determined lock on her hand as they approached the line of Wests.

"I'd offer to introduce you to my boyfriend, Carson McKay, but I've heard you've already met."

"You have a death wish showin' up here, McKay?" Harland snapped.

Her oldest brother had been born angry. Normally she tiptoed around him, but not anymore. "Why are you even here, Harland? You don't live here. Who I date doesn't concern you, so butt out."

"The hell it doesn't! You're my little sister and I'm protecting you. Not only that, you stepping out with a McKay puts us all in a bad light."

Carson's hand tightened, as did his jaw, but he didn't speak.

Darren, her blond-haired blue-eyed bruiser of a brother, stepped forward. "We thought we all made it clear that you're expected to stay away from Carolyn."

"Yeah, what we said to you weren't suggestions," Stuart tossed out. "But God's honest truth, turn around and drive away from here or we'll fulfill all of them promises."

"Times five," Marshall added.

Thomas said nothing.

Carolyn held her breath when her father opened his mouth.

"Go on and get in the house, Carolyn. We'll talk about your lapse in judgment later."

"No. I'm not a child. You can't send me to my room. I'm dating Carson. End of discussion. You all better find a way to deal with it, but if you can't that's your issue, not mine."

"Bullshit. You're so damn naïve, Carolyn. You haven't been around. You have no idea what kind of lowlife scum he is."

She glared at Harland. "You haven't been around me either, so I won't allow you to sit in judgment of me. Or him. Worry about your own love life and go home to the wife you have waiting there."

Her brothers huffed and puffed but didn't retort.

Then her father spit a stream of tobacco juice that almost landed on Carson's boot tip. "I'm just supposed to accept you're with him? No can do. I raised you better than this."

"Near as I can tell, you didn't raise her at all," Carson said evenly. "You sent her off to Catholic school to be raised."

"So we should've expected because she was sheltered that she'd fall for the first big, dumb cowboy to come along?" Harland sneered.

Carson faced Carolyn. "Sugar, you didn't tell me you were datin' someone else before you met me."

She bit her tongue to stop the laugh.

"See you got the same smart mouth as your father," her dad said.

Enough. Carolyn pointed at her brothers. "Move so I can get dinner on the table before it burns."

"You go on in. But him?" Her dad gave Carson the stink eye. "A McKay ain't welcome in my home. Ever."

"That's enough."

Her brothers and her father turned and looked at Clara West, venturing out the front door.

Carolyn hid her shock. Her mother wore a dress and shoes—not pajamas and slippers. She'd fixed her hair and put on makeup. She leaned heavily on her walker but she was also smiling.

"But Ma—"

"Hush," she said to Harland without taking her eyes off Carson. "Excuse my sons' behavior. Perhaps we should've sent them off to Catholic school too."

Carson removed his hat. "It's a pleasure to meet you, Mrs. West. I see that Carolyn inherited her beauty and gentility from you."

She ignored her brothers rolled eyes, snorts and hostility at the comment as she was focused on the pleasure shining in her mother's eyes.

"Carolyn is a fine cook. I'm pleased you'll get a sample of that today. Please come in and share a meal with us." She looked at her husband. "This is my home too and he is welcome in it. So bring another chair to the table."

"Won't need it," Harland said. "I lost my appetite and I ain't staying."

"Me neither," said Darren.

Their rude behavior hurt, mostly because she didn't understand it.

Stuart and Marshall looked torn. They'd have to pay for food in town if they took off. Shooting a last look at their departing brothers, they started up the porch steps.

Only Thomas offered Carson his hand. "Glad to see you came to your senses—even when it looks like most of them got beat outta you last night."

"Sometimes that's what it takes."

Carolyn grabbed Thomas's sleeve. "Why were Harland and Darren here?"

"Father Dorian called to talk to Mom about you bringing such a nice Catholic man to church with you and Dad overheard the conversation. He called Harland and Darren for a family meeting. And he was pissed when he found out we all knew about you two seeing each other."

"Doesn't matter now." She tugged on Carson's hand. "Let's go."

Her mother sat at the dining room table, speaking in low tones with Marshall and Stuart. They both scowled at Carson.

Great. She'd have to leave Carson in their company while she readied the food.

"Only six place settings, *Liebchen*. Your father won't be joining us."

His loss. If he didn't eat now she wasn't feeding him later.

Carolyn couldn't keep track of the conversation with the electric mixer whirring as she whipped the potatoes.

While the gravy thickened, she stacked the place settings and delivered them to the table. Her family knew the drill and distributed plates and silverware.

She brought out the food—roast pork, mashed potatoes, gravy, wheat rolls and a medley of cooked carrots, onions and sugar snap peas. She slid in next to Carson.

"This surely does look like a feast," he said, his eyes firmly on the juicy meat.

"Before we eat, we give thanks," Marshall said. "McKay, since you're such a nice Catholic man, would you do the honors?"

Carson looked startled a split second before he smiled. "Be happy to." He removed his hat, set it on the sideboard, and bowed his head. "Lord, we thank you for this bounty we are about to receive. We thank you for the rain that sprouted the vegetables and the sun that grew them to their peak of ripeness, and Carolyn's cookin' skills that turned them into this mouthwatering delight. We thank you for the soil that nurtured the silage that sustained the pig, for the farmers who deal with the muck, mess and stench of a pig farm every day so that we might enjoy this tender, succulent roasted pork, simmering in its own juices and spices. We thank you for the wheat farmers who toil over their grain harvest every fall, for the mills that grind that grain into flour, and the skill of the baker who can mix water, salt, yeast, sugar and flour into the warm, crunchy, melt in your mouth buttery rolls before us. Thank you for the family you've seen fit to bless us with, and may we always remember to give thanks where thanks are due."

When Carson took a breath, as if to keep going, Carolyn lifted her head. She crossed herself and said, "Amen."

Her brothers and mother followed suit.

Her mother said, "Thank you, Carson, for such a lovely and heartfelt blessing."

Carolyn glanced at her brother who'd offered the dare and smiled to see he'd been put in his place. But her smile dried when she realized she was sitting too far away from her mother to help slice her food into manageable bites. Her arthritis made it difficult to hold utensils and she ate everything with a spoon.

But her mother had a lot of pride which is why she rarely left the house, or ate meals at the table, so Carolyn couldn't treat her like a child in front of company.

Stuart realized the predicament and dished her up potatoes before passing the bowl on. Same with the veggies. When the meat platter reached him, he quickly shredded the pork before he scooped it onto her plate.

Carson was too busy piling his plate up to notice. Neither did he pay attention when Stuart handed their mother a spoon. Only when Carolyn saw her mother eat several bites did she relax.

Not that the meal was overrun with chatter. Carolyn wondered what mealtime was like at the McKay table. She managed not to jump when she felt Carson's hand on her leg.

As soon as Marshall, Stuart and Thomas finished eating, they left the table.

Even Carson threw in the towel. "Thank you for inviting me for such a delicious meal, Carolyn. You are one helluva cook. If you'll pardon my language."

She blushed. "Thank you." Then she eyed the pile of dishes. It'd take an hour to clean this mess up—an hour Carson would be stuck with her family.

Her mother said, "I'll keep Carson company while you get these dishes soaking before you take off. I'm sure you two have better things to do than stay around here on such a lovely day."

At least she'd gotten a small reprieve.

There wasn't much food remaining. She stored the leftovers and stacked everything by the sink. The pie she'd baked sat untouched and she covered it with foil to take to Carson's father. Not much of a bribe but better than nothing. And her brothers and father didn't deserve pie anyway. The jerks.

She considered changing out of her church clothes, but she still had to meet Carson's family. She ducked into her room and fixed her hair and freshened her makeup.

Her dad sat in front of the TV. He didn't look away from it as she crossed the room. He said, "You're making a big mistake. You'll choose him over your own family?"

"Only if you make me."

She left and didn't look back.

Chapter Twelve
Carson

Carolyn kept pinching the pleats in her skirt until Carson stilled the motion by placing his hand on hers. "Sugar. It'll be okay."

"You don't know that."

She had him there. But Jed McKay wasn't the type to cause a scene—especially not with a woman. If he was displeased, at least in polite company, he wouldn't say a word. Sure as shootin' he'd light into Carson when they were alone.

He angled his chin to the pie sitting on the seat between them. "That'll go a long way into sweetening him up."

"I hope so. I've never done this before."

"I'm glad I'm your first for a lot of things."

She blushed and he grinned. He loved seeing that color on her cheeks because only he knew her entire body flushed that pretty shade of pink when she was naked.

He had to release her hand to downshift when they reached the gravel road leading to his folks' house. Trees used as a windbreak obscured most of the three-story house from the road. He cut to the left and parked in front.

"Wow. This is...big," Carolyn said, leaning down to peer through the windshield.

"My grandfather bought it from a bigwig who worked for one of the railroads. The guy started to have it built for his wife before they relocated from the east coast; evidently she demanded a big fancy house. But he died during a flu epidemic and she had no interest in moving here, so she sold it and the land for pretty cheap."

"This place looks to have plenty of room. Why don't you live here?"

"Dad didn't approve of the way I was spendin' my free time. He spouted off that *while you live under my roof* bullshit so I moved out. We can work together but I don't gotta live with him. Me'n Cal pooled our money and bought the trailer. In case the back roads confused you, it's about three miles across the way on McKay land."

"Your land stretches that far?"

It stretched a helluva lot farther than that. "Yeah. We've been buying parcels as they come up for sale. Every little bit adds up."

"But—"

"Can we talk about this later?" He curled his hand around the back of her neck and kissed her. "Let's have a slice of that cherry pie with the old man."

No surprise his father hadn't greeted them on the porch. Carson opened the screen door and knocked loudly on the inner door before he opened it. "Dad? I've brought someone I want you to meet."

"Where is he?" Carolyn whispered.

"Probably napping in the living room." He led her past the staircase to the kitchen.

Carolyn set the pie on the counter and wandered through the space. "This is lovely."

Carson moved in behind her and set his hands on her shoulders. "This was Mom's domain. Seemed weird to be in here without her after she passed."

"I love that you can see the rolling hills and the pasture as you're standing at the sink."

"This house didn't originally have indoor plumbing, so Dad had everything updated about fifteen years ago."

"And it's probably due to be updated again," Carson's dad said behind them.

Carson kept his hands on Carolyn's shoulders when they turned around.

His father stared at Carolyn without saying a word.

Her body tensed.

"This is my girlfriend, Carolyn West."

His scrutiny increased, but he remained mum.

"It's nice to meet you, Mr. McKay," Carolyn said.

"West. You Eli's kid?"

"Yes, sir."

"He still alive?"

What the hell?

"Yes, sir, he is."

"Thought he'd be dead by now."

Again. What the hell was wrong with his dad?

"Excuse me?" Carolyn said.

"Eli West had a big mouth and a lot of nerve. Not a good combination. I figured either someone would've killed him or he'd died due to his own stupidity."

"Jesus, Dad. Enough."

Those blue eyes—eyes just like his—narrowed into mean slits. "You meet her family yet, son?"

"Had dinner with them today."

"They welcome you with open arms once they learned you're a McKay?"

Carson didn't respond.

129

His dad's shrewd gaze gauged the damage to his face. "Any of them responsible for that?"

"No. Had a little trouble at the dancehall last night but me'n Cal, Casper and Charlie handled it."

"That's why them boys weren't worth a hill of beans this mornin'."

"*I* don't have a problem with them getting their work done during the week. But I can see why they'd wanna pull the covers over their heads if you were as much an ass to them as you're bein' to Carolyn."

They glared at one another.

"I'm takin' her on a tour of the house." He clasped Carolyn's hand in his and towed her behind him. "This is the dining room. Beyond that in the corner is a parlor, also my mother's space." He kept up a brisk pace. "Living room." Down the hallway, he opened the first door. "This is Dad's study." The next room was self-explanatory but he found himself explaining anyway. "This bathroom got added on when they put in indoor plumbing. It used to be a bedroom. On the other side of that wall is the washroom with a washer and dryer." He pointed to the end of the hall. "Around that corner is another entrance to the kitchen and also a door that goes out to the back porch. Let's go upstairs."

Carolyn stopped. When he turned to ask her what was wrong, she placed her palms on his chest. "Carson. Sweetheart. Slow down."

He exhaled and pressed his forehead to hers. "Sorry. It's just..."

"I know. It's okay. I wanted to throttle my family earlier too."

He tipped her face up and kissed her, meaning for it just to be a short tender press of lips. But the instant their mouths met, he needed more of her.

She pulled away. "Let's get back to the tour."

Carson led her up the wide staircase that opened onto the second floor.

"Are all of these bedrooms?"

He'd never really looked at the house he'd been born and raised in through someone else's eyes. "There are eight bedrooms up here now. Don't know if they had rooms for live-in staff or what. During the remodel they turned one of the rooms into a bathroom. My folks' room had two connecting rooms, with the smaller room being the nursery. Dad surprised Mom and had them put in their own private bathroom."

"I'd love that. We have one bathroom in our house, but I know that's better than an outhouse."

"Yeah, I don't miss that at all." He pointed to doors on the opposite ends of the long hallway. "Casper and Charlie both still live here."

"Did you have your own room growing up, with this many to choose from?"

"Since me'n Cal are twins we shared the biggest room until we were probably thirteen. Then we each got our own space."

Carolyn touched the wide mahogany molding. "Did your

grandparents have lots of kids?"

Carson shook his head. "They had four or five—I never can remember, but I do know that my dad was the only one who survived to adulthood."

"A shame."

"With this much space my mom always wanted to have more kids. Felt it was her duty."

"My mom did her 'duty' and almost died after she lost the last baby. That's the reason she and my dad have separate bedrooms. The doctor said the next pregnancy might kill her, so they had to stop..." She blushed. "I can't imagine my parents doing it anyway."

He ran his finger down her jaw. "I know what you mean. I'm sure all kids feel that way, thinkin' about their parents' bein' nekkid together. Our kids will probably feel the same about us." Dragging her against him, he kissed her, his mouth demanding. It'd be heaven to haul her into his old room, pin her to the mattress and fuck her until they broke the antique bed frame.

She moved her lips away from his. "I know what you're thinking, McKay."

"You do?"

"Uh-huh. And that wouldn't give your dad a very good impression of me, would it?"

"Well, he already doesn't like you because you're a West—"

Carolyn shoved him.

He laughed. "Just kiddin', sugar."

"Carson? You still up there?" his dad shouted up the staircase.

"Yeah. We're comin' down." He sighed. "And that is why I don't live here anymore. Snoopy damn man." They moved past the closed doors, taking the narrow set of stairs back to the main floor.

"They built this house with servants in mind, didn't they?"

"I guess. These stairs came in handy when we were sneakin' back in after curfew."

She gasped. "I can't believe a good Catholic boy like you would do that."

"Just because Father Dorian called me that don't mean it's true."

His dad was waiting in the kitchen. The aroma of coffee filled the air.

Rather than hanging back, Carolyn walked over to the counter. "If you'll get plates and a pie cutter, I'll dish up."

Carson didn't offer to help. His dad needed to make up for being an ass. If he'd had his way, his father would've been denied pie, just like her family had been.

They carried their plates and cups into the dining room. After a couple of bites, Jed McKay said, "This is good. Thanks for bringing it. I hafta get my sweet fix at the diner."

"You tick off all them women who were dropping off coffee cakes, pies and cookies?"

His father iced him with a look. "Yep. Not interested in getting married and that's what they were all angling for." He looked at Carolyn.

She smiled. "Rest assured, Mr. McKay, I'm not interested in marrying you." She shoved a bite of pie in her mouth.

Carson about choked on his coffee.

"You don't look old enough to get married. How old are you?"

"Dad—"

"That's fine, Carson, I'll answer. I just graduated from St. Mary's. I'll be nineteen soon."

"You sticking around these parts?"

"We'll see. I'm here over the summer."

He sipped his coffee. "How's your mother?"

Then everything started to fall into place. Talking to Carolyn's mother after lunch, she'd asked about his dad. Obviously they knew each other. How well? Then he remembered the story Thomas told him about Eli West putting Jed McKay in the hospital years ago.

Had that been over Carolyn's mother? That made the most sense. No wonder the men hated each other. And it had nothing to do with the supposed blood feud between Eli and Jed's fathers.

"Right, son?"

He looked at his dad. "What?"

"I asked if she'd been at the dancehall last night when you mixed it up."

"I told him I'd already left and he said it was a good thing," Carolyn inserted.

He wasn't about to let his dad deliver a lecture about fighting. He'd been hearing that same lecture since his first fight at age ten. He finished his coffee and stood. "We gotta run."

Startled, Carolyn pushed back from the table and said, "Excuse me. I need to use the facilities," and disappeared down the hallway.

As soon as she was out of earshot, his dad warned, "Don't go getting serious about her."

"Why not?"

"She's too damned young for one thing. She's the daughter of Eli West for another."

"She's also Clara's daughter."

"Don't matter. I don't want you seein' her again."

"What you want don't matter to me because I *am* seein' her and I'm already serious about her."

His father crossed his arms over his chest. "It should matter because I hold all the cards for your future. Be a mighty bleak one for you if you see her in it."

"So you're...threatening me? You get off on makin' me jump through hoops. So go on and tell me, Dad. If I don't break it off with her, you'll disinherit me? Kick me off the ranch?"

"You mark my words, boy, that girl will—"

"I left you a slice of pie, Mr. McKay," Carolyn said as she breezed back into the dining room. "I promised the rest to your son."

"I'll just bet you did."

Would Carolyn think less of him if he took a swing at his old man?

Probably.

"Come on, sugar, we got places to be."

Carolyn held the pie in one hand and he grabbed her free hand. "Nice meeting you, Mr. McKay."

They were out the door before they heard his dad's response. They were out of the driveway before Carson spoke. "Sorry about that."

"What did he say to you that prompted our quick exit?"

"Nothin' worth repeating." He pulled off to the side of the road. "When I talked to your mom today she asked about my dad. Doesn't it seem odd that my dad would ask about your mom?"

Her eyes went wide. "Do you think they...?"

"Dated? Snuck around? Maybe. Maybe even behind your dad's back when he was dating your mom. Seems to be the reputation McKays have." He paused to breathe. "Years ago Eli put my dad in the hospital."

"I didn't know that! How'd you find that out?"

"Thomas told me. He overheard it from Roscoe."

"Then it's true because Roscoe is my dad's one decent friend." She looked at him. "I thought all the bad blood was between your grandfather and mine."

"It was. But it appears that's not where the bad blood ends between the Wests and McKays."

Carolyn set the pie on the dash and scooted closer, uncurling one of his hands from the steering wheel. Then she curled that hand around her face. "Maybe we'll be the generation that ends it."

Or maybe by being together they were starting a third-generation feud.

Carson didn't give a damn about what'd happened in the past. When he looked in Carolyn's eyes, he saw his future.

"That's a pretty intense look you're giving me, McKay."

He smiled and gently kissed the inside of her wrist. "Better?"

"Sweeter, definitely. So where to now?"

"I'm supposed to be meetin' my brothers at the Silver Spur."

"You hang out in a bar on a Sunday?"

"Yep." And just to be ornery, he said, "I've been to your church today, now it's time for you to come to mine."

Somehow he'd forgotten she could hit that hard.

Cal had taken their usual booth in the back. He stood when they approached.

"Cal, this is Carolyn West. Caro, this is my brother, Cal."

"Nice to meet you."

"Likewise."

"Cal is short for...?"

"Calvin. Can I get you a drink?"

"I'll take a Coke."

Carson gestured for her to sit on the inside. "I'll take a double shot."

Cal raised both eyebrows in a silent "That bad?" and Carson nodded before he slid in next to Carolyn.

"Where are your other brothers?"

"They'll be here soon." She was looking at him strangely. "What?"

"You and Cal aren't identical twins but you look an awful lot alike."

"And?"

"And I'm just wondering if your other brothers look like you two."

"Why such a curious kitty?"

"Because you've met my brothers. None of us look anything alike. My sister Kimi is blonde like me, and she's the spitting image of our mother, but Harland is the only one who looks anything like our dad."

"Huh. Same thing happens with cattle. Once in a while we get some weird color mixes."

She laughed.

"What?"

"I think that's the first time you've brought the conversation around to cows."

"I can pretty much guarantee it won't be the last time."

Cal returned with the drinks.

It was hard for Carson to sip his double shot of whiskey and not slam it.

Cal and Carolyn hit it off right away. He relaxed a little.

"Well, who we got here?" Casper said, grabbing a chair and flipping it around before he straddled it. "Didja bring dates for all of us? 'Cause if we get to pick, I'm choosing her." He offered his hand. "Casper McKay."

Carson batted his brother's hand away. "This is my girlfriend, Carolyn, so keep your paws off her."

Casper lifted his in hands in surrender. "No harm in tryin'."

Charlie slid into the booth next to Cal. "I told you they wouldn't sell to me. Go up there and buy your own damn beer."

"Fuckin' little brat. What good are ya if ya can't keep the booze flowin'?"

"I drive your drunken ass home, remember?"

"Right. Guess you are good for something." Casper stood and

headed to the bar.

"He is pissin' me off today," Charlie said. "Ever since we fought them guys last night, he's been talkin' about knockin' fool heads together." He snorted. "Big fuckin' talker. He's usually passed out in the truck when the real fightin' starts."

Carson didn't want to dissect last night's dust up, or anything about last night. "Carolyn, this is my youngest brother Charlie. He's usually more polite than this. Charlie, my girlfriend, Carolyn."

"Shit. Sorry. Sorry for sayin' shit." He rubbed his hand on his jeans before offering it to Carolyn. "Nice to meet you. What'd you say your last name was?"

"It's West."

Charlie's eyes nearly popped out of his head. "West? As in…"

"Yeah, that West," Carson finished.

"Now I know why Dad was bein' such an ass when we stopped at home to get some money before we came here." His gaze slid to Carolyn. "No offense."

Cal rubbed his hands together. "Who wants to play pool?"

"What's the bet?"

"Same as usual. Buck a game."

"I'll play ya," Carson said. He tugged on a hank of Carolyn's hair. "You can be my good luck charm."

Carolyn didn't say much as they played pool. She seemed more amused than bored.

Cal beat Carson. Then Cal lost to Charlie. Charlie then lost to Casper. Carson challenged Casper and Casper beat him.

Normally Casper would've been impossible to sit with after winning. He wasn't acting the least bit cocky, which threw Carson off. Then Casper offered to teach Carolyn how to play and she surprised them all by accepting.

"So what the fuck did Dad say to you today, Carse?" Cal demanded. "You had two damn doubles."

Without taking his gaze off his brother and his girlfriend, he said, "Dad threatened my future with the ranch. He didn't come straight out and say he'd kick me off and cut me out, but he sure as fuck implied it."

"That's a crock of shit," Cal said. "He knows he can't run the ranch without you. He also knows if he cuts you out we'll all walk—at least I will."

"Me too," Charlie said. "But I ain't so sure about Casper."

"He's too fuckin' lazy to step up," Carson said. "And if we all walked? Dad would be forced to hire men, which we know he ain't gonna do."

"Only McKays work McKay land," Charlie mimicked their father's favorite edict.

"He'd have to sell, which won't happen because he just bought two new sections in the last year."

"I knew he was bluffing as soon as he opened his mouth," Carson said. "Still pissed me off. He just had to speak his piece when Carolyn was in the next room."

"Did she hear him?"

Carson shook his head. "But she knows something happened."

"How'd things play out with the Wests today?" Cal asked.

"Worse than with Dad. Eli wouldn't even eat at the same table as me. Only reason I sat to the table at all is because of Carolyn's mother."

"I dunno, Carson. She's pretty and she seems real sweet, but is she worth the trouble?

Carolyn laughed right then and the sound flowed through him like liquid happiness. He wanted to say, "She's definitely worth everything I have to go through to make her mine," but his brothers would rag on him endlessly for such a sappy comment, so he merely said, "Yep."

Chapter Thirteen
Carolyn

Carolyn waited on the front steps of Carson's trailer, her leg bouncing as she tried to focus all her restless energy in one place. She probably could've gone inside—she knew neither Carson nor Cal locked the door—but waltzing in without an invite would feel like trespassing.

The sun beat down, frying the top of her head, making the skin on her arms sting. Thankfully she hadn't worn stockings or they'd be melted to her legs.

She should've gone home. The sun porch would've cooled off by now. She could strip, lie on her bed and let the breeze wash over her, hoping it'd wash away the ugly words that'd been tossed around today as if she wasn't there.

She'd done an onsite first fitting in Moorcroft for Missy Ludwig, the bride, and her two bridesmaids, Tammy and Edie, the catty women Beverly had pointed out to Carolyn. And to make matters more fun, the first bridesmaid she fitted was the brunette, Edie, who Carson had his arm around. Her nasty glower could've torched Carolyn's hair.

Carolyn had stayed professional, just like her aunt had taught her, when Edie started asking questions.

"So you're really dating Carson McKay?"

"Yes, I am."

"How long has that been going on?"

"Three weeks."

"Longer than most. That's probably just because you're not from around here."

"My parents live here."

"But you didn't go to school here. Where'd you go?"

"A Catholic academy in Billings."

"You were studying to be a nun?" She laughed. "That would be a challenge for Carson McKay. Trying to sweet talk a nun candidate out of her habit."

"Turn to the left please."

Edie paused as she admired herself in the mirror. Then, "You sure Carson hasn't dumped you and you just haven't realized it yet?"

Do not let your hand slip and jab her with this pin.

"He was downright hostile to you that night at the dance when he had his arm around me and invited me back to his place."

Tell her you and Carson had a fight and he was just using her to make you jealous.

No. She wouldn't stoop to that level. "We've been out almost every night for the last two weeks. I'm surprised you haven't seen us."

"But I didn't see you out with him last night. Looked like he was having a good old time without you. And he wasn't alone." Edie smirked at Carolyn's look of surprise. "Oh, sorry, you didn't know?"

"I know what I need to." After Carolyn finished pinning the hem, she said, "Turn."

"Yeah, right. Bet you don't know what kind of man Carson really is. He's using you; he uses everyone. It's a game with him. He'll see if he can get you to fall into his bed and he'll fuck you over as you're falling for him. Then he'll drop you like a bad habit—not that he's dropped any of his own bad habits. He's done the love 'em and leave 'em thing so many times, with so many girls, it's no wonder he had to go looking elsewhere for fresh meat." Edie's piggy eyes scanned Carolyn head to toe. "Young meat."

Carolyn blinked at her.

"Oh, sweetie. Are you gonna cry?" she cooed maliciously.

Like I'd give you the satisfaction. "Of course not." She jerked on the bodice. "Maybe you should think about wearing a padded bra with this dress so there's not such a huge gap in the bust line. There's nothing I can do to fix that." She couldn't manage a smile. "You're done. Go ahead and hang the dress on the back of the door and send in the next bridesmaid."

Edie unzipped the dress and let it fall to the floor. She kicked it at Carolyn. "You hang it up. You're nothing but the hired help around here."

Heat blazed in her cheeks as she shook out the dress and hung it up.

The *don't let her get to you* self-advice didn't work.

Tammy the bridesmaid was equally nasty.

As Carolyn packed up her notions bag, she overheard them in the room next door, talking about her as if she couldn't hear every blasted word.

What is she thinking, screwing around with Carson McKay? Does she think she's got a chance with him? Please. The only person that man will ever commit to is himself.

I know she's not from around here, but is she stupid? He'll use her and move on.

I wonder if she's seen the notches in his bedpost? A friend of mine swore me to secrecy that she's actually seen them.

I bet after he dumps her she'll slink away in embarrassment.

I heard their families have some kind of feud going on and Carson only took her out on a dare from his brothers to make her family mad.

But had Carolyn stood up to them? No. If she spoke her mind she'd come off as a screech owl. Better just to smile and move on.

She'd knocked on the bedroom door and all conversation ended like someone had sucked the oxygen out of the room. "I'll be back in two weeks for the final fittings. God bless and have a peaceful evening."

Then she'd driven to Maxine's shop and ditched the dresses. At loose ends, she backtracked here.

Even as her tears fell she knew they were stupid and pointless. Crying never solved anything. Did she really want Carson to find her sobbing on his steps? Then he'd have another one of those "you're too young for me" moments—which were becoming rarer by the day. But still.

Carolyn wiped her eyes and stood. Before she made it to her car, Carson's truck barreled up the gravel road, a dirt rooster tail trailing behind him.

He slammed on the brakes and bailed out of his truck almost before it stopped. "Well, ain't you a pretty sight to come home to."

She threw herself into his arms.

"Hey, now. Much as I love havin' you wrapped around me, I just got done workin' and I reek to high heaven."

"I don't care. I just need..."

He covered her mouth with his. He tasted like coffee and man. She held onto the back of his neck, keeping those full, soft lips on hers when she sensed he wanted to pull away. The sweet and slow kiss kept the passion between them on simmer rather than starting out as a raging inferno. It was exactly what she needed.

All of a sudden Carson bent forward, hooking her knees in his arms and lifting her up. Still teasing her lips with nibbles and soft smooches, he carried her into the trailer straight to his bedroom and lowered her onto his bed.

"Don't move. I'll be right back."

"Where are you going?"

"To take a shower." He grinned and let his hungry gaze wander over her. "A quick shower."

Carolyn stretched out. Sex aside, she wondered what it'd be like to spend the whole night in Carson's bed and not just a few hours. Did he sleep naked? Would they fall asleep in each other's arms? Would he want to have sex with her first thing in the morning? Beverly told her morning sex was the best. Then she'd gone into a little too much detail about how Mike had woken her up.

That *would* be a great way to wake up; Carson's tongue licking and teasing, his lips sucking on her tender flesh. He kissed her down there with as much skill and enthusiasm as he kissed her mouth. He liked making her squirm until she begged.

Which she always did. Without shame. Then he launched her into that pulse-pounding rush of heaven and gently brought her back down.

Just thinking about all the wonderful sensations her body was capable of under his tutelage sent a tingle down her spine and dampened her panties with want.

When the bedroom door shut, she pushed up on her elbows.

Carson stood by his dresser, small towel wrapped around his hips, rummaging through the top drawer.

His naked back was a sight to behold. His muscles flexed even with the smallest movement, sending the water droplets still clinging to his skin rolling down his sinewy muscles.

Then he faced her. "Caro? You okay?"

She automatically answered, "Uh-huh," but she was more focused on the impressive tent at the juncture of his thighs. Right then she wanted to feel that hardness in her mouth. Kissing him the same way he kissed and tasted her. Scooting to the edge of the bed, she gazed up at him.

He eliminated the space between them and curled his hand around her face. "Interestin' look on your face, sugar. Whatcha thinkin' about?"

Carolyn didn't break eye contact. "I want to put my mouth on you, but I don't know what to do. Will you teach me what you like?"

His blue eyes went molten. "What prompted you into wantin' to give me a blowjob?"

"Seeing you naked pretty much did it," she admitted. "I love it when you put your mouth down there and I want to know what it feels like to do the same thing to you." There. That hadn't been so hard.

"I want that too. But before we get to the next stage, I wanna hear you say the words."

"What words?"

Carson yanked away the towel. He circled his free hand around the base and stroked up. "This is my cock. Say it."

Her cheeks burned. "That's your cock."

"I know you've got issues sayin' dirty words, but when that bedroom door closes and it's just you'n me nekkid? Those words ain't dirty. They're body parts—our body parts—and I expect you to tell me what you want."

You can do this. "I want your cock in my mouth," she said softly.

Carson groaned and he moved his hand faster. Then he realized what he was doing and stopped. His hand tightened on her face and he swept his thumb over her cheekbone. "So fuckin' sexy that you want this."

"Show me what you like," she whispered. She placed her hand over his as he stroked himself.

"You can keep a pretty firm grip." He removed his hand, placing hers on that hard shaft. "Slow is good until I need it fast."

Without waiting for instruction, Carolyn angled her head and licked the tip.

He sucked in a breath and said, "More of that."

She swept her tongue across the slit, wetting her tongue with the clear liquid seeping out but it didn't really have a taste. She enclosed the entire tip in her mouth and sucked. Then she backed off and traced the edge of the head with her tongue.

Carson didn't direct her; he just let her explore, apparently not minding that she was so tentative. His hand was still curled around her face and his other hand played with her hair.

Bolstered by his patience, she took the tip in her mouth again and let her lips slide down the length, not stopping until her gag reflex kicked in. This close to his groin she caught a whiff of his musky male scent that even the soap from his shower couldn't mask. She eased back and swallowed him again to where her hand gripped the base.

Some instinct told her to kick up the pace; to move her hand up and her mouth down in tandem.

"That's it, just like that. God that feels good, sugar. So good."

She focused on pleasing him, knowing by the harsh sound of his breathing that she was doing something right. She took a chance and glanced up at him, expecting he'd have his eyes closed. But that burning blue gaze zeroed in on her, not her eyes, but watching his dick disappear into her mouth.

When Carson started bumping his pelvis forward, that was the sign he'd spoken of to go faster.

She bobbed her head, sucking hard when his length was in as far as she could take it. She had a quick thought: *why did they call this a blowjob? There was no blowing involved. It should be called a suck job.*

"Caro. I'm gonna come...pull back when I tell you."

His deep moans and the tighter grip on her hair made her squirmy and anxious. Doing this to him had already soaked her panties.

"Now."

As soon as she'd released him from her mouth, he wrapped his hand around hers and pulled on his dick so hard and fast, she wondered if it hurt, especially when the look on his face seemed pained.

"Watch," he said hoarsely.

His body began to shudder. She watched as thick ribbons of milky white shot out of that slit and coated both of their hands. He kept pumping and pumping until the spurts ended.

"Fuck." Carson blindly reached behind him and braced a hand on his dresser, acting as if he needed something solid to hold him up after that.

What a sense of satisfaction that response gave her.

As he caught his breath she asked, "Why did you have me pull back?"

"Since this was your first time...you ain't ready for me to come in your mouth."

Carolyn wondered how it'd feel having those powerful spasms on her tongue. Curious as to what that tasted like, she enclosed the head of his cock in her mouth and sucked.

"Jesus, what are you doin'?"

She showed her disapproval about his language by lightly sinking her teeth into his softening flesh.

"Shit. Sorry. That just... Damn, woman. I'm feelin' a little shaky after that." He sat beside her on the bed. Snagging the towel off the floor, he wiped off her hand before cleaning up his own.

"I'm buck assed nekkid and you've still got all your clothes on. How did that happen?"

She kissed the cup of his shoulder. "Oral sex education, remember?" she said, suddenly feeling shy. "So how'd I do?"

Carson dipped his head. Against her lips, he murmured, "I'd say since you made my knees weak you did pretty damn good, wouldn't you?"

"Mmm-hmm."

"You wanna slip them britches off and let me have a go at you?"

"If you want."

He nuzzled her neck. "Gonna be shy now?"

"Maybe."

"Can't have that." Carson put his hand in the center of her chest and pushed her back until her spine hit the mattress. He slipped her pedal pushers to the floor, then her panties.

When Carolyn started to scoot into the middle of the bed, he clamped his hand onto her thigh.

"Don't move."

"But how—"

Dropping to his knees, he brought her legs over his shoulders, burying his face between her thighs.

"This sweet juice tells me you liked havin' my dick in your mouth."

Then she couldn't answer because her mind was focused on his lips, his teeth and his tongue. Lapping and sucking, his hot breath washed over her, sending tingles up her belly.

Carson didn't tease her, leaving her hanging on the ragged edge as he'd done before. He built her into a frenzy of need and then finished her off with that rhythmic sucking thing he did with his lips that sent her soaring.

Her entire body quaked. She had a strange whooshing in her ears and she thought she might've...yelled out his name, with maybe a couple of loud *yes, yes, yeses.*

He released her legs and set her feet on the floor. "Sugar, put your britches back on or I'm afraid we won't leave this bed the rest of the night."

She watched him putting on clean clothes, which was almost as sexy as seeing him strip out of his clothes.

"I could use a beer. Come on." He offered his hand and led her down the hallway and into the kitchen. "Sorry that I forgot to pick up Coke for you."

"I'll just have a sip or two of your beer."

Carson raised his eyebrows. "Didn't think you drank."

"I do sometimes."

He let her have the first drink.

She swallowed the bitter brew. "Thanks."

"Let me know if you want more." He took a healthy swig. "What happened today? You seemed a mite melancholy."

"I was. Just..." *Don't go whining to him.* "No big deal. Just forget it, okay?"

"Nope. I'll keep pestering you until you talk."

Carolyn fought the need to fidget under his probing gaze. "I had a fitting for a bridal party today. Remember that woman you had your arm around that night you were so cold to me? She's in the wedding. And she said some stuff about you."

His eyes narrowed. "What'd she say? Because I never did nothin' with her. Never even kissed her."

"I believe you. She said the only reason you were with me was because I'm a challenge to you and you'd dump me like you've dumped everyone else. In fact, maybe I was too stupid to know I'd already been dumped because she saw you at the bar last night and you weren't alone."

"Are you askin' me if that's true? Yes, I was at the bar with my brothers, we had a couple of beers and left. That's it."

Carolyn placed her hand on his chest. "I wasn't accusing you. I believe you. I know you like to go out and rip it up. Edie's comments about you and me started this whole nasty conversation and they were acting like we weren't a couple."

"What'd you say about that?"

"Nothing. I overheard them. They didn't say it directly to me."

"They're idiots. We are a couple. Everyone who's seen us out and about knows we're a couple." He tugged on her hair. "As long as you know I'm with you and only with you, then I don't give a damn what anyone else thinks or says."

Easy for him to say. Turning a deaf ear to the rumors was harder to do.

He's a McKay. You'd better get used to dealing with rumors.

"How about I buy you supper?"

"Someplace quiet?"

"I was thinkin' more along the lines of the diner in Moorcroft. Show people we are a normal couple out on a date." He grabbed her hand and kissed it. "I haven't wanted to share you or our time together, but now I see I've gotta show off my beautiful girlfriend."

"Carson, you don't have to."

"I want to. It's past time I take you out someplace besides a bar."

Chapter Fourteen
Carson

"You gonna keep beatin' the shit outta that post? Or maybe we can move on to the next one?"

Carson swiped the sweat from his forehead with the back of his glove and let the hammer fall. "Sorry."

"Whatcha thinkin' about so hard?" Cal asked.

He didn't answer. Instead he picked up a shovel.

"It's her, ain't it?"

"Yep."

A moment passed and Cal sighed. "Come on, Carse, what's goin' on? I don't involve myself in your love life, but it's affecting your workin' hours so I have a right to know why you're so damn distracted."

Carson leaned on the shovel handle and gazed across this new section of grazing land, covered in scrub cedar. How did he say this without sounding like a sap?

Cal said nothing. He just waited.

"I want my ring on her finger. I want everyone to know she's mine. It's the first time I ever felt this way and I don't know what to do."

"Marry her."

"Just like that?" He scowled at his brother. "I'm bein' serious."

"So am I. Isn't that what you told me you planned on doin' the first night you saw her? And the first night you brought her over here? And after you introduced her to us? Or didn't you mean it?"

Carson struck the ground's hard crust with the shovel. The clang reverberated up his arm. "I meant it. Didn't know how much I meant it until I'd gotten to know her and she's...everything."

"Still don't see the problem."

"Yeah? How about her family will be pissed, maybe pissed enough to permanently cut ties with her if she marries me. How about she's young. How about we've only been together four fucking weeks."

Cal shrugged. "You said yourself that she seems older than her years. Most people get married young—you'n me are about the only ones in our class that ain't hitched. Doesn't matter how long you have or haven't been together. You'll have deeper feelings for her if you wait another year to make it official? And not to be a jackass, but there are plenty of families in these parts that wouldn't want you marryin' their daughter either, so that family bullshit is another moot point. Quit fightin' with yourself. Cowboy up and make her your wife or walk away."

"Just like that?"

"Just like that," Cal repeated. "You ain't one for half measures."

"No lie there." He rubbed his chin with the back of his hand, deep in thought. "I don't know how to do this. Do I buy her a ring? Or does she go with me to pick one out?"

"Doesn't Dad have Mom's rings?"

"Yeah. But remember he inherited them from his mother. She made Dad promise her jewelry would go to the first girl born into the McKay family."

"Damn. I'd forgotten about that. You bein' the first one to get married won't count."

"Nope."

Cal cocked his head. "Any money left over from the bank loan after we bought that section from Harvey Buckholz?"

"Since closing costs were less than we'd estimated...yeah. But I thought I'd use it to make the first payment."

"Looks like you've found a better use for it." Cal squinted at the sky. "Let's pack it in for today. It's hotter than a demon's cooch out here anyway."

Carson and Cal ended up driving into Rapid City for an engagement ring. He'd look cheap if he picked one with a little diamond chip. Carolyn was worth more than that. At the last store he found a round stone, the size of the end of a pencil eraser, in a platinum setting, that managed to be simple yet eye-catching.

"So when are you askin' her?"

"Tonight." Carson shot him a look. "You can make yourself scarce, right?"

"I suppose I'd better find someplace to live, so the newlyweds can have their privacy."

"The Buckholz house ain't in that bad of shape except for the broken windows and the critters that've moved in."

Cal glanced at him sharply. "I thought you wanted that place."

"It won't be ready for me'n Caro. So I'll stay in the trailer and let you have it."

"We'd better measure them windows and order replacement materials straight away."

They didn't speak again until they'd passed by Spearfish. Sometimes they could jaw on all day; other days they'd barely speak two words to each other.

146

"You plan to ask Carolyn's dad about marryin' her?"

"And give him a chance to say no?" Carson shook his head. "After we're engaged I might ask for his blessing. But I doubt he'll give it."

"Does that bother you? Or I guess maybe the real question is do you think it'll bother her?"

Carson hadn't considered that. "Shit. I don't know." He paused. "I hadn't thought about how Dad will react either."

"Good luck with that. I'll be hidin' in the barn during that yelling match," Cal said.

"And to think I was gonna ask you to stand up for me." He scratched his chin, as if deep in thought. "Charlie is a better bet than Casper for my best man."

"Piss off. I'll do it."

He laughed. "Then if Dad's an ass about it you better back me up."

"Don't I always?"

Since Carolyn's family was aware they were dating, he could call her at home. Still, he was relieved when she answered the phone and not one of her brothers. "Wests."

He smiled just at the sound of her voice. He was so gone over this woman. "Hey, sugar."

"Hey yourself, cowboy."

And yep, he heard that answering smile in her voice.

"How was your day?"

"Short. Yours?"

"Better than yesterday."

"Good. What's goin' on tonight?"

"Not much. Supper is done. Mom had a rough day so she's already tucked in for the night. Why?"

"Got time for me?"

He heard her move and in his mind's eye he saw her twisting the phone cord around her finger. "Always. What did you have in mind?"

"How about if we meet at the Ice Cream Palace."

"You've got such a sweet tooth, cowboy."

"Mmm-hmm. But you're about the sweetest thing there is."

"Smooth, too."

"Now I'm thinkin' about what smooth, sweet thing is my favorite to eat."

"Carson McKay," she hissed in a whisper.

"What? I was talkin' about tastin' your sweet pu...ddin'."

"You are ornery tonight."

"Just anxious. How soon can you be there?"

"An hour."

"See you then. Drive safe."

Damn case of nerves had him pacing. He stopped and studied the living room and kitchen area of the trailer, wondering what it'd be like having Carolyn living here. No doubt she'd fancy the place up. The kitchen would see more use. He grinned. So would the bedroom.

Imagining them being together all the time, for the rest of their lives didn't scare him, it seemed...right in ways he'd never had faith in before he'd met her.

For once Carolyn hadn't arrived before he did. She'd parked in the back of the lot, away from the families with rambunctious kids.

The woman was a ray of sunshine in a dress the color of lemons. When she beamed that glorious smile at him, he almost dropped to one knee and proposed right then.

Not exactly romantic.

He couldn't help but pick her up and spin her around before he kissed her. Her soft mouth opened beneath his with sweet heat and he didn't fight the possessive growl that no other man would ever know her kiss.

She gently touched his cheeks. "What?"

He let his mouth drift to her ear. "I missed you today."

"I missed you too. Thank you for last night. You've taken me out to eat two nights in a row."

"Been my pleasure." She clung to him, which was unusual since they were in public. "Something else goin' on?"

"Just having a moment."

"What kind of moment?" Carson tipped her chin up. "Tell me."

Those beautiful blue eyes locked to his. "I can't believe I've only known you four weeks."

"Is that good or bad?"

"Honestly? Both. Good because I like being with you. If we're not together then I can't wait until we are together again."

"What's the bad part?"

"I don't have experience with this so I don't know if it's...normal."

"Normal," he repeated. "Not sure I follow."

Fire flashed in her eyes. "Is it normal to be in love so soon? Or am I just reading too much into it because you're my first—"

"Boyfriend?" he supplied.

"No. My first lover," she said crossly.

Another growling sound escaped. "First lover? Got news for you sugar, I'm gonna be your *only* goddamned lover. Ever. No man besides me will ever touch you. Understand?"

"What are you saying?"

"I'm sayin'..." Shit. What was he saying? Everything he'd wanted to tell her just vanished. He closed his eyes.

Think. Focus. Throw it out there even if this isn't the way you wanted to do it.

"Carson?"

His heart thumped. He cleared his throat, trying to dissolve the lump of fear blocking his vocal chords. The instant he stared into her eyes, he calmed. "Marry me, Carolyn West."

Her mouth fell open.

"I'm not kiddin' around this time, not that I was when I asked you the first night we met, because I think that's what led us here. To the real deal." He brushed soft kisses across her mouth, taking advantage of her shock, thoroughly tasting the velvety pillow of her lips. "Marry me."

She continued to gape at him.

Jesus. Did he have to hard sell her? "I ain't rich, but we're building up our cattle business a little more every year." He nuzzled her cheek. "I'll make a good husband to you, I promise."

"Why?"

"Why what?"

"Why do you want to marry me?"

Carson reclaimed her eyes with his. "Because I can't imagine my life without you in it."

Tears welled and then they spilled free. "For real?"

"For real. Forever." He swiped the wetness away with his thumbs. "Say yes. Say you'll be my wife. Say you'll be mine."

She whispered, "I'm already yours. So yes. I'll marry you."

"Thank God." He managed to keep his kiss tender, despite the urge to give in to the passion that erupted between them. After several soft, sweet kisses, he murmured, "Give me your left hand," against her lips.

Carolyn placed her left hand on the side of his face. The simple, loving touch stirred everything inside him.

Carson kissed the inside of her wrist and stepped back. He shoved his hand in the front pocket of his jeans and pulled out the ring. Taking her hand, he slid the platinum circle on her third finger. "If you don't like it, we can take it back and get you something else."

"I can't even see it with your hat blocking my hand."

"Sorry."

She raised her hand to eye level. She gasped, her right hand flew to her mouth and the waterworks started again.

How the hell could she even see the damn thing through her tears?

"Sugar? You okay?"

She shook her head yes, then no... And then she started hiccupping which made her cry harder.

He had no experience with this stuff. What was he supposed to do?

Figure it out because you'll be dealing with this woman's emotions—

good and bad—for the rest of your life.

"C'mere." Carson wrapped her in his arms and held her until she calmed down.

She stepped back and wiped her face. "I'm probably a mess. I need a tissue. Just a moment." She rummaged in her purse. She gave him her back as she blew her nose. Then she brushed some sort of powder over her face before she faced him again.

"Better?"

"In shock. Huge surprise, McKay." She smiled shyly and walked back into his arms.

Carson kissed her forehead. "I'd apologize for popping the question in the parking lot of the damn Ice Cream Palace, but it's probably a good indication."

"Of what?"

"Of the fact I ain't a romantic kinda guy. I'll try to be that guy. But I ain't good at that hearts and flowers shit."

Carolyn laughed. "I guess time will tell, won't it? I'll forgive you for not being a romantic if you'll overlook that I don't have the faintest idea what it means to be a rancher's wife."

His mouth brushed her temple. "You'll spend a lot of time nekkid in our bed." His lips traveled, skimming the top of her ear. "I can't wait to wake up with you every morning and hold you in my arms every night."

"That was pretty romantic." She studied her left hand pressed against his chest. "The ring is beautiful." She bit her lip and that stemmed another round of tears. "Is it something that's been in your family?"

"Why would you think that?"

Her gaze hooked his. "It'd make sense that you could propose on the spur of the moment if you already had the ring."

"Like I had it on hand and I was just waitin' on the right woman to give it to?"

She nodded.

"Wrong. I bought this ring specifically *for* you. Today."

"You did?"

"Uh-huh."

"That's seriously romantic."

Carson placed his large hand over her smaller one and traced the stone with his thumb. "So you like it?"

"I love it." She pecked him on the mouth. "I—" a kiss, "—love—" another kiss, "—you."

"I love you too."

She teared up again. "That's the first time you've said that to me."

His eyebrows rose. "It is? Huh. I thought I'd said it before."

"It doesn't count when we're naked."

"Sure it does." He chuckled and kissed her nose. "What're we doin' tonight?"

"I'm still in shock. Can we go someplace quiet where we can make plans?"

"You don't wanna tell your family?"

She shook her head. "It can wait until tomorrow. I don't want anyone to ruin tonight because it's ours."

Happy as he was that she didn't have rose-colored glasses on when it came to their family situation, it put him on edge knowing big obstacles were in front of them. "I'd offer my place—which will be our place soon enough—but once we're alone I'm gonna be all over you."

"How well I know that." She smirked. "How happy I am about that. Let's have a sweet treat here while we talk. And if we get through all that..." her lips teased his ear, "...we'll see about you getting a taste of my sweet pu...dding."

Damn, he loved this woman.

Later on that night, Carson couldn't very well say that men didn't give a shit about wedding planning stuff—even when it was true.

"We'll need to meet with the priest right away and I'll get started making my dress." She fiddled with her ring. "How long of an engagement do you want? I was thinking the first part of October for the wedding."

"October? Not happening, Carolyn. That's too damn long."

"When do you see us getting married?" she countered.

"Within a month. But if I had my way? We'd apply for a marriage license tomorrow and make it official as soon as the law allows."

That stubborn chin came up. "We *are* getting married in the Catholic church. End of discussion."

"Fine. There shouldn't be a problem since I don't have to convert. We'll be husband and wife no more than one month from now. That's my end of discussion point."

"But...why are you so adamant on the short time frame?"

Carson took her hand. "I want to start spendin' my life with you now. Not months down the road. Why don't you just admit the only reason you don't want this wedding to happen so soon is because you're afraid people will gossip that we *had* to get married."

Her eyes flashed guilt.

"I don't give a damn what anyone thinks, Caro. The sooner you learn that about me the better."

"That's not the only reason you want it done in a month. You afraid I'll change my mind?"

He smiled at her. "No, I ain't afraid you'll change your mind. It's just...this is the slow time of year for us. That means I can spend a lot of time with you."

"During that free time you'll teach me things so I'm not a

151

greenhorn ranch wife?"

"Yep." Carson ran the pad of his thumb over her knuckles. "But why're you a greenhorn? My dad said the Wests owned Ag land?"

"We did. I mean we do. The land was my grandfather's and he passed it on, but Dad had no interest in ranching. He started working in the coal mine when he was sixteen. He and my mom lived in the ranch house until Stuart was born and they needed something bigger. That's when they bought the place we live in now."

"So they just abandoned the house and the land?"

"Dad leased it out until Harland was old enough to take over. I wasn't raised around cows. Or horses. They sorta scare me."

Carson grinned. "I'll have you ropin' and ridin' in no time, Mrs. McKay."

"That sounds weird."

"No, sugar, it sounds perfect."

Chapter Fifteen
Carolyn

She was up at five a.m. when her father came into the kitchen to grab his lunch pail. He grumped around, half asleep, so maybe it wasn't the best time to talk to him, but he needed to hear the news from her.

"Dad. I need to talk to you about something."

He froze, his hunched shoulders straightened when he turned around. His brown eyes were sharp, the cloud of sleep gone. "If this is about Kimi comin' back early, like I told you ten times before, it ain't happening."

"It's not about Kimi. It's about me. And Carson." She thrust out her hand and couldn't help but smile at how the diamond shone even in dim light. "We're getting married."

Then her father was right in her face. "Did that son of a bitch knock you up?"

"What? No!"

"Don't you lie to me. I see how he looks at you. A man only looks at a woman that way after he's sampled what's under her skirt."

"I'm not pregnant," she said softly, hoping it'd dampen his rage. "We're getting married because we're in love."

"In love?" he sneered. "Bullshit. The McKays don't know nothin' about love. They know lust. Carson's asshole father knew how to talk his way into the ladies' drawers."

Including Mom's? jumped into her head unbidden.

"He was a tom cat, laying down with any woman who was breathing. The reason he married a woman from out of state is because no decent, moral woman in Wyoming would have him. That's the legacy he's passed onto his sons. Not love."

"You don't know anything about him. You can't judge him on the actions of his father."

"The hell I can't! I can judge him on the actions of his father and his lyin', cheatin' grandfather too!"

"So you're willing to let your sons be judged on your actions? And on your ancestor's reputations?"

"The Wests' reputation was silenced with blood...by the McKays.

Why do you think that McKay didn't ask me for my daughter's hand in marriage? Because he's a dishonorable, disreputable man," he spat, answering his own question. "I'll never bless this marriage. Never."

She'd expected this, yet it still sliced her to the bone. "It doesn't matter. The only blessing I care about is the one we'll get from the priest."

"I never should've let you come back here this summer. I should've made you stay with your aunt. She never let you run wild like your mother does."

"Run wild? I don't even know how to run wild since I basically grew up in a convent!"

"A lot of good that did you—or us, trying to teach you morals. What do you do? Fall in with the first man who pays you the littlest bit of attention."

Carolyn hated seeing this nasty side of her father. She always scurried away when he started spewing venom. Not this time. She stood her ground. "I'm marrying him no matter what you say or think."

"Then you're no longer welcome in this house."

"Dad. That's enough," Thomas said from the doorway.

Her father whirled around. "Don't you defend her."

"I'm not. I came in to get my lunch pail and to tell you we've gotta go or we'll be late."

Then her father iced her with one last look before he stormed off.

Thomas slipped his arms around her as she stood shock-still. "I'll always defend you, Carolyn, and your right to make your own decisions. Don't worry; I won't let him kick you out. I'll smooth this over and we'll talk more later." He grabbed his lunch and headed out.

She wandered to the window above the sink and watched the sunrise, a hundred thoughts racing through her mind.

Carolyn didn't head to her mother's room until she'd gotten off the phone with Father Dorian and set up the meeting for early evening. By the end of the night she'd know whether it'd just be her and Carson saying their vows to each other in front of an empty church or if they'd stand before a judge.

She rapped on the door. "Mom?"

"Come in."

Once inside the always cluttered room, she realized her mom had tidied up the space. "Good morning. How do you feel?"

"Decent, actually. I slept well for a change."

"Good. Would you like breakfast? There's banana bread and I could make you hot tea—"

"*Liebchen.* Don't fuss. Sit down." She pointed to Carolyn's hand. "And for heaven's sake, show me the ring."

Carolyn had a burst of pride, although nothing about the ring was ostentatious. The setting was simple and elegant and perfect.

"This is beautiful. He knows you, sweetheart. And that's how love is supposed to be..." She sniffled and reached for a tissue. "Sorry. Tell me how he proposed."

When Carolyn finished the story, they were both crying and laughing.

Her mother placed her misshapen hands on Carolyn's cheeks. "Is this what you want? A life with Carson McKay? Life as a rancher's wife?"

"Yes. I'm surprised I fell for him so fast." She smiled. "Carson wasn't. He said he knew when he saw me I was meant to be his."

"So the gruff rancher is a romantic at heart?"

"He swears he isn't. He even warned me he wasn't that type of man."

"Actions always speak louder than words." She let her hands fall away and used one to cover her mouth when she started to cough.

"Mom, are you okay?"

Her mother waved her off and it seemed to take a while before she stopped hacking. "Speaking of words. Your father didn't take the news too well."

"Did you hear him?"

"I think everyone in the county probably heard him. I..." She sighed. "His reaction is not unexpected. But this is my home too, so I promise I won't allow him to kick you out, no matter how much he blusters." She sighed again. "I wish I could tell you that he'll come around, but he won't."

"Are you happy for me? Even if Dad isn't?"

"I am." She offered Carolyn a weak smile. "My happiness is partially based on selfishness. By marrying Carson you'll live close by and I'll still get to see you. I missed you so much when you were at school."

Then why did you send me away?

"Have you discussed wedding dates?"

"We'll be married within a month, if Father Dorian okays it. If not, then Carson will insist on a judge. He wants to do this soon so we can spend time together since it's the slow season for him." And after this morning, she couldn't wait to get out of this house.

Her mother frowned. "That doesn't leave much time for planning."

"What's there to plan? I'm asking Kimi to stand up for me; I need a wedding gown and boxes to pack what little stuff I have."

"That's what I mean. You shouldn't be going into this marriage empty handed. Someone needs to throw you a bridal shower. What about that friend of yours, Beverly?"

"Mom! I can't ask her to do that!"

"Of course, you can't. I'll think of something. Now I have an engagement gift for you." She reached for a velvet box on her nightstand. "This was my mother's and one of the few things she brought over from the old country. She'd already passed on by the time I married your father but I'd like to think she would've given this to me to celebrate finding a husband." She opened the box. "Go ahead and take it out since my fingers don't work so well."

Carolyn pulled out a beautiful silver bracelet with colorful crystals centered between each link. "I've never seen you wear this."

"I wore it all the time until it became too difficult to work the clasp." After Carolyn had it on her wrist, her mother stroked the delicate bracelet with the tip of her gnarled finger. "Don't be afraid to wear it every day. It's stronger than it looks."

"Thank you. I'll cherish it forever." She brushed her lips over her mother's cheek, getting a whiff of Evening in Paris, her mother's favorite perfume. For a moment she spiraled back in time to when she was a small child and the pride she felt seeing her mother outshine all the other mothers. Whether attending church with her children or just going to the store or school events, Clara West prided herself on being smartly dressed and well-coiffed. She refused to be stereotyped, especially since she had seven children and her husband was a coal miner.

"Now let's call your sister and Aunt Hulda with your exciting news!"

When Carolyn and Carson met with Father Dorian, he mentioned the required couples' course before he'd agree to marry them, a class that lasted six weeks.

Carson refused to take the class. Then he laid on the cowboy charm, emphasizing how important it was to both of them to get married in the church, but he understood there had to be rules. But since they'd both been raised Catholic—Carolyn had even recently graduated from Catholic high school—and both sets of their parents had been married in the church, and they intended for their children to be raised Catholic, then didn't they more than fit the criteria? After a few pointed questions, the priest agreed to marry them on a Sunday afternoon in three short weeks.

Three weeks until she became Mrs. Carson McKay.

It seemed surreal—it was as scary as it was exhilarating.

"Engaged a few days and we're already actin' like an old married couple, shopping for groceries on a Friday night."

"I'll remind you I shopped for groceries on Friday nights when I was single too."

Carson kissed her hand. "You ain't single anymore."

Like Carolyn's mother had warned her, her father had not had a change of heart about her marrying Carson. But he still expected her to pull her weight in the West household for as long as she lived there. For the first time he hadn't given the weekly grocery money to her directly; he'd left it in a sealed envelope on the counter.

"I can't wait to have your home cookin' every day and night."

"I promise I won't be making meals like that for you." She pointed to Carson's section of the shopping cart—TV dinners, potpies and canned goods. "You're not just marrying me because I can cook, right?"

His lips brushed her ear. "Partially. But the fact you're a hellcat in the sack weighed heavily in your favor too."

She elbowed him in the gut. "Behave."

"Never."

"Carson McKay. In a grocery store. On a Friday night. Seems God saw fit to bless me for saying the rosary today."

They both looked at the gray-haired woman who'd blocked the aisle with her cart.

She stepped forward. "You must be Carolyn. The rumor mill is churning about you, dear. No one knows anything about the mysterious woman who is marrying Carson McKay."

Carson put his arm around Carolyn's shoulder. "This is the lovely woman I've asked to be my wife. Carolyn West, meet Mrs. Agnes Varlo."

"So respectful, Carson. Your mother would be proud." Mrs. Varlo offered Carolyn her hand. "Please call me Agnes. And what Carson didn't tell you was his mother Helen was my dearest friend for over twenty years."

"I'm sure you miss her."

"I do, every day, even when she's been with the Lord for six years." Agnes kept hold of Carolyn's hand. "Tell me about the wedding."

Here was the first official test with people outside their families since they'd become engaged. "Mr. Impatient insisted we get married as soon as possible before his busy season starts. Not that I know what that means," she said with a laugh.

"So you're not from a ranching family?"

"No, ma'am. But I'm sure I'll catch on fast to being a rancher's wife. Anyway, to answer your question, Carson and I are getting married in Gillette at Our Lady of Perpetual Help in three weeks."

"Wonderful! I know Helen would be so happy Carson found a Catholic girl. Father Dorian is officiating?"

"Yes, ma'am. It will be a very small ceremony, just family and a few friends, but we'd be honored if you could attend since you are a family friend."

Agnes teared up. "That would mean a lot to me. Thank you. Now is someone hosting a bridal shower for you?"

Carolyn shook her head. "My mother has health issues and I've spent the last six years attending school at St. Mary's in Billings, so my friends don't live around here."

"Why, that's not right. Every bride-to-be deserves a bridal shower." She paused. "I tell you what. The ladies circle from St. Ignatius excels at these last minute events—I'll admit we're more prepared for funerals than weddings—but since I'm the president of circle, we'll hold a shower for you at the church."

"Really? I mean, that is so kind of you to offer, but at this late date I wouldn't want you to go to any trouble."

"No trouble at all. Especially for a new incoming member to the St. Ignatius congregation." Agnes paused and cocked her head. "I assume you will transfer to our church in Sundance and not drive clear to Gillette every Sunday?"

Carson ended his silence. "We're still discussing it, bein's Carolyn's family has long-held ties to that church."

Carolyn wanted to elbow him. They weren't even married yet and the man was already looking for ways to get out of going to church.

"I understand." But it was clear Agnes didn't understand.

"I am thrilled you're considering hosting a bridal shower for me. It would be wonderful to have my own household items to help make Carson's house our home."

"Consider it done. If you'll give me your phone number after I meet with the ladies circle I can call you with a firm date. I'll suggest Saturday afternoon, a week from tomorrow."

"That would be perfect." Carolyn recited her number, watching Agnes write it on the back of her green stamps booklet.

Agnes tucked the booklet in her purse. "I'll be in touch. It was so good to meet you, Carolyn."

"Good to meet you too."

"Carson," Agnes said.

"Nice seein' you again, Mrs. Varlo."

She waited until Agnes was out of earshot, before she said, "Wow. That was generous of her." She smiled. "A bridal shower is so exciting! My mother still has things from hers."

"I'm glad you're excited, Caro, but I told you I'd buy you anything you wanted."

"I know, but a bridal shower is a rite of passage for women. And it'll be good for me to meet women in the community since I don't know anyone."

"Agnes is thoughtful, but don't think for a second she isn't already assigning you to several church committees," Carson warned.

"I'm grateful, but don't think for a second I'd pass up a chance to tout my seamstress skills for a price."

Carson laughed. "But you don't have to take in sewing jobs after we're married. It's my job to provide for you."

"I know. But I'll go crazy without some sort of work to keep me occupied." She frowned. She was not looking forward to Missy's final fitting tomorrow. Might not be so bad if it was just her, but the nasty bridesmaids duo was sure to be there too. "I hope the alterations fit perfectly and I can be in and out of there in fifteen minutes."

"These are the women who questioned whether me'n you were really dating?"

"Yeah."

"Where's the fitting?"

"At the Methodist Church in Moorcroft."

Carson picked up her hand and kissed her engagement ring. "Guess when they see this that'll squash any argument that we ain't really a couple." He released her hand. "Let's get these groceries paid for. Is someone home who'll help you carry them in?"

"I'm sure one of my brothers is," she lied. Even if they were around they wouldn't help her, simply because they wouldn't think of it.

Part of her wondered if Carson would be that way after they'd been married a while.

But she watched him unload the groceries from the cart into the trunk and then hold the door open for an elderly woman after he'd returned the cart; she knew his gentlemanly side was ingrained.

At least in public.

Carolyn arrived early at the church the next day.

The alterations for Missy's dress were perfect. They waited for what seemed like forever before Tammy and Edie made an appearance.

Missy lit into them. "You're both hung over? That is just great. If you puke on the bridesmaid's dress during the fitting you will not be in my wedding, understand?"

"You're crabby today. You on the rag or something?" Edie said with a yawn.

Which sent Missy into another tirade, and Tammy joined in to defend Edie.

Carolyn wanted to crawl under a rock. These women considered themselves friends?

"Enough. Get your dresses on," Missy commanded.

Both Edie and Tammy dressed in the small church nursery. First Carolyn checked the hems. Good to go. Then she checked the lace panel on the bodice.

Edie snatched her hand. "What's this?"

Tammy leaned over to look. "Is that an engagement ring?"

"Yes. Carson and I are getting married."

"When?"

"In three weeks." Carolyn yanked her hand back.

"Are you pregnant?" Edie demanded.

"Are you always this rude?" Carolyn said. "That is none of your business."

"Ooh. Testy." Tammy and Edie exchanged a knowing look.

"Since the dresses fit, I'll be going."

Carolyn exited the room and stopped when she saw Carson leaning against the wall. Looking like a million bucks in his dark jeans, a blue plaid shirt that brought out his eyes, and his dress cowboy hat. "Carson? What are you doing here?"

He ambled forward, his eyes never leaving her face. When he reached her he slanted his mouth over hers for a lingering kiss. "I knew my beautiful bride-to-be had an appointment in town so I thought I'd swing by and take you to lunch." He pushed a section of hair behind her ear and caressed her jaw—a gesture more intimate than his kiss. "I was just missin' you, Caro."

No, the sweet man just wanted to show these doubters that he was entirely hers.

"That's a great idea. Let's go." She didn't turn around and see if Edie and Tammy were watching; frankly, for the first time she didn't care.

Seemed Carson's attitude was rubbing off on her.

Chapter Sixteen
Carson

Carson's job today was chasing after stray calves that broke away from the herd as they moved cattle to a different grazing area. Casper led the herd, Charlie handled keeping the first third in line, Cal the second third and Carson the back third. They'd had a good go of it so far, but he didn't like the way the clouds were forming. A spooked herd was a scattered herd, and since they still had one road to cross, that could be problematic.

Jed usually waited on the road for them with the horse trailer. He'd open the gate to the next pasture and warn the few souls who used that road there'd be a delay.

But today the man was being a jackass and left them to deal with it on their own.

Fine. They'd show him they didn't need his help.

They moved down the bottom slope that led to the rise where the road bisected their land. From here Carson could see the whole herd.

Casper kicked his horse to a gallop so he could get the gates open. They'd decided he'd position himself on one side of the road once the first few head of cattle passed through the gate and the herd mentality would keep the flow going. Then Charlie would flank the opposite side while Cal drove the main part of the herd forward.

It went like clockwork—until that first boom of thunder. Then the last twenty cow and calf pairs bolted. Half went to the left. Half went to the right. Running right down the middle of the damn road in opposite directions.

Carson whistled at Cal and pointed left, while he reined his horse right, kicking it into a gallop. He didn't get the runaways stopped for a quarter of a mile. After he'd gotten them turned around, he half-hoped for another boom of thunder to get them back to the gate quickly.

No thunder, but it started to rain. Which didn't bother the cattle; in fact, it got rid of the flies for a while. They didn't have much farther to go. Once they settled the herd near the small stock dam they could ride back to Cal's place. After all this shit had started with his dad, Carson had moved his horse and his tack to his brother's barn.

The rain didn't let up. It became a torrential downpour. Good for the land so he wasn't complaining. But the temp had hovered near eighty-five and the rain cooled him down right quick. Since the ground was slippery, they'd slowed the horses.

At least the wind wasn't blowing.

Yet.

Cal yelled at him, "Ain't this ridin' horseback in the rain shit romantic? You and Carolyn oughta try it."

"Piss off, Cal." Then he smiled for the first time in an hour, remembering that hot, wet night he and Caro had spent in the rain.

It took two hours to get back to Cal's. Carson tried to put it out of his mind that it would've taken them ten minutes to load the horses and fifteen minutes of driving time if their dad had helped out today.

After feeding the horses and hanging up the wet tack, they trooped into Cal's house.

The place was big and it needed a lot of work. They'd fixed what they could until the rest of their building supplies arrived.

Once inside the main living area, Carson noticed Cal had placed buckets everywhere. "At least we'll know where to patch the roof when it dries out."

"I'm thinkin' the whole thing needs replaced."

"It's pretty flat, probably won't take that long. Order the shingles next time you're in town and I'll help you roof it before summer's end."

"Won't you have to ask the little wifey if you can hang out with your brother first?" Casper asked with a sneer.

"Nah. I'm hopin' maybe she'll help."

Cal and Charlie laughed.

"Maybe once she learns the the truth about the ranch she won't stick around," Casper said slyly.

"What truth?"

"Oh, haven't you heard? With the most recent land purchase and you getting married that Dad is changing the legal parameters for inheriting the ranch."

Carson stared hard at Casper. "What the hell are you talkin' about?"

"Dad had an appointment on Friday with the trust attorney at the bank."

"What?" Carson and Cal said simultaneously. Then Carson demanded, "Why the fuck would he do that and not tell us?"

"Because you're legally tyin' yourself to a member of the West family. He knows blustering about cuttin' you off and kickin' you off the ranch are meaningless threats. He can't run the ranch without you. And I sure as hell don't wanna pick up the slack."

"No surprise there," Cal said.

Casper glared at him. "Poor Cal. Twin to Carson but even that don't get you close to the pedestal the first born son has been placed on." Casper smirked at Carson and took a long swallow of beer. "But you tarnished that halo and even put a fuckin' dent in it by finding the one woman guaranteed to send Dad into a red rage."

"How long you been sittin' on this information, Casper?"

"I overheard part of the conversation...a couple days after you informed Dad you were marryin' Carolyn West. I don't know what all he decided to change but it's a done deal."

Carson looked at Charlie. "Did you know about this?"

Charlie put his hands up. "First I've heard of it, I swear."

Goddammit. It was so fucking typical of Jed McKay to do what he wanted and his sons just had to live with the consequences.

But what if you can't live with them?

Then he'd leave. It'd serve his father right if his oldest son found a job working as a ranch hand for someone else. Yeah. He'd stick around just to make Jed McKay look like an idiot.

Casper stood. "I'm goin' home. See you tomorrow. Come on, Charlie."

Charlie didn't say anything. He just put his soggy hat back on and followed Casper out.

After they left, Cal said, "Wanna get drunk?"

"No. I wanna hit someone."

"I ain't helpin' you with that. But if you crash here tonight, we'll confront Dad first thing in the mornin' about this inheritance change bullshit." Cal handed him another beer. "You think Casper might be full of it?"

Carson shook his head. "He was goddamn gloating, so no. He knew about it ahead of time and purposely told us after the fact so we couldn't do anything to prevent it. He's such an asshole."

Several moments passed where they didn't speak.

Cal said, "Come on. Get outta them wet clothes and stop makin' that huffing noise. It's annoying as hell. There's nothin' we can do about it tonight anyway."

"So you might as well crack open the whiskey."

Early the following morning Carson and Cal found Jed in the dining room drinking coffee.

"So what's this bullshit about you talkin' to the estate lawyer at the bank and makin' changes without tellin' us?" Carson demanded.

"Mornin' to you too."

"Cut the shit. I ain't in the mood."

Jed motioned to Cal. "Get your brothers up. If we're talkin' about this now, I'm only sayin' it once."

When they were all seated in the dining room, Jed said, "Seems you've all heard I met with the attorney. I had language added to the original settlement deed and current land holdings."

"Which is what?"

"Everything is still solely in my name, so before you get pissy, I didn't have to ask, inform or consult any of you on my decision. Now the only person or persons who can lay claim to part of the McKay Ranch are McKay descendants, and even then, if any of you were to have daughters their claim isn't recognized.

"In simplest terms, whoever you marry—" Jed looked right at Carson, "—will never inherit an inch of McKay land. You have sons? They're part of the bloodline, they're eligible to inherit. Any daughters you might birth aren't eligible because their children won't be McKays."

"That is the dumbest thing I ever heard," Cal said.

"Don't care if you think it's dumb. It's how it is from here on out."

"Why'd you do this?" Carson asked.

His father slammed his hands on the table. "To protect the ranch! Dammit, boy, pull your head out. If this marriage don't work out between you and that West girl, she could sue you for her fair share of the ranch in the divorce settlement. Over my dead body that's ever happening. This change don't keep any of your kids from inheriting, but it will keep your wives from ever havin' any control."

"I think it's a good idea," Casper said. "Ranching is men's business anyway."

Cal and Carson exchanged a look and Charlie rolled his eyes.

"Like I said, the ranch is still in my name so—"

"Put up or shut up?" Carson snapped. "Fine. I'll shut up. For now. But here's some advice, old man. You ain't gonna live forever. So while you're tryin' to protect the ranch from scheming women, maybe you oughta be thinkin' about how you're gonna parcel it out before you're dead and buried and we have to sell every inch of land to pay the inheritance taxes since you didn't specify an heir."

At that point Carson picked up his hat and walked out.

Chapter Seventeen
Carolyn

When Carolyn heard a car door slam, she ran out the front door and picked up her little sister in a big hug. "I'm so glad you're here!"

Kimi was a tiny thing, six inches shorter than Carolyn, and a carbon copy of their mother. "I can't believe you're getting married. Let me see the ring."

Carolyn held out her hand.

"That is beautiful! You are so lucky." Kimi stood on tiptoe and peered over Carolyn's shoulder. "So where is the man who stole your heart?"

"He'll be here later." That's when Carolyn realized she hadn't even acknowledged her aunt. She skirted the front end of the car and gave the stout woman a big hug. "Aunt Hulda. Thanks for coming."

"Happy to be here. Where is everyone?"

"Dad and my brothers are working. Mom is inside. I thought you could stay in her room, if that's okay?"

"It'll be fine. After we have some lunch, let's talk wedding plans."

Her mother had dressed and joined them at the table. She and Hulda chatted easily, not like they hadn't seen each other in three years since her aunt had last come to Wyoming.

"Kimi. How has your summer been so far?" their mother asked.

"Good. I don't have the eye for detail that Carolyn does, so I'm mostly tending the gardens." She smirked. "I still haven't convinced Aunt Hulda to raise chickens."

Hulda harrumphed. "And who would gather eggs, take them to town and feed those loud buggers when you're back in school?"

"I told you I'd be happy to drop out of school," Kimi said sweetly. "It's not like I'm a top student anyway."

"Your aunt is generous enough to pay for your schooling, so you will stick it out, Kimberly," their mother said sharply.

Kimi raised her chin. "I go by Kimi now, Mom. And I'm fully aware who is paying my tuition and why." She pushed away from the table and started clearing plates.

When their mother opened her mouth, Aunt Hulda shook her head. It occurred to Carolyn that in many respects their aunt was more their mother than Clara West. Did their mother resent her for that? Or after raising five boys was she secretly happy to hand off the job of raising her two daughters to her widowed, childless sister?

"We'll get the dishes done and leave the two of you to visit." Carolyn picked up the leftovers—there wouldn't have been any had her father and brothers joined them—and headed into the kitchen.

Kimi had already started running the water and squirted in the soap.

"I'll dry," Carolyn said.

"But you always wash."

"Yes, I always wash *and* dry when I'm home in the summer so it'll be nice not to have to do it all myself." She wrapped her arms around her sister and squeezed. "I'm so happy you're here. Even if it's only for a couple of days. And just think, next time you come back? You can stay with me."

Kimi turned her head and grinned. "The West girls getting wild! So when do I get to meet my future brother-in-law? Geez. That sounds so weird."

"I still can't believe he'll be my husband."

"Bet you're looking forward to the wedding night."

Carolyn's cheeks heated and she focused on drying the first plate.

"Holy shit, Caro, you already did it with him!"

"Ssh!" She threw a look over her shoulder. "Not so loud!"

"Oh, hell. It's not like they can hear us."

"Language!"

Kimi rolled her eyes. "So, I wanna know all about it. What it's like. If it's as—" she pressed the back of her wrist to her forehead and swooned back dramatically, "—rapturous as all the girls claim it is."

The image of Carson staring so intently into her eyes as his body moved inside hers sent a blast of heat through her.

Then Kimi got right in her face, blonde curls shaking. "Aha! It is! You're thinking about it right now!"

"Can we talk about this later?"

"Fine, but you know I ain't gonna let this go."

The phone rang and Carolyn walked over and picked up the receiver. "Wests."

"How's my beautiful fiancée?"

She smiled and sagged against the wall. "I'm good. Surprised to hear from you. Kimi and my Aunt Hulda are here. We just finished lunch. What are you doing?"

"I've actually gotta pick up a part. I wondered if you could meet me for a half an hour or so. I wanna run something past you."

Carolyn glanced over at Kimi. "Is it okay if I bring my sister? She wants to meet you."

"Sure. In fact that'll work out because Cal is ridin' along with me."

"What time and where?"

"Say an hour at the Ice Cream Palace?"

"Can't wait."

"Me either. Later, sugar."

"Bye."

"You are grinning like a cat licking cream, Caro."

"He just makes me happy." She wandered back to the sink. "Let's get these done. I need to pretty myself up since I'm meeting my fiancé. Oh, and he's bringing his brother."

Kimi scrubbed a handful of silverware. "Go. I'll finish this."

Carolyn changed into a sleeveless shirt covered in daisies and white pedal pushers with a ruffled hem below the knee. As she fashioned a headband out of a silk scarf, she watched Kimi fluff up her shoulder-length ringlet curls. She hadn't changed out of the Bermuda shorts and white eyelet blouse she'd traveled in.

"How is it that you look older than I do?" Carolyn complained.

"Right. I look like a chubby-cheeked cherub." Kimi slicked pink lipstick on her lips. "The eyeliner makes me look older. And I don't know why you're complaining. You always look sophisticated." She gestured to Carolyn's outfit. "Did you make that?"

"Yes. You like it?"

"I love it. I'm jealous that you're so talented with a needle and thread. I think Aunt Hulda has given up that I'll ever be a seamstress of your caliber."

"Oh pooh. You're just impatient."

Kimi looped her arm through Carolyn's. "I'm impatient to get the hell out of here. Let's go."

Aunt Hulda appeared to be dozing in the rocking chair. No sign of their mother. She must've gone back to her room. As they passed through the living room, Aunt Hulda said, "Carolyn, when you get back we need to work on your wedding dress since the wedding is in two days."

"I know. We won't be gone long."

Once they were in the car, Kimi pulled out a pack of cigarettes. "Thank God. I'm dying for a smoke."

"Kimi!"

"What? Everyone smokes." She lit up and blew a stream of smoke out the window.

"But you're sixteen."

"So?"

"Swearing, smoking... Are you drinking too?"

"Sometimes." She took another drag. "But I'm not having sex...unlike *some* people."

"I'm almost nineteen." Her grip tightened on the steering wheel. "Besides, we *are* engaged."

"Uh-huh. Bet you weren't engaged when you did it with him the first time."

Carolyn did not want to have this conversation with her little sister.

"How was it? And if you don't talk to me about this I'll assume it was bad."

"Not even close to bad. It was...intimate."

"There's a brilliant statement."

"I'm serious, Kimi. Being skin to skin, with all the kissing and touching and the urgency. It *is* rapturous."

"Did it hurt?"

She grinned. "Not bad enough to make me not want to do it again."

Kimi laughed. "Fine. So it really is one of those things I have to experience for myself?"

"Yes." She changed the subject. "What's the gossip from St. Mary's?"

"Not much. Aunt Hulda keeps me busy so I don't get to see anyone. But the rumor is you're pregnant and that's why you're havin' the hurry-up wedding."

She shrugged. "Pretty much the consensus around here too."

"That doesn't bother you?"

"It bothered me worse when people assumed I'd let Carson use and discard me." She smirked. "But I'm the only woman wearing his ring."

"Doesn't it scare you to know you're going from taking care of one household to doing the exact same thing with him?"

Carolyn looked at Kimi sharply. "That doesn't sound like something you'd say. Is that what Aunt Hulda said?"

Kimi inhaled another drag and flicked the cigarette butt out the window. "She talked to me about it. And I know she wants to talk to you too. So I'm giving you a warning that it might not be the *I'm so happy for you* conversation you expected."

"She's far from the first one to express her unhappiness or disappointment in the marriage."

"Well, I, for one, am happy for you."

She smiled. "Thanks."

They pulled into the Ice Cream Palace but she didn't see Carson's pickup. Kimi hustled inside while Carolyn waited in the parking lot.

Carson roared into a parking spot—the man drove like an idiot. He hopped out and strode toward her. She couldn't see his eyes beneath the brim of his hat but she felt the heat of his gaze. He blocked her with his big body and without so much as a hello, lowered his mouth to hers and kissed her.

And kissed her.

When she tried to break free, he made that growling noise and said, "I'm not done," against her lips.

Finally he lifted his head and grinned. "Hiya, sugar. You looked so pretty standin' there I just needed me a little taste."

She placed her hand on his chest and found his heart beating like mad. Seeing her got him excited? Or kissing her got him excited? Either way, she loved that about him. "Hiya yourself, cowboy." She saw Cal leaning against the building by the door, waiting for them.

Carson pressed his hand into the small of her back, guiding her forward.

"Hey, Cal."

"Hey, Carolyn. You're lookin' good today." He leaned forward. "You sure you wanna marry this guy?" He jerked his thumb toward his twin. "He's kinda bossy. I'm much more laid back."

"I'm gonna lay you out flat if you keep tryin' to steal my woman, jackass."

"She's fair game until you say them vows, so I just want her to be sure."

She gazed at Carson, knowing her face shone with adoration. "I'm sure."

They walked into the Ice Cream Palace.

At that moment, Kimi turned around. She offered Carson a cursory look, then her focus was entirely on Cal. She gave him a little finger wave and took a long lick of her ice cream cone.

He sucked in a sharp breath. "Sweet mother of God, I think I'm in love."

"Oh for Christsake," Carson muttered.

"Language."

"*Please* tell me that's your sister."

Carolyn got in Cal's face. Or she tried to, but he couldn't tear his gaze away from Kimi. That forced her to snap her fingers in front of his eyes. "Hey, McKay, focus."

"What?"

"Yes, that's my sister, my younger sister. She's sixteen. Do you hear me? *Six. Teen.*"

Cal bestowed the slow, sexy grin that had women falling at his feet. "Well, darlin', she ain't always gonna be sixteen."

Kimi sauntered over, ignoring everyone but Cal. "Please tell me you're not my future brother-in-law?"

"I'm not. But darlin' girl, I'm damn near certain I'm your future husband."

She blinked coquettishly. "Then maybe you and me better get acquainted...?"

"Calvin McKay. You can call me Cal. Better yet, call me anytime you want."

"Jesus, Cal. Give it a rest."

Carolyn elbowed him in the ribs.

"Sorry." Carson offered his hand. "Kimi? Glad to finally meet you. Caro has told me a lot about you."

"Likewise." Kimi tore her attention away from Cal and narrowed her eyes at Carson. "Make my sister happy or else I'll gut you like a trout."

"Kimi!"

But she'd already refocused on Cal. "Let's leave the lovebirds alone and you can tell me why such a handsome man as yourself is still single."

"Because I was waitin' for you." Then, as they walked off, he whispered something in Kimi's ear that made her laugh.

"Well, that was unexpected," Carson said.

"No kidding. Kimi is the biggest flirt I know. I hope he doesn't put stock in anything she tells him."

"Cal's the same way. We'll let them hash it out. There's something I wanna run by you."

"Sounds serious."

"Not really. You want a cone or something?"

"Just a Coke."

"Sit. I'll get it."

Carolyn sat where she could keep an eye on her little sister and future brother-in-law.

Then Carson scooted into the booth seat across from her and blocked the view. "Here."

"Thanks. So what's going on?"

"We hafta scale back the honeymoon. I planned to take you to Denver for a few nights. Stayin' at the Brown Palace and headin' down to Colorado Springs to ride the Pike's Peak Railway. But Dad's bein' a controlling asshole. He knew we'd be on our honeymoon, and yet he set up a meeting next week with the Timmons family. They want to sell their homestead a little ways south of here. It's a great piece of land and if anyone can charm them into sellin' it's me, not my old man. So instead of goin' to Colorado, I thought we could spend a few days in Yellowstone. You ever been there?"

She shook her head.

"Me either." He picked up her hand and brushed his mouth across her knuckles. "So you're okay with it?"

"Of course, Carson. I don't care where we are as long as I'm with you."

"You're sure?"

"Positive."

"You won't mind spending our wedding night at the trailer? Because it's too far to drive to Cody after the wedding Sunday."

"That means you can take me to bed sooner, doesn't it?"

He bestowed that wicked grin and her stomach cartwheeled. "I suppose that is an upside."

"Are you staying at Cal's the night before the wedding?"

"Yeah. Why?"

170

"I need to drop off the rest of the stuff from my bridal shower the day of the wedding and it's bad luck for the bride and groom to see each other before the ceremony. I just want to make sure you won't be there."

"I won't be. In fact, I'll be so busy between now and then, not only with my regular day-to-day stuff, but tryin' to make Cal's place habitable since I've kicked him out of the trailer, that I probably won't see you until the wedding."

She breathed in deeply and let it out slowly.

"What, sugar?"

"It's just exciting to think that after today the next time I'll see you is when you're standing at the altar waiting for me, ready to become my husband."

Carson kissed her ring. "Damn, woman, do I love the sound of that." He slid out of the booth. "Wish I could stay but I gotta git." His eyes narrowed at Kimi and Cal, practically sitting on top of each other in the corner. "Go ask the manager if he's got a hose. I think we'll have to spray them two down to get 'em apart."

After they'd finished supper, Kimi shooed Carolyn away from the dishes, reminding her that she had a wedding dress fitting with Aunt Hulda.

Thoughtful of her sister, but Carolyn suspected Kimi only volunteered so she wouldn't have to spend time with their mother.

Her aunt sat in the wicker chair in the sun porch fanning herself, her sewing basket by her side. "Let's see what you've come up with."

"It's not really a custom wedding dress. Maxine had a base form in satin and I thought a lace overlay on top and tulle netting on the bottom would fill it out. It's simple, but I'm wondering if it's too simple?"

"Put it on."

Carolyn pulled the plastic bag down the dress hoping she hadn't created a mess of static. Keeping her back to her aunt, she stripped to her bra and undies. She took the dress off the hanger and stepped into it. The lace sleeves were the hardest part to get on.

How hard would it be for Carson to take off?

Not something she should think about with her aunt in the room.

She walked backward to the chair. "Can you zip me up?"

"Bend down just a little, child." *Zip.* "There. Now turn around."

When Carolyn turned, the bottom made a swishing noise against her calves. Because the base form was short, she'd opted for a tea-length dress rather than a full-length gown. She peeked at her aunt from beneath lowered lashes, half afraid she'd see disapproval. The sight of her aunt's tears shocked her.

"Carolyn. You look beautiful."

171

"You really think so, Aunt Hulda?"

"Yes." She dabbed at her eyes with an embroidered handkerchief. "I came prepared because I expected this."

"I'm just happy you're not crying because you think the dress is ugly."

She laughed. "No. But I will suggest a few adjustments. I like what you've done with the lace overlay and how it leaves the strapless satin base visible. But I think the neckline is too high. A modified boat-style with rolled lace will accentuate your graceful neck. Show it off while you can, sweetie, because you'll have an old lady wattle like mine before you know it. Where's the extra lace?"

Carolyn picked up the bag containing scraps. "So just add that on?"

"First clip the top section. That'll be easier than trying to cut the side seam and roll it since you've added sleeves." She had a long piece of lace that she'd gathered and draped just below Carolyn's collarbones. "Like that."

"Can you pin it please?"

She reached for the pincushion. "I also think you should add something to the waist. A sash perhaps, in a wide swath of gathered satin that mimics the drape of the lace. You've got such a trim waist. Be a pity not to draw a little extra attention to it too."

They'd worked in silence for many years, so the quiet never bothered her. But an expectant pause hung in the air this time. "Is there something on your mind, Aunt Hulda?"

"Child, are you sure you want to marry this man?"

"Why would you ask me that?"

"Because I'm an old meddling busybody." She pulled another pin from the pincushion. "Or because it happened very fast."

"I'm not pregnant," Carolyn said defensively.

"Of course you're not. This suddenness brought to mind that old saying 'Marry in haste, repent in leisure' so I want to hear that you're entering into this marriage for the right reasons."

"What are the right reasons?"

"There aren't any besides love."

"That's why I'm marrying him; I love him."

"It's also important you have things in common. I was very happy to hear he's a Catholic boy."

Carolyn smiled, wondering the last time someone called Carson a boy. "I understand that, but I also think we'll find common interests after we get married."

A moment of silence followed as her aunt pinned the lace.

"You know, I'll grant you that argument, Carolyn."

"Thank you. But I'm not trying to be argumentative, I promise."

"I realize that. And I hope you realize I'm not trying to discourage you from marrying him. I worry you don't have anyone to talk to because you're isolated here. Kimi is living with me; your friends from high school are in Montana. And your mother... Has she been helpful at all in offering you advice or even just lending a willing ear?"

"About Carson?"

"About him, about marriage."

"She has, actually. I told her about Carson the night after we met. She told me not to let past grievances with his family be a deciding factor in whether I pursued a relationship with him."

Her aunt harrumphed. "Smart advice from my sister for once. But I'll remind you since there's bad blood between your families, there will be a dividing line between those who will accept your marriage to this man and those who won't. Are you prepared to forego a relationship with your brothers and possibly your father to be with Carson?"

Carolyn didn't even hesitate. "Yes."

"That right there gives me the answer to all of my questions." She paused. "Turn."

Then Carolyn was facing her aunt. "Thomas said something to me a few weeks ago about you."

"And what was that?"

"That you offered to pay for mine and Kimi's private Catholic education because you felt guilty about taking something away from the church and wanted to give something back by turning us into nuns."

"Your brother is wrong. I paid for your education because I didn't want you to be an indentured servant to your family."

"There's nothing wrong with pitching in and taking care of your family," Carolyn said defensively.

"When you're an adult. I saw the responsibilities your family piled on you at age twelve because your mother was too frail to continue to run her household." She squeezed Carolyn's hip. "Your father and your brothers would've let you slave away for them and not thought twice about it. Without you here they had to step up. With your mother's failing health...your father had two built-in housekeepers and caretakers. Even your mother didn't want that for you. She's the one who asked for you to be educated not only in the Catholic school, but for me to teach you a useful skill."

Carolyn twisted her ring around her finger.

"You've been a blessing to me, child. I always hoped with as talented as you are that you'd take over my business one day." She paused. "So if this marriage doesn't...work out, remember you can always come live with me."

"You sound like you don't expect it to last."

"Physical attributes change. I hear he's a handsome man. You sure you're not in love with the way he looks? He won't look like that in ten, twenty, thirty years."

"I'm not in love with his looks. Though it certainly helps that he's nice to look at."

"It's more than lust and passion between you two?" her aunt pressed.

Carolyn blushed. But she wouldn't back down. "What do you know of lust and passion?"

Her aunt laughed. "I got a priest to leave the church and marry me, so I know plenty—*plenty*—about lust and passion. We only had ten years as husband and wife before he passed on, and God didn't see fit to bless us with children, but they were ten good years. I want you to be certain you're choosing the man you see yourself spending the rest of your life with and not him just because he's close by."

She locked her gaze on her aunt's. "Do you know what my father said to me? I'm an idiot to fall for the first man who pays attention to me. Now you're saying the same thing."

"No." She reached for Carolyn's hands and repeated, "*No*. I'd be remiss in my duties as your godmother if I didn't question you from every angle about this major step in your life."

"Did I pass the test?"

She managed a small smile. "Yes. You've got a bumpy road ahead. Let's pray your love will hold you together. Now let's get this dress gussied up for your big day, hmm?"

The next two days were a blur.

The wedding had been small. Just her family and his. Not all of her family. Her father hadn't shown up. She'd hoped he'd have a last minute change of heart—but he'd stayed away. As had her brother Harland. It surprised her to see Harland's wife, Sonia, in the church, sitting next to Darren's wife, Tracy. Darren, Marshall and Stuart filled up the front pew with their mother, who sat next to Aunt Hulda.

Maxine, Beverly and Mike rounded out Carolyn's side of the church.

Carson's side was even sparser than hers. His dad hadn't come either, just his brothers. Agnes and her husband Ed were in attendance as well as an older couple who lived across the road from Carson's trailer. Plus a few of Carson's drinking buddies had shown up, acting as if they were attending a funeral, not a wedding.

Because Thomas walked her down the aisle, Father Dorian skipped the "who gives this woman to this man" spiel.

Her gaze briefly registered on her sister Kimi, serving as maid of honor, and then she looked across the altar to see Carson's twin Cal flanking him. Then her eyes locked onto Carson's and that's all she'd seen. Him. Standing there in his western cut suit, hat and boots, looking so proud and yet anxious as he waited for her, ready to pledge his forever love for her in front of God and everyone.

After they'd repeated their vows and were introduced as husband

and wife, they'd had a small cake and coffee reception in the church basement.

And now here they were. Home. Their home.

"Caro? You all right?"

She turned and smiled at her husband. She couldn't believe this black-haired, blue-eyed handsome devil was completely hers. "I'm perfect."

"Yes, you are." Carson picked up her hand and kissed it. "As beautiful as you look in that dress, I need to strip it off you."

"Now?"

"The second we get in the house."

Her belly fluttered as it always did when that wicked gleam entered his eyes.

"Stay right there." In a flash he was out of the truck and on her side, opening the door. He slid one arm under her knees and the other around her waist, lifting her out with ease.

Carolyn wrapped her arms around his neck and held on. Pressing a kiss to that strong jaw, she murmured, "Carrying me across the threshold is romantic."

"Mmm-hmm. And it's also tradition that brings good luck." He managed to hold the screen door open while opening the inner door. He kicked the door shut behind him and kissed the top of her head. "Welcome home, Mrs. McKay." Keeping her in his arms, he headed down the hallway to the back bedroom. He hesitated inside the doorjamb. "What's all this?"

"I added a few things."

Since Carson had stayed at Cal's last night, Carolyn and Kimi had shown up early to redecorate the bedroom. Carson had already cleaned out half the closet and given her half the drawer space in the built in cabinets.

Since this was now her home too, she wanted the bedroom to reflect them, not just him. She'd bought new sheets, cream-colored linen with pale lilac and mint green flowers, and added a chenille bedspread in the same soft green. Then she'd rummaged through the closet that held her mother's abandoned sewing projects and found four fabric panels that she added to the front side of an old, tattered quilt. She made matching pillowcases and a new curtain out of the leftover scraps. This morning she'd finally assembled all the new pieces: the layers of bedding, window coverings that actually covered the windows. The space did look very *Better Homes and Gardens*, if she did say so herself.

"Do you like it?"

He nuzzled her cheek. "This looks so damn nice I'm afraid I'll dirty it up."

"Isn't that what we're supposed to do in our own bed? Get as dirty as we want?"

Immediately after she said that she felt Carson's hardness pressing into her hip.

"I like this raunchy-talkin' side of you." His lips grazed her ear. "How about we test that out right now?" He lowered her feet to the floor.

Before she could twine her arms around his neck and kiss him, Carson faced her forward, toward the bed. "What—"

"As your husband it's my right to peel this wedding dress off you, and I'm takin' my time." He placed a soft kiss on the nape of her neck. "You looked beautiful today, Carolyn."

Her entire body trembled.

"So perfect with the fancy hairdo and the lacy gown. But what's beneath all this finery is what I want." He stilled behind her, his fingers gripping her hips, his breath flowing over her damp skin.

The zipper made no sound as he slid it down to the rise of her buttocks. Then the rough tips of his fingers followed her spine, over the clasp of her bra to the band of her crinoline slip. As he pressed soft kisses across the sweep of her neck, setting every nerving ending alive, he slowly dragged her dress down. Tugging the lace at her wrists to release her arms, then pausing at her hips to caress that sensitive section of flesh with the back of his knuckles.

"Everything about you is so soft," he said, kissing the ball of her shoulder.

Carolyn turned her head and brushed her mouth over his temple. "And everything about you is so hard."

"Some things harder than others."

She smiled.

"Lose the slip, sugar."

One quick tug and the slip covered her dress on the floor.

"Hang on to my arm. Step out, I've gotcha. One more. Now stay just like that." Carson picked up her wedding dress and moved it. "Let me see you."

Her nerves didn't make sense. She'd been naked with this man before.

But never as his wife.

A kiss landed on the small of her back.

When Carolyn turned, Carson was on his knees before her. A shiver started at the top of her spine and worked its way down, setting off goose bumps as his hot gaze catalogued every inch of her.

She'd worn a plain white satin bra, a small pair of white satin underwear, a lacy white garter belt with white satin garters and the sheerest white stockings she could find.

"Is this new?" He traced the garter belt with the tip of his finger, stopping at the tiny pink rose at the top of the garter.

"Yes."

"You look like an angel in this and I'm havin' a devil of a time not tearin' it off you with my teeth."

The sensations he aroused in her just with words, or the hungry way he looked at her were still new enough to take her by surprise. The quiver in her belly spread between her legs, making her sex hot and slick. Her nipples tightened and her breasts felt heavier. Even her lips felt fuller, moister. And her pulse pounded everywhere.

Carson's hands curled around her hips and he urged her backward. "Sit."

Her rear met the edge of the bed.

He stood and took off his hat. Shrugged out of his suit coat. Unbuttoned his vest and tossed it aside. Untied his western tie, letting the ends hang loose. Popped the snaps on the top two buttons of his white dress shirt and untucked it from his pants.

A tiny thrill of possession rolled through her when she had peeks of his shiny new wedding band as he unsnapped his cuffs.

Carson removed his boots with practiced ease. Not once during his strip down had his eyes left her body.

Carolyn reached to slip off her right shoe, but his hand stayed the movement. "Leave 'em on. And open your knees wide so I can see what belongs to me."

Heart racing, she adjusted her heels and parted her thighs.

"Let that sexy ass hang off the bed a little and brace your arms behind you."

"You always gonna be this bossy?"

"Yep." He lowered to his knees. "Just tellin' you what I want."

"What do you want, Carson?"

"My mouth on my wife's pussy."

Her cheeks heated. She fought the urge to hide her face. Would she ever not blush when hearing him say such blatantly sexual things?

You like it. That's why you're blushing.

Then he opened his mouth over the satin covering her mound, delicately tracing the edge of her panties and her inner thigh with his tongue.

She sucked in a breath.

He continued to lap at her, getting her panties wetter and wetter—inside and out. He'd nip with his teeth, blow a stream of hot air, and suck; all the while his hands were caressing the skin between her stocking and garter belt. Finally he tugged at her panties but they didn't budge.

After making a displeased growl, Carson rested on his haunches and dug in his front pocket. He lifted his pocketknife into view and she gasped.

"What are you—?"

"Can't tear these off with my teeth so I need to cut 'em off." One quick slice by her hip, a firm tug and her underwear were dangling from his hand.

"Carson!"

"I'll buy you a new pair," he said offhandedly and whipped them behind him.

His devastating mouth paused over her mound. She watched as he breathed her in. Then petal soft kisses landed on the petals of her sex. Whisper light and tinged with devotion.

Oh, it was such a glorious sight, Carson's dark head between her legs and the sounds his mouth made as he ate at her. Feasted on her really. His tongue licked and teased, swirling and flicking. His soft growling noises vibrated against her sensitive flesh, pushing her arousal to a new level.

Carson sensed the change and focused entirely on her hot button. It didn't take long before her pelvis tingled in warning. Pleasure slammed into her in waves so strong her entire body bowed. She gasped when he wouldn't relent; he just flicked that skilled tongue faster and faster until it set her off again. Once the second wave slowed to a dull throb, she thrust her hand into his silky hair, lightly tugging to get him to back off.

He lifted his head and their eyes met. He offered her a grin and feathered kisses over the inside of her knee. "You like me doin' that."

"You know I do."

"One of these days—soon—I'll stay right here for an hour to see how many times I can get you to come. But for right now..." He pushed to his knees. Then his hands glided up the tops of her thighs, over her hips and the garter belt, stopping on her rib cage.

Carolyn watched as his fingers traced the bottom band of her bra and disappeared behind her back. Those deft fingers of his unhooked the clasp.

"Ditch the bra."

She slid the straps down and peeled the cups away from her breasts. The instant the air hit the tips, they shriveled into hard points and she was tempted to cover them up again.

"Damn. You are perfect everywhere." He angled forward and enclosed her right nipple between his lips. Then his wet mouth and silky tongue worked her over. Soft sucking where it felt as if he tried to stuff her entire breast into his mouth. He released her flesh slowly. "You like that too."

"I like everything you do to me." She ran her hands through his hair. "I like everything you let me do to you."

Carson tilted his head back.

The fire blazing in his eyes made her mouth go dry.

"I want you from behind. I know it's our wedding night and you were probably expecting sweet love makin', but I need more than that." He rose up, looming over her, and snared her mouth in a soul-searing kiss.

She could scarcely catch her breath when he released her lips to

178

attack her throat.

His lips grazed her ear. "I want you to feel my possession, Carolyn. So when you look back, you'll remember this as the night you became mine in name and body."

She whispered, "Show me."

Carson stripped and she sighed at seeing his muscular body, his sex jutting out, fully aroused and ready for her. Then he rolled her onto her belly. His hands, his mouth, his body brought every nerve ending alive from the nape of her neck to her backs of her heels. She was a mass of need by the time he raised her hips into the air. He spread her pussy open with his fingers and impaled her in one stroke.

Then he caged her body beneath his and remained like that for several long moments. His hipbones pressed against her butt cheeks, his belly and the hard wall of his chest plastered to her back, covering her completely. His strong arms alongside hers. His mouth on her ear.

This position was overwhelming—the possession and the intensity when he began to slam in and out of her. Hard and deep. Their skin grew slick. The sounds in the room were the squeak of the bed, their harsh breathing and the slap of flesh against flesh.

Her body seemed electrified, tingles zipping across every inch of her skin. The swollen pulse of her pussy around his cock dangled her on that edge between pleasure and pain—a dizzying sensation she liked far more than she would've believed.

Carson shocked her by placing whisper soft kisses on the sweep of her shoulder even as he hammered into her. "I love you, Carolyn. You're mine forever." Then he fastened his mouth to the side of her throat and sucked, his hips bucking against hers wildly.

Between the love bite, his rapid-fire thrusts and the fiercely sexy way he came, her name a deep growl that vibrated to her core, she went sailing off into ecstasy again.

She collapsed on the bed and he followed her down, his hips still slowly pumping. She winced when he pulled out, but she knew he was right about one thing; she'd never forget how he proved he owned her—heart, soul and body—straight down to the marrow of her bones.

Then they were face to face. His eyes were filled with so much love she couldn't breathe.

"Thanks for marryin' me. I promise I'll spend the rest of my life makin' you happy. I'll always put your needs and your happiness above everything else."

"Even the cattle?" she teased.

"Even them."

And she believed him.

Chapter Eighteen

Present Day... Hospital, Day 2

After being in the hospital thirty-two hours, Carson had had enough of his own company.

He'd made a list of people who he'd welcome in the ICU waiting area: anyone with the last name McKay or Donohue. He'd half-expected/half-hoped that Keely would show up to rip into him.

But no one had stopped by. His phone hadn't rung even one time.

So he stared out the window. Or he sat in his chair in the corner, deluding himself that he could nap while he waited for his first hourly five-minute visit.

"Hey, Uncle Carson."

Carson turned and saw his youngest nephew, Dalton, leaning against the wall. He eyed him from his ball cap to his steel-toed boots. Dalton was a strapping guy with the rugged good looks the McKays were known for. He'd left Wyoming a few years back to get his shit together after taking the term "hell-raising McKay" to a new level. Word among the family was Dalton liked to fight as much as Carson used to.

"How's the newlywed?"

Dalton grinned. "Happier than a pig in shit. And if you tell my beautiful wife I phrased it that way, I'll deny it."

"So noted." Carson lowered into a chair. "Got time to keep your old uncle company?"

"Of course." Dalton sat across from him. "I realize it's the dumbest question in the world, but how are you holdin' up?"

"I'm here. Beyond that, I don't know. It's a blur."

"Uncle Charlie mentioned you get to see Aunt Carolyn?"

"Not for the first twenty-four hours. In a bit they'll let me see her for five minutes. Which is better than nothin', I suppose."

"Your kids still givin' you grief about not sharing your time with them?"

Carson glanced up. His eyes narrowed. "I figured they would've sent Tell or Ben here as the peacemaker to try and talk some sense into me, not you."

"Whoa. I'm not here on anyone's behalf except my own. While I'd be pissed off if it was my mom in there, my dad wouldn't have gone all guard dog for his wife or anyone else. So I don't understand where they're comin' from. And not to be a dick, but you've been layin' down the law for years. Why in the hell are they so surprised you're doin' it now with so much at stake?"

"That's the question I've been askin' myself the past thirty-two hours. Enough about that. How was the honeymoon?"

"Great. But I'll admit we were bit by the travel bug. Rory is already planning our next trip."

"Is she here?"

"She's at her mom's. Rielle said to tell you that you're in her and Gavin's thoughts. And once you and Carolyn are home, she'll bring by a meal or two for you."

"Tell her thanks. How long are you here for?"

Dalton adjusted his ball cap. "Just a couple of days. Now that the honeymoon is over, we both gotta get back to work. There's plenty of stuff to do on the house we bought." He groaned. "Don't know what the hell we were thinkin'—the place is a money pit."

"I'm sure repairs are no problem for a man with your skill level. Kyler brags on you all the time. Says you can do anything."

"Ky's a great kid, but what he saw me doin' as far as a remodel at the house in Sundance was a cakewalk compared to what this house needs." He shook his head. "After all me'n Rory went through to be together, I swear it's fightin' about house stuff that'll break us up."

He raised an eyebrow. "That bad?"

"The crazy-assed woman threw a hammer at me."

"What did it hit?"

"The wall I'd just sheet rocked. I suspect stress from her new job and planning a wedding made her hypersensitive—" he leveled Carson with a look, "—and according to my lovely wife, *hypersensitive* is a word I don't ever get to use in our household either, so between us, I'll use the term bat-shit crazy to describe her there for a few weeks. But I know livin' with me when I ain't workin' in the winter months ain't a picnic either. So I'm hoping that now we're married, we'll settle in and it'll be smooth sailing. They always say the first year is the honeymoon phase, don't they?"

Carson laughed. A little meanly.

"What? Christ, Uncle C, you scare me when you laugh like that."

"I'll just say that the first year Carolyn and I were married we hit rough waters. Right away. We made it through, but it wasn't pretty."

Dalton wore a skeptical look. "You and Aunt Carolyn? Really? But you two never fight."

"We never fight in public. Except for a few times during those early years, but if anyone ever mentioned specific incidents to our kids, we lied like hell about it."

Dalton laughed.

"Anyway, we've had our throwin' hammers and settin' the curtains on fire moments. Getting over those moments and not dwelling in the past is why we'll hit the fifty year mark in our marriage next month."

Carson refused to consider Carolyn wouldn't be around or sentient enough in a few weeks to celebrate that milestone.

"That's an accomplishment. Congrats."

The nurse walked over and put her hand on Carson's shoulder. "It's almost time, Mr. McKay."

"Good. Thanks."

He and Dalton stood at the same time.

"I'll get outta your hair." Dalton clapped him on the back. "Give Aunt Carolyn a squeeze from me. Rory was so excited to get that book of McKay family recipes as a wedding gift from you guys. Mighty thoughtful."

"All Carolyn's doin', I promise. I still can't cook a lick."

"Too bad she didn't teach you to man the stove in the first year of marriage like Rory's threatening to do with me." Dalton offered his hand. "Take care of yourself."

"I will. Safe travels back to Montana. Tell that pretty bride of yours hello."

After Dalton left, Carson slipped on his sterile gear. His mind drifted between the here and now and the past he'd been lost in the past day and a half.

Finally, he was here with her. Where he was supposed to be.

Inside her room, he rolled the chair next to her bed and ran his gloved fingers down her forearm, threading his fingers through hers. He rested his forehead on the metal side rail. Between the hissing of the respiratory machine and the other noises, he figured this angle was the best for her to hear him. He had to speak loud, since the faceguard he was required to wear covered his mouth, protecting her against airborne germs.

"Hey, sugar. I'm sittin' here beside you. I know you can hear me. I *need* you to hear me. Come back to me. I need you to know that I'm right here, I ain't goin' anywhere.

"It's quiet out where I am in the waitin' room. There's really not a whole lot for me to do except sit around and think. Dangerous, right? I don't care if everyone thinks I'm an old fool for talkin' to you like this, because I know you can hear me. I *know* it. I feel you—my Carolyn— stirring inside there. I can't explain it any better than that and I don't even bother tellin' the nurses or doctors, lest they believe me to be a crazy old coot and kick me outta here."

He cleared his throat. "I've been thinkin' about our courtship, but as fast as things went between us, we shoulda called it a rocket ship." He paused because he knew she was laughing inside at his lame joke. "Anyway, Dalton just dropped by and said to tell you that him'n Rory are holdin' you in their thoughts. I'll admit I was surprised to see him." He let his thumb sweep over her knuckles. "Guess they had a nice honeymoon. Wish I'da taken you someplace fancy. So I'll make you a deal; when you come outta this, I'll take you anywhere in the world you wanna go for our fiftieth, okay?"

He paused. Forcing himself to slow down.

"So Dalton was tellin' me his house remodel project is a big job. He kinda hinted around that him'n Rory have had some cross words about that. I'm afraid I laughed at him when he said now that they're officially married things will go right as rain between them. I couldn't help but remember that first year we were married... It's a miracle we stayed married. Yeah, I know it wasn't all bad. It made us stronger as a couple goin' forward, that's for damn sure. Makes me cringe to think you couldn't even buy your own birthday shot that year. Christ. I cannot believe you were only nineteen. You looked that young, but sugar, you never acted that young. Especially with what you had to deal with growing up."

The door to the room opened. "Mr. McKay? Time's up."

He acknowledged the nurse with a wave.

"Come back to me. I'm right here. Where I've always been, where I'll always be. I love you. Please. Come back to me."

Carolyn felt as if she was suspended in a box. Trapped inside the four walls, aimlessly floating up, sinking to the bottom or floundering in the middle. Every once in a while she'd get a sharp pain in her head from being too close to the top. She'd reach up and push herself down and the pain would fade.

A spike lanced her brain. Before she moved, she heard it.

Heard him.

And I don't care if everyone thinks I'm an old fool for talkin' to you like I do, because I know you can hear me. I know it. I feel you—my Carolyn—stirring inside there.

She pounded her fists on the ceiling, yelling, *I'm here! Right here! I can hear you! Don't go! Stay here with me!*

But the louder she yelled, the fainter his anguished voice became so she went motionless again.

I couldn't help but remember that first year we were married...

She listened to the cadence of his voice, needing it to tether her. But she found herself spinning headlong into that memory even as she tried to reach out to hold onto him for a little while longer...

They'd been married three glorious weeks.

Carolyn had never been happier. Carson left early in the morning, came home for lunch, and did mysterious "ranch stuff" until supper, or he'd knock off mid-afternoon. He never mentioned if the tension and anger between him and his father had been patched up. Occasionally he'd mention a dumb thing that one of his brothers had done, or more accurately what they'd left undone. He came down hard on Casper and seemed to forgive Charlie because of his age. Even though Carson and Cal were twins, Cal deferred to his older-by-just-a-few-minutes brother.

Although there were only six weeks until the end of summer, Carolyn convinced Carson to till up a section of dirt behind the trailer. He brought her a truck bed full of good black dirt to mix in with the red clay soil and fenced the area off.

She'd planted peas, beans, lettuce, radishes and other vegetables with shorter growing times. She drove to see her mother twice a week and checked on that garden because her brothers had no interest in maintaining it. In her mind that meant half the yield of whatever she grew and canned belonged to her.

Since it was her birthday, Carson insisted on celebrating by taking her out. After supper they headed to the dancehall to meet Cal, Charlie, Casper, the McKay's neighbor Jerry Jenkins and his girlfriend Brenda, Beverly and Mike, who were officially engaged, and her brother Thomas and two of his friends.

Booze flowed freely and as the birthday girl she nursed a beer just to keep people from nagging her about not drinking. Carolyn chatted with Beverly about her upcoming wedding and her excitement at being a military wife. When she looked up she noticed Carson had disappeared.

At the half an hour mark when Carson hadn't returned, when her brother Thomas asked her to dance she said, "Sure."

Out on the dance floor, she knew Thomas had something on his mind. "What's going on?"

"Remember that stuff we talked about the first night you met McKay?"

"About me moving to Denver with you or to Chicago with my friend Cathy?"

"Yeah. I told Dad tonight that I'm going to Denver and I gave the mine my two-week notice."

She felt as if he'd punched her in the gut. "You're really doing it."

"I really am."

"What did Dad say?"

"Some smart thing about not being surprised because I've always been too good to get my hands dirty for very long. Not much I could say to that, was there? Anyway, Mom started crying about another of her kids flying the nest. But she wasn't upset, just...resigned."

"I don't want you to go."

Thomas squeezed her hand. "Don't look at me like that. You're a married woman now, with a life of your own. Denver's not that far away. Carson wanted to take you there for your honeymoon and you know you can visit me anytime."

Her eyes searched his. "But that's the only way I'll ever see you, isn't it? Because you're not coming back here."

"Maybe I will. Chances are I won't."

"Because of Dad?"

He sighed. "Yeah. Mom's gotten way worse in the last year and Dad won't..."

"But he took her to the doctor last month."

"Did either of them tell you what the doctor said?"

Carolyn shook her head.

"The rheumatoid arthritis is in her lungs."

She frowned. "What does that mean?"

He said nothing.

"Thomas. You can't spring something like that on me and then clam up."

"Do you think I wanted to share this with you on your birthday?" he demanded. "No way. And here I am... Just forget it."

"Because it's bad, isn't it?" she whispered.

"Yes."

"How bad?"

"If she goes on oxygen they're giving her another two years to live at most. Without oxygen...a year."

That's it? "How'd you find out?"

"They were fighting about it. She's refused to go on oxygen because she doesn't want to move into a nursing home just to prolong her miserable life—her words, not mine."

She rested her head on her brother's shoulder, too shocked to even cry.

"I'm sorry. I was the only one home during their fight so I'm the only one who knows. And now you."

"Even knowing she'll probably be dead in a year, you're still going to Denver?"

Thomas locked his gaze to hers. "Yes. I can't change anything and I've watched this situation deteriorate long enough. You weren't here and I didn't say that to make you feel guilty. We have to make our own choices. You did. Now I am."

"What am I supposed to do with this information? Mom and Kimi had a fight after the wedding and she left in a huff, saying she wasn't ever coming back. That she'd finish out her schooling and work for Aunt Hulda until she turned eighteen." Carolyn wanted to scream, *who's going to take care of her?*

But in that moment, she knew. Caring for her mother as she was dying would fall to her.

"I've always been closer to you than anyone else in the family," Thomas reminded her. "I couldn't not tell you."

Did he think passing along the bad news somehow absolved him of the guilt of leaving?

The only one who feels guilty about anything in the West family is you.

When the song ended, she hoofed it back to the table and ignored Thomas's shouts calling her back. Still no sign of Carson, but he'd left his whiskey.

Good. She picked it up and drained it.

Beverly grinned. "That's the spirit, birthday girl! Mike, get her another shot. And one for me."

"Oh, no, that's okay."

"I insist," Beverly said. "Who knows where I'll be on my birthday so we're celebrating yours and mine tonight."

Carolyn knew better than to argue. And besides, wasn't that what this crowd did? She needed to learn to drink. Especially if she wanted to keep up with her husband.

Where was he, by the way?

She tapped Charlie on the arm. "Where's Carson?"

"Went out to talk to Earl about something. Why?"

"He's been gone a while."

"You know Carson. He gets to talkin' and drinkin' and loses track of time."

No, she didn't know that about the man she'd married.

"Come on sis-in-law, you wanna dance with me?"

"Sure. After the shot I'm doing with Beverly."

Charlie's eyes widened. "Didn't think you drank."

"I'm trying it on for size tonight."

He slid his full lowball glass over. "Since I'm too young to buy you a birthday shot, you can have this."

"Why aren't you drinking?"

He shrugged. "Not feelin' it."

"Thanks."

Mike returned with two shot glasses. Beverly leaned over to whisper, "To marriage; we fold our man's socks because we want to hold their cocks."

Carolyn grinned. She chased the whiskey burn with the last of her warm beer. Then she clapped Charlie on the shoulder. "Let's dance."

Charlie was a great dancer. She didn't think anything of it when the "Do-Si-Do" started, requiring dancers on the floor to change partners. She danced with half a dozen different men. During the last minute or so, she ended up with a guy who was drunk. He kept trying to pull her closer and she tried to rip herself away from him entirely with a terse, "Let. Go."

"Sorry." Instead of releasing her, he clamped his hand on her butt cheek and angled his head like he wanted to kiss her.

Her reactions were slower than usual, courtesy of the booze, so she turned her head away.

But the guy's lips didn't land.

Because Carson had inserted his arm between her and Mr. Grabby Hands.

186

"What the hell? Move it, buddy," he slurred.

Carolyn watched as Carson pushed the guy back. Then he punched him hard in the stomach and followed through with an uppercut that rocked the guy on his feet. When the guy didn't go down, Carson hit him two more times until he did.

Then he loomed over him. "You ever put your filthy fuckin' hands on my wife again I will break every fuckin' bone in your body. Every. Goddamned. Bone. And then I will make you bleed. Are we clear, you sorry son of a bitch?"

The people who'd been on the dance floor had gathered around. A woman dropped to her knees beside the man and glared at Carson. "What did my husband do to you?"

"He touched my wife."

"We were dancing, you moron—of course he touched her," she snapped.

But Carson hadn't looked at the guy's wife even once. He was too busy trying to set him on fire with his gaze of hatred. "Last I knew his hands on her ass and him tryin' to lock lips with her wasn't part of dancin'."

Carolyn touched Carson's arm. He still didn't look away.

Charlie moved in and Carson immediately stepped between them, shoving Carolyn behind his back. "Don't ever come up behind her like that."

"Because you'll what? Knock me on my ass? Wouldn't be the first fuckin' time. You done with this now? Or you waitin' till he stands up and then you'll take it outside so you can keep beatin' on him?"

She froze. Carson wanted to keep fighting this guy?

"I'm done." Carson put his hands on her shoulders and steered her away.

The murmurs and mutterings of what'd happened passed through the crowd.

By the time they returned to the table, she knew Beverly had heard about the scuffle because she'd plastered on a fake smile. "Now that you're back I can tell you happy birthday one more time before we leave." Beverly hugged her and whispered, "Watch your step with Carson."

"What do you mean?"

"He's never needed a good reason to start a fight. But now that you're his wife? You're reason enough."

"Beverly, Carson would never hit me."

"I know. But that doesn't hold true for the men who are looking at you. And if they touch you? They may as well start picking their teeth up off the floor. The man has a possessive streak as wide as the state of Wyoming when it comes to you, Carolyn."

"You make it sound like a bad thing."

"A man wants you that much and wants other men to know it?

Never a bad thing...as long as he shows you—behind closed doors—and it's not all just male swagger in public."

"The swagger is entirely justified."

"Lucky you." Beverly hugged her hard. "Take care. See you soon."

When she turned, she caught Carson staring at her. "What?"

"You drank my whiskey."

"So? You weren't here. And why were you gone for so long?"

"Wasn't that long."

"Almost an hour." He frowned. "Yes, I was watching the clock. According to your brothers, you take off like that all the time."

"I was doin' business, Caro. That happens."

Rather than chew him out in public, she put her mouth on his ear. "It *used* to happen. Now that you have a wife, you don't get to disappear off to heaven knows where for heaven knows what. It's rude to take me out on my birthday and ditch me. You know how I feel about getting ditched."

Carson adjusted his stance so he backed her against the wall, blocking her from everyone at the table and anyone in the vicinity. "How much have you had to drink tonight, sugar?"

"A beer, your whiskey, Charlie's whiskey and Beverly bought me a shot. Why? I'm not drunk."

"You are actin' more belligerent than usual."

"Says the man who punched a guy four times," she retorted.

"I wanted to hit him more than that, so he oughta consider himself lucky." He rubbed his cheek along hers. "I put the off-limits sign on you the second you started wearin' my ring and when you took my name. He—and all the other assholes eyein' you—needed a reminder that no one, and I mean *no one*, touches what's mine."

"Then maybe you should take me home and prove that I'm yours."

"In a bit. Let's stick around and celebrate your birthday. We've got years to act like an old married couple."

As it turned out, Carson celebrated her birthday harder than she did; she had to pour him into his truck, but not until after last call.

Then once she dragged him home, he passed out as soon as his head hit the pillow.

That night set the tone for their first year of marriage.

Carson worked hard and played harder. They spent Friday and Saturday nights out. She'd insisted since he dragged her to the bar and the dancehall that he better not complain that she expected him to accompany her to church.

After they'd been married three months, Clara West's health took a turn for the worse.

Carolyn had just finished sewing the lace on a christening gown, when she heard a loud thump in her mother's bedroom. She raced in to find her mother lying on the floor, hacking so violently blood spilled from her lips.

Trying to remain calm, she picked her mother up and settled her back in bed. "Do I need to call an ambulance?" *Or Father Dorian?*

Her mother shook her head.

"Don't tell me you're fine, Mom. I know you're not." She paused. "Thomas told me what's going on."

Her mother lay in her bed and wheezed for several long minutes before answering. "He shouldn't have told you."

"You're right. *You* should've told me."

"Why? There's nothing you can do. Nothing anyone can do."

Frustrated, she said, "You can't be left alone every day. You need daily medical care." Why didn't her father see that?

"I sleep a lot, *Liebchen.*" She closed her eyes. "I'm tired now. We'll talk later."

Her mother didn't wake up for the remainder of the day. But Carolyn waited around to speak to her father, which would be awkward since they hadn't seen each other or spoken to each other since before the wedding.

She waited on the front porch so he couldn't avoid her.

Late afternoon, Eli West hauled his bulk out of his truck and stopped at the edge of the stairs; his eyes held an accusatory gleam. "You already leave that McKay bastard?"

It took every bit of patience not to rise to his taunt. "No. How long are you going to let Mom suffer alone? She fell out of bed today. What if I hadn't been here? And don't lie to me, Dad. I know the arthritis is in her lungs."

"Why do you care? You left here—left her. Her problems ain't your concern."

"They don't seem to be your concern either."

"Don't you take that smart tone with me."

"Do you want her to die? Because that's how it's coming across to me."

He raised his hand and it would've connected with her face if she hadn't ducked. "As usual you don't know nothin'."

"Put her in a nursing home where she can get the care she needs."

"She refuses."

The way her father looked away guiltily...something else was going on. "Or are you refusing?"

His angry gaze snapped back to her. "I can't afford long term care for her, okay? Unless I abandon her as a ward of the state and then they make all the medical decisions for her. I'll lose everything I've worked for my entire life. And you know what? I'd gladly give it all up, but she won't let me. She says she'll die in her home with dignity, not among strangers who only want to prolong her life to eke more money outta me."

Tears rolled down her face. Once again Thomas had gotten

everything wrong. Their dad wasn't the villain; he was a victim of his wife's stubbornness and circumstance too. "What can I do?"

She noticed his eyes were moist. His voice was so scratchy when he finally spoke. "Be here with her during the day until I get home from work. I can't quit and lose my job and pension this close to retirement. But my boss said I can knock off two hours early until..."

She dies.

Just thinking about that was a knife in her heart. Carolyn swallowed the lump in her throat and said, "I'll be here."

"Thank you." Then his gaze tapered to a fine point. "I need your word that you won't tell McKay about this."

"Dad—"

"Your word, Carolyn. I promised your mother I wouldn't tell you kids nothin' about this. And McKay knowin' that I don't have the money to give my wife..." His voice broke. "Please. I need some dignity in this too."

None of this sat well with her, but she didn't have a choice. Since Marshall had taken a job in Cheyenne and Stuart moved down south to build houses, she had no help—emotionally or physically—from any of her siblings. Taking a chance her father might rebuff her, she hugged him. "Okay. I'll keep this between us."

He hugged her for a long time.

Carolyn stepped back and wiped her eyes. "I'll be here in the morning."

So her every-other-day visits became daily visits. She'd go home late in the afternoon, exhausted, wishing she could tell Carson why she was spending more time at the home she couldn't wait to leave, rather than the home she'd made with him.

Lying to her husband—a lie of omission was still a lie in her guilty mind—ripped her up inside.

She thought about seeking solace and advice from Father Dorian, who visited her ailing mother every other week. But Carolyn suspected he'd remind her that she'd willingly taken on the burden of her mother's care and her family's secret—and it was her Christian duty to honor her father and mother.

At first, Carson didn't say too much about her absence because fall was a busy time. He'd crash right after supper and be up at the crack of dawn the next day. She'd come up with reasons why she had to be at her mother's; canning and preserving food took up a lot of time, as did the extra sewing projects she'd taken in for Maxine. Their trailer was too small for sewing equipment so the work had to be done where her equipment was—at her mother's.

Eventually she didn't have to create excuses because Carson stopped asking.

Christmas rolled around and they exchanged gifts, then he went to his father's house and she to her parents' house because their family situations remained at an impasse.

During the lull before calving began, Carson started hitting the bars three or four nights a week. He'd be gone in the late afternoon when she returned and he'd stay gone until after midnight. Sometimes he'd come home on his own. Sometimes Cal dragged him home, which always meant Carson had been fighting.

Even the passion between them had cooled. The only time Carson reached for her was in the middle of the night. She welcomed his hands and his body on hers, but after the time she'd tried to seduce him and he'd passed out on her, she'd been too gun shy to try again.

This wasn't how she'd envisioned their life together.

She felt them drifting farther apart. She'd stopped buying her groceries in Sundance because she'd run into ladies from church circle, or the women she'd met from the bars and the dancehall who knew her husband was out drinking and fighting, while she, the dutiful young wife, stayed home. Their looks of pity shamed her.

When calving started, Carson all but moved in with Cal. Yes, she knew it was the busiest and most critical time of the year on the ranch, but she had no idea how long calving season lasted.

So she let him be. She cooked for him and cleaned for him and tucked him in on the couch those nights he was too drunk or too tired to stumble to the bedroom.

But the last straw was the night she'd gotten a phone call from the Weston County Sheriff informing her that Carson was in jail on a drunk and disorderly charge. He'd called Cal first to bail him out but his brother had refused.

That's when she'd had enough. They'd either fix this or end it.

They made the ride from the jail home in utter silence. Carson had sobered up in the eight hours he'd spent behind bars.

As soon as they were inside the trailer she confronted him. "Jail, Carson? Really?"

"I didn't start the fight."

"No, but you didn't walk away from it, either."

"What's your point?" he said coolly.

"I'm sick of it. You're out all the time, drinking and fighting. When will you stop with the fighting?"

"When guys stop bein' assholes."

"So never."

He glared at her. Then he said, "What do you care? You're over at your folks' place every damn day. I'm surprised you even noticed I wasn't here."

"I'm gone during the day but I'm here at night. Every night. But you head out to the bar before I get back." She tried to contain her anger. "Do you do that on purpose? Because it's such a chore to hang out with me and you'd rather be with your bar buddies than your wife? If you wanted to lead the partying and fighting lifestyle, why did you marry me?"

Another hard glare.

"What do you think people are saying, with you being out at the bars alone?"

"I don't give a damn what other people think."

"That's apparent because everyone thinks we're on the verge of divorce." She swallowed her rising tears. "How long before you find some woman...or have you already—"

"Goddammit, Carolyn, don't you go there. I made a vow to you and by God, I'm gonna keep it."

"Why? We never should've gotten married because we're both miserable." She shook her head. "I can't do this anymore."

In an instant Carson's hands were around her biceps and he loomed over her. "Don't you even *think* about walkin' out on me."

"But—"

"No, you will talk to me before you take a single step toward that door." He closed his eyes for several long seconds. "Please. Tell me what in the hell is goin' on with you. I hear you cryin' in the night, Caro, and it rips me in two. I hate that I'm the cause of them tears."

"You're not the sole reason for my tears, Carson." She took a deep breath and asked God to forgive her for breaking a promise. "I've been keeping something from you."

"What?"

"The reason I'm spending so much time with my mom..." Her voice broke. "...is because she's d-dying."

All the anger bled from his eyes. "What?"

"She's been going downhill for months. I found out late last summer she had about a year to live."

"Last summer?" he bellowed. "Why am I only hearing about this now?"

"Because that's how she wants it." She closed her eyes. "Thomas told me right before he left for Denver. My dad made me promise I wouldn't tell anyone. Not my brothers, not Kimi, not my Aunt Hulda." She looked at Carson. "Not even you."

"How bad is it?"

"The arthritis has gotten into her lungs." She blew out a breath. "She can't go into a nursing home for a number of reasons."

"So that left you, Carolyn the dutiful daughter, to see to your mother's needs as she's dyin'. And that lets your father off the hook to care for his wife on her deathbed. He can just skip off to work, knowin' you're shouldering the burden. And you're keeping her secret from your siblings, which means they ain't lifted a single finger to help you care for her, have they."

The way he phrased it didn't make her sound noble, but like a chump. A doormat.

"So you've taken this whole weight on yourself for the past few months."

She nodded.

Carson started to pace. "In the fall I knew you were busy clearing out the gardens and canning, and I had to deal with sortin' and shippin' cattle. But after the first snowfall you kept goin' over to your mom's and I thought..."

"What?"

"That you regretted marryin' me so quickly. So I took to feelin' sorry for myself. Thinkin' booze would numb the pain. And if that didn't work, I used my fists."

"Carson. You're the best thing that's ever happened to me. What I meant when I said I couldn't do this? I'm scared I'm losing you. You deserve so much more than the little you've been getting from me. Things are slipping out of my control and everything is falling apart and it's too late..."

That's when she started to cry. For the secrets, for the misunderstandings, for the lies they told themselves and each other. For the realization she'd fallen into the pattern of her parents' marriage: no communication, keeping her mouth shut and not causing any strife. Turning away from her husband instead of relying on him. Half-wondering if her father had manipulated her, knowing that keeping such a big secret would cause problems with her new husband.

"Please let me be what holds you together." Carson crushed her against him. "It's not too late—never too late for us. We'll get through this together, like we should've from the start."

"I love you," she whispered against his throat. "So much."

"I love you too, sugar."

"Promise that we'll never let things get this far out of hand again."

"That's a promise I can make." He rested his forehead to hers. "With all this family stuff between us, you caretaking your mom and me workin' with my dad and brothers day in and day out...we have to learn to put us first. I'll do that from here on out. Like your father should be doin' with your mother. So I hope you understand that I can't forgive your family for this, Caro. Don't even ask me to try."

"Carson. They don't know what's going on with Mom."

"The hell they don't. Don't tell me Eli hasn't blabbed to Harland and Darren about their mother's condition. Don't tell me they haven't been sitting back like they always have and letting you carry the load."

"What do you want me to do? She's dying. This isn't a time for me to be petty."

"No, it's not, but it's time for your father to face up to the reality of his wife's situation. You are not a nurse. What if something happens when you're with her and you don't know how to handle it?"

Last week her mom had had a coughing fit that left her too weak to speak. She worried even if she called for an ambulance that it wouldn't have gotten there in time.

"I won't have you livin' with that guilt for the rest of your life—of our life."

More tears fell because she knew Carson was right.

"Clara needs to be in a place with qualified professionals." Carson framed her face in his hands. "The woman sent you away when you were a kid so you didn't end up doin' this for her. I can't imagine she wants this for you now."

"She sleeps a lot. Sometimes I don't know if she's aware I'm even there."

"Then it's definitely past time."

She touched the puffy skin beneath his eye. And the knuckle-shaped bruises on his jawline. His mouth had escaped punishment this time and she stood on tiptoe to kiss him. "Thank you."

"We'll get through this."

"I believe that now."

"Sweet Jesus, woman, I've missed you. Missed everything about you. About us."

"Show me."

Then Carson led her to their bedroom.

Their reunion, emotional and physical, was beauty and passion and sweetness. It was love. It was a promise.

It was perfect.

And in the months that followed their reaffirmation of prioritizing their life together, and three months shy of their second anniversary, they created a new life.

Before Carolyn saw the image of her holding sweet baby Cord, everything went black and she was sucked back into darkness.

Chapter Nineteen

One thing about staring out the window? Carson saw some sweet moments.

Like the young man who helped his extremely pregnant wife out of the car. Then they both disappeared into the main hospital entrance. But the guy had left the car parked half on the curb, with both doors open and the engine running.

Carson remembered being that flustered when Carolyn had gone into labor with Cord. Both the terror and the thrill of it as she'd struggled for nineteen hours to bring him into the world. And the instant Carson had held that helpless baby—his son—in his hands, his whole world had changed.

He'd celebrated Cord's birth with his Dad, with his brothers, with anyone, really, who offered to buy him a celebratory drink.

It'd shocked the hell out of him when Eli West showed up at the hospital to meet his grandson.

Too bad Eli and Jed crossed paths in the waiting room afterward. Rather than taking the opportunity to bury the hatchet, the men had argued so loudly security tossed them out.

So much for Cord being the healing bridge between the McKay and West families. It'd taken a tragic death to do that years later when a new life should have.

"Carson?"

He'd been so lost in thought, he hadn't heard anyone approach. He faced his daughter-in-law, Macie. "Hey, darlin', what're you doin' here?"

"Checking up on you." She set a brown paper bag on the chair. "Feeding you since I suspect you're living on Dr. Pepper."

"It keeps me awake and satisfies my sweet tooth."

"Like father like son. Carter can't get enough of the stuff either. And before you ask, Carter isn't here. He went home for a few days since..."

"Since I won't let him see his mother."

Macie shook her head. "He supports your decision. I don't know if you remembered him telling you that during the big blow-up."

"I remember. I just wasn't sure whether he'd changed his mind and had thrown in with the others."

"No. He's working on a big commissioned piece that's due the end of the month and he can block everything out when he's got the welder going." She smiled, but it didn't warm her brown eyes like usual. "Though I doubt it'll be easy for him to keep his head from spinning this time. He's freaked out about this situation with Carolyn."

"Everyone is."

"How are you holding up? Really."

Carson plunked down and she settled into the chair beside him. He didn't know Macie as well as his other daughters-in-law since she and Carter lived in Canyon River. What he knew of her he liked; she was passionately protective of Carter and had supported them financially through the lean years of Carter's career as an artist. Now that his son had made a name for himself in the world of western art, as well as earned hefty commissions on his pieces that provided a high standard of living for Macie and their four children, Macie could've quit her job managing two restaurants. But she claimed she enjoyed the work and messing around in the kitchen—and that attitude reminded him of Carolyn. His wife still tried new recipes for him as well as cooked meals for shut-in members of the church, new parents, grieving families—anyone in the community in need.

"Carson?"

His gaze connected with hers. "Sorry. I'm prone to driftin' off into a trance-like state without warnin', which tells you how I'm holdin' up. Poorly."

"What can I do?"

"Tell me about my grandkids."

"They're all healthy, so I'm not dragging some kid crud along with me."

"Is Thane helpin' out his Grandpa Cash with the bull ridin' school this summer?"

"As much as my dad will let him and Ryder help out. Sometimes Thane comes to the restaurant with me. He thinks loading the industrial dishwasher is big fun."

"Caro's trained me to do that. 'Bout the only thing I can do in the kitchen besides make a mess. What's Parker up to?"

"The kid loves baseball. I swear we could spend every weekend at the ball fields and he already practices three times a week."

"Me'n Gran-gran had planned to visit in a couple of weeks to watch him pitch. Has Spencer been bitten by the baseball bug this summer too?"

"He's all about the rodeo. He keeps warning us he's gonna be a bulldogger." She mock shuddered. "The thought of my child throwing himself off a horse onto another animal at breakneck speed almost makes me break out in hives."

Carson smiled. "Carolyn used to say the same thing. I'm pretty sure she closes her eyes when her grandsons do it. What's my sweet little Poppy seed been up to?"

"Rescuing critters. She found motherless kitties and a nest of baby mice last week. She put them all in the same box in the barn so they wouldn't be lonely. It'll be interesting to see if the mice become catnip. Carter wanted to tell her trying to make them one family wasn't a good idea, but I said to let her be. If anyone could get kittens and mice to coexist it'd be our daughter."

"Sounds like the kids are all good. They to the fightin' stage yet? I remember it drove Carolyn crazy in the summer when the boys were together all time and they'd start fightin' constantly."

"That hasn't happened. But sometimes I feel our kids aren't as close as they should be. I hear all these fun stories about Carter's growing up years and wonder if our kids will have those kinds of memories."

"I think the memories always seem better in hindsight. I know some of the stuff they reminisce about wasn't the great time they make it out to be."

"As an only child I don't have anything to compare it to. So I'm like, *go outside and build a tree fort together! Make some memories!* They just look at me like I'm crazy and ask if they can play video games."

"It's a different world. Makes me an old timer to say that, but it's true. And you can't force your kids to like each other. You hope they do, but there's gonna be times they can't stand the sight of one another. If you're lucky they'll outgrow it. Sometimes we don't."

Macie's gaze turned shrewd. "You're talking about you and Casper."

He shrugged. "I won't lie. None of us particularly liked him, even from the time we were kids." Carson looked down at his hands. He'd automatically clenched them into fists thinking about his brother. After Charlie had told him and Cal about the physical abuse Casper had inflicted on Dalton as a boy, he'd wished he could dig up that bastard so he could beat the fuck out of him one last time. He'd never hated anyone as much as he hated his brother in that moment. That old rage surfaced, tempting him to go looking for a fight. But he was pretty sure no one would take on a seventy-four-year-old man unless he cased the local retirement center.

"I'm glad that Casper's sons have overcome brother-hating issues." She patted his arm. "I'm really glad that none of your sons feel that way about each other either."

"Me too. Luckily Colt's got a forgiving nature or this'd be a different conversation, 'cause we screwed up with him even after he cleaned up his act."

"Carter hated that he wasn't around for any of that."

"I'm glad he wasn't. It put me, Cord and Colby in the judgmental asshole zone."

197

"But you straightened it out. As much as Carter loves having his own studio close to the house, I know he wishes sometimes we lived here, closer to his family."

When Macie looked away quickly, Carson said, "And you feel guilty about that?"

"Well, yeah. I get to see *my* dad every day. Dad's kids with Gemma and our kids are growing up like cousins, but that doesn't replace the connection we both want them to have with their McKay cousins. Carter had that growing up and he wants that for our kiddos."

"You're visiting here at least every couple of months, and with your crazy schedules I'm happy your family can get here at all," Carson pointed out.

"It requires a lot of juggling, but it's worth it."

"How many of my kids visit your family in Canyon River?"

"Colt and Indy and their brood were the most recent ones. But since they have the fewest kids of Carter's siblings, it's easier for them to get away. Jack and Keely used to come more often, but it got harder for them after they had the twins. Colby is helping Dad out with the bull riding school for a week this summer and Channing and the kids usually tag along. That's always fun. Total chaos with ten kids. Then Ryder, Ella and Jansen don't wanna be left out, so they're usually over too."

"Good thing you built that big house a few years back." Carter and Macie's sprawling ranch-style home was located on a beautiful vista on the outskirts of Gemma and Cash's ranch and could easily accommodate all of the McKays.

"It's a big change from the tiny trailer we lived in after we first got married and had the first two boys."

"I remember them days. Only our first two boys remember livin' in the trailer. Then again, we tend to play musical houses in the McKay family."

Macie's eyes narrowed on the paper sack on the chair beside Carson. "I've been so busy yammering I didn't let you eat your sandwich."

"I'd rather talk to you while I have the chance. Eatin' alone don't bother me."

"Has anyone from the family come to check on you?"

"Dalton. And now you. I appreciate you stopping by. Tell the *artiste*—" a private joke between him and Carter, "—I'm glad he backed me."

"I will." She paused again. "Carson, I'm asking you one favor on Carter's behalf. Maybe it seems strange coming from him, but I promised I'd mention it to you."

"What's that?"

"If Carolyn needs physical therapy during her recovery, please ask Keely to work with her. Not only is Keely really good at her job, it'd go a long way in proving that your reasons for keeping Carolyn isolated were situational and short term."

That was something Carson hadn't considered. He was just trying to get through each hour. It didn't surprise him that Carter was trying to mend fences. He had so much of his mother in him: a kind heart, a fierce love and a stubborn streak. Sometimes as the youngest son his brothers had called him a mama's boy, intending it as an insult. But Carson couldn't think of a better compliment or a better person to aspire to be like than Carolyn McKay. "Not to worry. If Carolyn needs rehab, our daughter is the first one I'll call."

"Excellent."

"Although, that girl did torture me after my hip replacement surgery with all her blasted exercises."

"How is your hip?"

"Better," he lied.

"Good. Take care of yourself. Know you and Carolyn are in a lot of people's thoughts and prayers."

After she'd gone he tore the paper wrapper off the sandwich. Although he was starving, he savored each bite.

Contemplations about sibling solidarity and rivalry had him thinking about Casper. How in all the years he thought he knew his brother...he really hadn't. While he'd never excuse how Casper had treated his sons, Carson knew his brother's life hadn't turned out the way he'd expected. But as usual, Carson had borne the brunt of Casper's bad decisions...

Half the time Carson didn't know why his dad summoned him for his help. The man grumped around like an old bear. Today was no exception. Carson had been delegated gate opener. With Cord propped on his hip, he shut the gate and walked over to where his dad unsaddled his horse.

His father didn't look up when he said, "Ain't exactly handy carting a kid around when we're supposed to be movin' cattle."

"Carolyn was too damn sick to even get outta bed this mornin'. What was I supposed to do? Leave Cord bawlin' in his crib?"

"Shouldn't she be over mornin' sickness by now?" he demanded. "This is the second time this week you've had to drag Cord along."

Like Carolyn had purposely spent the morning throwing up because she wanted to inconvenience Jed McKay. "If she ain't better by tomorrow I'm takin' her to the doctor."

"So you'll miss a day of work."

"Last I knew you had three other sons who could take up the slack for one damn day," Carson retorted.

"Cow! Mmmooo," Cord said, pointing to the cattle slowly making their way to the stock tank.

"That's right. A cow says moo. What's a horse say?"

"Giddy up!"

Carson grinned. He loved that Cord had started to talk. "A horse says *neigh*. Think Grandpop will let you feed his horse some oats?"

"Sure I will," his dad said. "Get the bucket while I'm finishing this up."

"Down," Cord said.

"Nope."

Cord's little booted feet kicked. "Daddy. Down."

"Do you wanna feed the horse?"

He nodded.

"Then you gotta stay close by me. I can't have you runnin' around and getting hurt, okay?"

"'Kay."

For all of Jed McKay's blustering about having the boy underfoot, it amazed Carson that he was so patient with Cord. Showing him things outside. Setting up the wooden blocks and toys inside. Sneaking him ice cream. Jed just came over and plucked Cord from Carson's arms and headed into the barn.

Since he'd become a father himself, Carson wondered how much his dad helped his mother when they were babies and toddlers. He couldn't imagine having two little Cords to keep track of—like his mother had dealt with, with him and Cal. Having two kids in two and a half years would be hard enough.

He waited by the fence for his dad and son to return, wondering how to broach the subject of a pay increase. Things were tight and he was making the same money now as he had when he and Carolyn first got married.

They wandered out of the barn, Grandpop in a deep discussion with Cord about something when a Buick tore up the driveway and slammed on the brakes in the middle of the yard.

Then a tall, gray-haired man climbed out of the driver's side and angrily stormed toward them.

The potentially dangerous situation had Carson snatching Cord away from his dad.

"You!" The man pointed to Jed. "Are you Casper McKay's father?"

"Who wants to know?"

"I do."

"And who the hell are you?"

"Patrick Tellman." Then he sneered at Carson. "Another one who can't keep his pants zipped. You're populating the whole area with McKays, ain't ya?"

"You're about to meet the business end of my shotgun, comin' on McKay land and insulting me and mine."

"Is Casper your son?" he demanded.

"Yes, he is. What's he done now?"

"He knocked up my daughter, that's what he's done."

Carson glanced at his father, but the man didn't show a lick of emotion.

"Who's your daughter?"

"Of course you gotta ask that since rumor has it all of your sons are notorious for catting around in three counties."

"Stop with the insults and get to the point," Carson warned.

"Who is your daughter?" Jed asked again.

"Joan Tellman."

Not a name Carson recognized. Last he knew Casper had been seeing a woman in Spearfish named Donna.

"So your daughter Joan is pregnant and she claims Casper is the father?"

"Claims?" Patrick Tellman moved in toe to toe with Jed. "Casper *is* the father. My Joan is a good girl and swore to me Casper was the only man she's ever been with. But I can understand why you'd be suspicious since a sweet Christian girl ain't your sons' normal type.

Wrong. Carson thought of his Carolyn—a good Catholic girl to the core. She embodied decency and goodness. He accompanied her to church hoping some of her ways would rub off on him. God knew he could use it.

"Don't seem like she's showing such good Christian values if she's pregnant outside of wedlock," Jed said evenly, and Carson knew he was trying to retain his cool. "Has your daughter mentioned this to Casper?"

"No. That's why I'm here. Father to father. I'm telling you I expect Casper to marry Joan as soon as possible."

Jed McKay didn't say anything. Then he gave Patrick Tellman a resigned look. "I'll talk to Casper today and I'll have him contact Joan tonight."

"And if she doesn't hear from him?"

"She will. I guarantee it. You have my word."

That seemed to satisfy the man. He nodded, spun on his heel and marched back to his car. His exit from the ranch was more subdued than his entrance.

Carson really wished he'd been long gone when this went down.

"That dumb fucker," his dad said and Carson knew he wasn't referring to Patrick Tellman.

"No kiddin'. I didn't know he was seein' this Joan woman."

"Never heard her name before today. But that don't mean nothin'. Only woman you ever brought home was Carolyn. And you had your share of rumors long before that." Jed sighed. "I need a goddamned shot of whiskey."

Here was his chance to escape. "I'll leave you to it. Let me know what happens."

"I already know what'll happen—Casper is getting married." He

201

pointed at Carson. "You ain't goin' nowhere. In light of this there's some ranch business to straighten out."

Cord fussed and Carson set him down. "What ranch business?"

"Something I wanna run by you before I tell Casper and Charlie. The Ingalls place I'm buyin' has a house. Since you and Cal work so well together, I'm leaving you both here and I'll be sendin' Casper down there. Charlie too. Eventually."

Carson had a brief flash of anger. That house was way nicer than the trailer he and Carolyn lived in. Now with a baby on the way and a busy two-year-old it'd be an even tighter fit for four. Why hadn't his father considered giving him the house?

Because he's punishing you for moving out after your mother died.

He knew better than to complain, so he deflected. "When we have this discussion, I don't want you to let on that I'd heard about these change in plans before they heard it from you."

"Why's that?"

He watched Cord picking up rocks. "Because they already accuse me of getting special treatment from you."

"They meaning Casper."

Carson shrugged.

"Last I checked I'm still makin' the decisions for the ranch. It ain't favoritism if I decide it's what's best."

"So will I be headin' down there to work those new sections? Will they still be comin' up here?"

"We'll do what needs done."

That was his dad's answer to everything. *We'll do what needs done.*

Meanwhile Casper would skate by with the minimum amount of work and get paid the same amount as Carson did. And now he'd be adding travel to his day.

Doin' what needs done, my ass.

He'd make sure the new sections of land were ready for cattle, but he would *not* help Casper get his house ready for his bride.

Just then Casper and Charlie pulled up with Cal following behind them in his truck.

"Now's as good a time as any to talk to them."

"You plan to pull Casper aside afterward?"

"Nope. He done what he done. Ain't no reason to hide it."

Fuck. This day just got better and better.

As soon as Casper, Charlie and Cal were out of their vehicles, their dad said, "Meetin' in the dining room."

Carson felt his brothers' curious gazes but he focused on Cord. "Come on, son, and leave the rocks. We're goin' inside."

"Don't wanna!"

I know how you feel, kid.

He held his hand out and Cord took it.

Once they were seated at the table, their father zeroed in on Casper. "What kind of fool are you? Man named Patrick Tellman paid me a visit today, informing me that you knocked up his daughter, Joan."

Casper's face turned bright red and for a second Carson worried his brother was about to have a stroke. "She's pregnant?"

"So it seems. She swears you're the only man she's ever been with."

"She says she was a virgin, but I don't see how that could be. She's one of those women who'll do anything in bed. And I mean *anything*. She had to learn that kinky shit someplace."

"How long have you been dating her?"

"I never dated her," Casper shot back.

"Fine. How long have you have been proddin' her?"

"I met her five months ago. But I ain't been with her for over a month and a half."

"You just fucked her when you felt like it and walked away?"

Casper glared. "I wouldn't be the first man to take what was offered."

"You'll be the last man when it comes to her."

"What are you talkin' about?"

"You're doin' the right thing for once in your life and marryin' her." He looked at Cal. "Seems you're the only one who hasn't impregnated a woman, so let that be a lesson to you to keep your goddamned pants zipped."

Carson shot Charlie a questioning look and Charlie seemed equally confused.

But Casper interrupted before Charlie could speak. "You can't make me marry her."

"Yes, I can. You will take her as your wife or you're out."

"Out. Out of what? Out of favor?" He aimed his glower at Carson. "Too fuckin' late for that."

"I'll kick you out of the house. You're off the ranch and on your own. Since I own your truck, pay your wages and you've been livin' in my house your whole life, you got a lot to lose by thinkin' you can get around this. I'm done putting up with your laziness and lies. It's time you own up to your responsibilities, Casper."

"So I'm bein' punished."

Yeah, some punishment. By being a fuck up you're giving him a house and land of his own? Maybe I oughta fuck up.

"Since you'll soon have a wife and a child, you're movin' down to the Ingalls place. Charlie will eventually live down that way too, but for now he'll be makin' the drive every day from here."

Charlie stood. "This is bullshit. What'd I do? Nothin'. Now you're sendin' me thirty miles away?"

"Like I told Casper. Your options are to do what you're expected to or you're out."

"Yeah, yeah, I get you've got the biggest set of balls in the McKay family. But I also know why Casper is such a big prick. He gets it from you." Charlie left.

Carson's eyes met Cal's. Charlie had been in a funk since his jailbait girlfriend had suddenly moved away a few months ago. With the way Charlie talked, they half-expected to show up one morning and find him gone. Their youngest brother was the smartest of the lot. He owned his truck so he did have the means to leave if he so chose.

"You got anything to add?" their dad asked Cal.

"Just the same thing that me'n Carson have brought up several times. Dividing the land so we're each workin' our own section. The way it sets now it's not equal pay for equal work."

"You just had to get a shot in at me, didn't you?" Casper demanded. "You act like I don't do nothin' around here."

"You do about half as much work as Carson, get paid the same and he has a wife and kid to support," Cal snapped. "That ain't a shot, that's the honest truth."

"Enough," their father said. "Only thing that's changing is Casper is getting married and movin' out."

Carson looked at his son, wearing secondhand clothes, and swallowed his pride. "So this ain't the time to ask for a pay raise?"

"Not when I just bought the Ingalls place."

"Even if we have a good year?"

"Depends. A bonus might be in order, but you know any profits pay off existing debt and then what's left goes in the expansion fund. It's about the long term and the future."

Think before you speak.

But Carson couldn't hold it in. "So in the short term, I have three mouths to feed, plus soon a fourth, on the same salary you're payin' yourself and your single sons. Think on the fairness of how we're raising beef for other folks to eat, while your grandkids and the future of this ranch are eatin' canned beans and powdered milk because that's the only food I can afford to buy for my family." He glanced down at Cord. His lip quivered and his blue eyes were enormous with fear. Great. Now he'd scared his son. He picked the boy up and nuzzled his cheek. "It's okay. Let's go home to Mama."

Carson had made it to his truck when he heard Cal say, "Wait up."

He opened the passenger door and set Cord on the seat. "Stay down, okay?"

"'Kay."

Then he faced his twin. "What?"

"Is it really that rough for you and Carolyn?"

He felt his cheeks heat and he looked away. "Yeah."

"Dammit, Carse, why didn't you say something?"

"Because it's embarrassing. I put off askin' him and now I see I shoulda kept my mouth shut. Jesus. I hate that I damn near begged for a few extra bucks and he didn't even consider it." Carson closed his eyes. "Casper fucks up, knocks up a chick that he doesn't even like and he gets a house? I don't know where Casper gets the idea I'm the favorite child because from where I'm sittin' in my cramped trailer? He is."

"I'll give you some of my salary if it helps. I just spend the extra on stupid shit anyway."

Between his frustration and his brother's kindness, he might just break down. He took in a deep breath and let it out before he patted Cal on the back. "Thanks. I mean it. But I can't take your money."

"Carson—"

"But I will let you buy me a bottle or two of whiskey if you promise to drink it with me when I drown my sorrows about bein' broke."

"That I can do."

"Gotta get home and check on my wife."

Cord had sacked out by the time Carson pulled up to the trailer. He carried the boy inside and placed him in the crib—boots and all.

Carolyn was stretched out on the bed in their room, a washrag over her eyes, a package of saltines on the dresser next to a Coke.

He perched on the edge of the bed. "Hey, sugar. How you feelin'?"

"A little less like dog poop than I did when you left."

"Sorry. What can I do?"

She lowered the cloth from her eyes. "Where's Cord?"

"Sleepin' off a drunk on the tractor. That boy needs to learn how to hold his whiskey."

"Funny."

"He crashed." Carson slipped off his boots and crawled up next to her. "C'mere. I need to hold you." He tucked her under his arm and she rested the side of her face on his chest. He closed his eyes and breathed her in. Within a few minutes the world of the McKay ranch faded. She gave that to him. Calmness. Softness. She was the one thing in the world that was completely his.

"Carson, sweetheart, what's wrong?"

Money is tight, my father is a controlling ass, I'm pissed off at Casper, money is tight, I'm worried about you with this pregnancy and have I mentioned money is tight?

But he couldn't—wouldn't—add extra stress on her. He'd sworn to her on the day they married he'd spend his life making her happy, and taking care of her, so he'd keep his worries to himself.

"Nothin'. Everything is as it should be when we're together like this."

"I agree. But you're not telling me everything. So start talking, cowboy."

Where to start? "Looks like you'll be getting a sister-in-law in the next couple weeks. I'd say she's lucky since she'll be movin' into a real house down on the new south section of the McKay Ranch and not a shithole trailer, but the fact of it is, she'll still be married to my asshole brother Casper no matter where they live, so maybe she ain't as lucky as she seems. I just wish..."

Carolyn sat up.

Carson kept his eyes closed. Then he felt her straddling him and her hands landed on his chest.

"You wish what? That I hadn't gotten pregnant again?"

His eyes flew open and he put a protective hand over her belly. "God no. I love that we're adding to our family."

"You wish we were moving to that ranch house you showed me? Because to be honest? I'm happy we're staying here. This is our home. It's small but it's ours. I love my garden spot. I can drop Cord off at Agnes's place whenever I have work to finish for Maxine."

"I wish I was makin' enough money that you didn't have to take those jobs. It feels like I'm failing to support you and our family."

She slammed her hands down by his head on the mattress so they were eye to eye. "It falls on *both* of us to provide for our family. I won't watch you kill yourself while I'm sitting here twiddling my thumbs whenever Cord naps. Doing piece work keeps me sane, keeps my skills fresh. I imagine things will get busier with a new baby, but I don't ever want to hear you say you don't support this family. You love me. You love our son. You work hard. You make me happy. If that's not support I don't know what is."

"Caro—"

"You listen to me. Everything I want—everything I need is right here. With you. It does not matter *where* we live. It matters *how* we live when we're together."

Maybe her pregnancy hormones were contagious because her sweet, heartfelt words made him misty-eyed. "I love you. So damn much."

"Show me." She swept her lips over his in that not-so-innocent way that he craved. "You needed to hold me? I need this."

"You sure?" He stroked the swell of her belly. "You were sick—"

"Hours ago. I brushed my teeth, washed myself up and I need your mouth and your hands on me."

Instant erection.

Carolyn shed her blouse and oh yeah, she hadn't worn a bra. Her tits were enormous during pregnancy.

"Gimme."

"Huh-uh. Take it if you want it."

So she wanted to make him work for it? Fine by him. He jackknifed and nestled his face in her cleavage. He slid his hands down her naked back and beneath the waistband of her pajama bottoms. His fingertips connected with more bare skin—no underwear either. He started his assault on her nipples. Softly sucking on the rigid tips, using his teeth, then backing off to rub his face against that abundant flesh and not giving her nipples any attention at all. He followed her ass crack to the wet opening of her cunt, slipping two fingers into her from behind.

"Carson."

He grabbed her hand and placed it over her mound. "You want it, sugar, take it."

She tightened her other hand on his shoulder, letting her head fall back as she rubbed that spot. Her hair swayed, teasing his forearm as she bumped her hips forward.

"Sexy fuckin' woman. That's it."

Carson plunged his fingers into her pussy, sucking her nipple, then easing back to lightly flick it the same way he did when his mouth was on her clit.

The woman was so in tune with satisfying her sexual needs, her body so responsive to his, that it wasn't long before goose bumps beaded across her skin. She released a tiny whimper, the one that drove him insane because he knew she was about to come. He loved watching her get off.

Her fingers began to move faster on her clit. When he felt the first spasm, he shoved his fingers deep, moving his mouth to her other nipple, sucking it in tandem with the pulsing of her pussy muscles around his fingers.

A gasp tore from her throat. Her hold on his neck increased to the point of pain. But he fucking loved that almost as much as when she damn near pulled out his hair when his face was buried in her cunt.

Abruptly Carolyn stopped moving. She shoved at his hand.

"What? Did I hurt you?"

"No. I need more. I'm still..." She released a frustrated noise and went straight for his belt buckle. "Take them off."

"Sugar—"

"Now!"

The primitive need to satisfy his mate fired every cell in his body. He forced himself to be gentle as he set her aside and stripped, blood and possession roaring through him. He wanted to fuck her from behind, needing to prove to her that he could take care of her in the way that mattered most.

Since she was pregnant, he paused, waiting for the fog of lust to clear a bit. His Carolyn liked rougher sex. In the past she'd had teeth marks on her ass, finger-shaped bruises on her inner thighs, and purple love bites on her neck and chest as proof of the no-boundaries passion that exploded between them.

"What?" she asked in that husky, *fuck me now, what are you waiting for* tone.

"Just tryin' to figure out how I want you first."

"Hurry up and decide."

Carson crawled across the bed, rolling her onto her side, then spooning behind her. He shifted her top leg back over his hip, sinking his teeth into the nape of her neck as he sank his cock into her hot, slick pussy. "Fuck, that feels good."

"Harder."

"I haven't started to move yet."

"I know. And I'm dying here."

"Look at me."

Carolyn turned her head. Her face was flushed and those blue eyes of hers were wild with need.

He was the luckiest damn man in the world.

"Hard and fast?" he murmured.

"Please. I love the way you fuck me with that big cock of yours, Carson McKay."

Might send him straight to hell for loving the rare curse word coming from his good-girl Catholic wife, but so be it. So he pushed her to say it again. "I'm sorry, sugar, I didn't quite hear that."

"Fuck me. Make me come so hard I pass out from the sheer bliss of having your cock pounding into me."

"That I can do."

And he did.

He sent her over the edge twice—multiple orgasms for her was another benefit of pregnancy—and he roared like a beast when his balls finally released his seed.

Carolyn bore down with her cunt muscles, milking him so hard he swore he came twice in a row. Sweat coated his body. Her breath drifting across his skin as she spiraled down from her orgasm sent a shudder through him.

She sought his mouth, shifting their position so he was on his back with her laying half on top of him. She whispered, "I love you," against his lips and peppered kisses from his chin, up his jaw to his temple. "I am so lucky."

He snorted. "Because I fucked you like an animal?"

"No."

When she didn't elaborate, he said, "You goin' someplace with this? 'Cause woman, I don't think my brain is firin' on all cylinders."

"I'm lucky because you are mine." She bit his earlobe. "Everything about you is just...mmm. This long sweep of your neck? Drives me crazy. It's warm and strong. Yet when I do this?" Carolyn sucked on the section of skin where his pulse pounded closest to the surface and he groaned. "I can make my big tough cowboy go weak in the knees."

"You love that power," he murmured.

"I love that I can spend just as much time worshipping your chest with my hands and mouth as you do worshipping mine."

Then she proved it. Mapping the cut of his muscles with her

tongue. Licking and sucking. Doing that nuzzle and bite thing on his pectorals and his nipples that could make him shoot all over his belly.

"I love that this hard body of yours is mine to play with whenever I want. Other women still look at you and want you. I can't help but feel a little smug that these muscle-bound arms are around me every night." She feathered her thumb over his lips. "That this sinful, playful, skillful mouth knows every inch of my body."

"That's definitely...mmm for me."

Carolyn locked her gaze to his. "Nothing in my sheltered life prepared me for what it means to love Carson McKay, the gorgeous blue-eyed cowboy, third generation Wyoming rancher, hell-raiser of the first order. But nothing in my sheltered life prepared me either for the way you look at me, for the way you love me. With everything you have, with everything you are. I can't believe with all the women you could've had who understand this ranch stuff, you picked me to build a life with." She pressed her cheek against his heart. "I'm grateful for you, for this life and sometimes I forget to tell you that."

This sweet, wonderful woman gave him so much and got so little in return. "I'm getting the better end of the deal, trust me."

They stayed entwined together.

"You must've worn Cord out," she said. "He never naps this long."

"He acted a little scared when me'n Dad had words."

"Wasn't the first time, won't be the last."

He stroked the curve of her hip. "So you sayin' Cord had better get used to it?"

"You tell me. Our son is the first born of the fourth generation of McKays. If he chooses to stay in the family business, he'll have the same types of things weighing on him that you do with your father."

"I can promise I'll never be like my dad was to me to our kids. Never."

Carson shifted in the hospital chair.

That hadn't been a promise he'd been able to keep. As much as he'd hoped things would improve with his father and the ranch over the next couple years, the situation deteriorated even more.

Chapter Twenty

Hospital, Day 3—morning

Carson stared out the window.

Again.

He'd done solitary work a good part of his life. Normally he had no problem spending time alone. But he was really sick and fucking tired of his own company.

You've done this to yourself, even if it's for Carolyn's benefit.

His kids were sticking together as far as he could tell. None of them had called. None had stopped by.

They'd all rallied around their mother during his surgery a few months back.

But Caro didn't bar them from contact with you. Not even after you coded on the table for two minutes.

But it wasn't the same.

The nurses left him alone—not that he expected them to entertain him. He'd never been much of a TV watcher, and having the boob tube on, even low volume, grated on his nerves. But he was so...bored he'd turned the damn thing on just for the company.

"Uncle Carson?"

He turned to see his nephew Quinn struggling with three bags. He crossed the small space. "Here, lemme help you."

"Thanks. The nurses already checked them."

Carson peered inside. The two heavy canvas bags contained stacks of magazines and the third bag food.

"Libby raided the retired periodical stacks at the public library, lookin' for men's magazines. But don't be hopin' for *Playboy*," he said dryly.

"I'm afraid I was the blush and stammer type if I ever came across those, even in my youth."

"Me too."

"Tell Libby thanks. The distraction will be good. Not a helluva lot to do in here."

"Ma made you a couple of sandwiches and other stuff. To 'tide you over', she said."

"Vi's gone above and beyond. Tell her thanks too."

"Sure thing." Then Quinn plopped down. "Go ahead and eat if you're hungry."

Carson remembered he hadn't eaten today. "You're sure? Looks like there's plenty to share."

"I just ate breakfast with Ben and Gavin. They wanted me to let you know that you're in their thoughts."

He nodded and removed the first sandwich—roast beef on rye— from the sandwich baggie and took a big bite.

Quinn rambled on about the ranch, not delving into anything too serious. Carson was grateful for the chatter while he polished off a sandwich and a slice of rhubarb pie. Vi's pies had the tastiest crust— not that he'd ever tell his wife that.

"I probably shoulda told you first thing that Adam and Amelia are both one hundred percent healthy. I heard the docs are concerned about even a simple infection somehow getting to her."

"That's good, especially for you and Libby. In our house it seemed like one of the kids always had some kinda crap."

Quinn grinned. "That's because you had three times as many kids as we do, three times as many germ carriers."

"My brothers reminded us of that when we were lookin' for babysitters."

"You'll never catch me complaining about my kids. Me'n Lib waited a long damn time for those blessings. For a while there...I wasn't sure we'd make it, especially not after I realized she was serious about kickin' my ass out." Quinn adjusted his hat. "Sorry to be babbling on. I forget all that past stuff with me'n Lib has passed through the McKay gossip channels and you know all about it."

"Only because we're aware that every couple has problems and we were glad to see you two worked it out."

"No McKay couple that I know of hit the skids as hard as we did," Quinn said.

Carson uncapped his second Dr. Pepper of the morning and drank. "That's because you weren't around when me'n Carolyn hit the skids."

Arms crossed over his chest, Quinn looked as if he wanted to call bullshit on that statement. "Oh yeah? You and Aunt Carolyn?"

"Yep. The first year we were married was pretty rough, dealing with all the West/McKay family bullshit, and her mother bein' so sick and dyin'. But we pulled through. Then we had Cord. Things were okay for a while after Colby was born, Round about years five and six, she threatened to kick my ass out on numerous occasions—every one justified, but I sweet-talked my way back into her good graces. Don't get me wrong; I worked hard, but then I partied hard, leavin' her alone with two kids. Real fuckin' peach of a man I was during that time. I'd straighten up for a while, then go back to my same drinkin' and fightin' ways. Until she'd had enough. By that time we'd been married...about seven years."

"Jesus, Uncle Carson, I had no idea."

"No one does. Well, Cal and Kimi did because they lived close by and Cal had to deal with my drunken ass and Kimi with her sister's tears. That was right before your mom came back and married your dad, so poor Charlie got sucked into bein' my partner in crime sometimes."

"You never told your kids?"

"Just Colt, and not the particulars, only to let him know I'd headed down that destructive path he'd been on. I've been of the mindset that problems between a husband and wife should be dealt with in private." Then again, he hadn't that luxury with Carolyn. Her blow-up had been very public.

"While normally I'd agree, in this case me'n Libby bein' separated and then getting back together forced my mom to do some soul searching. Like you said, I wasn't privy to my folks' intimate relationship before that, I just know it affected their marriage for the better afterward."

"And I'm glad of that too."

Silence stretched between them for the first time since Quinn had sat down. When Carson glanced at the clock, he realized thirty minutes had passed. In ten minutes he could sit with Carolyn.

Quinn chuckled and rolled to his feet. "Guess I get the award for bringing the least amount of cheer into the waitin' room, huh?"

"Nah. It's good to reflect. And trust me; I've had plenty of time to think. No surprise that memory ain't one I'm lookin' to revisit."

"Take care, Uncle C. Tell Aunt Carolyn we're pullin' for her. And if you need anything, call."

He wouldn't call, but he appreciated the offer. "Thanks Quinn. Give my best to Libby and tell her thanks."

"Will do."

Carson used the bathroom and returned to staring out the window, counting the minutes.

It seemed forever before he heard, "Okay, Mr. McKay. Let's get you suited up."

This time when he entered the room he loomed over her, studying her beautiful face, rather than just plopping down by her bedside.

"Hey, sugar. I'm here beside you. I know you can hear me. I *need* you to hear me. Come back to me. I need you to know that I'm right here, I ain't goin' anywhere.

"Not that I'm talkin' about anything earthshattering while I'm in here." He caressed her forearm. Then he dropped onto the rolling stool. "Quinn brought by some magazines. Maybe I'll find a fascinating article to talk about. I heard the docs say it's the sound of a familiar voice, not the words that are said, that matters, but I think that's a bunch of horseshit. I want you to hear what I'm sayin'.

"Vi sent me food. Sweet of her. It was good—not as good as yours, but I'm thinkin' you won't be up for cookin' after you wake up and we bust you outta here. Somehow Quinn got on the subject of the problems he and Libby had a few years back. He seemed embarrassed by it so I said that we'd been married a few years when I about fucked it all up. And yes, I told him the blame landed square on me. I hadn't thought about it in years, so I'm hopin' that time in our married life is a blur to you..."

Carolyn had been bobbing along in the dark currents of her mind, her thoughts disappearing beneath the surface as soon as she had them. Then she'd hear his voice and pop back up, fighting the undertow. It wasn't lost on her that she was swimming against the tide—but she'd never learned how to swim.

She flailed around until she latched onto the memory, praying it'd keep her afloat in this pseudo-reality for a little while longer because even bad memories were better than no memories at this point...

"Mama."

Carolyn turned from the stove. She adjusted Colby on her hip and looked at Cord, playing with his barnyard animal set on the living room floor. "Whatcha need, sweetheart?"

"When's Daddy comin' home?"

Good question. As it was well past dark the man should've been home two hours ago. "I don't know. Maybe something came up." Lying to herself was one thing, but she didn't want to lie to her son about why Daddy preferred to spend his evenings elsewhere.

Carson McKay, you are in for it when you stumble your drunken self home.

During the slow season, her husband spent a few evenings a week in town. Having a few drinks and laughs with other ranchers, guys he'd known all his life. Carolyn didn't begrudge him that time. The man worked hard throughout the year and deserved to kick back.

But in the past, he'd always gone out with Cal. Since Kimi was seven months pregnant with twins, Cal went straight home to his wife every night.

Remember when Carson used to do that?

Yes. Even after Cord had been born he'd rather be home with them than chugging beer with his buddies, even for one night.

When had that changed?

During her second pregnancy. After his fight with his father.

Caring for Cord all day and the constant nausea and tiredness with baby number two had given her less energy for her husband. Carson's weekly trip to the Silver Spur had changed into twice a week.

Then after Colby's birth, in addition to taking care of a two-year-old and a baby, she tended their enormous garden, took on sewing projects for Maxine, and with Agnes's encouragement, she'd become involved with Ladies Circle at St. Ignatius.

So the fact Carson could entertain himself seemed like a blessing. Then last year after Kimi returned to Wyoming, had a whirlwind affair with Cal, ended up pregnant and married and practically living next door, she spent her free time with her sister. Carson didn't seem to mind, and even if he had she would've happily pointed out all the time he spent outside ranch work with his brothers.

But it hadn't come up.

They'd been married seven years. They had a five-year-old, a three-year-old and—she placed her hand over her belly—another one on the way. Something she hadn't told her husband because he hadn't been around lately.

The sound of stomping boots brought her out of her woolgathering. She glanced over to see Cord reaching for the door handle.

"Whoa there, little buckaroo. What's the rule?"

"Don't go outta the house without askin'."

"Right. So what are you doing?"

Cord's sweet face formed a scowl. "Mama, I asked if I could go lookin' for Daddy and you didn't say nothin'."

"Because I didn't say no you figured that meant yes?"

He nodded.

She'd have to be much more literal with her boys from here on out. "Sweetie, your daddy isn't close by."

"Why not? Where is he?"

"I'll call Uncle Cal and see if I can't find out." She kissed Colby's forehead. "Play with your brother."

Another scowl.

Just as she reached for the phone to call Kimi, it rang. Sometimes it was uncanny how much she and her sister had the same train of thought. "McKays."

"Carolyn. It's Francine. How are you?"

Not her sister, but the head of the Ladies Circle, calling to discuss the care packages they'd been assembling for missionary purposes. "I'm fine, Francine. How are you?"

A pause. "I'm doing well, thanks for asking. And I have...something that I need to discuss with you."

She knew they needed another coordinator for catechism class, but she really couldn't add another thing to her duties. "I'd be happy to talk about it next week after the meeting; right now—"

"Carolyn, dear, this has nothing to do with your volunteering at the church. This is personal. And I feel the need to preface this by saying I'm not telling you this out of malice or spite. This isn't some two-bit gossip I'm passing along thirdhand. This is something I witnessed myself, just last night."

"What?"

"I saw your husband with another woman."

Her lungs and her vocal chords seized up, but somehow she managed to squeak out, "Where?"

"We had supper at the Silver Spur. I had to use the facilities and when I passed the back room, I saw Carson." A pause. "With some woman."

"Who?"

"To be completely honest, I'm not sure who the woman was. It was dark back there. And they were..." She cleared her throat. "Cozied up together is the simplest way to put it."

Carolyn half sat/half fell onto a kitchen chair. "You're sure it was Carson?"

"I wouldn't be calling you if I wasn't sure. I wrestled with telling you, but I thought you'd want to know. I know I would if it were me."

Her head spun. Carson. Her Carson. The man who claimed to love her more than anything, the man who swore he'd spend his life making her happy...was cheating on her?

The bottom fell out of her world.

Francine said, "I haven't told another soul. Trust me, I won't. I hope it's a misunderstanding and I saw the situation out of context."

"I hope so too, Francine."

"If you need anything, *anything*," she stressed, "please call me."

"I will. And thank you for your honesty and your discretion. I'll get to the bottom of it right away."

"Blessings to you dear, you're in my prayers."

As soon as Carolyn hung up, the sick feeling that'd taken root grew ugly, thorny stems and began to spread. She folded her arms on the kitchen table and laid down her head, squeezing her eyes shut against a flood of tears.

Had her attention to the boys, and her sister, and her other responsibilities driven him into another woman's arms?

She scrolled back the past week or so, trying to remember if Carson had acted weird. Or guilty.

He'd been freshly showered when he came to bed last night.

To wash off the scent of another woman's perfume?

She'd chalked up his distance to him being tired and stressed about money.

You're making excuses for him.

No. But she hadn't been much of a wife to him lately either.

And how is that? You cook for him, you wash his clothes, clean his house and raise his children.

What about sexually? She hadn't seen to his needs—or he to hers in the past month.

Because he's getting what he needs from someone else.

A sort of red rage began to build in her, supplanting the feeling of desolation.

How dare he. She would not be cast aside. She was more to him than a cook, maid and babysitter. How long had it been since he'd acted like she mattered? When had she accepted that an occasional glimpse of the loving man she'd married was better than none?

She couldn't even remember the last time they'd had a conversation that didn't involve ranch work or kids. She couldn't remember the last time he'd done something sweet or thoughtful for her.

But you've done plenty of sweet and thoughtful things for him.

A little finger poked her in the side. She lifted her head and looked into Cord's enormous blue eyes. Serious eyes. Eyes like his father's. Love for this child swamped her and she hugged him tightly. He reached up, wreathing his arms around her neck and she rubbed her cheek against the baby-smooth softness of his skin.

"Me too!" Colby shouted and tried to worm his way between them.

Cord whispered, "Mama, why you sad?"

She leaned back. "How could I ever be sad when I have such wonderful boys to make me smile?"

Colby scooted under her arm and rested his head above her breast with a sigh.

"I have an idea. How would you guys like to spend the night with Aunt Kimi and Uncle Cal? Then tomorrow after I pick you up we'll get ice cream."

That brought a sweet smile to Cord's face. "With marshmallows?"

"And a cherry on top." She kissed Colby's dark head. "Let's get jammies and your toothbrushes."

"And Bully," Colby said.

Her son loved the stuffed bull Carson had won for him at the fair last year. "Wouldn't dream of leaving Bully behind."

The boys tore off and Carolyn dialed her sister's number. Before Kimi even said hello, Carolyn said, "I need you to watch the boys tonight. That's all I can say right now."

But it wasn't Kimi on the line. Cal said, "No problem." A pause. "Is this about Carson?"

"Yes."

"Ah hell, Caro. Do you know what you're doin'?"

Did Cal know about Carson's recent activities at the Silver Spur? Did Kimi know that Carson might be stepping out on her? How long had it been going on? Was she the last to know and the laughingstock of the town? Sweet, obedient Carolyn McKay sitting at home popping out kids while Carson McKay ran wild and made her look like a fool? "Why didn't you tell me?"

"Because I don't know what's goin' on with him either, so don't assume nothin', okay? Carson has been a real jackass to me the last two months. If we ain't directly workin' with each other, then I avoid him 'cause I don't like the way he's been actin'. I'm glad you're callin' him on his shit."

This was why she loved Cal. He was loyal to his brother, while not willing to kiss his ass or overlook his faults. "Thanks. I'll drop the boys off in ten minutes."

After she returned home it took forty-five minutes to get ready. But she wasn't certain if dolling herself up would even matter. One last swipe with the eyeliner and another coat of siren red lipstick and she studied her reflection. Not a trace of frumpy housewife stared back at her. In fact, she looked so different in these clothes and heavy makeup she wondered if Carson would recognize her. She wondered why she didn't put more effort into looking like this all the time.

Turning sideways she only noticed a slight swell in her abdomen. When pregnant with Cord and Colby she hadn't started showing until five months.

Too bad she couldn't knock back a shot of whiskey to calm her nerves. She slipped off her wedding rings and headed to the car.

The Silver Spur had a decent amount of cars in the parking lot for a Thursday night. Carson's rig was parked up front. As if he'd been there a while.

Her heart raced as she sauntered in, but she held her head high. The normal buzz of anticipation filled the smoky air as the band tuned up. She hadn't been in here in ages and scored a spot at the end of the bar, within view of the back room. Standing on tiptoe, she saw a hatted head in the last booth, but with the amount of cowboy hats in Wyoming it could be anyone.

The bartender stopped in front of her. "What can I get you tonight, beautiful?"

"How about a whiskey Coke—hold the whiskey."

He grinned. "Comin' right up."

Carolyn didn't study the people to see if she'd recognize anyone. She leaned an elbow on the bar and checked out the space, as if it was the first time she'd been in.

"Here's your drink, darlin'."

She tried to pay him but he waved her money off. "You're doin' me a favor by classing this place up."

Two minutes later the first guy approached her. "You new to town?" he asked. "Because I haven't seen you in here before."

"You sure?"

"I'da remembered a fox like you."

She smiled. "You spend much time at the Spur?"

"More than I should, probably." He sipped his beer. "What's your name, pretty lady?"

"Sugar," she lied. "What's yours?"

"Tater."

"Interesting name. Are you from around here, Tater?"

"Yep. But I'm on the road a lot."

"Oh. Are you a truck driver?"

"Nope. I'm a rodeo cowboy."

Carson's choice words about the guys who ran the circuit jumped into her head and she affected an awed look—totally fake—not that the guy noticed. "For real? What's your specialty?"

"Ropin'." Then he launched into an explanation of the strategy involved that was complete crap.

Carolyn saw movement in the back room. Carson stood to let the dark-haired home-wrecker out of his side of the booth.

The band launched into "Your Cheatin' Heart".

How appropriate.

Despite the rage boiling her blood, she managed a calm, "Tater, I feel like dancing." It'd been a couple of years since Carson had taken her out. Since before Colby had been born.

"Anything you want, darlin'." He reached for her left hand—it felt weird not only to have her ring finger bare, but to hold another man's hand besides Carson's.

Tater didn't smash her body to his or let his hands wander. He was all about the dancing, performing all sorts of twists and fancy turns, dips and double twists. By the time they returned to the end of the bar, she was thirsty.

"Need another?" the bartender asked her.

"Water would be great."

"And a Coors," Tater said.

The bartender sent him a dirty look. "You oughten be here tonight, Glanzer. Shouldn't you be home with your family?"

"Not your business. Just hurry up with the damn drinks."

Okay. That was rude. And what did the bartender mean that Tater should be home with his family? Was he married with kids? Good Lord. Maybe this bar had become the place to openly cheat on your wife. When Carolyn caught him salivating over her cleavage, she fought the urge to cross her arms over her chest.

The band launched into another tune and couples headed for the dance floor.

"You're a good dancer, Sugar."

"Thanks. So are you. You have all kinds of moves I've never seen."

Tater leaned in, his eyes zeroed in on her breasts. "I have more moves than that. I'd love to show you the best ones. Course, those are done horizontally."

And...they weren't talking about dancing. Her cheeks flamed and she looked down. But her gaze landed on his gigantic buckle.

"Like what you see down there?"

Her head snapped up.

He laughed, as if he'd caught her checking out his crotch.

The bartender slid her drink over and handed Tater a bottle.

Carolyn was trying to come up with something that'd make Tater leave when someone pushed into her from behind, sending her careening into Tater. The glass crashed to the floor but not before water soaked her front side. It seemed everyone in the bar had turned around to look at them.

"Damn. Are you all right?"

She glanced up when Tater brushed droplets from her chest. Why was his other hand gripping her butt cheek? There wasn't water back there.

"Get your fucking hand off my wife's ass right fucking now."

Tater released her immediately. "Wife? What the hell is goin' on here?"

Carson was right in Tater's face. "Yes, she's my wife. Touch her again and I'll rip your fuckin' arms out of the sockets. Understand?"

"Sugar, you shoulda told me you were married. Not that I blame you for bein' out lookin' for something better, since this guy is an asshole."

"Shut your mouth," Carson snapped.

"Or what? You'll punch me? Bring it, fucker. I ain't been in a fight for weeks and I'm more than happy to take out that pent-up aggression on you."

Carson shoved him.

Tater started to charge but a big guy stepped between them, placing a meaty hand on both of their chests.

"Take it the fuck outside or I call the sheriff. Dig?"

After snagging his beer, Tater started walking backward. He grinned at Carolyn. "Fun while it lasted." He vanished into the crowd.

Immediately Carson wrapped his fingers around her upper arms and hauled her to the tips of her boots. "What the fuck are you doin' here?"

"Having a night out."

"Like hell you are. Get home where you belong."

"No."

"Tryin' my patience, woman."

"Your patience?" Carolyn jerked out of his hold. "Spare me. I'm the queen of patience when it comes to you. So where'd your friend go?"

"Who?"

"The woman I saw you with earlier. I didn't quite make it to the back booth to see if she was sucking you off or if you preferred to fuck her."

Carson's eyes widened.

"Surprised to hear me say that word?" She stepped in close enough to poke him in the chest. "Fuck, fuck, fuck, fuck, fuck, fuck, fuck. Fuck her and fuck you if you've been fucking her. How's that?

Did I get the fucking point across you fucking cheating asshole?"

"I'd never..." His face had turned mottled red and he looked ready to commit murder.

The bouncer returned and inserted himself between them. "Ma'am? Are you okay?"

"No, I am not okay. Not even close to okay."

"What can I do?"

"If you could get me some napkins so I can dry myself off that'd be appreciated."

"Sure thing. Be right back."

Carolyn reclaimed her place at the bar, giving Carson her back, thankful there weren't mirrors so he could see her face.

He didn't make a move toward her. Nor did he speak. But she sensed him seething.

Good. *Let's see how you fucking like being ignored, you dumb fucker.*

Another guy moved into the open space on her left. "Ma'am. You all right?"

Lord, save her from gentleman cowboys. "I'm fine. Just spilled on myself."

"That happens to me too when I drink tequila."

She released a brittle laugh. "Wish I could blame it on booze."

"Can I buy you a drink?"

Then Carson stepped up and loomed over the man. "I'll shove a bottle straight up your ass if you don't get the fuck away from my wife."

"Sorry, man. I thought—"

"You thought wrong. Beat it."

After the guy left, Carson moved in close enough she could smell the whiskey and cigarettes on his breath. "Goddammit, Carolyn, what are you doin' here?"

Somehow she'd masked the hurt and let her anger show. "You spend so much time here lately I wanted to experience the appeal of it for myself."

"Where are my sons?"

"In the car. Locked in the trunk. With guns and the candy I used to lure them in." She got nose to nose with him. "Don't you ever, ever, *ever* question that I'd put their safety, happiness and wellbeing above everything else in my life."

Shame flashed in his eyes. "I'm sorry."

"Yes, you are. You've been a sorry excuse for a husband and a father and I'm done putting up with it."

"What are you sayin'?"

"You know exactly what I'm saying."

"Carson? Is everything all right?" a female voice inquired.

He shook his head at whoever was behind her.

220

Carolyn turned, her stomach plummeting when she realized the dark haired woman she'd seen Carson with was Edie. The same woman she'd caught him with seven years ago. The same woman who'd taken every opportunity to make Carolyn miserable whenever they ran into each other.

Edie's gaze winged between them. Then she offered Carolyn a smirk. "I didn't know you were here."

"Obviously I am, so now you can buzz off."

"There's no need to be rude. Carson and I were just...talking."

"I don't care."

Edie's eyes went comically wide. "You don't believe me?"

"I believe I asked you to leave."

"I didn't mean to cause problems." Edie sent Carson a pleading look. "It's not what you think. I needed someone to talk to and a shoulder to cry on. And since Carson has such big shoulders...he obliged me."

Carson made an irritated sound.

As Carolyn studied Edie's smug face, the situation became clear. She suspected Edie had heard Carson had been hanging out at the Silver Spur a lot lately. And Edie knew perfectly well that the gossip mill would churn with news that she—the recent divorcée—was spending time alone in the back room with Carson McKay.

How long had it taken for the news to reach Carolyn?

One. Day.

So Carolyn knew Carson hadn't been stepping out on her—at least not with Edie. Given the size of this town? If he had been cheating on her, she would've heard about it long before now.

"I'll oblige you too by reminding you that Carson is my husband. He's a good man. But that's the thing, he's *my* man. *Mine.* He's not your friend, he's not your confidante, so back off."

She eyed Carolyn's wet blouse. "Apparently you've had too much to drink. No matter what you've heard—"

"Oh, I heard all right. The gossip about you two being cozied up last night already got back to me."

Carson swore behind her.

"I'm here to put a stop to it."

"Honey, I don't have any control over gossip. If folks around here are saying your man is looking to scratch an itch that he ain't getting scratched at home? You can't blame me if he's sniffing around because I got me some nice claws."

That did it.

Carolyn took a swing at her and was the little witch ever surprised when the punch landed right on her smart, lying mouth.

Edie stumbled and Carolyn struck again.

This time she socked Edie in the gut with everything she had. When Edie doubled over, Carolyn pounced on her, knocking her to the floor.

Carolyn went down with her, on top of her, continuing to strike her with body shots even when Edie curled into a ball to escape the blows.

Hands landed on her back and Carolyn twisted away, determined to keep swinging until her fist connected with solid mass.

While the anger still churned inside her, Carolyn grabbed a handful of Edie's hair and tried to jerk her head up. "Look at me," she demanded.

Edie shook her head.

Carolyn bent closer to Edie's ear. "Look at me or I will start yanking out chunks of your hair in bloody clumps."

That got her attention. Edie moved just enough that Carolyn could see her scared eyes and her bloodied face.

"The reason you weren't successful in seducing my husband is because he'd sooner fuck a diseased sheep than you. Stay away from me and mine or I will finish this and fuck you up until you're unrecognizable. Do you understand?"

She nodded.

"Say it out loud so I and everyone else can hear you."

"Yes."

Breathing hard, Carolyn slowly stood. Pushing the hair back from her face, she noticed a circle surrounding them. But the inner circle was all women, who seemed to be stopping the men from breaking up the fight. She recognized several of the women, and they were nodding at her with approval.

Holy. Cow.

"Back up and get outta the way," the bouncer barked and crouched next to Edie.

The bartender stomped over. "That's it. So much for me thinking you'd class up the joint—you started a damn bar fight! Get out. Don't ever come back because you are banned for life."

Her jaw dropped. "What do you mean banned for life?"

"Just what I said. I ever see your face in here again I'm calling the sheriff."

Infuriated, Carolyn threw up her hands. "I'm banned?"

"Yes."

"Is she banned?" She pointed to Edie, still curled up on the floor.

"No."

"Why not?"

"Because she's bleeding; you're not."

Carolyn opened her mouth to argue or maybe lunge at the guy who'd decided—unfairly—to toss *her* out, when Carson's strong arm created a band across her chest.

"If my wife is banned, then you'll never see me in here again, understand?"

The bartender went bug-eyed. "She's your *wife*?"

"Damn straight she is."

"Sorry, man, we'll miss ya, but I can't let this slide."

She jabbed her elbow into Carson's gut with enough force he loosened his hold on her. "Fine. I'm gone." Holding her chin up, she marched to the front door and the crowd parted for her.

The shame she expected to feel? Strangely absent.

Maybe for the first time she understood why her husband liked to fight. It was cleansing.

She'd almost made it to the parking lot when hands landed on her hips and pushed her into the shadow of the building, then spun her around.

Carson wrapped his hand around the back of her neck, holding her in place. The fierceness in his eyes...wow. Been a long time since he'd looked at her that way.

"That was the most magnificent thing I've ever seen. Except for the two times you brought our sons into the world."

"I'm mad at you, Carson McKay. So don't you dare try and charm your way out of this mess."

"I'm not. I'm tellin' it like I saw it, sugar. You were spectacular. *Spectacular.* Callin' me on my shit. Not backin' down from me or anyone else. Reminding me of why I fell in love with you."

"Maybe you ought to remind *me* why *I* fell in love with you," she challenged. "Because a man who claims to love his wife doesn't avoid coming home."

"I know."

"What is going on with you?"

"Besides the obvious that I've been drinkin' too much?" He pressed his forehead to hers. "I've been a lousy husband and a shitty father." He inhaled. Exhaled. "Fuck. It's like stabbing myself in the heart even sayin' that to you because you are such a damn good wife and mother. You are the most important thing in my world. And if I lose you..."

Carolyn watched his chin wobble as he fought to retain control. Her gut clenched and her heart hurt to see this strong man start to crumble. But she let him struggle.

"Truth is, my life is over if I'm dumb enough to lose you. So I ain't gonna let that happen. Ever. I fucked up but I'll do whatever it takes to fix this. Whatever it takes." He stared into her eyes. "Say you'll give me another chance."

"Then you need to come clean. During all the time you've spent away from home and at the bar, did you step out on me?" Her breath remained trapped in her lungs as she waited his answer.

"No. *Fuck* no. I'd never do that to you. Or to us."

"So Edie...?"

"I swear I had no idea what she was doin'. Last night she and two of her friends sat at the booth in the back room while they were playing pool. When her friends left she was sitting next to me and she didn't move. By then I was pretty deep in the bottle. Doubt I spoke more than a dozen words to her. So what she said about cryin' on my shoulder was complete bullshit."

"That doesn't explain tonight."

His eyes brimmed with anguish. "She told me she was worried her ex would show up and asked if she could sit with me for a bit. That happened when Charlie was drinkin' with me. Then he took off with her friend."

"And Charlie didn't think anything of leaving his drunken brother alone with a recent divorcée?"

"Charlie knows I worship you. He knows even if Edie had been nekkid I wouldn't have touched her."

Men were so stupid sometimes. "You know that doesn't mean *she* wouldn't have tried to touch *you*."

He blinked as if that hadn't occurred to him. "I see that now and I'm really sorry I didn't see it before."

"Do you have any idea know how horrible it is to get a phone call from a friend who's seen you out with another woman?" Her tone turned bitter. "Then I get here and find out it's Edie? That made it worse. You know the crap she's said to me over the years. So is this one of those times you tell me you don't give a damn what anyone around here says or thinks about you?"

"No." He brought his eyes in line with hers. "*No.* I give a damn because this hurt you. *I* hurt you. I have to live with that. I have to prove that it'll never happen again."

"There's an easy way to prove it."

"How?"

"As of right now your going to the bar days are over, Carson McKay. Not just the Silver Spur but every other bar in the vicinity and the entire state of Wyoming."

He said, "Done," without a moment's hesitation.

"You want to drink? You'll drink at home. You want to go out? You'll go out with me. Those are my stipulations for us moving on from this."

"That won't be a problem. I want to be the man you deserve." Carson framed her face in his callused hands. "I love you, Carolyn. You are it for me. You have been since the moment I met you. There ain't a woman alive that can give me what you do."

"What's that?"

"Passion that has marked my heart and soul as yours, and yours alone."

This brusque man wasn't big on professing his feelings beyond telling her he loved her. So when he said things off the cuff and from a place of truth? She cherished every word.

Then his mouth was on hers. His hunger, his driving need didn't surprise her; it inflamed her.

She shoved her hands into his hair, knocking his hat to the ground. Carson didn't pause in the ferocious kisses; if anything, he kissed her harder. Pushing her backward until her spine connected with the building.

"There's another way you can prove it," she panted against his throat. "Fuck me. Right here, right now."

"But, Caro, if anyone comes out here—"

She grabbed his chin in her hand, forcing him to meet her gaze. "They'll see you fucking me—*your wife*, not some two-bit bar whore. And I don't give a damn who knows that you wanted me—*your wife*, so desperately that you fucked me right outside the front door."

"Good God, do you have any idea how fucking much I love you?"

"Show me."

After he thoroughly ravished her with intense kisses that left her breathless, his mouth skated down her neck. His razor-stubbled cheeks scraped her skin, which he soothed with sucking kisses. "Fuck, woman. Never get enough of you," he panted. "I'll be an old man of a hundred and five and I'll still want this—need this—from you."

She moaned when he zeroed in on the section of her neck that nearly sent her into orgasm. "More."

He sucked harder, letting his teeth and tongue come into play while his fingers found the first button on her blouse. He yanked and the snaps gave way, exposing her torso to her belly button. Then he placed his hand over her heart and she went weak-kneed. She spiraled even deeper under his spell when his fingers slipped beneath her bra and started plucking her nipple.

Against the upper swell of her breast, he growled, "Will I find my pussy wet if you put my hand between your legs?"

She loved that he called her pussy his. "Yes."

"Do it."

The shock of his demand fed the inferno raging between them. She circled her fingers around his wrist and tugged his hand beneath her skirt.

Carson's kiss stayed at the teasing level as he pushed two fingers inside her and swept his thumb over her clit.

The band began to play again and the bass from the speakers reverberated against her spine. It seemed as if her blood mimicked the *thump, thump, thump* rhythm of the bass. She let her head fall back and squeezed her eyes shut as her midsection tingled and tightened. So close. So, so, so close... How long had it been since passion had exploded between them this fast?

"Caro. Look at me."

"Carson, please—"

"Sugar, I need you to look at me when you come."

She opened her eyes and fastened her gaze to his. There was the look she'd missed seeing on him; his complete possession of her, his utter devotion to her.

That's all it took.

Her nails scored the back of his neck when the orgasm steamrolled her. The slow, steady *thump, thump, thump* prolonged each throb around his fingers and against his wickedly stroking thumb. Not until the last pulse did she look away.

Carson's mouth brushed her ear. "Turn around." As soon as she did, he stretched her body out, keeping her hands against the building. "I wanna fuck you face to face so I can see that look of bliss when you come again." He nuzzled her neck. "But I need it fast and hard and deep. I need to remind you, to remind myself that you married a man, not a loser who drowns his sorrows in a bottle. A man whose idea of heaven is bein' balls deep in this hot cunt. A man who'll never give you reason to doubt him again."

With one hand he tilted her head so he could kiss her, while the other hand pushed her skirt to her hips. Then he angled his pelvis, connecting his hardness with her soft, wet tissues.

"Pull your panties out of my way," he growled against her lips.

Managing to brace herself with one hand, she reached down and pulled the soaked crotch of her underwear aside.

The hot, slick tip of his erection bumped her hand before finding her opening. Carolyn waited for—craved—that first thrust as he impaled her fully.

But Carson eased himself inside her little by little, changing the kiss to a soft sweep of damp lips and the heated exchange of breath. Then he was seated inside her, waiting.

"Carson?"

"Promise me you'll give me another chance."

"I will."

"Promise me you won't leave me."

"I won't."

"Tell me you still love me."

"I still love you."

That's when he unfurled all that coiled male need. Pounding into her like a battering ram.

Oh how she'd missed this. Carson's sexual energy unleashed on her. His breath hot in her ear, his whiskey-rough voice telling her how good her pussy felt. His hand kneading her breast and one squeezing her hip. His mouth on the nape of her neck sending every fine hair on end with deceptively gentle kisses.

He knew what got to her. Knew how to propel her to the edge where she teetered precariously. Where one nudge would send her soaring into pleasure.

"One more, sugar. Give it to me."

Then he pulled out and followed the seam of her sex with the broad tip of his cock. His hand slid down to hold the thick head against her clit. Every pump of his hips sent the rim rubbing against that swollen nub exactly where she needed it. Faster and faster until that dizzying sensation coalesced, spinning her into orbit in a hot throbbing rush. His mouth caught hers in a brutal kiss as he muffled her cries. As she came back down, she feared her legs would give out.

"I've got you, beautiful. I've always got you."

He pushed his cock back through her plumped folds and he reentered her in one deep thrust that caused her clit to spasm one more time.

The long strokes became short jabs. There was no warning besides a groaned, "Fuck," and Carson's deep rumble in her ear as his orgasm overtook him.

She clamped her inner muscles down on his shaft and felt every scalding spurt of his seed. Every hard pulse.

But there were no sweet kisses or tender moments in the aftermath. The front door slammed against the building and people started streaming out.

Carson had her skirt down and her panties back in place. He turned her around and said, "Your shirt," while he zipped and buckled. He reached down to retrieve his hat.

When he realized she hadn't started to fix her clothing, he offered her a soft smile. "Flustered ya, didn't I?" Then he tackled the snaps on her shirt himself.

Such a sweet man; sometimes she forgot how much she needed that tender care from him. "You always fluster me when you put your hands on me. You have since that first time."

Their eyes met.

"Let's go home and I'll put my hands on you some more."

As they crossed the parking lot, she said, "How much whiskey did you have tonight?"

"A lot. Then I went completely stone cold sober the instant I saw you."

"I imagine your wife going on a rampage in your favorite watering hole will do that to you." She stopped. "You do realize us banging against the side of a honkytonk doesn't change the fact that we have a lot to talk about?"

"Yeah." He smirked. "But I love me some hot makeup sex. And that you demanded it from me? Made it even better, sugar."

"And don't you forget it. Get in the car."

"I'm fine to drive my truck."

Carolyn shook her head and pointed at the passenger side. He looked about to argue, but thought better of it and climbed in.

On the way home the silence between them was especially awkward. Carolyn kept both hands on the steering wheel and her eyes on the road. In her peripheral vision she saw him gazing out the window, his face unreadable. When she dropped her right hand on the seat, Carson immediately picked it up, kissed her knuckles and kept hold of it.

Oh, troubled man of mine, what's going through that brain of yours?

Carson seemed surprised when they pulled up to the trailer. "Aren't we stoppin' to get the boys?"

"And wake Cal and Kimi when they were nice enough to take them at a moment's notice? No. I'll send you over to get them in the morning so you can properly apologize to my sister and your brother for being an inconsiderate jackass and thank them for taking care of our sons."

"Caro—"

"I don't want to hear it. Right now I want you to pull your jeans and your boxers down to your knees."

He lifted that one, sexy eyebrow. "Why? You gonna spank me?"

"You'd deserve it. Drop your drawers, *sugar*, I ain't gonna ask again," she mimicked in his cowboy drawl.

"This mean and nasty streak from that sugar sweet mouth of yours is givin' me wood," he said as he unbuckled his belt and tugged his clothing down to the tops of his boots.

"Undo all the snaps on your shirt and spread your thighs as wide as the seat." She held her hand up. "And no, you don't get to ask questions. Just do what you're told."

"Yes, ma'am."

He hadn't been kidding about getting hard again. She twisted sideways in her seat, rising onto her knees, bracing one hand on his thigh and the other on his rock-hard abdomen. She sucked his shaft to the root, loving the musky scent of his pubic hair and the taste of her sex juices mixed with his as she held him deep in her throat.

"Jesus Christ, Carolyn!"

She sank her teeth down, showing her displeasure at his choice of words.

"Shit. Sorry. But damn, woman, I wasn't expectin' that."

She couldn't help but smile as she started to work him over. Using her teeth, her tongue, her wet mouth to make him groan, to make him sweat.

To make him beg.

Carolyn reached between his legs to fondle his balls. Then she brought them up and sucked on them. One at a time, then together, letting her face rub on the side of his shaft.

His belly rippled and she felt his legs quivering.

She licked up the front side of his cock, flicking her tongue around the rim but not in the spot he wanted. She delved her tongue into the slit, lapping up his taste.

Carson gently pushed her hair over her shoulder so he could

watch her.

Then she showed him all her passion and skill, but no mercy. She started a rhythm with long, deep strokes and gradually quickened her pace so her mouth only slid halfway down. Sucking. Swirling her tongue around the head then back to that fast movement in and out of her mouth. No hands, just her lips and teeth and tongue and hard suctioning power to drive him to that pinnacle of pleasure.

His hands landed on her head, grasping handfuls of her hair as his hips bucked up. A stream of muttered curses rent the air.

Carolyn lowered her mouth to the root again, deep throating him, swallowing around the head of his cock as he started to come. She slid back to the tip and sucked the last spurt, needing the familiar taste of him on her tongue.

She kissed her way up his torso, smiling at how hard his lungs labored and how fast his heart raced. She loved to nuzzle and stroke him after a blowjob, but this time she gripped his chin, forcing his attention to her. "Carson."

"Hang on. Lemme get my head unscrambled."

"No. Look at me. Now."

Those beautiful dazed blue eyes opened.

She grabbed his softening cock and lightly squeezed. "Who does this belong to?"

"You."

"And who am I?"

"My wife."

She inched closer to him. "Remember that the next time floozies are sniffing around you. Remember who fucked you outside a bar. Remember who sucked you off in her car. Remember that you'll never find a woman who gives you what I do in and out of bed. Remember you're mine and I take care of what's mine. But if you *ever* fuck around on me I will cut off your cock and wear it as a necklace." She smashed her mouth to his, her kiss brutal. Relentless.

Carson's rough-tipped fingers tenderly caressed her cheeks, her throat, drawing her out of the place where she had something to prove.

His gentleness was her undoing. His mouth moved over hers sweetly as he whispered promises against her lips. "I love you more than life itself. You don't ever have to worry that I'll stray. You own me; heart, soul, mind, body and cock. Forever."

"Good. Come on, let's go inside."

He walked behind her. When she slipped the key in the lock, he kissed the back of her neck. "Need you. Skin to skin. Slow and sweet."

Turned out she needed that too.

Afterward, they were spooned together on the couch, her back to his front. "That was...like it always used to be between us."

Carson kissed the ball of her shoulder. "Yep." He stopped idly stroking her nipple to spread his hand out on her belly.

Somehow her earlier self-assurance that she hadn't started showing yet was a lie. She had a fairly substantial pooch.

"Carson?"

"Mmm?"

"I'm pregnant again."

"I know you are."

Carolyn turned toward him. "How?"

He kissed her nose. "We've been through this twice before, so I recognized the signs. I'm bettin' it happened that night...?"

"During calving when you were nearly frozen solid and I used blankets and body heat to get you warmed up."

"You got me downright hot. Three times if I recall correctly."

"Four if you count the blowjob."

He laughed. "Of course it counts. Speaking of...you sucking me off in the car pretty much blew my mind."

"Been a while since I've done that. It's a little hard to do with the boys along." Her smile faded. "You okay about the baby?"

"Completely okay. So that makes you..."

"About four months along. I've been holding off going to the doctor."

"Why?"

She shrugged. "Like you said. I've been down this road twice."

Carson became quiet and she knew he didn't buy her reasoning. Finally he said, "You're not goin' because of money."

"It's not a big deal. By the time I'm closer to delivery and I need to see the doctor you'll have sent the cattle to market and we will have the money."

"You have no idea how much this eats at me."

"What?"

"Bein' a shitty provider for my family because the cattle business is a damn crapshoot on a good year. Christ. I can't afford to get you the proper medical care. We're still livin' hand to mouth and in this cramped damn trailer. Happy as I am that we're adding to our family, where are we gonna put another kid?"

Carolyn rolled to face him. She searched his eyes and saw such guilt and shame. "Carson. Sweetheart. What's going on? You're never so negative about ranching."

"Maybe it's never seemed this dire before."

"Is that why you've been drinking?"

"Yeah. As much as I know it don't help, it dulled that panicked feeling."

"How long have you been panicked?"

"Since the cattle sale last year barely covered our yearly operating expenses."

She pressed her palm over his heart. "Why didn't you say anything to me?"

"Because it's my job to worry about money, not yours."

"There's your problem. It's not a *you* thing or a *me* thing, but an *us* thing. We've been down this keeping secrets road before and it didn't go well for us, remember?"

He kissed her furrowed brow. "I don't know how the hell I forgot."

"So talk to me."

"Dad is still expanding the ranch, which is good in theory, but in reality, it don't make sense to buy land when it'll sit unused because we can't afford to buy extra cattle. Not only that, we don't have the manpower to run more livestock. Cal and Charlie are good workers. Casper sucks most days. Dad ain't as spry as he used to be. And I can't work anymore than I already am."

Some of what he was saying made sense; some didn't. Carolyn decided right then she needed to be more involved with the ins and outs of the cattle business.

"To make matters worse, whenever I question him, he reminds me the name on the land deed was his and the decisions about the ranch are still his. I've been thinking if I'm ready to pop my old man in the mouth every day, if maybe it's time to go."

"Go?"

Carson tucked her hair behind her ear. "Sometimes I wonder what it'd be like just to pack up and go somewhere else. Be someone else."

How long had her man been wrestling with this? It tied her up in knots that he had kept it all inside. "I like who you are, Carson McKay. I really like that you're talking to me about this. But I have to ask why it's the first time you've opened up to me in pretty much the last year?"

He kept stroking her lower back. "I know how happy you were when Cal and Kimi got married. Your sister is back in your life and she lives next door. And don't take this the wrong way, sugar, but I suspect you and Kimi share everything and there's some stuff between a husband and a wife that shouldn't be shared. Especially if that sister is married to my brother. He don't need to be findin' out stuff about the ranch and finances secondhand from his wife—it should come from me. So I'll admit I've kept the problem with the ranch stuff close to the vest."

He didn't say *kept it from you*, but he didn't have to. "I'd never do that. Sure, Kimi and I gossip, but it's about our family—and I haven't shared those West stories with you. Sometimes we talk about people at church or in the community that annoy us. We talk a lot about babies and the boys. We swap household tips, recipes, and sewing and knitting patterns—things you'd tune out fifteen seconds into the conversation."

He smiled.

Carolyn put her hands on Carson's cheeks. "My loyalty is to you.

From the minute we married, now, and in the future."

Silence stretched between them. Then in that gruff voice she adored, he said, "Sweet God in heaven, what did I ever do to deserve you?" He gifted her with a kiss so full of love her tears arose.

"Sugar, don't cry."

"Get used to it. You know how much I bawl when I'm pregnant and hormonal."

"Never again. I'll never give you cause to doubt me again. I promise."

"I've heard that before."

"I know. But I'm done. It's past time I step up to the responsibilities of bein' a father that our sons can be proud of. Be the kind of son my dad takes pride in. My priority is to make sure you're happy above all else."

When the image wavered, Carolyn screamed *no.*

The next part was the good part. Where Carson lived up to his promises and then some. Where their marriage became stronger than ever. Where they added to their family, a baby boy they'd named Colton who was the spitting image of his father.

And like before, when she boomeranged back to the dark place, she questioned whether she'd ever really left it and if her mind was just playing cruel tricks on her.

Chapter Twenty-One

So Carson was thinking about sex.

Nothing new there.

But he wasn't fantasizing about the hot and sweaty pulse pounding moment when bodies connected, but the importance of touch. How even in their most intimate moments, he had to have his hands on Carolyn. Feeling her skin and reveling in her reaction to how he touched her.

So although he caressed her arm every second of those five minutes every hour, it wasn't the connection he needed from her.

Reciprocation.

During his last hourly visit he'd barely spoken to her. He'd held her hand, willing her to squeeze it. He'd stroked her cheek, silently and stupidly begging her to turn toward his touch. He couldn't lower his protective face shield to nuzzle her temple, hoping for just a hint of the scent of her skin or her makeup or her shampoo. A shower-cap looking apparatus covered her head from her eyebrows to the nape of her neck. It was a wound care protection that kept the wound draining and the area around it sterile.

Today her stillness bothered him. It reminded him of the days following his father's first heart attack. The doctors had kept Jed sedated and on oxygen. Back then diagnosis took much longer, so for those few days, he and his brothers had no idea whether their father would live or die.

As hard as that wait-and-see time had dragged on for them, it'd had one positive outcome. When Jed McKay finally came to, he realized he wasn't invincible. He understood changes had to be made to the existing structure of the McKay Ranch. So in the months that followed, Jed parceled out individual sections to all four of his sons. Carson ended up with the most land and cattle. Casper grumbled about it even when Jed explained the pro-rating system he'd been compiling over the years.

So the bottom line was Carson's hard work hadn't gone unnoticed and he'd finally been rewarded for it.

"Carson."

He snapped to. His eyes flew open and he realized his daughter-in-law was right in his face. "Channing. Warn a guy, next time, will ya?"

"I said your name like four times."

He eased back and scrubbed his hands over his face. Three days' worth of whiskers scratched his palms. His neck hurt, his eyes burned, his stomach growled, his hip ached. Hard to believe he slept at all when he felt like a caged animal. "Sorry. I'm a little out of it."

"That's understandable. I'm assuming no change in Carolyn's condition?"

"Nope."

Channing backed off and perched in the chair across from him. She eyed the stacks of magazines. "I'm glad Quinn brought you a distraction."

"Is that why you're here, darlin'? To distract me?"

She cocked her head. "Not even close. But we'll get to that in a bit."

"Now you're scarin' me."

"The almighty Carson McKay scared of little ol' me?" She laughed. "That'll be the day."

"So what's on your mind?"

"Besides the sad fact that the most thoughtful, generous, caring, sweetest, fiercest woman I know is lying in a hospital bed, fighting for her life? That's pretty much all that's on my mind, and anyone else's mind who loves her. And who loves you."

Uncomfortable, he looked down at his hands. "I know how Colby feels about her, Channing. But that don't change nothin'. He can't..." *See her like that.* He could at least admit to himself that it wasn't only the threat of germs keeping everyone out of her hospital room, but the knowledge that Carolyn had always taken such pride in her appearance and she wouldn't want people gawking at her like she'd become a science experiment.

"I didn't show up to browbeat you about the parameters you set for your adult children regarding *your* wife; that, as adults, they should accept without question and understand since they're all married themselves."

He glanced up at her. "Well, that's a relief."

"However...I am here to browbeat you about something else."

Shit. "What now?"

"While I know you've not let your personal hygiene slide entirely, you're skating on that thin line. You haven't been home, which means you've been wearing the same clothes since you rode here in the ambulance...three days ago."

"So?"

"So, you need to go home and shower, shave off the raggedy beard you're sporting, and put on some clean clothes."

He bristled—rightly so. "What part of *I ain't leavin' her* is confusing to you kids?"

Again, Channing got right in his face. "What part of you smell bad, you look like a hobo, and after three days of constant wear, your dirty, germ-laden clothes might be putting your wife at risk is confusing to you? Not to mention that Carolyn would seriously kick your ass if she saw you out in public like this."

That gave him pause. Serious pause.

"You said yourself that nothing has changed with her condition and nothing will change for several more days. The doctors won't attempt to wake her while you're gone. So take a couple of hours. Get some fresh air. Clear your head and clean up, you'll feel better for it. Plus, you left in an awful damn hurry so do a walkthrough of your house and give yourself piece of mind that all is safe on the home front. Get your cell phone charger since your phone is dead. And yes, I know that because my husband has bitched about not being able to get in touch with you. Not that you want to talk to him or your other kids. But at least if you had your phone charged you could check on cattle futures and play Farmville on Facebook."

Right. Playing games on his phone? Never gonna happen. The only reason he'd gotten a smart phone was so he could get pictures of his grandkids.

But he could admit that itchy feeling between his shoulder blades had been building all day. Seemed a lifetime since he'd seen something besides these walls. He imagined filling his lungs with real air, not this sterilized oxygen.

"If nothing else, grab some fresh clothes for Carolyn to wear home from the hospital while you're there."

That cinched it for him. He'd go. Wait. He didn't have a vehicle here. But Channing did. "You'll lend me your SUV?"

"I'll go you one better." She reached in her pocket and handed over his set of keys. "Good thing you ranchers are a trusting lot and leave your keys in your truck."

"Damn good thing. Did Colby take you over to our place?"

Channing rolled her eyes. "Are you kidding? AJ picked me up and dropped me off. Your sons are being a special brand of difficult right now, so we're letting them stew and following our own agenda." She jabbed her finger at him. "Don't you dare rat us out, Carson McKay."

"You have my word I won't. Thanks. I..." His gaze moved to the door to Carolyn's room, indecision tearing at him. Last night, Lissa, the nurse who'd warned him it'd be better if he didn't leave the ICU waiting room for the duration, had recanted her original advice and told him to get some fresh air today.

"Go," Channing said softly. "I will sit right here in your spot until you return. I won't let anyone in. I won't go in myself." She took his hand. "Let me be your fill-in guard dog for a few hours. Please. You deserve a break, and stinky man, you *need* a shower."

Carson squeezed her hand. "Bold as brass you are, girlie. I never woulda thought you had it in you. Then again, you gave me what-for when I asked about you and Colby that weekend we first met in Cheyenne."

"You are an intimidating man. I knew you didn't think I was right for him, but you didn't know me, and it just made me mad that you assumed."

"I remember. But you've proved me wrong over the years, and that's gotta feel good."

When she cocked her head again, he knew he was in for it.

"What?"

"You may feel that way now, but after Colby's injury, whenever I called to check on him, you didn't deliver my messages. Why is that?"

"Stuff like that needed to be said in person, not passed from you to me to my son."

"So you weren't trying to keep me from Colby?"

"Of course I was."

Her lips flattened.

"But it didn't work, did it? And darlin', if I would've scared you off? Then you weren't meant to be with him anyway."

"You sneaky-assed man. I hope Carolyn punished you good for your meddling. Colby said she could put the screws to you way worse than he ever could."

Carson thought back to the hours he'd spent digging Carolyn's two new flower beds—in an area she knew was comprised mainly of rock, making it backbreaking work for him. She told him every time he looked at those beds of blooms in the future that he'd remember that given the right foundation and a lot of care, beautiful things could sprout from even the rockiest ground.

In that moment he ached with how much he needed her; every bone, every blood cell, every breath, every fiber of his being.

"Carson?" Channing rubbed his shoulder. "Are you all right?"

He cleared his throat. "Seems I get sucked into memories pretty damn easily. After fifty years with her, there are lots of memories to scroll through."

"I imagine."

"Thanks for kickin' my behind. Carolyn would be proud you done it in her stead. You're a good woman, Channing. My son's lucky to have you." He paused. "So am I." Pushing to his feet, he ignored the sharp pain in his ass after sitting in one place for so long. "I'll be back. And when I get back, we're gonna talk about why Gib is usin' a second-rate horse for ropin' when it's obvious the boy has skills and needs to upgrade."

"Talk to his father about that."

"I'll be talkin' to *you*, bein's that his father and me ain't currently speakin'."

She laughed. "Anything else?"

"Seems Austin has roped Beau, Spencer and Dimitri into tryin' to convince me to take them all fishin'. Where'd they get the fool idea that I'm the grandpa who enjoys sittin' out in the sun, slapping mosquitos and baiting hooks?"

"Not from me. But Gib, Braxton and Miles tried to get Austin to remember the time you and Carolyn took all four boys camping in that motor home you had for what...two days?"

"Don't remind me. I'll figure out something fun to do with them but it ain't gonna be fishin' or campin'. I learned my lesson there. How's my youngest grandson?" Channing had suffered a miscarriage when Keely was pregnant with her first child. At that point both Colby and Channing thought they were done adding to their family. So no one was more surprised—or thrilled—than they were three years later when their little "oops" Duncan was born.

Channing sighed. "He's the perfect baby. I am so lucky to have his brothers as my helpers because I'm so much more tired having a kid at my age than I was when I had Gib. Colby is a lot more mellow around him too, especially now that Duncan is six months old and doing cute baby stuff." She nudged Carson with her knee. "Talia is still asking when you're coming over for another tea party."

Carson smiled, thinking about Colby's shocked face last year when he'd walked in on Grandpa and Talia having a tea party, complete with Grandpa wearing a rhinestone crown and a glittery purple feather boa.

Colby had frozen in the doorframe, his mouth hinged open like a busted gate. "Dad? What's goin' on?"

"Me'n Princess Talia are havin' tea."

"B-but..." Colby's wide-eyed gaze had winged between them. "Since when do you do that sort of thing?"

Carson raised his eyebrow. "Since my last child was a girl who liked havin' tea parties and her mama couldn't always oblige her. And since I've been blessed with six granddaughters who are old enough to host tea parties, and three more girlies that'll be of that age soon enough. Why?"

"You did this with Keely?"

"More times than I can count." Carson pretended to sip his tea. "You oughta try it. Talia makes a mean pot of tea."

"Carson?" Channing prompted.

"Sorry. Told ya I've been tripping down memory lane."

"It's okay." Channing settled in his chair with a stack of magazines. "Get going."

Carson walked out of the hospital in a daze.

The sun shone from a cloudless blue sky. A soft breeze rippled the leaves on the trees ringing the parking lot. He squinted at the vehicles lined up in neat rows, searching for the familiar tailgate with the extended ball hitch.

No sign of his truck.

Where the devil had Channing parked it?

Rather than wander aimlessly, he hit the panic button on the key fob and followed the bleating horn noise to his dusty Dodge.

The interior was the same mess. He adjusted the seat and the rearview mirror and pushed up the sun visor.

Carolyn's sunglasses fell onto the dash. He snatched them up, staring at the black plastic dotted with rhinestones, overwhelmed by the absence of her. The little things might just do him in. Set him on that path of tears he'd managed to avoid. So far he hadn't broken down entirely, not out of some macho need to show no emotion, but simply because he feared if he started crying he wouldn't be able to stop.

Get moving. The sooner you get this done the sooner you can come back to her.

Starved, he hit the drive-thru at McDonald's. After that, he stopped into a convenience store and bought a pack of cigarettes. Whenever stress got to him, he smoked. Carolyn never judged him—she'd always claimed she'd rather him smoke every once in a while than be a fulltime tobacco chewer. He hadn't kicked that habit entirely either. Some days he needed a pinch of Redman—not that he told his wife that, but she probably knew anyway.

The nicotine from those first few puffs gave him a head rush. But he'd made the trip from Spearfish on I-90 heading toward Sundance so many times over the years he could've driven it with his eyes closed.

His thoughts jumped from one thing to another, but they never strayed far from Carolyn. If she had any awareness at all. If she was suffering any pain—despite the doctor's assertions the medications handled that.

He didn't meet any vehicles on the road that led to the ranch. Out of habit he checked out the pasture on his left, even when he knew the cattle had been moved to different grazing areas weeks ago.

Before Carson turned into the driveway, he pulled up to the mailbox and grabbed the stack of mail that'd accumulated over the past few days. Then he whipped a U-turn and headed up the gravel road that would bring him home.

Home.

He'd lived in this house most of his life. From birth until age eighteen. Then he and Caro and their oldest three boys had moved in after Jed's heart attack and this place had become too much house for one man. As the oldest McKay heir, albeit only by a few minutes, he'd stood first in line to inherit. His only brother who'd complained about that was Casper—until their father pointed out that over the last decade, Casper, Charlie and Cal had received houses and Carson hadn't.

So their dad had taken over Carson and Carolyn's trailer and this had become their home.

As he sat and stared through the dirty windshield, he remembered the day they'd moved in...

They'd left the boys with Cal and Kimi. The back of his pickup was loaded down with boxes. Even after nine years of marriage, they didn't have much stuff to move because they'd had no room for much besides the necessities in their cramped trailer. Carolyn hadn't complained when her sister and both her sisters-in-law had actual houses; she'd just made do.

She wouldn't have to make do any longer. If Carson had his way, she wouldn't have to make do with less than what she deserved ever again.

After they'd pulled up, Carolyn hadn't bounded out of the truck with the enthusiasm he expected. He glanced at her, sitting in the passenger's seat, staring at the house with the oddest expression on her face. "Sugar, you okay?"

"I don't know. There's part of me that can't fathom this enormous house is really ours now."

Carson reached for her hand. "It is." He kissed her fingertips. "So how about we go check it out?"

Carolyn managed a wobbly smile, as if she was trying not to cry. "Okay."

They met at the start of the sidewalk and paused, reaching for each other's hands at the same time. Side by side they walked up the wooden steps to the covered porch. He studied details with a keener eye now that he owned the place. The front door needed fixed; it definitely needed a coat of paint. As did all the wood trim around the windows. Probably Carolyn would like a screen door at the front of the house to catch the evening breeze, so that'd be first on his agenda.

But the very first thing...

Carson turned her toward him. He kissed her very softly and murmured, "Ready?" against her lips.

"Very ready."

"Good. Hang on." Then he swept her into his arms and carried her inside.

He knew she appreciated his romantic gesture when she nuzzled his throat and sighed. After setting her on her feet, he took her beautiful face in his hands and said, "Welcome home, Mrs. McKay."

Her tears fell as she fit her mouth to his and she gifted him with a kiss filled with sweet gratitude.

It'd struck him hard then, as it did every so often, that ranching was his livelihood, but this woman was his life, his heart, his home. Loving her had shaped him into the man he'd become.

Carolyn broke free of his hold with a soft laugh. "Sorry. This is all just too much."

"It's everything you deserve." He kissed her again. "Ready to check out your house?"

She smiled. "Kitchen first."

"Of course." He enjoyed watching her prowl the enormous space. Opening cupboards and running her hands over the counters with an expression akin to awe.

Finally she looked at him. "It's so big."

"That's what all men love to hear."

She swatted his biceps. "I can't believe your dad left us all the dishes and pots and pans."

"He won't need 'em. This is the one room he didn't clean out after Ma died."

"We won't need to buy anything besides food to stock this kitchen." She looked at him curiously. "What else did Jed leave behind?"

"Pretty much everything with the exception of his favorite chair and TV," Carson admitted. "And to be honest, he's relieved we're movin' in. He said he was tired of rattling around in this big old house like a lone BB in a shell."

"He apologized to me that the house needs so much cleaning. But I don't mind. I'll know every nook and cranny by the time I'm done."

"Come on." He kissed her forehead. "Let's see what you've got to work with."

Carson listened with amusement as Carolyn rattled off the changes she wanted to make. The living room furniture would do for now, but she envisioned something far less formal for a house with three boys. She loved the dining room and swore they'd eat every meal in here and not at the small table in the kitchen. She commented on stripping wallpaper and adding new paint. Every room needed new rugs as well as different curtains. She immediately declared the parlor off the kitchen as her space, muttering to herself about placement of her sewing machine and needing more shelves in the closet.

They finally ascended the stairs, which opened up to the middle of the hallway.

Carolyn stopped.

"What?"

She pointed at the closed doors. "Do we let the boys choose their own rooms?"

He scratched his chin. "I dunno. Do you think they each need their own room? We've got the space now, but Cord and Colby have always shared. Maybe they'll just want to put the bunk beds in one room until they're used to the place and then they can pick."

"Good idea. The one good thing about the trailer was Colton was self-contained with his brothers in a small bedroom."

"Only when he wasn't tryin' to convince his big brothers to release him from his cage." Their third son had started walking and talking early. Cord and Colby dragged him everywhere with them so the kid seemed a lot older than two and a half.

"Don't remind me."

Carson placed his hand on Carolyn's belly. "We'll need that crib for this baby pretty soon anyway."

"Not for four months."

He kissed her temple. "Like I said, soon."

"Since there are two staircases, maybe we should install locks on the outsides of the boy's doors." When Carson raised his eyebrow, she said, "I'm kidding. But I have all these worries I didn't have before."

"It'll be fine. Me'n my brothers survived growin' up in this house, our boys will too."

"I know. It's just..." She smiled. "Don't mind me. Hormone overload."

"Let's check out our bedroom." He rubbed his lips across the top of her ear. "I've got a surprise for you."

The door to the master bedroom was ajar. He moved in behind her, placing his hands over her eyes. "No peeking until I say."

"Carson McKay, if you—"

"I can put a hand over your mouth too, so zip it."

She huffed out an exasperated noise.

He steered her into the room and kicked the door shut behind them. Then he dropped his hands. "Now you can look."

Carolyn gasped and walked toward the brand new king-sized bed. He'd sprung for a new headboard and he watched as her fingers trailed across the curved center, flanked on both sides by tall rounded posts in a rich mahogany. Then she ran her hand across the sheets and looked at him. "You did all this?"

"I picked the mattress and the headboard, but Kimi helped with the sheets. We figured you'd want to buy or make a new coverlet for it, so I'm leavin' that part to you. I also didn't buy new furniture 'cause I wasn't sure what style you'd want."

"The sheets are perfect." She smiled. "This bed is huge."

"And sturdy." He grinned. "I made sure the headboard wasn't too close to the wall like in the trailer."

"In a house this size it's not like the boys will hear the headboard banging anyway."

Then that sexy, heavy-lidded look darkened her eyes and his dick instantly went hard. "What?"

"Let's break the mattress in."

"Now?"

"Right now. Before we get too busy unloading boxes and we're too tired later."

"Damn, woman, I love how you think." His lips teased hers as he undressed her. His hands mapped every naked curve, the heavy weight of her breasts, the swell of her abdomen, and the curve of her ass, hips and thighs. Then he explored her with his mouth. Sucking her nipples as he kneaded the flesh surrounding them. Since she'd nursed three babies she'd lost sensitivity in them, which was why he used his teeth. Her soft gasp indicated she liked that a lot.

Carson kissed his way down that beautiful bump in her belly. He rubbed his razor-stubbled cheeks and jaw across the firm flesh, amazed as always that a new life had taken seed inside her. "You're so damn sexy when you're carryin' my child."

"I'm sure it increases my appeal that I'm also very horny when I'm pregnant."

He chuckled against her belly button. "There is that too." His hands circled her hips. "Sit and spread your legs for me. I want my mouth on you." He dropped to his knees and inserted himself between her thighs. She had to lean back on her elbows so her belly didn't block his access to that slice of heaven.

Her entire body twitched at the first long stroke of his tongue.

"Goddamn do I love the way you taste. Sweet and hot. Sticky. But when you're pregnant, it's a darker flavor." He suckled her pussy lips and dipped his tongue into her opening, lapping up all that sweet, rich juice. Pulling that soft, fragrant flesh open wider with his fingers, he licked and sucked every inch of her swollen sex. Nibbling on her clit. Licking her slit up and down in a light tease and then plunging his tongue in as deep as it'd go.

She came hard, those pussy muscles spasming around his tongue while he rubbed her clit with the tip of his nose. That set off another orgasm and he slid his mouth up her hot and slick skin, fastening his mouth around her clit, lashing that pulsing nub with his tongue.

As Carolyn came down from back to back orgasms, he nuzzled the bottom of her belly and the tops of her thighs. He had to reach down and unbuckle his belt and unzip his Wranglers since the denim was strangling his cock.

She pushed upright, a dazed smile on her face. "How is it you seem to get better at that every time?"

"Lots of practice on you, sugar."

She laughed. "Get nekkid, cowboy, and let's mess up this new bed."

"Yee-haw."

After he shed his clothes, he bounced in the middle of the mattress. "Hey, it is springy."

Carolyn crawled across his body. "You didn't test it first?"

Greedily, he cupped those luscious swinging breasts in his hands. "Nope. I just bought the top of the line model. And I don't mind tellin' you, I hope we wear this bed out fast."

Her fingers circled his cock and she swirled the tip around her pussy, getting it wet with her juices before she filled herself with his hardness.

They groaned in unison.

She leaned as far forward as her belly allowed and locked her gaze to his. "Thank you for buying us a new bed, Carson. But I'd be happy sleeping on a sack of straw as long as it was with you."

"That pretty much describes our old bed." He pushed a long strand of hair over her shoulder. "Lots of good memories in that bed. And in that house."

"You gonna miss it?"

"Some."

"Me too." She smiled that secret smile and started to move on him. "But I am looking forward to all the different places we can make memories in this house."

"Good. 'Cause I was thinkin' the next memory I'd like to have is bending you over the counter in our bathroom and fuckin' you in front of the mirror." He slapped her ass. "So get movin' and ride me hard, sugar; time's a'wastin'."

A loud caw startled him out of the memory.

Carson shook himself, grabbed the pile of mail and headed inside.

They'd made a lot of changes to this house over the years. Kids had come and gone; now grandkids wreaked havoc whenever they came over. Carolyn loved the chaos. Since the moment they'd moved in, she'd said a house this size should be filled with kids. He'd done his best to make that dream come true for her, for both of them.

Now it was quiet most days. Never more so than in that moment he walked into Carolyn's kitchen and noticed the baking goods she'd laid out the morning of her accident. Cocoa, sugar, flour, chocolate chips, a bag of wrapped caramels, and the dark pan she swore was the reason her brownies were always so good.

His gaze landed on the dishes in the sink. It'd drive the woman nuts if she knew they'd been sitting there stinking for three days. His steps faltered when he saw her coffee cup, half full, pink lipstick stain on the edge, sitting in the same spot in the kitchen where she read the paper and planned her day.

Why seeing that lone coffee cup hit him like a mule kick in the gut, he had no idea. Why he placed his lips over that lipstick mark, hoping for a taste of her when he downed her three-day old coffee, made no sense either, but he found himself doing it anyway.

The coffee was the bitterest he'd ever tasted.

Old fool. Acting like she's already gone. Instead of lamenting the fact she ain't here, why don't you do something useful and clean up her space so she don't have a conniption fit when she does come home?

Carson rolled up his sleeves, needing to touch the things she'd last touched, and got to work.

Chapter Twenty-Two

Hospital, Day 3—early evening

After he'd taken a hot shower in his own bathroom, donned fresh clothes and packed for himself and Carolyn, Carson returned to the hospital.

Still, he felt guilty for his three-hour absence and the fifteen minutes he'd missed spending with his wife.

Had she noticed?

Don't be ridiculous.

But he vowed the next time he left the hospital to go home he'd be taking Carolyn with him.

Day dragged into early evening. Each visit to Carolyn's room brought up another memory. The last two hours he'd talked about Cam, how his normal birth weight didn't indicate the kid would be such a bruiser. Even at age two he'd been freakishly strong but surprisingly gentle. Especially with Carter.

There were only a little over two years between the last two boys. Five kids kept both of them busy. But their older sons, being typical boys, could care less about a new baby. Yet Cam had been fascinated by Carter and showed zero sibling jealousy. He loved his baby brother. Loved him so much he wanted to take Carter everywhere.

Carson would never forget the day he'd come inside and found Cord watching *Petticoat Junction* with Colby and Colt and not keeping an eye on his two youngest brothers while Carolyn took a shower. He'd scaled the stairs to see Cam giving four-month-old Carter a ride; he'd wrapped Carter up like a burrito and raced up and down the hallway, dragging the baby behind him.

His wife might've fainted on the spot if she'd seen it, even when Carter was perfectly fine, cooing happily. So Carson hadn't told her about that incident. Or the time when Cam and Colt were playing jungle in the playroom. They'd rigged several sheets between the curtain rods and two light fixtures on the ceiling to create a hammock for Carter. A hammock on a pulley system that lifted two-year-old Carter almost to the ceiling, near the exposed light bulbs and next to the open window.

That might've been the day he'd found his first gray hair. Even looking back now, he wasn't sure how his sons had managed to do that.

Right as he'd started to drift into the memory of Colby shooting out four windows from *inside* the house, he heard a loud voice bouncing off the walls down by the nurse's stand.

"Seriously? I've fixed lots of those over the years. Usually a flower is easiest because the lettering you want covered up can be incorporated into a vine or a stem." A pause. "Absolutely. Here's my card. Call me and we'll set up a consult."

Carson remained in his chair, knowing if he stood up he'd probably collide with his daughter-in-law India. How she sat for hours inking tattoos baffled him because when she wasn't working, she hustled around as if she was afraid she'd get arrested for loitering if she stopped moving.

Just then she barreled into the waiting room. A tank-top showed off both sleeves of her tattoos. Her short hair was subdued—subdued for her. Not streaked with vibrant blue, neon green or shocking orange, but the shiny burgundy color of wine.

She marched right up to him, her round-toed combat boots bumping into his cowboy boots. "Give me a hug, grumpy old man. I'm sure we both need one."

He flat-out adored Colt's wife. Outspoken and in your face, India's *take me as I am or get the fuck away from me* attitude charmed him, mostly because they were cut from the same cloth. In Carson's opinion, India Ellison was the greatest thing that had ever happened to his son.

"Nice hair," he said after she released him from a tight hug.

"Wouldn't want to get boring in my old age as a mother of three. Although my hair should be bright red and I should have horns growing out of my scalp since I've given birth to hellions." Her piercing eyes sought his. "Carson, can I just say this situation fucking sucks all around?"

"Yeah, darlin', you can."

"Any change?"

He shook his head.

"I don't have to ask how you're holding up because I can see it in your eyes, old man. Have you been sleeping at all?"

"Some. In the middle of the night they let me piggyback the time I spend with her, so I get ten minutes and I sleep for two hours instead of one."

"Big of them." Scowling, she gestured to the empty bottles of Dr. Pepper scattered around. "Dude. Pick that shit up. If I would've wanted to talk to you in a mess, I would've invited you over to our place."

Such a little ball-buster.

"I'm grabbing us each a soda. I need some damn caffeine."

Carson tossed the trash and settled in the corner seat.

India returned with two bottles of Dr. Pepper, and four candy bars. She tossed the Butterfinger, the Snickers and the Salted Nut Roll in his lap, keeping the Twix for herself. "How about we call that my version of baking cookies since you know I'm a sucky cook."

He smiled. "Works for me."

They didn't speak until they'd polished off a candy bar each.

She flopped back in her chair and jammed a hand through her hair. "So your kids are being dickheads, huh?"

"I get why they're pissed off but it ain't gonna make me change my mind."

"Hudson, Ellison and McKenna are all healthy little pigs. Colt told me to make sure to tell you that I wasn't carrying germs to you."

"I appreciate it. How is Colt?"

"Worried sick about his mother. And you. He's cut himself off from his brothers and Keely. I take that back—he talks to Carter because they're the only ones who aren't assholes."

"Tell Colt I appreciate it."

"The reason he hasn't come by isn't because he's following Cord's stupid edict of 'all of us or none of us' but because he's hurting, Carson. He's hurting real bad. He's always seen you and Carolyn as invincible. This is the second time in the last four months that he's had to face that you're not. He... Never mind."

Something else was going on that caused Indy such distress. Carson set his uneaten candy aside and leaned forward. "Tell me what's worryin' you."

"It's been a very long time since I've seen Colt this close to...wanting to take a drink."

His stomach dropped. "Has he touched the stuff?"

India looked him in the eye. "No. He's talking to me, which is good. He's going to AA meetings every day and talking to his sponsor, which is even better."

"I am so fuckin' relieved to hear that."

"I know. Most people probably wouldn't have dumped that extra worry on you when there's so much weighing on your mind right now, but I'm not one to pretend stuff is sparkly fucking rainbows when it isn't."

"Which is one of my favorite things about you, Indy darlin'. So how is Colton coping if he ain't hitting the bottle?"

"He'd like to beat the fuck outta someone. Kane even offered to mix it up with him, but wisely Colt declined. So he's chopping wood. Lots and lots of wood." She smirked. "And that gets him a better coping mechanism because seeing that sexy man with his shirt off, muscles dripping sweat, does it for me every damn time." She laughed. "TMI, I'm sure."

"Funny thing? Carolyn used to say the same thing about me." He grinned. "TMI, I'm sure."

"Touché, old man."

"Now tell me about my grandkids."

India groaned. "Pigs in clothing, that's what the three of them are. I should start calling them the three little devil pigs. I do not understand how they can make such a huge freakin' mess in such a short amount of time. I about fell on my ass this morning because they'd left markers all over the floor. I stepped on a huge ball of paste they'd just dropped on the carpet. Then I looked around and thought, where the hell was I when the bomb dropped? My house is destroyed. As easy as it'd be to say the place becomes a pigsty when Colt is home with them, that's not even close to the truth. The kids aren't ever left unattended and we're both at our wit's end on how to deal with it."

"If I had a nickel for every time Caro said the same thing to me? I could've hired a maid for her a long damn time ago." Carson cracked open his soda. "Darlin', no offense, but Hudson is old enough to know better. He's the ringleader, ain't he?"

"Yep."

"Over the years the kids were growin' up, I came home a coupla times and found my lovely, calm wife threatening to buy herself a bullwhip to use on her sons."

"Did Carolyn spank them?"

"Neither of us did unless the kid did something life threatening, but that was only when they were little. Spanking never had any effect." He chuckled. "One time when Cord was probably nine or so, he decided to build a mud wrasslin' pit out past the barn in a shallow spot where water collected. Evidently he and Colby and Colt were havin' a big old time out there, mucking around like pigs in..." He paused. "Anyway, they came strolling up to the house, near dark, clothes covered in mud, acting like it was no big deal. Carolyn was very pregnant with Carter at the time, and Cam was two. She'd hit the end of her rope. She lined them up on the sidewalk and sprayed them down with the hose. And by that time of day it'd started to get cold."

"Go on, I'm taking notes."

"After she'd hosed them down, she made them strip to their underwear and sprayed them down again, warning them to stay outside until they dried off, because if she found even one speck of mud anywhere in her house, she'd drag them back outside by their ears and spray them again—but they'd be buck-assed nekkid."

India grinned. "She find any mud?"

"Nope. What I'm tryin' to say is she had patience with the fact they were messy boys—up to a point. She knew we'd be pickin' up after them, that goes along with havin' kids. But if the messes were extreme or frequent, the kids had consequences. Sounds to me like a little hosing down might do your hellions some good—figuratively speakin', of course."

"You're right. I'll mention the mud pit wrestling incident to spark Colt's memory."

Carson asked about India's Ink—her tattoo shop—and they

chatted for another ten minutes or so. But as always, Carson kept an eye on the clock as his time with Carolyn crept near.

"I probably better go home and check if the boys roped and tied up the dining room chairs with the vacuum cleaner cord again. Or if McKenna tried to flush something else down the toilet since her attempt at flushing her blanket failed last week." She threw up her hands. "What is girls' obsession with that? I remember Eliza doing the same damn thing."

"No matter what anyone tells you? Girls ain't easier than boys."

India reached in her purse. "I did bring something for you. It might be a little stupid and corny, so don't laugh, okay?"

"Never, darlin'."

She handed over a small cloth envelope. "It's a sachet I made using Carolyn's favorite scent from Sky Blue. I thought you could...I don't know, put it in your pillow out here or something. Maybe if it smells like her you'll sleep better."

Carson was too choked up to say anything when the sweet scent of his wife filled his lungs.

"Sorry, stupid idea, I'll just go now."

He clamped his hand on India's knee. "You are just a sentimental little angel under all them devil tattoos, ain't ya?" He looked up at her and didn't bother hiding the moisture in his eyes. "It's perfect, Indy. Thank you."

"You're welcome." She squeezed his hand. "I do ask that you don't ever show it to Carolyn, master seamstress, because my sewing skills leave a lot to be desired."

"You got it." He kept hold of her hand, not knowing how to even ask her what he needed to.

"Carson? What is it?"

He sucked in a big breath and slowly let it out. "They shaved Carolyn's head, all the way to the top of her scalp except for the very front. She'll need a scarf or something to hide it when she comes out of the coma because she won't want anyone to see her like that. I went home today and just grabbed a bunch of stuff, not knowin' what I should bring her. Since you're good with hair and accessories stuff, I know she'd trust you to help her, and not fall into a blubbering wreck like Kimi and Keely would if I asked them."

"I'd be honored to help her." She firmed her quivering chin. "Bet she never thought she'd be so tight with a foul-mouthed tattoo artist after that first time she called me out on not being the appropriate woman for her precious son."

"Don't kid yourself for a second she didn't love how fast you rallied to Colton's defense and bitch-slapped her down to reality—her words, not mine."

"I'm just glad you both see Colt as the amazing man he is now, and not the fuck up he'd been. It means a lot to both of us." India pushed to her feet. "Take care of yourself, old man. Give our love to your better half. And for god's sake, eat something more than just candy bars for supper, will ya?"

"No promises."

Carson dusted the Snickers and used the facilities. By the time he returned to the waiting room, the nurse was ready for him.

Inside the room, he parked the rolling stool next to Carolyn's bed, placing one gloved hand on her forearm and covering her hand with his other.

"Hey, sugar. I'm sittin' here beside you. I know you can hear me. I *need* you to hear me. Come back to me. I need you to know that I'm right here, I ain't goin' anywhere."

He launched right into his one-sided conversation. "It's your lucky day. India stopped in. She was goin' on and on about the new tattoo she designed for you. A gigantic bear, its jaws open and dripping saliva. She thought the image appropriate since you've always been a scary mother bear when it comes to your cubs—no matter how old they get. We were thinkin' she could ink it above your McKay brand. That way you'd have a tat above and below your belly button. And you know how much I love tracin' that tattoo with my tongue."

Sometimes he still couldn't believe his wife had gotten herself tattooed, between her hipbones right above her mound.

He laughed. "Okay, sugar, that was a total lie. Indy sends her love, as does Colt. I think she showed up because she needed someone to complain to about her kids bein' pigs. Devil pigs in clothing, was how she phrased it. I know you felt that way a time or twenty when the boys were growin' up. I told her about the time you hosed the boys down..."

As soon as Carolyn heard Carson's voice she stayed still, soaking up every syllable. It seemed as if she hadn't heard from him in days, but she knew it might've only been hours since she existed in the void of nothingness. The doors to her memories were no longer visible and randomly accessible. That scared her. Those memories were her only hope of staying tethered to the life she had and the world she needed to return to. Now the only time she could access those memories was when Carson spoke of the past.

She remembered the mud hole incident, but that wasn't the memory that popped up first...

Boys.

Why did she have to give birth to all boys?

Five rough and tumble McKay boys.

Why couldn't she have had a sweet daughter? An angel who didn't have an aversion to baths, who wouldn't wrestle in the living room, who wouldn't constantly shove food in her mouth and five minutes later go looking for more? A little doll she could clothe in frilly dresses and darling hair ribbons. A quiet child.

But this is what she got.

Five destructive boys.

Who had wreaked utter havoc in the house in just four hours.

Someone had let the dogs in the living room—dogs with muddy feet.

Then the boys had left their manure-covered boots inside the kitchen door, so now her kitchen reeked like cow poop.

Dishes covered the counters. The last person who used the milk hadn't bothered putting it back in the refrigerator.

Carolyn followed the wreckage to the living room. Dirty socks, comic books, Ag magazines, toys and more pieces of clothing littered the floor. Not to mention wrappers from Halloween candy were everywhere—on the couch and chairs, the coffee and end tables. She even found gum stuck to one of the lamps. In two places.

Gum!

The dining room table was piled with book bags, textbooks, crayons, coloring books, glue sticks, school projects and papers thrown haphazardly on the floor, on the chairs and on the sideboard.

With her blood pressure rising, she headed down the hallway and poked her head in the small bathroom. The toilet lid was up; it looked as if someone had sprayed the toilet, the walls and the floor with urine—oh, and then had forgotten to flush the toilet. The sink was covered in grimy soap scum and the bar of Lava was on the floor. She glanced in the mirror—not that she could see herself clearly because someone had smeared soap everywhere.

That did it.

She'd been gone since one o'clock this afternoon to work the election polls. This was how her sons reacted to being unattended in the house...for just a few hours? She shuddered to think what she would've found if she'd left them alone all day.

Enough.

She stormed out of the house and found her five little pigs between the machine shed and the barn, on the old barrel they'd rigged up for Colby's bull riding practice.

"Cord, Colby, Colton, Cameron and Carter McKay, get your butts up on the porch pronto!"

When they weren't moving fast enough to suit her, she barked, "Now! Or so help me God I will get a switch and use it on each one of you!"

Even after they were lined up on the sidewalk, the five of them were screwing around, pushing each other and shoving. Cam was trying to bench press Carter over his head.

"You will stand there like statues and listen to every word I say. Is that understood?"

Mumbles.

"I said, *do you understand?*"

"Yes, Ma."

Carolyn glared at each boy in turn, from her oldest to her youngest. None met her gaze.

"My job is taking care of my family. It's a job I take great pride in. Raising good boys, making our house a happy place to live and to come home to." She paused. "Do you think I was happy to come home today and find that god-awful mess? It looks like I'm raising bears in that house, not boys. *Bears!* But I could forgive bears, because they are animals and do not know any better. But you boys are *not* wild animals and every one of you knows better. I will not let you disrespect what I do every day. I work just as hard as your father and you'd never do to him what you did to me. What do you think would happen if you just went into the barn and took his tack and threw it all over the place?"

They looked at each other warily but were smart enough not to speak.

"So why is it all right to destroy the inside of my house in four hours? Just because I'm not here to tell you not to? The *don't-be-pigs* rule is the same regardless of whether I'm here or not! Did you assume I'd clean it up like I'm the hired help? Or do you think because you're boys that you can just leave all the inside dirty work to women? I don't appreciate..." She began to melt down.

Just as Carson started up the driveway.

Carolyn hastily wiped her tears. This wasn't something she wanted him to see. Or deal with because he ended up meting out the boys' discipline most of the time.

"Ma. We're really, really, really sorry and we'll clean up our messes and do everything you want and it'll never ever ever happen again; just don't tell Dad," Colby said in a rush.

"Yeah, Ma, please don't tell him," Cord added. "We'll go in and fix it and we'll be really fast."

Colt was totally panicked. "We'll be grounded until next summer if Dad sees you cryin' 'cause he'll know it's our fault."

"Dad said any time we made you cry he'd whip our butts," Cam added. "He'll probably even take away Christmas!"

Three-and-a-half-year-old Carter didn't really know what was going on—not that he was innocent on the mess-making front, but he let out a horrified, "No Santa?"

Cam whispered something in his ear that had Carter blurting out, "Sorry, Mama."

She let them sweat it out until Carson parked. "Okay. You've got one chance. I want every bit of the mess gone, including the muddy dog prints, including the disgusting bathroom, including the barn boots that somehow ended up in my kitchen. You will work together, you will get it done in two hours, and then you will tuck yourselves in bed without any supper. Got it?"

"Yes, Ma, thanks, we're so sorry—"

Carolyn pointed at the house. "Get. Moving."

Their shoes left tread marks on the concrete they left so fast.

Carson meandered up to the house. Lord, she loved her husband's ambling walk; it allowed her plenty of time to check him out. Dressed in his new Wranglers and a white button-up shirt with subtle stripes of navy and gray, wearing a gray wool vest, his black hat and black boots, he was a man who turned heads—especially hers, since he was every bit as handsome and sexy as the day they'd married.

He kissed her first, like he always did. When he pulled away to ask questions, she pulled him back to deepen the kiss. Which only stalled him for so long.

Those blue eyes were mighty skeptical. "What's goin' on with the boys?"

"Nothing. I was giving them last-minute instructions."

"On what? 'Cause from where I was sittin' it looked like you were givin' them what-for."

Carolyn looped her arm around his waist, directing him toward his truck. "I told them since I'd dressed up to work the election, and you were in your cattleman finery after spending the day at the St. Onge sale barn, that you were taking me out for supper."

"That right?"

"Do you have a problem with that?"

"None whatsoever. Where you thinkin'?"

"Twin Pines." They had notoriously slow service, which just might save her boys behinds and give her a chance to cool down.

"Why there?"

"Maybe I wanted to dance with you. It's been a while."

"That it has." Carson helped her into his truck. On the way to the supper club he held her hand as they talked about their days.

As always, living in a small town they ran into several people they knew at Twin Pines. In the last decade the McKay Ranch had become a very successful cattle operation and Carson's advice was sought after. As for Carson's claim people had long memories around here, none ever brought up his wild drinking and fighting days.

The food was good. Carson teased her about choosing linguine with shrimp for her meal, but it was definitely something she didn't cook at home.

Afterward, they headed to the bar side. The piped-in music wasn't great, but she didn't care.

"That was a happy sigh, sugar."

"I'm happy when I'm with you and you're holding me close like this."

Carson put his mouth on her ear. "You think sweet talkin' means you're gonna get lucky tonight?"

His deep voice sent a shiver of want straight to her core. "I'm hoping."

"I'll warn ya. I like my women wild and I'll expect kinky things."

She nuzzled the edge of his jaw. "I can be kinky."

"How well I know that. And what a lucky man I am for it."

"But...between the kids and all the day to day stuff of being a wife and mother... What if I've forgotten?"

He leaned back to gaze into her eyes. "I'll remind you." Carolyn tried to duck her head, but he demanded, "Look at me."

She hadn't seen that sexual fire burning in his eyes recently and it instantly made her wet, needy and achy.

"How about if I just drag you home right now, haul you up to our bedroom and fuck you hard for an hour straight?"

Her stomach swooped. "I suggest if we wait another hour, the boys will be in bed and there won't be any parental duties to interfere."

He grinned that same wicked grin that'd charmed, infuriated and inflamed her the first time they'd danced together. "So for the next hour I can rub my body against yours and whisper all the dirty things I'm gonna do to you?"

"And I can do the same."

"Hot damn."

They stayed on the dance floor the entire time. Teasing each other with words and subtle touching.

By the time they left—they almost got it on in the front seat of his truck—Carson hinted he'd last longer if she gave him a hand job on the way home.

After she finished jacking him off and licked him clean, he swore she hadn't lost her kinky edge.

The house was dark and quiet. Carolyn's focus wasn't on checking to see if the boys had followed her edict. Her sole focus was getting naked with her husband.

As soon as he shut and locked the bedroom door, Carson was on her. Making short work of her clothes. The man hadn't even taken his boots off and he had her spread on the end of the bed, his mouth buried in her pussy. That lethal tongue driving her up, up, up and over. And then doing it again.

Carolyn had barely floated back down from that head rush when Carson's hot, hard, body was on top of hers.

His rough voice vibrated against her breast. "How kinky you feelin' tonight, Mrs. McKay?"

"You just made me come twice. I'm feelin' pretty loose at the moment."

"Then sugar, I'm gonna tie you up a bit." He pushed off her.

"Where are you going?"

The man's eyes held a depraved gleam. "Grabbing some rope."

And he wasn't joking when he returned from the closet, a length of rope dangling from his right hand.

"How long has *that* been in there?"

"A while. Been savin' it for a special occasion. Face and shoulders on the bed, ass in the air."

Even when Carson was a sexually charged man, the times he went even more over the top in the bedroom made her hotter than ever.

Carolyn rested the side of her face on the mattress, watching him eye her naked body. Birthing five kids should've made her self-conscious of her less-than-ideal physique, but the way her man ate her up with his hungry eyes gave her the sexual confidence to be in this position.

"Damn, woman, you're sexy. Arms behind you."

She crossed her wrists in the small of her back and the rope dragged against her side as he tied her. Then he moved in behind her, his work-roughened hands clamped on her butt cheeks.

She held her breath, expecting him to plow into her. But he fed his shaft in slowly and stopped. She wiggled to get him to move. But he remained like that, buried deep. "What's the holdup, cowboy?"

"Told you I was gonna fuck you for an hour. This way first, then we'll see how creative I can get." Carson stroked in and out of her steadily. And as always, she lost herself in him, in them, her world boiling down to his hands, his cock, his mouth, reveling in the sexual intensity that was only ever for her. It was heady stuff that after almost fifteen years she still satisfied his sexual appetite.

He reached around and lightly stroked her clit, purposely not giving her the speed or the pressure that'd get her off, just keeping her primed for what came next.

He pulled out and lifted her up by her shoulders. His voice rumbled in her ear. "I wanna suck on you as I'm fuckin' this hot pussy of mine."

She loved the way he treated her with such care, while at the same time turning her inside out with his insistent touches, raunchy words and blatant desire.

Carson sat in the middle of the bed with his legs stretched out in front of him. "Straddle me on your knees." As he helped her into position he latched onto her nipple; the rough scrape of his five o'clock shadow was a harsh contrast to how softly he suckled. He poised his cock at her entrance and held her hips, helping her lower down.

Feeling his fingers at her wrists untying the rope, she sent him a quizzical look.

"Enough kinky. I need your hands on me," he said gruffly.

Carolyn wrapped her legs around his waist. He couldn't move inside her much, but that was his intent, teasing her and prolonging this connection. While he sucked on her nipples and her neck, his hips rocked forward and she ran her fingers through his silky black hair.

She loved that he'd honed every muscle the hard way from ranch work. So strong in body, so strong in heart. Tough enough to go head to head with ornery bulls and mean mama cows, but gentle with their babies. She scraped her nails down his muscular back and squeezed his hard butt cheeks, then dragged her fingers up, curling her hands around his powerful arms.

His kisses grew fevered, his movements hurried. He said, "Hang on," and rolled down to the mattress so he was on top.

Carson plowed into her with the force of a battering ram. His solid body crushed her, filled her, moved her, owned her, destroyed her. As many times and as many ways as they'd made love, this was her favorite: face to face, mouth to mouth, eye to eye, heart to heart.

Hitting that detonation point happened simultaneously. She arched her neck; he panted against her as the stormed surged through them both. When that rush abated, he smiled against her throat.

"What?"

"Who needs kink when we've got this?"

He kissed her and eased out of her, rolling to his back and tucking her against his side.

Sated and sleepy, she rested her chin on his chest and played with his chest hair. "You always know."

"Always know what, sugar?"

"Always know when I need a reminder that I'm more than just a harried ranch wife with five rambunctious and messy boys. You remind me that I'm...yours."

"Damn straight you're mine, Carolyn McKay. You've been mine since the moment I saw you and you'll be mine until my last breath."

It overwhelmed her sometimes, how much she loved this man. She tried not to sniffle when the tears fell. But Carson's chest getting slick gave her away.

He tugged her head back and murmured, "Beautiful woman with the beautiful heart," and planted his mouth on hers, kissing her with the tenderness and possession he did so well.

She sighed when he finally ended the kiss. "Sorry for leaking all over you."

"I don't mind. It's part of the deal with a pregnant wife." He paused. "When's the baby due?"

"How'd you know?" Not fair that the man always figured it out before she had a chance to tell him.

"You've been testy. And horny as hell."

"That means I'm pregnant?"

"Two signs I've seen five times before. And Caro, you were cryin' during a baby food commercial last night. That's sort of a giveaway." He stroked her arm. "You okay with it?"

"I don't know. I'm not...*not* okay with it. I just never thought I'd have six kids. Especially not after seeing how it affected my mother's health. Then again, she didn't have her first baby until she was thirty-three."

"It's ironic that's how old you'll be when you have your last baby."

Carolyn lifted her head and looked at him. "We're done after this?"

"Ain't your life's work to pop out kids until you hit menopause, no matter what the pope says. I won't take the risk that you'll end up like your mother because I'm selfish; I want lots of years with you after the last kid leaves the nest. You've been lucky with every pregnancy, but that ain't always how it goes, especially the older you get. After this one, we're done. Don't care which one of us gets snipped or clipped, but it's gonna happen."

"Okay."

"So I want you takin' it easy this go around. It'll be over four years since you had Carter. You don't take any chances; the boys are old enough to help you out a lot."

"I agree. As long as we're on that subject, I want the boys to start having household chores in addition to ranch chores."

"I got no problem with that. Was that the issue earlier?"

She hedged. "Teaching them life skills is my responsibility too." She rubbed her face in his chest hair and breathed him in. "Speaking of, I need to check on them before I conk out." She pressed a lingering kiss on his lips. "I love you. Even the days when I look around and see messes everywhere in this house, and boys who'd rather roll in manure than bathe in water, and endless chores for both of us...then I see you and I know I'm exactly where I want to be and I can't imagine my life any other way."

His eyes softened. "Same goes, sugar. Now go check on them boys before I decide I need another helping of you before we hit the hay."

The boys had been on their best behavior during her pregnancy. A few minor incidents, including an escaped calf in the dining room during calving season, but they were trying to help out more.

But she'd reached the stage of her pregnancy where nothing was clean enough. She'd been scouring the kitchen when the first contraction hit. As strong as it was, it wasn't her first rodeo so she ignored it and finished scrubbing the refrigerator.

She'd made progress wiping down all of the cupboards when another contraction squeezed her midsection.

Okay. That one got her attention. As did the next two. But Carolyn was determined to cross every chore off her list today. Besides, the baby wasn't due for two weeks and in five other pregnancies she'd never gone into labor early.

She alphabetized her spices and breathed through the contractions that were coming closer together.

Who knew this false labor stuff could feel like real labor?

With a small squeegee in one hand and the spray hose from the sink in the other, she contemplated cleaning the window above the sink, versus how much it'd bug her if she just let it stay dirty, when angry footsteps came up behind her.

"Carolyn, what in the hell do you think you're doin'?"

"Trying to figure out the best way to wash the windows. I realize climbing on the counter and standing in the sink isn't an option. So I figured I could spray the glass with hot water and squeegee it fast."

"Huh-uh. Not happening. Step away from the cleaning supplies."

Carolyn whirled around, aiming the hose at him. "Back off. I have a list to complete. Don't you have chores of your own to finish without trying to tell me how to do mine?"

"Listen to yourself. And look around. The house sparkles from top to bottom. You've been nesting the past two weeks and, sugar, give it a rest."

Carter's head popped up beside Carson's hip. His blue eyes were enormous. "Who's mama makin' a nest for?"

"The baby."

"The baby sleeps in a nest?" Carter asked with interest.

Carolyn started to clarify the difference between nesting and a bird's nest for her very literal child, because he'd asked how the baby got in her tummy and Carson muttered something lame about the birds and the bees and fertilized eggs. But she snapped her mouth shut when the next contraction doubled her over.

As soon as it ended, Carson was in her face. "How long have you been havin' contractions?"

"Off and on."

"Off and on in the last hour?" he pressed.

"Off and on all morning. But I think it's false labor."

"Guess we'll see, won't we?" Carson picked up the phone and dialed. "Kimi? It's time. We're leavin' in five minutes." He paused. "Thanks. I'll tell Cord to expect you here in an hour." He hung up. "Get your bag."

"Carson, I'm not ready to have this baby so I haven't even packed a bag."

"Good. Then we can leave right now." He told Carter, "Go get your brothers. Quickly." Then he put his hand on her belly and kissed her forehead. "Let's hope I don't have to deliver this kid in the cab of my truck."

"Oh pooh. Relax. I'm not close to popping this baby out yet."

An hour later...

"Come on, sugar, you're almost there."

"I know," Carolyn snapped. "I've done this a few times, remember?"

Carson curled his hands around her face. "Don't snap at me,

beautiful."

Her hair was sweat-soaked; her skin was hot and bloated, and she smelled like cleaning supplies. "Don't look at me. Don't call me beautiful." She hissed. "Oh crap, this one's gonna be bad."

"Look at me and breathe. That's it. You're doin' good."

Afterward Carolyn slumped against the pillows. "Can I push? I need to push."

The nurse said, "I'm guessing about three more of those big contractions and you'll be there."

"Oh...here we go again." She stayed focused on her husband. When the next contraction came on the heels of the last one, medical personnel scrambled to get ready.

Doctor Haskell, who'd delivered all their babies, ambled in, chomping on a piece of licorice. He suited up and scooted to the end of the bed. "You've done all the work, now I just gotta get out my catcher's mitt."

The nurse repositioned the bed and Carson moved in to brace Carolyn's shoulders.

"All right, Carolyn, give that baby a big ol' push."

She grunted and squeezed the bed's railings as she bore down.

"One more push and we'll see if you cooked the stem on or the stem-less variety."

Carolyn lifted her upper half up and bore down with gritted teeth. Then she fell back against Carson with a huge sigh of relief.

Then Doctor Haskell started laughing. "I'll be damned. McKays, you have a daughter."

"What?" Carolyn scrambled upright. "A girl? Let me see."

"Doesn't sound like you believe me." The doctor laughed again. "You knew there was a fifty-fifty chance this would happen."

"Didn't even cross my mind after birthing five boys, my sister having twin boys, and my sisters-in-law only having sons."

Carson stood and peeked over the edge, completely dumbfounded.

"Michelle," Doctor Haskell said sharply. "Get a chair for daddy, he's about to pass out."

"I'm not some fuckin' pussy who's gonna faint..." But his face was ashen and he wobbled.

Carolyn watched with concern as the nurse pushed him into a chair. "Head between your legs and breathe."

After a minute or so he slowly raised his head.

"You okay?"

"Hell no. Might take me a decade or two to get over the shock."

"Lord, I never even considered picking a girl's name."

"At least you know it'll start with a C like all the others," he said dryly.

"Just for that smart comment, I'm not picking a C name," she retorted.

Doctor Haskell wandered over with a pink-wrapped bundle. "Your daughter is a healthy seven pounds, thirteen ounces. She's twenty-three inches long and passed all her prelim tests. So we'll give you a few minutes before we finish the medical stuff." He placed the bundle in Carolyn's arms. "Congratulations."

"Thank you."

Carolyn loosened the blanket. She pulled back the little pink and blue striped hat, revealing coal black hair. She murmured, "That's nothing new. Bet the girl has blue eyes too. Stem-less variety or not, she's still a McKay, through and through."

The baby didn't move or open her eyes as they checked her out. Carolyn hoped that meant she'd be sweet and mellow.

"She's beautiful, Mama, like you. You done good again."

"I can't believe we have a girl. The boys will flip."

"Everyone is gonna flip, sugar. She's the first McKay girl born in this country. I'd have to ask my dad, but I don't think his father had sisters in Ireland."

"Then she should have an Irish name."

"Agreed. Oh. Go ahead and contact that nunnery school you went to in Montana and get her enrolled now."

Carolyn laughed and kissed his cheek.

But she suspected Carson wasn't joking.

They brought their daughter home two days later. There was enough food from well-wishers to feed even their hungry army of boys. Enough pink clothing and toys to warrant the girl getting her own room.

Carson carried their precious bundle into the living room and sat next to Carolyn on the couch. She was exhausted and had spent a good portion of her time in the hospital sleeping. She suspected Carson had spent his time staring at the newest addition to their family with nothing less than awe.

Carolyn unwrapped the blanket. "Come on, boys, and meet your baby sister."

The boys gathered around, staring at her.

"What's her name?" Colt asked.

"Keely."

Cam and Colt exchanged a look.

"What?"

"That's a dumb name," Colt said. "Why didn't you name her something cool like Farrah?"

She heard Carson mutter, "Jesus. Farrah. Really?" and she elbowed him.

"It probably ain't too late to change it," Colby suggested.

"Her name is fine, don't listen to them, Mom," Cord said. "At least it don't start with a C."

Cam leaned over and poked her belly. "She looks scrawny to me. I bet she cries a lot, huh?"

"All babies cry. You cried a lot if I recall," Carolyn said.

Cam looked horrified.

That's when Carson noticed Carter had hung back. "Hey, Carter, come on over here and take a gander at your scrawny, bawlin', baby sister with the weird name."

Carolyn elbowed him again.

Carter pressed himself into Carson's side. "She's little."

"Yes, she is. And she's lucky that she has five big brothers to protect her."

"I made something for her. Don't go nowhere," he warned and raced off.

"Do you know what it is?" she asked Carson, since he'd been home with the boys at night.

He shrugged. "No idea."

Cord, Colby, Colt and Cam had already disappeared.

The back kitchen door slammed and Carolyn heard Carter huffing and puffing. He came around the corner carrying... Dear God, what was that? It looked like a gigantic bowl made out of mud. With bits of straw and twigs sticking out all over.

"I made a nest for the baby! A big one like an eagle's nest! And she can sleep in it in my room. I even used chicken feathers and picked all the worms outta the mud—"

In his excitement, Carter tripped and the nest went flying. It landed on the carpet with a wet thud and mud splattered everywhere. Hay and feathers floated in the air while she and Carson sat there in complete shock.

Then Carter started to wail about his broken nest. His crying startled Keely and she screwed up her face and began bawling too.

"At least we know her lungs work," Carson said over the escalating cries.

Hearing the commotion, the older boys tore around the corner, pushing and shoving each other as they jockeyed to be the first one into the room, not paying attention as usual, so a jubilant Colt became airborne after his feet connected with the muddy nest. Then Cord and Colby skidded across the carpet, knocking each other down. Cam managed to avoid the dog pile, but he fell into the coffee table, launching a glass of grape Kool-Aid into the air in a cloudburst of purple rain.

Carolyn closed her eyes and counted to ten. Then she pressed her lips to her sweet baby's head and whispered, "Welcome to chaos central, baby girl. I'd tell you it's not always like this, but that'd be a lie."

The light became dim again.

No! Don't send me back into that nothingness.

Carolyn fought to remember what happened next as she waged a silent battle with the encroaching darkness...and lost.

Chapter Twenty-Three

Hospital, Day 4—morning

"Ma'am? I'll have to see what's in the box."

A soft voice answered, but he couldn't make out the words—or who the voice belonged to.

Carson scooted forward and saw a tall, lithe blonde woman standing at the nurse's desk while they inspected whatever she'd brought him. While he appreciated their vigilance, he was pretty sure he knew what was in that box and his stomach rumbled.

Domini turned and faltered a step when she saw him staring at her. "Carson. I didn't expect you to be right there."

"Not a lot of other places to go." He eyed the package and felt a tug on his heart. The outside of the white box had been decorated in marker and crayon with hearts and flowers.

"I see that gleam in your eyes and yes, these are for you. Liesl baked them all by herself. Oxsana and Sasha decorated the box."

Across the top they'd written, *Love you, Grandpa!! Get Well Soon, Gran-gran!! Miss you!!*

"I'm a lucky man to have the best granddaughters in the world," he said huskily. "Tell my girls thanks and that me'n Gran-gran will treat them to ice cream when she's feelin' up to it." He opened the box. "Oatmeal raisin. My favorite." He snatched one off the top and bit into it. "Damn that girl can bake. Takes after her Gran-gran." He finished the cookie in two bites.

"I'll tell her you said so."

After he realized his rudeness—shoving a cookie in his pie hole without saying hello to his daughter-in-law, he brushed the crumbs off his shirt. As he took a swig of soda, he gave her a quick head to toe inspection. No wonder Cam called her princess. Domini had a foreign look about her—delicate features, icy blue eyes and white blonde hair that spoke of her Ukrainian heritage. In addition to running Dewey's Delish Dish, she was a cop's wife, and dealt with Cam's lingering effects from his stint in the army and his career—and nearly life-ending injury. Now she and Cam had six busy, rowdy kids. Not necessarily shy, but soft-spoken, Domini was the picture of calmness. It seemed nothing rattled her even in the sea of chaos that was their life raising a big family.

"Domini, you're lookin' as pretty and happy as ever. I trust my son is takin' good care of you?"

She blushed. "Always. And I'll say again, it's obvious where your son got his charm."

He smiled and swigged his Dr. Pepper.

"Any change with Carolyn?"

"Nope. They're still plannin' on slowly bringing her out of the coma whenever the hell they deem it so." That didn't sound bitter at all.

Domini gazed at the small space and his corner of the room where he'd literally set up camp. Those calm eyes bored into him. "What are you eating?"

"Some stuff from the cafeteria." When he remembered to eat. "I'm getting by."

"Have any of your children been by to make sure you're all right? Or are they boycotting this place like Cam is?"

"Haven't seen any of them." He reached for another cookie. "Is it an organized boycott?" Carson had a funny mental image of his grown children holding protest signs, marching in front of the hospital, shouting at passersby that they wanted their mommy.

Getting punchy, McKay.

"I have no idea. And no offense, but I'm just as mad at your other kids as I am at your son. So you can quit wondering if I'm here to plead for visitation rights on his behalf."

Carson bit into the cookie. Chewed. Swallowed. "Domini, darlin', I don't want to put you at odds with Cam."

"I'm at odds with him because he's a freakin' hypocrite." She rattled off a Ukrainian phrase he doubted flattered his son. "Anton and Liesl are steering clear of him after he went on a tear about his rights and they asked if he'd apply that same argument if I was in the hospital."

"What'd Cam say?"

"Nothing. He just snapped at them. But Oxsana informed her father that if Grandpa wanted to ban everyone from Gran-gran's room, that he shouldn't argue because he's supposed to honor his mother and father no matter what, no matter how old he is."

Touched, he said, "My little I-haven't-found-a-rule-that-can't-be-broken Oxsana said that?"

"Yes. Evidently she's been paying attention in Sunday school," Domini said dryly. "And Dimitri told Cam he should listen to you because you know *everything*. And he emphasized *everything* twice."

Carson grinned. "Bet that put a knot in Cam's shorts."

Domini laughed. "Yes, it did. I thought you ought to know your grandkids have your back." Her smile slipped away. "That's not to say that the kids aren't worried about Carolyn. We told them what happened. And trust me, they're all super healthy right now—" she knocked on the wooden chair leg, "—or even I wouldn't have risked coming here."

"I'm glad you did. And not just because you brought me cookies." He paused. "Why'd you call Cam a hypocrite?"

"He made decisions after his war injuries about keeping his family away due to health issues that served his needs. Not just for a few days, but for years. He can't fault you for making a decision that serves your needs first."

"He'd still be pushin' us away if not for him findin' you, darlin', I fully believe that."

"Thank you. Cam is a strong man, but he's a worst-case scenario guy. I don't know if that's because he's in law enforcement or what. Even if he could see Carolyn, I'm not sure I'd want him in there because he'd be a Negative Nancy."

"Cam has been that way since he was a kid. One time he had Colt convinced that the mosquito bite on the back of his neck was filled with an egg sac and if he scratched it a hundred bugs would fly out and bite him a hundred more times."

"Good Lord. Now I know where Markus gets it."

Cam's youngest boy was a serious little kid. A deliberate thinker. Oddly enough, he reminded Carson of Cord, not Cam. "What else is goin' on?"

"Anton is competing this weekend in Gillette. Since Cam is on duty, I'll probably end up driving Anton and Gib to the event to get them registered. Channing and Colby plan to come later, depending on..."

What happens with Carolyn.

As far as Carson was concerned, he'd be loading up his wife and taking her home. "Tell the boys I'm sorry I won't get to watch them compete. Anton has come a long way in his bull doggin' skills this summer."

Domini sighed. "It's because he's shot up four inches in the last six months. With this growth spurt I cannot keep enough food in the house for that boy."

"I remember them days."

"Dimitri, Oxsana, Sasha and Markus have art and science camp at the community center all next week. Oh, and Macie and I decided to go to a restaurant management conference in Denver for four days at the beginning of August. Which will leave Cam home with the kids by himself for the first time. I've already informed him that I expect him to deal with our children by himself. No passing off babysitting duties to Anton and Liesl. No dumping them off with Aunt Keely or with Grandpa and Gran-gran or any of his other brothers."

"Aren't those decisions about what he does or doesn't do with the kids when you ain't around his choice?"

She picked at a stray thread on the bottom of her shirt. "Normally I'd agree with you. Cam is a great father. He's involved with every aspect of our kids' lives. But sometimes he says things before he thinks them through."

Now it made sense. "Jesus. What did my thick-tongued boy spout off about?"

"Something that made me want to punch him in his smart mouth. Hence the 'no relying on your massive family and overly kind sisters-in-law' to pull his butt out of the fire. He will deal with his children all by his little self if he thinks it's so easy."

Carson laughed. "Give me the days you'll be gone. We'll ignore his calls. Though, I gotta say, I feel for him. Carolyn left me with all six kids for five days once."

Her look of surprise was there and gone. "Really?"

"Yeah. Keely was...two. Cord was fifteen. Back then Caro did all of the house stuff. I mean, it wasn't that she raised the kids by herself while I ranched, it's just—"

"Carson, it's okay." Domini patted his leg. "No judgment from me. So what happened?"

"The better question is what *didn't* happen?"

She groaned.

"So when Cam is feelin' all kinds of cocky about how easy it is keepin' six kids in line with no break from the other parent for days on end, ask him about the time his mother left me in charge because I guarantee he'll remember."

Domini smiled. "Thank you. One of these days I'd like to hear what happened straight from the horse's mouth. I have a feeling I won't get the whole story from my husband." She stood. "I won't keep you. I do have munchkins to herd."

"Thanks for comin' by, Domini."

She crouched in front of him. "I know you have a dozen people you can call. But if there's anything you need, day or night, or even if you just need someone to listen to you, remember you can call me. Being married to Cam, being part of the McKays, has given me everything I ever wanted and if I can pay that back, even in a small way, let me know."

"I might take you up on that."

"I hope you do." She patted his hand. "And if you want to eat all those cookies in one sitting? It'll be our little secret."

Carson limited himself to two more cookies. The sugar buzz wore off and he started to crash. He stretched out, his mind flipping back and forth between what dumb thing Cam might've said to the mother of his children and that summer Carolyn had left him in charge...

Five days. With all six kids. By himself.

He could do this.

Couldn't he?

You deal with five hundred head of cattle every day. Wrangling six kids? Piece of cake.

Famous last words.

Carson stowed Carolyn's suitcase behind the driver's seat. The boys were lined up by age on the walkway to the porch, as Mama McKay said goodbye to her cubs. At fifteen Cord was already taller than his mother. A gangly kid, all arms and legs, and a deeper voice, but not yet to the stage where his mother's affection embarrassed him. At age thirteen Colby was almost the same size as Cord, with a stockier build, and he was obsessed with all things rodeo. Ten-year-old Colton was the instigator of the bunch, but he managed to charm his way out of trouble. The kid was also a brawler—such a chip off the old block; he and Cal had to bust up fights between Colt and Kane at least every couple of weeks. Eight-year-old Cameron and six-year-old Carter were still too young to be much help on the ranch, but they found trouble more often than not, which meant they were tasked with entertaining Keely.

Oh, his two-year-old baby girl had her five brothers twisted around her chubby little fingers. All she had to do was bat those big blue eyes, flash her dimpled smile, toss those black ringlet curls or stomp her foot and her protectors came running.

When Carolyn said, "Listen up," Carson refocused.

Carolyn picked Keely up and propped her on a hip. "You boys *will* bathe when I'm gone."

"Aw man, do we have to?" Colt complained.

"Yes. And dunking each other in the stock tank doesn't count."

Colby nudged Cord. Cord shoved him back, knocking him into Colt and Cam.

"Boys," Carson said sharply. "Quit horsin' around and listen to your mother."

"You will be respectful to each other, to the house, and most importantly you will help your father with whatever he needs."

"Hey, wait. Who's cookin' for us?" Colby asked suspiciously.

"Dad is," Cord said with a snicker.

"Dad?" Colt looked horrified. "But he don't know how to cook nothin'."

"There's plenty of sandwich fixings and meals in the freezer."

"And cookies?" Cam asked hopefully.

"Yes, cookies, but just like when I'm home, cookies only after chores are done."

"Mama, do I have chores?" Carter asked.

"Yes. You'll be in charge of feeding the dogs. Have your brothers show you what to do." Carolyn looked over at Carson and he tapped his watch. She nodded and kissed the top of Keely's head before she set her down. "Now, come and give me hugs."

They swarmed her. Then they shouted goodbye and raced inside, Cord bringing up the rear after he'd scooped Keely up and carried her into the house.

She stared at the closed door for several long moments before she walked over to him.

Carson pulled her into his arms. "Sorry about your Aunt Hulda, sugar."

"Thanks. I'm sure it'll hit me that she's really gone when Kimi and I are dividing up her belongings."

"You think you can get it all done in five days?"

"Aunt Hulda was very organized. Everything is in a storage facility, boxed and labeled where it's supposed to go. Kimi and I just have to contact the recipients. And meet with the lawyer to hear her will." Her shoulders shook and a sob escaped.

He rubbed circles on her back and rested his chin on her head, feeling so helpless and wanting to make her sadness disappear.

She tilted her head back and looked at him. "Sorry to be blubbering on you."

"I don't like wearin' your tears unless they're happy ones, but you've a right to your grief. I know she meant a lot to you." He curled his hands around her face and wiped away her tears.

"It'll be good for Kimi and me to be able to talk about her on the drive."

"Are any of your brothers goin' to the funeral?"

"No. That makes me sad because she's the only family we ever had besides each other."

"I know how that goes. My dad was my grandparents' only child to survive to adulthood. My mom's entire family got wiped out in the flu epidemic and she ended up an orphan. It's good you had your aunt as long as you did."

"You are such a sweet man." She pressed her mouth to his. "I'll miss you." Another couple of soft kisses. "So, so much."

"Don't know how I'm gonna function with my heart gone," he murmured gruffly against her mouth. "I love you, Caro."

"I know. You reminded me of that very thoroughly last night."

He grinned. "And I'll remind you again the night you get home."

"Counting down the days, cowboy." She stepped back and looked at the house. "I've never been away from the kids this long."

"I'm sure they're already missin' you."

"You'll be okay with them."

A statement, not a question. Was she trying to convince herself? Or him?

"I'll be fine. Keely's outta diapers, so it's all good."

Carolyn poked him in the chest. "I still don't know how you managed to get away without changing a single diaper after fifteen years of parenthood and six kids, Carson McKay."

Very careful and artful dodging if he did say so himself. "Drive safe. Call me when you get to the motel."

"I will." She paused. "I left lists on the refrigerator."

He didn't need lists. Wasn't like he was a stranger or just babysitting. These were his kids; he'd been around them every day of their lives. He knew how to take care of them.

"Go. I got this covered."

The first day? No problem. Carson dragged all the kids along in the feed truck when he did the late afternoon cattle check. They had sandwiches for supper. He figured it'd be hard to screw up sandwiches until he realized he had to make seven different kinds because none of them liked them fixed the same way. They also dusted two bags of potato chips and two dozen cookies.

After supper they watched TV. He let the *you have to bathe* rule slide tonight. His sweet Keely even curled up in his lap and fell asleep. Ten o'clock rolled around and the boys went to bed without arguing.

Piece of cake.

At two in the morning, someone shook him awake. He squinted at his oldest son. "Cord? What's goin' on?"

"Keely is cryin'."

Shit. Why hadn't he heard her?

Because Carolyn gets up with the kids at night if they need something, not you.

"Why?"

"I dunno. She's cryin' that she wants Mom."

"Okay. Lemme slip on some clothes and I'll be right there."

"Hurry. Cam said she's been screamin' in her crib for a while."

Jesus.

After Carson dug around in his dresser drawer, he found a pair of cotton pajama bottoms—he'd never worn the damn things before—and a T-shirt. Yawning, he walked down the hallway to Keely's room. She was too old for a crib, but the thought of her having free run of the house all night terrified Carolyn. She stood in her crib rattling the wooden bars like an ape at the zoo.

Cam was trying to talk to her through the wooden slats and she was screaming in his face. As soon as she saw him, she said, "Mommy?"

"Mommy ain't here, punkin, so you'll have to make do with me."

"Want Mommy."

"C'mere girlie." He picked her up and she burrowed into him like a tick, her little body shuddering. He looked at Cam. "You heard her cryin'?"

"Yeah."

Then he wondered how that was possible when Cam and Carter's room was at the opposite end of the hall. "Were you in the bathroom?"

Cam studied his feet.

A guilty look if he'd ever seen one. "What were you doin' up at two in the mornin', Cam?"

"I heard a noise on the back porch and it sounded like a mountain lion so I went down to check it out."

Cord snorted. "There ain't mountain lions around here dipsh—" he looked at his dad, "—stick."

"You went outside lookin' for a damn mountain lion at two o'clock in the mornin'?" Carson demanded.

"No. I climbed up on the counter and peeked out the window. Didn't see no eyes glowing back at me or nothin'."

"So you helped yourself to some cookies while you were down there," Cord sneered, pointing at the crumbs on Cam's *Indiana Jones* T-shirt.

"I was hungry. Then I came up here and heard Keely cryin'. She kept saying she wanted Mommy so I tried to tell her a story to get her back to sleep, but then she started screaming."

"What kind of story did you tell her?" Cord asked. "A monster story?"

Keely lifted her head and hiccupped. "Scawy monsers in my woom, Daddy."

"No, punkin, there aren't scary monsters in your room."

She nodded and pointed at Cam. "He tole me, *rawr!*—" she made a clawing motion with her hand, "—and den dey get me."

"For the love of God, Cameron, did you really tell your terrified two-year-old sister, at two in the mornin', that there are mon—them things in here?"

"I was trying to help her! She was cryin' and sad..." Then Cam's lower lip started to quiver.

Shit. He was such a big kid sometimes he forgot the boy was only eight.

"It's okay, son. Thanks for ah...tryin' to help. It's late. Just go crawl back in bed."

Cam came over and gave him a side hug before he raced off.

Cord shook his head and left without a word.

Carson brushed the curls out of Keely's eyes. "You ready to go back to bed, darlin' girl?"

She shook her head. "Hafta go potty."

"All right. But then bed, okay?"

"'Kay."

Of course it didn't work out that way. It was after three a.m. by the time he'd finished rocking her to sleep and slipped her in bed.

Day two started out well enough. Except for Cam insisting he could make his own toast. Only after the kitchen filled up with smoke and he refused to eat the slice of blackened bread did Cam confess that he'd never used the toaster.

Everyone got cereal at that point.

Carson left Colby in charge while he and Cord did morning chores.

They returned two hours later and Keely was running around the yard in just her underwear and her pink cowgirl boots.

No sign of any of her brothers outside.

Carson scooped Keely up and stormed into the house. "Colby! Why in the hell is your sister half nekkid outside all by herself?"

"What? She was outside? Me'n Colt were just, ah...doin' some stuff in here. I swear she snuck out on her own! She's always, uh, runnin' off on Ma."

Bullshit. His eyes narrowed. "What kinda of stuff were you doin'?" His gaze swept the living room. "Because it looks like a goddamned tornado went through here." That's when he noticed the hammer and a few nails on the coffee table. "What do you need them tools for?"

Colt said, "We hung up a picture for Ma. As a surprise."

"Where?"

He swore both boys looked at the ceiling and whistled.

Shit.

"Where?"

Colt pointed. "It's the one Carter drew her for Mother's Day and she put it in a frame and everything."

Keely squirmed. "Daddy. Down."

"Hang on." He walked over to the framed picture of flowers. They'd done a nice job hanging it straight and he would've been proud if not for the fact he could see the plaster buckling behind the frame. He lifted the picture off the wall the same time Colt said, "Dad, we can explain."

Sure enough. Behind the oh-so-thoughtfully hung picture was a fist-sized hole.

Keely said, "Uh-oh."

"You better believe uh-oh." He replaced the picture and counted to ten before he faced Colby and Colt. "What happened?"

"We stayed in the house like you told us," Colby blurted out. "And Colt bragged that he could punch as hard as Rocky Balboa. So I was holdin' a pillow—"

"And Colby thought it'd be funny if he pulled it away at the last second. My fist hit the wall and went clean through it," Colt finished.

"Jesus."

"Geezuz," Keely repeated.

"Dad. You ain't s'posed to swear," Colt pointed out.

"Least he didn't say the f-word. Though I think Ma hates *takin' the Lord's name in vain* swear words worse than the f-word or the c-word."

How the fuck did these boys know the c-word?

"It rhymes with lock," Cord said helpfully.

Okay, not *that* c-word.

"Ain't no one asked how my hand is," Colt grumbled.

"Or my stomach," Cam said from over by the couch. Which was missing all the cushions. Cushions that Cam was sprawled out on, on the floor, holding his gut.

"What happened to your stomach? And the couch?"

"Colt punched me. It's okay, Dad, don't get mad at him. I asked him to. But then it hurt really bad 'cause I'm pretty sure Colt does punch as hard as Rocky and I kinda...threw up."

"You threw up in the fuc—" *don't swear, don't swear,* "—in the livin' room?" Was that why the cushions were scattered to hell and back? Was he tryin' to cover it up? "On the couch?"

Cam rolled his head back and forth on the cushion. "No, I barfed in the bathroom. I got most of it cleaned up."

"You will get *all* of it cleaned up because I ain't on barf-mopping duty," he warned.

"How come Keely's still half-nekkid?" Cord asked.

"Good question." He looked at Colby, then Colt. "Why didn't one of you boys help her get dressed?"

"Ma always does that."

"Hey, I tried to get pants on her but she screamed in my face and tried to hit me," Colby said. "So I let her be nekkid. But she did get her boots on by herself."

On the wrong feet, Carson just noticed. "Girlie, you need to put some clothes on."

She rested her head on his shoulder and sighed. "'Kay. Wanna weaw a dwess. I'm a giwl, not like dem."

"And thank God for that," he muttered and shifted her higher on his hip. He glanced at the clock. It was only eleven a.m. Too damn early for a tumbler of whiskey.

Then he noticed he was one kid short. "Where's Carter?"

Colby and Colt looked at one another like they just remembered they had another brother. "Uh, he went to feed the dogs."

"By himself?"

"Yeah."

"You were supposed to help him and show him what to do."

"We sorta...forgot."

"How long ago did he go outside?"

They both shrugged.

Shit.

Carson motioned Cord over and handed him Keely. "Help her get dressed in a dress."

"Where are you goin'?"

"To find Carter." He pointed at Colby, Colt and Cam. "When I get back this place better not look like this, understand?" Then he leveled the only threat that would work. "I mean it, boys. No one is eatin' lunch or getting so much as a crust of bread until this place is cleaned up to your mother's standards."

That made them hop to it.

Then Carson went in search of his youngest son. The kid wanted chores like his brothers and Carson had been putting him off, it was just easier to do even the little things himself. He whistled for the dogs.

Weird they weren't around. They were always underfoot.

He headed to the barn. "Carter? You in here?"

No answer.

He cut to the last empty stall where they kept the dog food. The bag of dog food that'd been half full...was now completely empty. No sign of the dogs or his son.

That's when he noticed the side door that led to the back pasture was cracked open. He pushed it open all the way and stepped onto the packed dirt. "Carter?"

All at once a sobbing boy launched himself at Carson. Alarmed, Carson picked him up and said, "Are you hurt?"

"No, Daddy."

"What's wrong?"

"I think I killed Beast and Sassy!" Then he sobbed so hard Carson couldn't understand the rest of what he said.

"Slow down, son."

More hiccupped crying.

Once he'd settled, Carson said, "Where are the dogs?"

Carter pointed to the stock tank.

What the hell? "Where? I don't see them. Are they in the tank?"

"Behind it."

Still carrying Carter, he walked over and sure enough, the dogs were lying on their sides, bellies bloated, panting heavily. Then he caught the ripe scent of barf and saw two enormous piles of vomit, mostly comprised of undigested chunks of dog food. At least the dogs weren't laying in it. He wasn't cleaning up kid *or* dog barf.

"You wanna tell me what happened?"

"I went to get the scoops of dog food and Beast and Sassy followed me into the stall. And they started eatin' and eatin' and they wouldn't stop! Not even when I tried to pull them away. So I made a trail of food and they followed me outside. But then they started drinkin' and drinkin' from the stock tank. They wouldn't stop that neither. Then they started throwin' up, like a lot, and they laid down and I thought maybe they was dead."

"That's why you're hidin' out here?"

He nodded. "I didn't want them to die alone."

Carson pressed his lips to Carter's sweaty forehead. He was such a sweet boy.

Then Carter said, "But then I was scared that maybe you'd whup me for killin' them, so I was hidin'."

He had to work hard not to laugh. "You didn't kill them. They're pretty sick though. But that's their own doin'. They're greedy pups and they don't know better than to eat everything in sight. I'm thinkin' maybe they learned their lesson."

"Sorry, Daddy, I just wanted to help."

"I know. I'm sorry that you've been sittin' out here by yourself, while your brothers..." He sighed and set Carter down. "Let's make sure the door to the feed stall is shut tight before we head back to the house."

The morning of day three, Carson called Cal and asked if he wanted to come over with Kade and Kane for a couple of hours so he and Cord and Colby could get some work done. His brother laughed, said no way in hell, said it wasn't his problem that Carson had three times more kids than he did and hung up on him.

Asshole.

So as to not have a repeat of the previous day, leaving the kids unattended in the house, Carson and Colby saddled up. Cord drove the feed truck and his siblings rode along. He led the cattle through four pastures and Carson and Colby followed behind wrangling the strays. What should've taken two hours took four and a half.

By the time they returned home, the boys were starved and fighting, and Keely had a complete meltdown because Colt threw the wildflower she'd picked out the pickup window.

Lunch was a free for all and as he looked in the refrigerator, he wondered where the hell all the food had gone. And how they could be completely out of dishes when the boys complained that he wasn't feeding them?

He shooed the kids out of the kitchen and loaded the dishwasher just to have some peace and quiet, knowing Caro would probably fall over in shock if she saw him. It wasn't that he believed domestic chores were women's work—over the years he'd offered to help out, but his wife made it very clear that the house was her domain and any help she needed she'd get from their children. He figured her stance was because if she accepted his help then she'd have to reciprocate and help him with *cow stuff.*

Afterward Carson sat down with a cup of coffee.

Within five minutes he heard, "Dad?"

He glanced up from the newspaper—the first chance he'd had to read two-day-old news—and saw Colby leaning in the doorframe. "Yeah?"

"I need to work on my ropin' skills for junior rodeo."

"Ride and rope?"

He nodded. "Been workin' on stationary ropin' and I gotta step it up for the meet at the end of the month."

He'd been promising the kid since last week he'd help him get in some practice time. "All right. As soon as Keely is up from her nap we'll head out there."

273

Colby snorted. "She ain't sleepin'. She's been bouncin' and singin' ever since you put her in her crib."

Great. He drained his coffee. "Get saddled up. I'll send Cord to gather calves. Where is he?"

Colby jerked his chin toward the stairs. "In the bathroom. He spends more time in there lately than a girl. Me'n Colt and Cam have had to start goin' outside."

Oh hell no. Cord wasn't...

Yes, of course he was. He was that age. Where once he could whack off that's all he'd ever want to do.

"Tell him to get his ass out of the bathroom. I'll round up the boys and Keely. You okay with me bein' your hazer or would you rather Cord did it?"

"You."

"All right. But it'll be a short session."

Carson had Colt and Cam carry the bench from the picnic table outside the corral, while he carried Keely. With her mother being gone, the girl had serious abandonment issues. Or maybe she was just cranky from day two with no nap.

Piece of cake, right?

He told the smart voice in his head to fuck off.

The area offset from the barn was just a dirt pasture—not a setup per rodeo specs, but it'd work for Colby's skill level. Although he knew if any of the boys took a serious interest in rodeo, they'd have to invest in space and equipment.

He passed Keely off to Colt and squatted down so all three boys were paying attention to him. "Your butts don't leave this bench, understand?"

"What if I hafta go to the bathroom?" Carter asked.

"Hold it."

"What if a big rattlesnake comes out of a hole in the ground and its fangs are dripping poison and it acts like it's gonna attack us?" Cam asked with a straight face.

He gave Cam a level look. "Even then. And maybe you oughta back off the evil critter scenarios in front of the littler kids?"

Cam sighed and kicked at the dirt. "I told Ma that readin' would just get me in trouble."

Jesus.

"This ain't gonna take long, so you all just sit here and watch us." Carson hustled to ready his horse. Once he mounted up, he noticed four angry mama cows outside the corral bellowing at their calves. The calves were too busy frolicking inside the pen to pay attention.

Colby was working his rope, keeping his horse Bart reined in. That gelding liked to bolt and Carson didn't trust any of his kids besides Colby to handle the ornery thing.

Carson trotted over to him. "Since we ain't got space for a straight line, I'll work the outside of the corral and keep the calf in the center."

Colby nodded, already deep in competition mode.

They cantered to the far side of the corral and paused. Carson yelled, "Chute open," and Cord cracked the gate.

The first calf came out and looked around but didn't run. Still, Colby was immediately on the ball, rope ready. He tossed the loop, made the catch and bailed off Bart, piggin' string between his teeth as he tied four legs together and threw up his hands.

Too bad they weren't timing because that would've been a good score.

Colby untied the calf, it trotted off and he shouted at Cord to get the next one ready. In that moment Colby wasn't a thirteen-year-old boy, but Carson saw him as the man he'd become. Methodical, determined and competitive as hell.

Yeah, maybe he'd better plan on getting that rodeo space ready sooner rather than later.

Once the calves figured out they were about to be roped and dragged, they kicked up more of a fuss. After ten run-throughs, Carson said, "You're lookin' better. You won't have to adjust on the fly in an arena as you do here. But this practice showed you can do it." He dismounted and handed the reins to Cord. "Thanks for handlin' the chute."

"And takin' care of your horse," he added sullenly.

God save him from surly teens. Scary shit to think he'd have three of them that age at any given time for the next decade and a half.

As he crossed the dirt, Carson noticed his kids were sitting on the bench like he'd asked. Then Keely's beloved stuffed horse Buckles sailed over the corral onto the dirt. Just as he opened his mouth to yell at them to stay put, he'd pick it up, that little monkey Carter scaled the fence.

When Carter reached the top rail and turned around, most likely to taunt his older brothers with his derring-do, he lost his balance and hit the dirt inside the fence with a bone-crunching thud.

Carson was pretty sure he'd never run that fast in his life.

By the time he reached Carter, the boy was wailing. And Carson knew why; his left arm was at the wrong angle.

Fuck. Carolyn was gonna kill him.

Colt and Cam were shouting, Keely was blubbering about her horse, and a wide-eyed Carter, obviously in shock, tried to squirm away.

"Son. You gotta stay still."

"It hurts, it hurts, it hurts!"

That sad, pain-filled voice sliced through him. "Ssh. I know. We'll get you fixed up, I promise."

Cord and Colby both rushed over.

"Holy fuckin' shit," Cord said. "It's broke, ain't it?"

"Yeah. We'll have to take him into town. Cord, the keys are in the truck. Go get it and bring it around so we can get everyone loaded up here."

"We're all goin'?" Colby said.

"No choice. Now get them horses dealt with so we can go."

Colby took off.

Fifteen minutes later they were on their way into Sundance, with Cord driving and Carter on Carson's lap, curled into him. It was the quietest he'd heard the kids.

Not that it'd last.

Six kids in the hospital for over two hours? The staff was happy to see the ass end of them.

Too het up to worry about cooking, Carson had Cord stop at the grocery store and sent him in to buy frozen pizzas.

Glancing down at Carter passed out on his lap, he realized the pain meds had kicked in. He smoothed the boy's hair back, grateful the injury hadn't been worse. He noticed Carter clutched the black marker in his fist so his brothers could sign his cast.

Back at the ranch, Carter didn't move when Carson carried him into the house and situated him on his bed.

By the time he returned to the kitchen, the boys had opened all ten frozen pizzas. No doubt they'd devour them without tasting them.

He went straight for the whiskey.

Keely refused to eat pizza so he gave her applesauce and cottage cheese—most of which ended up in her hair, which required a bath. In the tub she leapt up and smacked her forehead into the soap dish, leaving a mini goose egg that would likely be a hideous shade of black and blue by the time Carolyn came home.

He just had to survive the next two days. The worst of it had to be over.

Didn't it?

Day four Carson ended up serving cookies for breakfast since they were out of breakfast food.

"What happened to all the cereal? There were five boxes when your mother left."

"We ate 'em when we got hungry," Colby said.

Which seemed to be all the damn time. Feeding these boys was a fulltime job itself.

Carson did a quick head count. Carter sleeping upstairs. Cord—in the bathroom again—Colby here, Keely here. "Where are your brothers?"

Colby's eyes were glued to the back of the empty cereal box. "Haven't seen them."

"At all?"

"I saw them when I was comin' out of the bathroom this mornin'," Cord offered as he strolled in.

"When?"

"Like seven."

That was an hour ago. "What were they doin'?"

"Didn't ask."

Two hours later, just as Carson was ready to call the sheriff, Colt and Cam ambled up the driveway like Tom Sawyer and Huckleberry Finn, fishing poles slung over their shoulders and carrying buckets.

"Where in the hell have you boys been?"

"Fishin'!" Colt said with pride.

"You didn't think to tell anyone where you were goin' at seven o'clock in the damn mornin'? You just took off?"

"We wanted to surprise you and catch fish for breakfast since we don't got no food."

Carson tried to remain calm and not thrash the crap out of them. Where the hell had they thought they'd catch fish around here? The stock dam?

"But we didn't catch nothin'," Cam said, dejected.

"That's cause you don't even know how to cast a line," Colt scoffed.

"Do too!"

"Do not," Colt mimicked.

Cam stopped. Holding his pole with both hands, he yelled, "Do too! Watch this!" Then he started wildly waving his pole around and let the fishing line fly. "Hey. Where'd it go?" He spun the reel and jerked on the line hard.

Colt screamed and bent over.

For the fifteen seconds it took Carson to reach Colt's side, he feared Cam had hooked Colt in the eye. He said, "Where'd it get you?"

"My leg!"

"Which leg? Son, stand up so I can see it."

When Colt straightened, Carson saw the hook imbedded in the back of Colt's calf, deep enough to have threaded through the skin in two places. It'd gouged out a chunk of flesh before it'd caught. This was beyond him being able to yank the damn thing out with a pair of pliers.

Fuck. Looked like he'd be making another goddamned visit to the emergency room.

Carson took out his pocket knife and said, "Hold still."

"Dad! It ain't that bad! Don't cut off his leg!" Cam yelled.

"For the love of God, Cameron. I ain't gonna cut off his leg. I'm cuttin' the fishin' line."

"Oh."

"Can you get the hook out?" Colt asked, craning his neck around to gauge the damage.

"'Fraid not. Gonna hafta take you to town."

Cam had dropped the pole and crouched to check it out. "Well, it don't look *that* bad. Ain't hardly bleeding at all. With how loud you screamed like a girl I thought I'd see the hook stuck in the bone and blood gushing everywhere."

Colt spun around and punched Cam in the eye, knocking him on his ass. "Ain't that bad? How'd you like it if—" he growled and lunged.

Carson was quick enough to stop Colt from pouncing on Cam, who was now holding his face and wailing. "Knock it the hell off, both of you. This is getting fuckin' ridiculous."

"What's goin' on? We heard screamin'."

Cord and Colby—holding Keely—stopped five feet from where Cam was curled into a ball. And Colt was bleeding.

"Colt has a fishin' hook stuck in his calf, so I'm taking him to the hospital. You all stay here. And stay in the damn house." He rested on his haunches in front of Cam. "Lemme see."

"I think he popped my eyeball."

Mr. Dramatic. The kid should be an actor. "Then you'd better let me look at it so I know whether I'll need to take you to town with us."

Cam moved his hand.

Carson sucked in a sharp breath. Already swollen. The kid would have one helluva shiner. "Can you see?"

"Sorta."

"Put something cold on it." He addressed his oldest sons. "Watch TV or something until we get back. If your mother calls, not a word about us bein' at the hospital, got it?"

"Yes sir."

He gestured to the poles and buckets. "Get this stuff put away." Then to Colt he said, "Stay put. I'll get the truck." He checked to make sure he had his wallet. In fifteen years with six kids they'd been to the ER once. *Once.* The first time he's left alone with the kids? He was on his second trip in less than twenty-four hours.

Yeah, his wife was gonna lose her mind.

Cord rapped on the driver's side window.

"What?"

"Probably better stop at the store while you're in town since there's nothin' to eat around here."

Colt ended up with four stitches but it'd taken the doctor longer than he expected to remove the hook. After the doc had cleaned the area, and Carson had seen the level of grime on Colt's skin, he swore that kid was taking a shower if he had to hose him down himself.

At the grocery store he'd ended up with a cartful of food—all quick, all junk, all of which would make his sons happy.

Luckily there wasn't big trauma at home. Things were somewhat normal except for Carter being loopy from his pain meds. Keely had crashed, face down on her stuffed animal in the middle of the living room floor—but at least she was napping. Cam had a bag of frozen peas on his face. Colby was sprawled out on the couch. Cord was in the bathroom. Again.

That's when Carson realized it was damn near two o'clock and he hadn't checked cattle. How the hell had he forgotten? Now he had to feed the horde before he could feed the herd.

Lunch was eight cans of Spaghettios, a dozen hot dogs, two bags of barbecue-flavored potato chips, a box of Twinkies—all washed down with a gallon and a half of chocolate milk.

As soon as he chucked the paper plates from lunch, he wandered into the living room. "I need to check cattle."

Cord sighed and stood.

Carson shook his head. "You're in charge...and hold off on your bathroom visits until we get back."

Cord's face turned bright red.

He pointed to Colby. "You're up. Let's go."

Despite the gusts of wind that sent the cattle looking for shelter, they finished an hour and a half later. Colby hopped out to open the last gate, Carson drove through and waited, watching in the rearview mirror like he always did to make sure the gate actually got shut.

That's when a gust of wind shook the truck and he watched as the wind caught the gate, slamming Colby's hand between the gate and the post.

Carson bailed out of the truck and barely stopped the gate from smacking into Colby again as he rested on his knees, cradling his arm.

"Fuck, fuck, fuck, fuck," Colby yelled. "That fuckin' stupid fuckin' gate."

"How bad is it?"

"I don't know."

"Can you move it?"

Colby shook his head.

"Come on." Carson opened the passenger side and helped Colby in before he went back and secured the gate.

After he'd climbed in the truck, he saw Colby's tears before he tried to blink them away. This kid never cried. Not even as a baby, so he must be hurting bad. "Show me."

Wincing, he moved his left arm.

Carson's stomach bottomed out, seeing that Colby's right hand had already swelled and was turning red and purple. A long raised welt had darkened on the center of his forearm. "Christ, kid. How are you not screamin'? That fucker looks painful."

"I didn't..."

"Son, you don't gotta act tough around me. I'd rather you were honest so I have an idea of what we're dealin' with."

"It feels like all the bones in my hand are broken."

A hand injury with multiple broken bones could mean multiple surgeries—and from what he'd heard, they were painful and incapacitating.

Carson left Colby in the truck when he went in to explain what'd happened and why he had to make his third trip to the emergency room.

On the drive into town, Carson kept up a steady stream of chatter because Colby's pain-filled silence was more than he could take.

Sure he'd been upset holding onto Carter and hoping there weren't complications when they reset the break. But the poor overwhelmed six-year-old had all but passed out.

Then today with Colt, the kid had cracked fishing jokes all the way into town. The only time his charm faltered was when the nurse had numbed the area with four separate shots. Carson had seen one single tear escape while the ten-year-old gritted his teeth.

"Dad," Colby interrupted. "It's okay. I don't really think Ma will skin you alive when she gets home. This was an accident."

His thirteen-year-old boy having to console his forty-one-year-old father just made him feel worse.

This trip to the hospital took longer. He'd be damn surprised if the medical personnel didn't call Wyoming Child Protective Services.

He remained by Colby's side through all the X-rays and waiting for the on-call specialist to give a diagnosis.

The good news? No broken bones but a couple of hairline fractures that required Colby to wear a cast for six weeks. The bad news? Since he'd injured his riding hand the kid couldn't compete for the rest of the summer. Better than not being able to compete for a few years because of surgeries.

By the time they finished three hours later, Carson was exhausted. They stopped at Dairy Queen and picked up burgers and fries and ice cream for supper.

The mood at home was subdued, although it hadn't affected their appetites. His nerves were shot. He sat on the couch and Keely immediately crawled into his lap, snuggling into him. Then Carter did the same thing on the opposite side. Then all the boys were piled on the couch next to each other or on the floor in front of it. No bickering or shoving, and he finally relaxed.

Carolyn arrived home earlier on day five than Carson expected.

He caught her in his arms as she alighted from the truck, holding onto her tightly—then he kissed her with the passion he usually saved for behind closed doors. When he finally released her mouth, she sighed. "You really did miss me."

"Like you wouldn't believe." He heard the screen door open and knew the time of reckoning had come. His gut tightened, as did his throat. And he was man enough to admit even his balls shrunk a little, as he ran through everything he had to tell her.

"Mom's home!" Cam said with glee.

And still he didn't move.

"Carson? Sweetheart, what's wrong?"

"You'll see. And uh, don't judge me too harshly, okay?"

Carolyn ripped herself away from him. She froze after she'd only taken two steps.

All six kids were in a line, like before. Carson tried to see it from her eyes. Cord, the only one without obvious injury, unless she looked close enough to see the chafing on his right hand from continual jacking off, held Keely, who was sporting a goose egg on her forehead. Next was Colby, his hand in a cast. Next was Colt, a bandage wrapped around his calf. Then Cam, with a vicious black eye. And finally Carter, with a cast on his left arm.

Silence.

Then Carolyn slowly faced him.

And Carson blurted out, "I swear I can explain."

"Mr. McKay?"

Carson blinked at the nurse. "Yes."

"It's time if you want to go in."

"Thank you."

Yeah, that wouldn't be a memory he'd bring up with his wife.

Chapter Twenty-Four

Hospital, Day 4—afternoon

"I'm headed down to the cafeteria," Carson told Tori, the day charge nurse.

"The special today is Salisbury steak. And it is good."

"Thanks. I'll give it a try." He rode the elevator down to the first floor. The doors opened and he was surprised to see his sister-in-law—or was she his ex-sister-in-law?—Joan McKay standing there.

She said, "Just the man I wanted to see. But it looks like you're leaving?"

"Only to grab lunch in the cafeteria. You're welcome to tag along if you'd like."

"Sure, if you don't mind."

"Not at all. It's this way."

Joan got into the beverages only line. Carson loaded up his plate knowing he wouldn't eat again today. He chose a spot in the corner away from everyone since he'd become a real germaphobe.

"You look surprised to see me," Joan said.

"I'm surprised to see anyone, if you wanna know the truth. The kids aren't taking the 'no visitation' rule too well."

"I don't imagine they are. I knew I'd better stop in before I see my grandkids. Georgia mentioned Jackson and Carly had the sniffles. Which means Tucker, Wyatt and Bethany probably do too. Brandt and Tell said to let you know you and Carolyn are in their thoughts."

"Tell 'em I said thanks."

Joan leaned forward. "I'm sorry this happened to Carolyn. I've always admired her. Although she didn't like Casper, she treated me well. She still treats me like part of the family, even after…"

"You and Casper got divorced? Or after Casper died?"

"Both." She sipped her coffee. "But I was thinking more of when she birthed kid after kid and I struggled to get pregnant and stay that way. Then when it finally happened, she welcomed my boys. I know we didn't get included in a lot of McKay stuff in those early years, but I never resented her for it."

"Why not?"

"Because she was protecting you. She didn't want you to have to deal with Casper in your own home. He went out of his way to make you feel like shit during the work day and she wouldn't put up with that in a place that's supposed to be your refuge."

"She's put up with a lot over the years."

"She took it all in stride and she lived those Christian tenets so many—including my ex-husband—paid lip service to. She and Kimi and Vi were completely supportive after Luke died and all the rest of the crap that happened afterward. Very few people know how instrumental she was getting me settled when I left Casper." She smiled sadly. "Carolyn just wanted to get me the hell away from him."

Carson had to tread lightly. Joan didn't only have rotten memories of her time with Casper, but what he'd learned of the man had tainted everything. He couldn't fake letting bygones be bygones.

"I don't know if I ever really thanked you for what you did for Brandt, Tell and Dalton as far as the ranch. I mean, I know you didn't retire because you wanted to."

"Oh, you'd be surprised how eager we were to pass the reins over," he said dryly.

Joan smiled again. "It went above and beyond. It changed everyone's life."

"Ours too, but I'm happy to hear that." He picked at the meat soaked in gravy. The food was okay, but it wasn't as good as Carolyn's. "Dalton stopped by. Sounds like him'n Rory had a good time on their honeymoon."

"They're leaving for Montana tomorrow. It's a good fit for them up there. Especially after all that happened."

His gaze moved to hers.

Anguish distorted her face. "You know, don't you?"

"About Casper secretly beatin' the fuck outta Dalton? Yeah. Charlie told me and Cal."

"Does Carolyn know?"

Carson shook his head. "Charlie debated on even tellin' us. I didn't talk to my kids about it. Neither did Cal. We figure if Dalton wants people to know, it's his business to tell them, not ours or anyone else's."

Relief swam in her eyes. But it was there and gone. "I didn't know it was going on. And I'm sure you're thinking, how could she not know what was happening with her own children? Living in the same house..."

"You don't gotta explain or defend yourself to me, Joan."

"Why not?"

"Because it ain't my place to judge. There's a lot of guilt to go around. If I hadn't been so pissed off at Casper about ranch stuff, I might've recognized the signs. Me'n Cal and Charlie. We didn't. We were too wrapped up in our own lives. If not for Luke callin' us out, things would've stayed the same."

Joan looked confused. "What did Luke do?"

"He said just because Casper was an asshole didn't automatically make his sons assholes. They worked hard and had as much McKay blood as their cousins—our sons—did. Casper kept them out of the loop on ranch happenings and Luke asked that one of us keep at least him apprised of what was goin' on so they didn't look like lazy idiots."

"How old was Luke?"

"Seventeen."

She closed her eyes. "Luke wasn't perfect, but I'd like to think he would've gotten his act together if he'd had more time. I miss him every day." She sniffled and looked at Carson. "Sorry. Not exactly a happy topic."

"No, it ain't. But sometimes we gotta look back to go forward. Whatever mistakes you made, you've atoned for them from what I can see. It seems your sons have forgiven you or at least gotten to a place where the past don't have a stranglehold. That says a lot about how you raised them and what kinda men they are."

"Thank you. We've moved past a lot of it and I'm thankful every day my sons have their heritage as part of the McKay Ranch. If Casper had had his way..."

Carson's gut clenched. "Yeah. I remember that time all too well. Though, I try not to think about it."

"Casper had such extreme reactions when it came to death." She paused. "How did he react after your mother died? He never spoke of it to me."

They'd all been in shock. There was no sickness or downward health spiral like Carolyn's mother. Helen McKay had been fine one day and dead the next. Their father had dealt with his devastation by working his sons even harder, so at age eighteen Carson and Cal bore the brunt of Jed's grief.

"Casper simply shut down. He'd been closer to Ma than any of us. She let him get away with everything. She took Casper's side even against our father's."

"But Charlie was the baby, and he was sickly, so I would've guessed he would be spoiled," Joan said.

Carson shook his head. "As the oldest boys, me'n Cal knew Dad had greater expectations for us. He never expected much out of Casper because Ma made excuses for him. I think if she'd lived longer Casper wouldn't have stayed on the ranch. He had aspirations to go to college but after Ma passed on he was lucky he graduated at all. Then he figured out he didn't have to work very hard and he'd still get paid the same as the rest of us. By age twenty he was completely apathetic. After that he just got plain mean."

"I'm familiar with his mean side. Whenever he was...annoyed with me, he'd say his mother never would've allowed him to marry me because she would've known I was a liar, and a whore who'd be a sorry excuse for a wife and a lousy mother."

"How you stayed with him as long as you did..."

"I made the best of the situation. I'm not the first woman to do it, likely I won't be the last. My sons gave me joy. And at times, they gave him joy too. It wasn't all bad. I'm not making excuses or coloring the past as I'd like it to've been, but there were happy times in our house." She stood. "This wasn't what I had in mind when I decided to visit."

"Joan, it's fine. There's never gonna be water under the bridge where Casper is concerned. For either of us."

"I know that. Take care of yourself, tell Carolyn she's in my prayers, and I'll be in touch."

Carson lumbered back to the ICU waiting room. As he donned the space suit, his thoughts had drifted to that dark place he'd avoided and he didn't want to drag that into Caro's room.

Your life has hardly been sunshine and rainbows. Besides, just because you remember it a certain way doesn't mean she will.

Inside the room, he hooked the rolling stool beside the bed and sat down wearily. "Hey, sugar. I'm sittin' here beside you. I know you can hear me. I *need* you to hear me. Come back to me. I need you to know that I'm right here, I ain't goin' anywhere."

Then he waited a beat to gather his thoughts.

"I had another visitor. Joan. She sends her love and best wishes. As I was talkin' to her, it hit me that even when she's been part of our lives since Cord was what? Two? That until she left my brother, I didn't really know her. But then again, with all the stuff that's come to light in the past few months, I don't think I ever really knew Casper either.

"It was weird, Joan askin' about Casper's relationship with our mother. I hadn't thought of that in years. But it reminded me how Casper reacted after Ma died, which was totally different than his actions after Dad died." He paused. "Still burns my ass how I found out that our father was dead..."

Without warning, almost against her will Carolyn popped up at the listening place like a cork, roused by the sadness in Carson's tone. Disoriented, she only caught bits and pieces of what he was saying because his voice kept fading in and out.

What made him sound so sad?

She focused on the words, not the emotion, as she tried to avoid slipping back into the gray matter.

The word *died* leapt out at her.

What? He was talking about death? Who died?

Dear God. *She* wasn't dead, was she? Was that the reason for his sadness?

No. He'd be inconsolable if it were her.

Concentrate.

Eerie silence surrounded her.

Then...*burns my ass how I found out that our father was dead.*

It clicked. And she was spun into another memory...

Seeing Casper's truck pull into the drive so early in the morning set off Carolyn's warning bells. He always made Carson go to him if something needed to be discussed about the ranch.

That man was more than a little off. She'd considered asking if Casper had been the deranged kid pulling the wings off butterflies, or torturing barnyard animals, but part of her didn't want to know. She decided to give Carson a little time with his brother before she wandered outside. She had a legitimate excuse for interrupting; she'd talked to Joan two days ago and baby Dalton was fighting some kind of respiratory infection.

She got sidetracked by Carter looking for his baseball cleats, and then by Cam searching for his library card.

Ten minutes had passed when Carson stormed into the house, right past her, went into his office and slammed the door.

That'd never happened before.

She hovered by the closed door, trying to hear who Carson was talking to. She waited until several minutes of silence passed, then she knocked once and stepped inside the room.

Carson had his back to her as he stared out the window.

She closed the door and started toward him. "Sweetheart, is everything okay?"

He shook his head.

"What happened with Casper?"

"He came to tell me, to gloat really, that our father is dead."

Carolyn froze. "What?"

"Evidently Jed died during the night. For whatever reason they couldn't get ahold of Cal so they called Casper."

"And he's just letting you know *now*?"

"Claims he wanted to tell me in person."

"Does Cal know?"

"He does now. I just called him. And Charlie. Fuck."

She went to him, nestling her cheek against the rigid line of his back, wreathing her arms around his waist. "I'm sorry."

"Yeah, well, so am I. I hated putting him in that fuckin' nursing home. Even after that last stroke and Cal and Kimi couldn't take care of him..."

His entire body was rigid even as it shook.

"The man who spent his life outside, battling the elements, putting his blood and sweat into the land so he'd leave behind some kind of legacy for us, died alone in a tiny windowless room."

Her tears fell. Carson wasn't looking to be absolved of guilt; he was in one of those rare moods where he needed to vent.

"My father, a man I admired my whole life even when he could piss me off like no one else...is gone. Who the fuck would ever be happy about that?"

Had Casper acted happy that Jed McKay had died? Had the idiot said that to Carson?

"I know Dad ain't been the same for a few years, but he was always there. Goddammit, I just saw him yesterday. Now I'll never see him again. Keely is four; she won't remember him. He was so damn tickled to have a granddaughter. He won't see Cord graduate or take on more ranch responsibilities. He won't know that I..."

"That he did know. Jed McKay knew exactly how much you cared about him, about this family. How much blood, sweat and love you've poured into this place over the years. That's why he put you in charge, Carson. He understood you have the drive and the love of the land, and the cattle business, and will make sure the legacy he built will be passed on to the next generation of McKays. He was proud of you. He told me that himself. We both know the man wasn't prone to handing out any kind of praise unless it was earned. You earned it and his respect."

He didn't respond for the longest time. When he finally said, "Thank you," in such a quiet and sad tone she scarcely heard him. Then he disentangled from her embrace and faced her.

His eyes were dry. Not that she'd expected him to be sobbing, but beneath the sadness Carson was seething.

"I've gotta meet up with Cal and Charlie and go over the funeral stuff."

"What do you want me to do?"

"Tell the kids. Then we'll talk about it later."

She shook her head. "You—we—need to tell them before you leave."

"Caro—"

"He was your father; this crappy job shouldn't fall on me. And we broke it to the kids together last year when my dad passed on."

"Fine. They all here?"

"Except for Cord. You sent him to town."

"Hell, he's probably already heard the news about his grandpop at the hardware store. Round the rest of 'em up."

The kids lined up on the couch, from Colby to Keely, and Carson matter of factly informed them their grandfather was dead.

Carolyn understood the man was in shock, but still, it was a pretty abrupt way to break the news, especially to children. Gently, she said, "How about if we say a prayer for Grandpop, since he's at peace and in a better place."

Keely blurted out, "Grandpop Jed is at *Disneyland*?"

Carson cracked a smile at that. "No, punkin. Grandpop is in heaven now."

"Oh."

It was clear by the look Cam and Carter exchanged that they thought Disneyland was a much better option than heaven.

They all bowed their heads, Carolyn said the prayer and before they hit the last consonant in amen and crossed themselves, Carson had booked it out the door.

He didn't come home until late that night. But Carolyn hadn't been worried because Cal and Charlie were both out with him, doing whatever.

She'd talked to Joan, who'd been even more subdued than normal. Evidently Casper hadn't been with his brothers. In fact, Joan hadn't seen Casper at all.

The next morning Carson bounded out of bed and out of the house before Carolyn. During the day the phone rang off the hook. Friends and neighbors wanting the details on the funeral service and if they should bring food to one place so the four McKay wives could divvy it up for the McKay sons' families.

When her husband hadn't shown up for supper, and Cal and Charlie were mum on his whereabouts, Carolyn figured Carson had gone looking for a fight.

She knocked on Cord's bedroom door.

He barked, "What!"

"I need your help."

Cord immediately opened the door and stepped into the hallway—probably so she couldn't see the mess inside his room. "Ma? What's goin' on?"

"I need to find your father. You're driving. I'll meet you downstairs." Next she knocked on Colby's door.

He barked, "What!"

"I'll be gone a while. Cord's coming with me so you're on babysitting duty."

Colby immediately opened the door and stepped into the hallway—probably so she couldn't see the mess in his room either. "Babysitting *again*?"

"I'm not a baby!" Keely yelled from her room.

"Me neither," shouted Carter from the bathroom.

"Just watch your younger siblings, okay? I don't know when I'll be back."

Cord didn't say anything until they were halfway to town. She'd directed him to Moorcroft rather than the Golden Boot in Sundance—Carson's usual hangout. "I ain't surprised Dad's takin' Grandpop's death so hard. I haven't seen him since yesterday and he never disappears like this."

"Not in recent years. But before..." She shot Cord a look. "Let's just say you boys come by your fighting nature naturally."

"I'd heard rumors about Dad bein' like that...but I never put much stock in 'em."

"Why?"

Cord's look said, *Duh. Because he's old.*

"I hope he's just drowning his sorrows and not getting his pretty face messed up by some kid twenty years younger than him."

"Ma. Are you okay? Because you never say sh—stuff like that about Dad."

"Yes, I do. You boys just don't hear it." Where did these sons of hers think their good looks came from?

"When was the last time Dad got into a fight?"

She closed her eyes briefly, trying to remember. "Six years ago? A guy who was bitter about some cattle deal called him out on the cheating way the McKays did business. Two things your dad won't stand for. Someone tearing down the McKays or some guy coming on to me. Anyway, this guy wouldn't pipe down."

"Dad took a swing at him?"

"Eyes on the road, son. Yes, your dad went after him. And that ended it."

They drove through the Ziggy's parking lot first. No sign of Carson's truck.

"You don't think he could've left his truck somewhere and rode to the bar with someone else?"

She shook her head. "He doesn't hide it if he's out looking for trouble. He's probably at the Rusty Spur."

Cord gave her an odd look. "You've been there?"

If he only knew. "You do realize your father and I had a life before we had children?"

"Well, yeah, but I don't see you and dad tearing it up, getting wild and shit."

"Because we're old?"

"I didn't say that."

"You didn't need to."

He sighed. "I know where the Rusty Spur is."

They found Carson's truck. Carolyn made Cord stay in his vehicle while she went inside.

Carson had taken a seat at the end of the bar. A full shot glass sat beside a bottle of Coors.

The bartender caught her eye. "What'll it be?"

"A whiskey Coke—hold the whiskey."

"Coming right up."

Carson picked up the cigarette smoldering in the ashtray and took a drag. "You worried you'd find me fightin'?"

"That's been the case in the past. So I thought I'd see if you needed someone to have your back since your brothers aren't out with you."

"Except Casper was. Long enough to take a couple of shots at me. Then I took a couple of shots at him. More than a couple." He faced her.

Carolyn winced, seeing the fat lip and the beginnings of a shiner around his right eye. "I'm assuming Casper looks worse than you?"

"You're goddamned right he does. I hope the asshole is pissing blood." His feral grin sent a shudder through her.

She'd seen Carson fight, so she knew what kind of physical damage he was capable of inflicting. But the lingering anger rolling off him was new; usually he was much calmer after a fight. She laid her hand on his cheek. "Tell me what's going on, McKay."

He closed his eyes and leaned into her touch—another unusual reaction from him. "We ain't even buried Dad yet and Casper is already talkin' about selling the ranch. That was the first fuckin' thing the asshole said to me after he told me about Dad bein' gone. The first fuckin' thing."

She didn't know what to say to that.

"Casper is a big talker. But this time he actually followed through. He contacted a lawyer about dividing up the ranch and the assets."

"Can he force you, Cal and Charlie to sell?"

"He thinks he can. But the whole reason he's doin' it is because he knows we'll do anything to stop that from happening. He thinks he can force us into borrowing against what we own to buy him out." He picked up the shot and drained it. "We ain't got that kind of cash. We're land rich and cash poor. All of our profits go toward payin' ourselves and payin' off the yearly operating loan. With the way the Ag business is right now, family farms and ranches goin' under, there's no way any bank would risk it."

"So what happens now?"

"If I had the money I'd buy him out and not give a shit if I ever see him again. But that ain't an option. So we're stuck with him."

"Sweetheart. Why didn't you talk to me about this?"

"Because I've been too pissed off. The kids don't need to see me this way either."

Her heart ached for him. Because of Casper's machinations, Carson couldn't even grieve his father. Rather than ask more questions, she sat next to him and sipped her soda.

Carson gestured to the bartender for another beer.

Carolyn was about to head outside to tell Cord to go home, when someone behind them said, "If it ain't another drunken McKay."

When Carolyn started to turn around, Carson put his hand on her forearm, stilling the movement.

"You drowning your sorrows because Daddy died?"

He ground out his cigarette.

"Bet that puts the future of the McKay Ranch in question."

Carson slowly turned around on his barstool. "First of all, Timmons, fuck off. You don't know nothin'. And I ain't that drunk, so tread lightly."

She couldn't help but spin to see who was stupid enough to taunt

Carson.

The guy was big. Easily six foot four, but skinny as a telephone pole. Over the years she'd become familiar with most of the families in the area, but she'd never seen this man.

"I'd like to tread all over your goddamned spine. I owe you payback," he sneered.

"For what?"

Timmons shuffled closer. "Don't play dumb. You know what for."

"It's been almost twenty years and you nursing a grudge ain't my problem."

"Nursing a grudge over what?" popped out of Carolyn's mouth before she stopped it.

"None of your business, bitch. Turn the fuck around and shut up."

Carson's boots were on the floor and he was in the guy's face. "Speak to my wife like that again and I will shut that fat mouth of yours."

"You always did bandy around like the cock of the walk." The guy loomed over Carson. "Too bad it don't hold water no more. You don't—"

Before the guy knew what hit him, Carson's fists connected several times in a row. The last crack to the jaw rocked him back and Carson charged him, knocking him to the floor.

He pummeled the guy, but not without consequence. Timmons got in a couple of good shots. Which only served to infuriate Carson more.

As she watched fists fly and blood spurt and heard the dull thud of flesh smacking into flesh, it seemed ten minutes passed before a bouncer intervened, when in reality it'd only been a few minutes.

The bouncer shoved Carson back. "For Christsake, McKay, ain't you old enough to know better by now?"

Carolyn tried to hand Carson a stack of bar napkins to mop up the blood and sweat dripping down his face, but he angrily smeared his face across his shirt sleeve.

"You keep letting assholes like him in here and I'll keep wiping the floor with them."

"What the hell did he do to you anyway?"

Carson glared at the man wheezing and bleeding on the floor. "The dumb fucker insulted my wife. That ain't ever gonna go well for any man, no matter how old I get."

Carolyn wanted to blow him a kiss but she refrained.

"Evidently he's still got a beef about something that happened nearly two decades ago."

"Damn right we do. You McKay fuckers took advantage of my grandpa and bought his land right out from under us. That parcel should've been passed down to his family. But no. You dangled a fat check in front of him and he sold to you without discussing it with any of us. That's sneaky shit."

"You're just pissed off that your granddaddy sold his land and pocketed the money to enjoy his retirement rather than pass down a heritage none of you gave a damn about. He was happy to sell to us because he knew we'd take care of it and keep it productive. That's what burns your ass. Your granddaddy preferred sellin' to strangers rather than entrusting it to his own family."

Timmons huffed and puffed as he maneuvered himself upright. "No one around here trusts any of you McKays and we're all laughing that Jed finally kicked it. Good riddance to that manipulative bastard. We're all hoping the rumors are true—rumors comin' from your own brother—that you're all about to get your comeuppance and be forced to sell everything."

The next thing happened in slow motion.

Cord stepped forward, hitting Timmons with such force in the sternum that the man dropped back to his knees. Then he clocked him in the ear and the guy was back on the floor, writhing in pain. Cord stood over him, vibrating with rage. "Shut your fuckin' mouth about my grandpop. You ain't fit to speak his name. And I can guarantee you the McKays are gonna be around for a long goddamned time, so get used to it."

"Out," the bouncer said to Carson and Carolyn. Then he pointed to Cord. "You ain't old enough to be in here anyway, pup, so beat it."

None of them said a word until they were in the parking lot.

Cord spoke first. "Dad. It's not true, is it? That we stand to lose the ranch?"

"No, son, it's not true. Your Uncle Casper is tryin' to pull some shit, but that's all it is: a big pile of horseshit 'cause he's got no other play. Makes me sick that my own brother is running his big mouth all over the place because he can. Puts all the McKays in a bad light."

"Pissed me off what that guy said about us."

"I noticed that," Carson said dryly.

"This happened a lot to you, didn't it? Havin' to fight when some asshole started talkin' shit about the McKays."

Carson wiped his bloodied mouth on his other sleeve. "It's still goin' on. I expect it always will. The bouncer was right about one thing. I'm getting too damn old to fight."

"Not from where I was standing."

A beat passed and then Carson grinned at Cord. "Your old man's still got it, eh?"

"Looks like. Lucky thing you've got five sons, one daughter and five nephews to set folks straight on what it means to mess with the McKays."

Carolyn frowned. Why hadn't Cord included Casper's four sons in that tally?

Because he sees them as part of the problem, not the solution.

Those kids couldn't help their parentage, and they were only little boys. But guaranteed they'd turn out bitter like their father if they didn't have a better influence. In that moment she knew she'd try to foster a relationship between the cousins—even if she had to fight her husband to make it happen.

She tuned back in to hear Carson say to Cord, "Nah, we're good. Your Ma is gonna take care of me, right, sugar?"

Her eyes met her husband's. The lust glittering in those blue depths liquefied her bones. As soon as they were alone the man would have her pushed up against the side of his truck pounding into her, or he'd have her bent over the tailgate slamming into her.

And she couldn't wait.

She rested her hand on Carson's chest. "Let me grab my purse from Cord's truck and then we're good to go."

Carson didn't respond, but the sexual heat and urgency rolled off him.

Carolyn grabbed Cord's sleeve. "Come on."

After she'd shouldered her purse, her oldest son got right in her face. "Ma. Dad is scaring me with the way he's actin'. There's a look in his eye I've never seen before so I think it'd be better if he rode home with me."

Cord was on the cusp of manhood; she suspected he already had experienced the pleasure found in a woman's body. And even if it might embarrass them both, he needed to understand the full spectrum of the night's events. "Your father would never hurt me. Fighting revs him up. I know how to handle him and what he needs."

His eyes widened and then he blushed. Embarrassed by his blush, he retorted, "I don't know why I'm standin' here feelin' shocked about you and Dad getting..." He shook his head as if to clear the mental image. "It ain't like the walls upstairs are *that* thick between the bedrooms. Just drive safe."

"I will. Don't wait up."

After she'd become her grieving husband's refuge, letting him lose himself in the potency of their physical connection, welcoming his body powering into hers, she soothed him, bringing him to the calm after the storm.

Whether it was the booze or crashing from the post-fight and post-sex adrenaline high, Carson finally opened up about his father's passing. The man's tears were rare and that much more heartbreaking when he sobbed in her arms.

They didn't return home until the middle of the night.

Once they were in their bed, Carson reached for her again, almost desperately. He made love to her with such tenderness, with such sweetness, with such devotion, she couldn't stop the tears from falling even as she shuddered in pleasure beneath him.

Afterward he kissed her, keeping the physical connection of their bodies. "I love you, Caro. I ain't an easy man to love. I'm grateful every damn day that you see past what's on the surface and know the man I am down deep. It's never scared you—even when it's scared me. You give me more happiness and love in one day than I ever thought I'd have in a lifetime. Thank you."

She'd been married to the man nearly twenty years and he still had the power to surprise her. To move her. To remind her that she, too, was lucky.

The images turned fuzzy and then disappeared entirely. Then she floated in that gray matter again.

No! I want to go back. I want to relive what happens next. I have to remember it all!

But as Carson's words, "Come back to me. I'm right here. Where I've always been, where I'll always be. I love you. Please. Come back to me," registered as the end of their time together, the grayness became black, swallowing her completely.

Chapter Twenty-Five

"Funny, you don't look like the anti-Christ."

Carson jolted awake. God. How long had he been asleep? He squinted at the clock. Only fifteen minutes. Between the flashbacks and the dreams, he had a serious time disconnect.

"Dammit. I woke you up, didn't I?"

"Uh, yeah." He blinked and tried to orient himself. He looked at his daughter-in-law. "Hey, AJ. Sorry I'm out of it."

"Which I expected, given the circumstances. I won't ask if there's been any change, because even though you banned everyone from the ICU, you would've let someone know."

"Of course I would have." He paused. "They really are painting me out to be the anti-Christ, ain't they? I didn't ban them from the ICU waiting room, just the ICU itself."

AJ opened her mouth to say something, but then closed it again. "Why don't you sit over here?"

"That bad, huh?" he said as he lowered himself into a different chair.

She moved in behind him, setting her hands on his shoulders. "Just relax and let your head fall forward."

"What're you—"

"I'm massaging your shoulders and your neck because I can see your tension."

"AJ, darlin', you don't have to do this."

"I know. It's my way of contributing to your well-being since rumor has it you've already gotten plenty of cookies."

"Damn, girl, you didn't bring me cookies? You can just get the hell out of here, right now."

She laughed. "No secrets in the McKay family. But in all seriousness, I know my sisters-in-law have been here and have told you we're on your side in this decision. But I'll also point out that you passed on the stubborn male McKay gene to your sons, so it is partially your fault. The extreme reaction of them being unwilling to listen to reason is why we're all so ticked off. They've got it in their fool heads that you're just being petty because you can be. Granted, I didn't grow up in your household, but I've never seen you as that kind of man. Then or now. So they're just bein' jerks because they're scared."

He forced himself to breathe slowly and steadily as she dug her thumbs into the back of his neck.

"Your kids have had some tragedy in their lives, but they've not had to deal with the trauma of havin' a sick parent or losing a parent. I have. Macie has. Channing has. India has. Domini has. Jack has. And your McKay offspring don't know the sense of helplessness that comes with that loss. Or the feeling of desolation that eats at you, sitting in the hospital day after day, praying for a miracle. Please don't take that as we don't have hope Carolyn pulls out of this. We all do. It's just we all understand where you're coming from in having to make hard decisions because we've seen similar situations and watched our parents struggle with it."

"I suppose you've tried to explain that to them?"

"Tried bein' the word. I let Cord have his rant and then I calmly pointed out his emotions were overcoming his common sense. That's when he stopped talking to me." She started a slow rub on his shoulder blade. "I'd say it's been quiet around our place, but Cord isn't the chatterbox in our family anyway."

"Speaking of... How is Miss Avery?" Carson asked slyly.

"Busy. She's almost got her father convinced to buy her a horse— no pony for her because she's a real cowgirl."

"I don't have a saddle to pass on to her, since Keely has claimed all her old tack. Not that I think Jack will let Piper get on a horse."

"That's too bad. I say hook them early on the love of horses. That way once they're older and they love riding above all else, when they need discipline, making them exercise and groom their horse, but not letting them ride it is the best punishment."

Carson turned his head to look at her. "Which of your kids is in need of discipline?"

AJ gently turned his head back where it was. "Will I sound bitter if I say all of them?"

"I don't know. What's goin' on?"

"Cord and Ky...I don't even know where to start with them." She started kneading harder. "Ky is a good kid. Sometimes he misses curfew, but I'm sure Cord did too at that age."

"Hell, that boy missed his curfew more often than he made it home on time."

"Seems my husband has conveniently forgotten that fact. It drives Cord crazy that Ky is on his phone all the time."

"Afraid I've got no experience with that, except the phone calls we got from parents demanding, 'Do you know what your sons have been up to?' which wasn't fun."

"That hasn't happened to us so far. And I don't want to interfere because I think Cord and Ky oughta figure it out themselves. If that was all that's been goin' on, it'd be enough. Except now Foster has decided to be a country singer. Since he got that guitar for Christmas all the kid wants to do is stay in his room and jam. Cord has to get after him to do chores. Then on a day last week when Cord and Ky were especially not fun to be around, Foster convinced Beau to do his chores."

"Ain't Beau a little young to be doin' anything by himself?"

AJ worked her way down his spine. "Yes. Which Foster knows, but Beau just wants Foster to pay attention to him, so he'll do anything he says. Luckily I caught wind of it before Beau took off with the BB gun to kill snakes out in the bull's pasture. I tracked Cord down and told him to deal with Foster. He turned pissy and asked why disciplining our sons always fell on his shoulders."

She'd become aggressive with her massaging. "Uh, AJ, darlin', you're getting a mite rough with my saggy old man skin."

"Oh. Sorry." Then she whapped him on the arm. "Saggy old man skin, my behind. I hope Cord's in as good shape as you are when he's your age—if I don't skin him alive first." She sighed heavily. "Anyway, where was I? Right. Cord passing the buck. I was like...what? You think *you* handle all the discipline? Bullshit. Who had to deal with Vaughn biting other kids at daycare? Who had to go to the school when Beau stapled Julia Ragland's dress to the bulletin board while she was still in it? Who had to attend a parent-teacher conference about why Foster's grades have slipped since he got that damn guitar? Me! All in the last two months of school when my husband was busy doin' ranch stuff."

Carson wondered if he was supposed to offer advice or if this was one of those *listen with your mouth shut* conversations.

AJ's hands stilled. "I just dumped my problems on you without even thinking."

"Which is fine, because other people's worries allow me to forget my own for a little while."

"Did you and Carolyn have this problem? Where one person has a different vision of what's goin' on than the other?"

"It was better and worse at different times as the kids were growin' up. Sounds like Cord is hardest on Ky, whereas I came down hardest on Colt. And look how that ended up. Colt hated me for a while and I didn't even know it. He was drinkin' and partyin' and sleepin' around to the point he wound up in rehab. I won't say the similarities are there between Cord and Ky, but I ain't gonna say it's not a possibility given the stubborn streak Cord has. I will say that even if Carolyn and I disagreed in private about discipline, we never let it affect our united front."

"So far we've been able to manage that."

"Then you're already ahead of the curve. What worked best for us was takin' the discussion outta the house. We went out to dinner where we knew we couldn't yell at each other."

She laughed. "I'll try that." She dropped her arms around his neck and squeezed. "Thanks for listening to me blather."

"Thank you for the massage."

"We all hate this."

"I know."

"Since no one is home at your place, I've been fielding phone calls from your friends. I guess as your oldest son's wife I'm supposed to be in the know. Got people who want to bring over casseroles and such."

"Tell them that their offers of food will come in handy when Carolyn is home recovering."

"I will." AJ moved to stand in front of him. "Carson, is there anything else I can do for you?"

"Yeah, there is. I watered the garden and the flowers on the porch when I went home...yesterday? Time is a blur in here. So if you have a spare moment or even if Ky's got time to do it I'd appreciate it. Carolyn wouldn't be happy if everything turned dead and brown on my watch."

"Since you've been right here by her side I think she'd probably cut you some slack. But I'll send Ky over to check."

"Thanks."

"Take care. I could say this a hundred times and ninety-nine times you wouldn't take me up on it, but if you need anything, call."

As soon as she disappeared around the corner, he wandered to the window, his hands in his pockets.

It'd be another fifteen minutes before he could pay Carolyn his hourly visit. He watched the comings and goings of the vehicles in the parking lot below. A fixer upper old Ford truck screeched into the lot. A teenaged boy hopped out of the driver's side and held the door as a blonde girl slid out, her high heels connecting with concrete. They indulged in a passionate kiss and a quick round of grab ass. Then after the couple cleared the tailgate, another boy exited the passenger side and joined them. The guys looked enough alike that they had to be brothers. The girl turned and laid a sloppy wet kiss on the second boy, keeping the first boy's arm looped around her waist and the other boy's arm draped over her shoulder.

Even in his wild youth he'd never shared a girl with Cal—it seemed creepy, in his opinion—but it wasn't for lack of offers. And if the rumors were true, his sons and his nephews had no such dilemma about sharing a woman or two. Or three.

Thank heaven those days worrying what his boys were up to were long behind him, because his sons were too damn young when they'd started sweet talking girls out of their clothing.

Carson still remembered how the first phone call about those *wild McKay boys* had turned Carolyn's world upside down. Like Cord and AJ, they'd been in a similar disagreement about which of their boys many sins were his responsibility to deal with...

The door to the machine shed slammed.

"Carson."

Not the *hey let's go upstairs and roll around between the sheets* tone he was hoping for from his wife whenever she sought him out. "Yeah?"

"Do you have any idea what your sons did?"

He hated conversations that started like this. "What?"

"Colby and Colt lied to us last night. They weren't at youth bingo night at the church."

"Where'd they go?"

"They picked up Karen Ayers and went to the lake. Get this; they convinced her since we're born naked that God prefers everyone swim naked as a way to honor him."

"And the girl fell for that cheesy line?"

"Yes! So both of our sons spent the evening frolicking naked, at a public lake, with a sixteen-year-old girl!"

Oh hell. He tried not to laugh and focused on fixing the lawn mower engine that'd crapped out again.

"Carson McKay. This is not funny. I received a very angry phone call from Karen's mother, demanding an apology from us, for letting our sons run wild. And an apology from our sons, to her *and* her daughter, for taking advantage of Karen."

"How'd Karen's mother find out about Karen sneakin' off and goin' skinny dippin' in the name of God with Colby and Colt? Because I doubt either of them boys were dumb enough to walk her to the door afterward when they were dripping wet."

"That is not the point! Did you even hear a word I said?"

He looked up at her. Yes, his wife was mad as hell, but she'd always been so damn cute whenever she got her dander up, so he was having a real hard time not planting a kiss on that pouty mouth. "What is the point?"

"Your sons are running wild."

"Sugar, they're teenage boys. They're gonna go a little wild sometimes. See what they can get away with. They'll do dumb shit. Same as we all did."

"You're excusing their behavior?"

"No." He stood and twisted his neck side to side to alleviate the throbbing in his head. "How did Karen's mother find out about her daughter's trip to the lake with the McKay boys? The town gossips?"

"I guess Karen confessed everything to her mother this morning."

"Everything? Was skinny dippin' all those three got up to last night? Or did something else happen?"

Her eyes widened. "You mean, like, did one of the boys have sex with her?"

"Did you ask Colby or Colt if they were messing around with her?" He didn't add: or if both of them were? At the same time?

"No. I came straight here to talk to you about this situation so you could deal with them."

That's when Carson lost his sense of humor. He wiped his hands on a greasy rag. "Why does this fall on me? Because I've got a dick? Or because I almost talked you into skinny dippin' with me when we were young and wild so I oughta know a young man's mind?"

She threw up her hands. "What has gotten into you?"

"Caro, I'm serious. I wanna know why when the boys do something wrong, that doesn't have to do with the ranch, I have to be the hardass about it and you get to swoop in and bake them goddamned cookies."

"If you ever stepped foot in the kitchen to actually cook something for your children, I might be able to laugh at that comment."

"See? You even turned the cookie-baking comment into another thing I'm doin' wrong."

"Being a little defensive, aren't you?"

"Do you blame me? Whenever one of the boys does something that requires discipline, it falls on me. That ain't fair. As I see it, *you* took the phone call from Karen's mother, so *you* oughta talk to Colby and Colt about what happened."

The confusion in her eyes made things clearer for him. She hated that her boys were growing up and keeping secrets from her, and she wanted to believe they'd done nothing wrong, but she was afraid to ask.

There were levels of wrong, but Carson didn't believe for a second either of his sons would ever disrespect a girl or a woman and force her to do something she didn't want to.

"Here's where I'm at. Our boys are good-lookin'. You know it. I know it. They know it. Hell, everyone in town knows it. I'm betting Karen climbed into Colby's pickup willingly, stripped off her clothes willingly, and had herself a good old time swimming buck-assed nekkid with our boys. But at some point she started feelin' guilty about it. Or her mother got nosy, demanding to know what Karen had been up to and Karen didn't want to admit she'd had fun, so she changed her story to one where the wild McKay boys forced her into getting naked and goin' swimming with them."

"I'm just supposed to chalk it up to boys being boys? Excuse my sons' behavior because they're McKays?"

"No, but it'll go a long way in tryin' to explain it."

"You are an exasperating man, you know that? This is why *you* need to deal with this. I have no experience with this wild teenage behavior, Carson. None. And you do. Lots of experience."

"If me'n Cal and Casper and Charlie had done half the crap that was blamed on us, we'd be in jail right now. Sundance is a small town, Carolyn. Rumors spread, and change so much that usually what the end person hears ain't close to the truth of what really happened. This won't be the only time *we'll* hafta deal with it. So we'd better come up with a way that I don't always end up bein' the bad guy."

"That's how you see it?"

"Yep."

"Bull."

"Excuse me?"

"You heard me. Bull. I'll agree when it comes to ranch work and chores you crack the whip. But how often do you have to do it? Hardly ever because the boys don't want to disappoint you, or get extra chores for leaving things undone. Whereas I have to ask five times to get the garbage taken out, and then whichever boy deigns to do it, mutters about me being a nag. Same thing happens when I tell them to put away their clothes. Or to pick up their rooms. Or to help with the dishes. I can't be the disciplinarian because they don't listen to me. I'm just the nagging mother."

"Caro, that's not true."

"It is."

"How long has this been goin' on?"

She rolled her eyes. "Years. So maybe I am using the gender argument when it comes to teenaged boys. But do you really believe they'll have an open conversation with their mother about sex? Cord wouldn't look me in the eye for two weeks after I found that *Playboy* magazine in the bathroom. He reacted the same way after that night at the Rusty Spur and I all but told him that fighting made you horny and you were about to ball my brains out in your truck."

He sighed. "All right, all right, I get it. I'll talk to them. But fair warning that if I do this, chances are slim Karen's mother is getting an apology."

Carolyn kissed his cheek. "Thank you. I'll tell the skinny dipping twins you want to see them in your office."

So that's how Carson ended up having the sex talk with his sons. It helped that he'd had three shots of whiskey before the conversation started.

Getting summoned into Dad's office sent the other kids scurrying upstairs to their rooms, because a trip to the office meant they were in big trouble.

Colby and Colt sat on the padded bench and the two of them nearly took up the entire thing. Carson remembered when he could line up all five boys on the bad bench.

"Have any idea why you're both in here?"

A moment of silence followed.

Then Colt said, "I know I was drivin' too fast. And I don't have any excuse except I wanted to see how fast that truck would do a quarter mile. Colby was just along for the ride."

Carson looked at Colby and the boy cracked like mud in the August sun.

"I know you said you didn't want me on the back of a bull because I'd break my fool neck, but I had to try it one time. And Colt didn't have nothin' to do with it besides drivin' me there and home."

Jesus. He wondered just how many confessions he'd get out of these two if he kept doing his stone-faced statue imitation.

"That's not why we're in here, is it?" Colby asked.

Carson shook his head.

"It's not?" Colt said, realizing he'd made an unnecessary confession.

"But keep goin'. Let's see what other shit you boys' have been pullin'."

"Ah, we didn't mean to get stuck up at Flat Top after the keg, and we'll get your tow chain back from Dag...tomorrow?" Colt offered.

"Jesus, Colt, shut your damn mouth," Colby snapped.

"Well at least I didn't tell him about us takin' Tina and Tonya to—"

"Shut up!" Colby said again.

Colt closed his mouth so fast his jaw popped.

"Since it sounds like we could be here all night with what you two have been up to, how about I get right to it." He paused. "The name Karen Ayers ring a bell? And before you decide to get cute, I'll just throw it out there that Karen's mother already called here and talked to your mother. So she knows that you skipped youth group last night and went skinny dippin' with Karen."

"Mom knows?" Colby said.

"We're dead, huh?" Colt said.

"You think your mother needs to get phone calls like that? Hell no. And not only because she passes the buck on to me."

"Is she madder about us skippin' out on church? Or about us goin' nekkid swimming with a girl?"

Carson stared at Colby. Hard. "What do you think?"

"We're dead," Colt said again.

"You boys cause her enough grief with her havin' to nag you constantly to get basic household chores done. Next time you start muttering under your breath when she asks you to do something? Imagine if you'd have the same reaction if I asked you to do something."

Colby and Colt exchanged a look.

"And feel free to pass that advice on to your brothers. Now. Karen Ayers. What in the hell were you thinkin'?"

A few moments passed. Then Colby said, "We weren't thinkin' beyond she's the prettiest girl in school with the wildest reputation."

"Was it her idea to go swimming nekkid? Or yours?"

"Mine," Colby admitted.

"But it wasn't like we had to beg her to take her clothes off or nothin'," Colt added.

"That's not the way she's tellin' it, least not to her mother.

302

Anything else happen you wanna talk about?"

Colby closed his eyes when Colt opened his mouth. "She let us touch her boobs. Not both of us at the same time, but one of us at a time."

Like that made it...better. Christ.

"That's all that happened, Dad, I swear."

Carson addressed Colby. "Why'd you think it'd be a good idea to take your fourteen-year-old brother along?"

"I'm almost fifteen," Colt protested.

"I took him because goin' to the lake was his idea," Colby said.

Colt tried really hard not to look smug.

And Carson didn't know whether to laugh or whap him upside the head.

"I ain't gonna pretend that you won't be tryin' to have sex as often as possible once you start down that path. I will say I expect you to be responsible, discreet and respectful."

Confusion filled Colt's eyes. "I don't get it."

"He means wear a condom, don't have sex on the school bleachers and don't go braggin' about which girls you're havin' sex with. Right, Dad?"

He wasn't surprised Colby knew the score, or how to score for that matter. "Yes, condoms, every time, even if the girl swears she's on the pill. We don't need a grandkid and you don't wanna get some crotch rot that's goin' around. Discreet also means I don't ever wanna hear about you skinny dippin' again, or where you're dippin' your wick, and I definitely don't want your Ma catchin' wind of it, am I clear?"

"Yes, sir."

"As far as respect? Girls who're willin' to have sex with you? Treat 'em right, not like they're just a warm place for you to stick it in. Sex ain't only about you getting your rocks off. The sooner you learn that—"

"The more sex I'll have?" Colby inserted hopefully.

How was he supposed to answer that?

Don't. Let that one go.

"Are we in trouble?" Colt asked. "'Cause you weren't real clear on that."

"If I could take away your dicks and give them back to you when you're old enough to use them responsibly, I would. But since that ain't an option..."

His sons looked at each other with relief, not like they'd gotten away with something.

"As far as the other shit you're doin'?" He leveled his gaze on Colt. "If I ever catch you drivin' faster than the speed limit, you'll be walkin' everywhere for at least a month, understand?"

"Yes, sir."

Carson's gaze moved to Colby. "I told you no bull ridin'. Period.

303

And that I'd consider lettin' you try it when you were eighteen. Until that birthday rolls around, I'd better never hear of you goin' against this rule I set. Never."

"Sorry, Dad. It won't happen again."

"Now go apologize to your mother and ask her if she needs help with anything."

They bolted so fast they tipped the bench over.

Carson reached for the flask in his bottom desk drawer. Good thing he had a few years before he had to have this same talk with Cam and Carter.

But no way, no how was he ever having this talk with Keely.

Chapter Twenty-Six

Hospital, Day 5—morning

He had a bad case of indigestion. Not a good way to start the day. But that's what he got for trying to eat something healthy; eggs and toast and fruit gifted him with heartburn.

He should've stuck to eating cookies. But he was actually tired of cookies. He swore he heard Carolyn's phantom laughter in his head.

The doctors had checked on Carolyn first thing this morning. No change. No plans to ease her out of the coma. They decided she'd "benefit" from two more days in stasis.

That really increased the churning in his gut.

Pacing hadn't helped.

Neither had catching up on world news on TV. If anything that'd turned his stomach a little more.

The nurses let him use the private shower and steam room on this floor. Ten minutes of hot water pounding down on him and slipping on a fresh pair of clothes made him feel better.

He returned to the ICU waiting room to find his grandson Ky hanging around.

"Hey, Grandpa. I wondered where you'd disappeared to."

Carson ran a hand through his damp hair. "Cleaning myself up so your Aunt Channing doesn't come back and hose me down like we used to have to do with your Uncle Colt when he was a boy."

"Uncle Colt? Really? Man, he's always like...so clean. Cleaner than anyone else, even when he's workin' cattle."

"Times change." He dropped into his chair. "So what's up?"

"Dad said I was supposed to tell you that me'n Anton and Gib are looking after your horse."

"I appreciate that. I'm sure your Gran-gran would say the same." As much as it pained him to admit, he'd have to get rid of Sheridan. That mare deserved an owner who could give her the care she deserved and that hadn't been him in the last year. Plus, he couldn't look at the horse without thinking of the accident.

Kyler shifted his sneakered feet and glanced at the closed hospital door. Carson couldn't count the number of times he'd heard the words "spitting image" used to describe a father and son, but Ky was such a carbon copy of Cord—at least in looks—that even he'd mistakenly called the kid Cord a time or ten.

"How is Gran-gran?"

"The same. I keep tellin' myself that's a good thing. Might be bad if she woke up before the doctors wanted her to."

Ky sat heavily in the chair next to him.

Didn't seem like the kid wanted to be here—not that Carson blamed him. Chances were he'd been roped into keeping Grandpa company.

Ky locked his gaze on Carson's. "Are you and Dad in some kinda fight? He wouldn't come here himself and tell you about us takin' care of the horse and we've been doin' it for four days. Then I heard him complaining to Mom about you."

"Not gonna repeat what names he called me?" Carson said with amusement.

"Nope."

"Probably wise. Your dad—and the rest of my kids—ain't happy about the 'no visitors' rule. They think I'm bein' controlling and paranoid. They believe the rules oughta be different for them since Carolyn is their mother. But she's my wife, my responsibility. My sole purpose is to do everything in my power to get her outta that hospital bed and home where she belongs."

Kyler didn't even blink at Carson's snappish response. "I don't understand why everyone is so bent outta shape about it. I know if it was Mom in there my Dad would be the same way. 'Cept probably worse."

Silence stretched.

Finally Carson said, "You don't need to stick around if your dad guilted you into comin' here."

"He didn't. I'm here because I wanted to ask you something."

"Ask me what?"

"What happened between you and Dad that made him move to Seattle?"

Not what he'd expected and he didn't know if he should answer. "Son, does your dad know you're askin' me about that? 'Cause that wasn't a happy time for either of us."

"He refused to talk to me about it, so I figured I could ask you since you don't pull punches."

Maybe this would be the one time he would.

"I wouldn't be asking if I didn't need to know so I can make a decision."

"You and your dad still goin' round and round about post-high school options?"

"We're still going round and round about everything."

Poor kid. Carson remembered what it was like to be at loggerheads with his dad and all the times he's been a stubborn jackass of the first order with his sons. "Tell ya what. Get us both a soda and we'll see where we end up." Carson dug in his pocket and pulled out five crumpled one dollar bills. "Damn soda here is higher priced than whiskey."

Kyler grinned. "Maybe we oughta be drinkin' whiskey. I've got some in my truck."

Carson gave him a level stare.

"Kidding. Dr. Pepper it is."

He returned with two bottles of soda, two candy bars...and three bucks. Carson raised an eyebrow when Ky passed the money back. "The candy is my treat."

"Thanks. You oughta be savin' your money to take out all them pretty girls swarming around you. Gas ain't cheap these days."

"Dad pays for my gas, so it's all good." Kyler cracked open his soda. Then he wolfed the candy bar before Carson opened his wrapper. "Why don't you tell me what's goin' on."

He sighed. "The team's already started football practice. Every morning from six to eight and then there's weight training and agility conditioning every afternoon from four to six. Coach thinks we can win state this year after we've finished second the last three years, which would be awesome since it's my senior year. I come straight home after practice and get chores done. Dad is passing off my evening chores to Foster, which is about time because I was doin' way more at his age than he is. Anyway, there's already been a couple of college scouts showing up to watch practice."

"The scouts are there for you?"

A tinge of red appeared on Kyler's cheeks. "Yeah. Anyway, I like the scout for UWYO. They're a division one school, but they'll never get close to a national championship. The scout who showed up last week was from Oklahoma State. He talked a good game and they've got the winning records to back up their claims."

"Did either of them offer you anything?"

"Both did. Full rides. Arizona State University offered the same thing with the option clause of expanding their offer, whatever that means." He wiggled the metal tab on the can. "So to throw more crap in the mix, last week, Marla called."

Since Cord had married AJ a dozen years ago, Ky had called AJ Mom, a fact his biological mother Marla wasn't happy about. But since the boy visited Marla in Seattle maybe once every two years, and AJ was in Kyler's life every day, Carson didn't see the issue. "What's goin' on with her?"

"She wants me to apply to Washington State."

"Huh. I didn't realize that team was on your radar."

"It's not. But as soon as Marla found out about the other teams throwing out offers, she contacted the athletic director and sent in an audition tape."

"Without asking you?"

Kyler nodded. "Kinda slimy, I know. She did it because she means well, but all Dad sees is manipulation."

"Is WSU sending a scout?"

"I guess."

"You interested in goin' there?"

"I don't know. I want to base my decision on which football team has the best shot at playing in a national championship the years I'm on the team. Dad says there's more to the decision than that." The soda can dented after Kyler squeezed it with obvious frustration.

"He tellin' you where you should go?"

"He says it's a no brainer; I should pick UWYO."

"What's his reasoning on that choice?"

Kyler looked him in the eye. "Sentimentality."

Whoa. Such an astute kid for seventeen. "You wanna explain that?"

"Because he could come to the games and because I wouldn't be far from home. But he also knows if I choose a bottom tier division one school then my chance of playing pro ball after college is practically none." He tacked on, "Not that I think I'm good enough to go that route now. But if I don't choose the best possible program, then I won't grow as an athlete." He blew out a frustrated breath. "And the other thing? I don't want to get a degree in Ag management."

"That's what he's suggesting you do?"

"Yeah. But sure enough if I earn that degree and come back here and try to ranch with him, he'll get pissy and remind me he's been a rancher for far longer than I have and there ain't nothin' wrong with the way he does things and most things about ranching can't be learned in books anyway."

Dammit, Cord, didn't you learn anything from me? Pushing that boy in one direction—your direction—is gonna push him away from you.

"Sounds like him." Carson sighed. "Hell. That sounds like me." He shot Kyler a look. "That's why you want to know what happened. So it doesn't happen between you and your Dad."

"I also wanna know if it's some freakin' pattern with McKays that I'm destined to repeat regardless of what I do."

"You askin' if I had the same issue with my old man?"

He nodded.

"Yep."

He groaned.

"It's just one of them things. Different personalities and differing philosophies creates friction. Can't tell you how many times when I was in my early twenties that I told my old man to fuck off and I'd never run the ranch the way he did." Carson's eyes narrowed. "You tell your Gran-gran I swore in front of you and I'll deny it."

Kyler snorted. "I'm pretty sure after being married for almost fifty years Gran-gran knows exactly how much you swear, Grandpa."

"She still gives me hell about it." More than anything in the world he wanted that woman to wake up and snap, "Carson McKay! Language!" at him.

"What did your dad say when you told him you didn't wanna be a rancher like him?" Kyler asked.

"Told me to pull my head outta my ass and get my work done because he knew I was bluffing. Sounds like sappy bullshit from an old man, but the truth is ranching is in my blood, although some years I'da happily traded in the hard work and low pay for a steady job workin' in the auto department at Sears." He sipped his soda. "Does Cord know you wanna do something else with your life?"

"That's the thing. I don't know if I do. Maybe four years away from here and my family will make me miss it."

Cord lasted almost three years in Seattle before he returned to Wyoming—not that Carson planned to mention it. "You have options. No one's gonna fault you for lookin' into them."

"Thanks, Grandpa." Kyler stood. "It's about time for your hourly visit with Gran-gran so I'll let you be." He jammed his hands in the front pockets of his jeans. "Will you, ah, tell her I miss her and I can't wait until she's better?"

Carson didn't trust himself to speak so he just nodded.

"Later, Gramps."

He cleared his throat. "I thought you wanted to hear about the big fallin' out between me'n your dad?"

"I do. But I'll ask him." He offered a sly grin. "Maybe it'll help him remember what it was like to be the one wanting to get away."

"Good plan. But remind him I told you that the way I handled it was wrong. All wrong. Maybe that'll prompt him to do things the right way."

After his grandson left, Carson pushed out of the chair, grimacing at the pain in his lower back. Getting old sucked. But at least his hip wasn't bothering him.

He stared out the window without really seeing anything, his thoughts focused on the fight he'd had with his oldest son right before he left Wyoming...

"No."

"Jesus, Dad, will you just listen to me?"

Carson reined his horse around. "So you can tell me that I'm an idiot? That you know so much more about what we oughta be doin' in this section?"

"It's not like I'm demanding we switch to raising all Angus or something. All's I'm sayin' is we oughta look at planting a different kind of grass mix here. We ain't had the yield we ought to in the last two years since we bought this acreage and you damn well know it."

He did, but how was he supposed to admit he'd been wrong?

Encouraged by his silence, Cord railed on. "And while we're talkin' about it, I don't think *because that's the way we've always done it* is the only damn answer you ever give me. But every time I've tried to talk to you, you shut me down."

"Then you'd think you'd learn to keep your opinions to yourself."

"You're an asshole and I've had enough of it."

"Because I won't listen to you?"

"You won't listen to *anyone*, Dad. When was the last time Uncle Cal asked for your opinion on anything?"

Carson dismounted. "Am I supposed to be keepin' track of that?" He sent his son a hard look. "Guess I don't need to since *you* seem to be doin' it for me."

"I can tell you even your own brother says you're bein' a stubborn fool—just like your dad—about some of this stuff."

"So you're polling my brothers now? I'll bet Casper weighed in heavily on the *I'm an asshole* side, didn't he?"

Cord's spurs jangled as he walked over to stand in front of Carson with his hands on his hips. "I think there are days when even Mom would be on that side."

"Watch what you say or you might find yourself eatin' dirt, boy. You may be younger, but I got a lot of fight left in me when it comes to people talkin' shit. And that's exactly what you're doin' right now."

They glared at each other. They'd been snarling and snapping at each other for the better part of a year. Cord working around him. Undermining his authority. If they weren't arguing about what type of grass to plant, they were arguing about the breeding program, the field rotation, land lease issues, what shoes to put on the horses and what color to repaint the barn. If there was something to have an opinion on, guaranteed Cord would have the opposite opinion of his father's. It'd gotten tedious and the back and forth was getting them nowhere.

"Real nice, Dad. Real helpful." Cord jabbed a finger at him. "You wanna know the truth? No one wants to work with you. Colby is off rodeoin' because he'd rather be anywhere than stuck here under your thumb. Cam joined the service as soon as he graduated from high school because he'd rather get his ass shot off than get his ass chewed every fuckin' day of his life by you. Carter is goin' off to college and you can bet your ass he ain't majoring in Ag management so he can return to the fold and help you out."

"What about Colt? You left him off your roll call of people who wanna get the hell away from me and my stubborn ways."

Cord snorted. "Colt gives a shit about two things: pussy and booze. He'll be the obedient son doin' whatever you say as long as ranching don't interfere with his afterhours pursuits."

Because Colt was easier to work with than Cord, it was also easier to ignore the similarities he saw between Colt and himself.

"I work my ass off. For years I've been tryin' to prove I'm worthy of the almighty Carson McKay's stamp of approval. But I'm never gonna get it. So I'm done."

"Done what? Done for the day?"

"No, done for good. Jesus, Dad. Half the time you don't even bother to listen to me. I think you suffer from old timer's disease."

"Old timer's?" Incensed about the low blow, Carson snapped, "I'm fifty-two years old and a long goddamn ways from old timer's. Just because what I tell you ain't what you wanna hear don't mean I'm some foolish old man rambling about nothin'."

"Well you can ramble on to someone who gives a shit. As of tomorrow, that ain't me. I'm gone."

"Yeah? Where you goin'?"

"I'll know when I get there. But it'll be a long way from here." Cord took off his gloves and threw them on the ground before he stormed off. Then his truck tires spit gravel as he tore off. Again.

Carson didn't say anything. He just hung up his tack and brushed down his horse. Then to calm himself down and clear his head, he set about straightening the tack room. Carter popped in to let him know he'd finished chores.

He had no idea how long he'd been in the barn until Carolyn showed up. "You missed supper."

"Sorry. Not really hungry."

"Carson, honey, what's going on? Keely tracked you down and said you were throwing stuff and swearing so she ran the other way."

He said just one word: "Cord."

"Ah. That's why he took off like the hounds of hell were on his boot heels."

"Yeah, well that fits since he all but called me the devil himself."

That's when she moved in and wrapped her arms around him. She didn't say anything, she always knew what he needed, even just a simple touch. Immediately everything was better in his world.

She kissed the side of his neck and purred, "Mmm. Dust and sweat and cowboy. My favorite."

"I'm a little more ripe than usual." From angry sweat—not that he'd tell her that. Then again, she probably already knew.

"Come inside. Once you get scrubbed clean let's see how dirty we can get."

Carson lifted an eyebrow. "On a Tuesday night with the kids home?"

She shrugged. "Why not? It's not like they'll notice."

Great plan. Things hadn't been spontaneous between them in a while... His eyes narrowed. "Hey. Wait a second. Is this a pity fuck? You tryin' to take my mind off me'n Cord havin' words?"

"Maybe. Besides, don't you always say a fuck is a fuck? And be honest, you won't be thinking about anything else when your dick is in my mouth."

He smacked her butt and she yelped. "Sugar, I love that dirty mouth of yours. Now march that fine ass of yours up to the bedroom."

The next day Cord hadn't shown up to work, which left him to do everything by himself since Carter and Keely were both in school. By the time he'd returned home, he'd found his wife staring aimlessly out the window. The breakfast dishes still in the sink, the house a bit messy; she always tidied up after Carter and Keely left.

"Caro? What's wrong?"

Without facing him, she said, "Cord is gone."

His gut clenched. "What?"

"He stopped to say goodbye." Her voice broke on a sob. He went to her to pull her into his arms but she waved him off. "Don't."

"What did he say?"

"That he'd had enough. He needed to find his own way. Find a way not to hate you."

That knocked the breath from his lungs. He reached for the back of the dining room chair to keep himself from passing out. He couldn't believe it'd come to this. That he and his son couldn't work this out. Carson figured Cord would go on a bender for a couple of days and things would go back to normal. That's what he'd done when his old man had pissed him off.

And how did that go for you? How many years did you spend resenting your father until you realized the man wasn't half the idiot you'd made him out to be?

"Cord told me what's been going on."

Carolyn's voice was quiet and controlled.

"I want you to know that I'm not taking sides. But to be honest, I don't want to hear your side. I thought—maybe I should say I hoped—that because you dealt with this very thing with your own father over the years, that you'd handle it differently when it came to your sons."

The silent, unspoken accusation lingered between them. He'd been married to this woman long enough that he knew what she was thinking, almost as if he was inside her head.

You swore to me you'd never have the kind of relationship with your children that you had with your father. And when the boys were growing up, you were there for them, teaching them, encouraging them. But as soon as Cord decided he wanted to ranch with you, you've slowly turned into that man. Nitpicking everything he says or does. Rarely listening to his ideas. Reminding him you're in charge and he'd better fall in line. And I've seen you acting the same way with Colton. How long before you chase him away too?

At that point he knew he'd fucked up in the worst possible way. And wasn't it a kick in the ass that the *doomed to repeat the same familial pattern* stuff that Keely yammered on about from her psychology class wasn't bullshit; he'd gotten sucked into it because it was familiar.

Yet even knowing that, he didn't know how to change it. What if he couldn't? What if his boys ended up hating him because he was too fucking stubborn to admit that he wasn't the infallible man they'd looked up to? Had that man ever really existed?

He'd never walked away from his wife when she was distraught. But she wanted nothing to do with him so he left the house, choking on a cloud of guilt.

That first year Cord was gone had been rough on everyone. Especially since Cord had joined a fishing crew based out of Seattle and spent months at sea and called home only twice. Carson suffered most of all because he'd had to do Cord's work and his. Colt, determined to prove his worth in the face of his brother's defection, worked hard enough for two ranch hands. But it still wasn't enough.

When Colby realized things were falling apart at the McKay ranch, he'd backed off on his rodeo travel schedule and helped out. But Colby declined to live at home and Carson allotted the funds for Colby to build his own place on McKay land.

Nine months into his personal hell, Carson had swallowed his pride and asked Cal and his sons for help, as well as Charlie and his two oldest boys.

Year two was better. Even though Cord spent months at sea working as a fisherman, he actually called to check in. But he never mentioned returning to Wyoming—even for a visit.

At the start of year three, Cord had called to announce he'd gotten married. Carolyn, who'd kept to her word and hadn't taken sides, lit into Carson like he hadn't experienced since his drinking and brawling days. She told him if their son planned to make his home and his life in Seattle, he deserved their support and they'd show it by paying him and his new wife a visit.

So they'd made the trip. Both he and Carolyn had disliked Marla, Cord's wife, ten minutes into meeting her. If that wasn't bad enough, Carson knew his son was restless in the big city, living in a tiny apartment when he wasn't cramped into an even smaller space on a fishing boat. Seeing that allowed Carson to make the apology he'd owed his oldest son.

Over a bottle of whiskey they'd made up and made plans. It seemed too good to be true that Marla was onboard for living in the "wild west" married to a real cowboy. A month after the Seattle visit Cord and Marla were back in Wyoming, living in Cord's old trailer. But in order to make his wife happy, Cord agreed to build her a house. It'd taken every penny he'd had and then some, and a little over a year to construct the house of her dreams. Then the woman had only stuck it out for a year after Cord had slaved to give her everything she'd wanted. No one had been surprised when she'd taken off or that she'd left their baby son with Cord.

"Mr. McKay?"

313

He blinked, jolted from the memory, and turned to face the nurse. "Yes?"

"If you want to get ready, I'll take you in."

"Thanks."

Carson washed up, slipped on the modified spacesuit, latex gloves and transparent hygiene mask that protected her, but allowed him to talk to her.

The sound of the ventilator no longer bothered him; it meant she was still breathing. The machines surrounding the bed kept up a steady hum and the occasional blip. He sat on the rolling stool next to the bed. Setting his hand over the top of hers, he squeezed, wishing they could be skin to skin. After this he knew he'd never take holding her hand for granted again.

"Hey sugar. I'm sittin' here beside you. I know you can hear me. I *need* you to hear me. Come back to me. I need you to know that I'm right here, I ain't goin' anywhere.

"My day is a whole lotta waitin' around until I get these five minutes an hour with you. Since our kids are MIA, I spend that time twiddling my damn thumbs, wondering what's goin' through your head. Or I try and watch TV but nothin' can hold my interest for more than a few minutes.

"Anyway, Kyler visited a bit ago. He wanted to talk to me about what's been goin' on between him and Cord. I needed you there so damn bad because you're so good at that talkin' it out stuff. I listened mostly, answered some of his questions, but I don't know if I helped him or not. We've always known Kyler is a good kid, but today I realized that he's special in a way that'll be tough on his family. Yeah, Cord and AJ are bustin' their buttons proud of him, but Ky's got ambition and drive...and after hearin' him talk today about some of the college offers he's getting, he's got the talent. I just wish I could save him and Cord from butting heads over this. Made me wonder how Charlie dealt with Chase bein' a star athlete. So if it comes to that I might enlist Charlie and Chase's help in talkin' to Cord."

Even on day five, Carson paused, expecting Carolyn to answer.

"Sometimes I look at Ky and can't believe he's all grown up. I think about Cord's pride the night Ky was born, presenting that bundle to us like he was handing us a crown prince." He let his thumb sweep her knuckles, hating how still her hands were. At home her hands rarely had an idle moment. "Our little Ky. First grandson. Still the same sweet boy though. Said to tell you to get better soon because he misses you."

The door opened behind him. "Mr. McKay, I'm afraid your time is up."

He faced the nurse. "Thanks." Looking at his wife, he said, "Come back to me. I'm right here. Where I've always been, where I'll always be. I love you. Please. Come back to me.'"

Carson walked backward to the door, keeping his gaze on her for as long as possible...

No! Don't go. Stay and talk to me. I know where I am when you're here.

Carolyn didn't always make it to the listening place. Sometimes she'd hear the rumble of his voice, but by the time she surfaced from the murky depths of her mind, silence greeted her. Distraught, she'd find herself sinking back into the darkness, but sometimes, she fought it.

Like now. She wanted that memory. She deserved it.

And then the moment was right there and she jumped into it with both feet...

Witnessing the pride and terror on her oldest son's face after he emerged from the nursery with a bundle wrapped in blue nearly sent Carolyn into a fit of giggles. Then when he'd handed that squirmy baby boy to his father first, and the look of understanding and acceptance they'd exchanged in that moment had her bawling as much as baby Kyler.

They'd gone home and touched base with their families after being at the hospital most of the day. Aunt Keely was fit to be tied that she couldn't see her nephew since she was spending spring break in Denver with her Uncle Thomas and cousin Sebastian.

Carson had broken out the good bottle of Irish, and she and Carson toasted the new generation in the McKay family.

After she'd drained a third shot—normally she limited herself to one—Carson picked up her hand and kissed her fingers. "What's goin' through that pretty head of yours, sugar?"

"A lot of stuff."

"Good stuff? Or bad stuff?"

"Some of both, to be honest."

"Such as?"

"Such as I worry that Marla will continue to be the same aloof, uninvolved woman we've seen. Babies are work and any kind of work has always been an issue for her."

"Yeah, I know what you mean."

"Cord will be an excellent father; how can he not be with you as an example—" Carson kissed her hand again, "—but he does have major ranch responsibilities. He can't be Kyler's primary caretaker. And then I feel guilty for assuming that Marla won't be a good mother. I've tried really hard not to be a meddling mother-in-law."

Carson sighed. "As much as I've been lookin' forward to havin' a grandbaby, I've wondered how I'd approach this with Cord if it becomes an issue."

She threaded her fingers through his. She'd always loved his hands, and now they were very much a middle-aged man's hands. Tough as leather, the skin wrinkled and covered in age spots. She caught him clenching and releasing his fists more frequently. Although he never complained, she knew his joints were stiff in the morning after another day spent in the elements. Sometimes she thought he wore his age on his hands rather than on his face.

Oh to be so lucky.

"Caro?"

She looked up at him. "Sorry. What did you say?"

"Just wondering where this melancholy is comin' from."

"Honestly? Thrilled as I am for our son, and as happy as I am to have a baby around to spoil, it makes me feel old. Good heavens, Carson McKay, I'm a grandma! How did that happen? It doesn't seem that long ago we were young parents. Now when I look in the mirror I see—"

"The most beautiful, amazing woman in the world? Because that's what I see whenever I look at you."

"You looking to get laid, silver-tongued cowboy?"

He grinned. "Always. But I meant what I said. I still find you sexy as hell. I still wanna throw you over my shoulder and race up to the bedroom and fuck you until I hear them whimpering moans you make when you come. Course, I'll be movin' a little slower as I'm hauling you up the stairs since I ain't the strapping young buck I used to be."

Carolyn gasped. "No, really? You'll start doddering around since you're a grandpa?"

"I'll show you doddering, woman." He stood and pulled her to her feet. Then he bent down and braced his shoulder into her belly before he lifted her. She hung over his shoulder like a sack of grain. He slapped her butt—hard—and made a beeline toward the stairs.

"Put me down! You'll throw your back out."

"And if I do I'll tell everyone who asks that it was from a sex-related injury."

"Carson!"

He laughed. And slapped her other butt cheek.

Then they were in their bedroom, staring at each other, breathing hard. That sense of anticipation heightening the air around them.

Carson lowered his head, placing one, hot, openmouthed kiss on the side of her neck in the spot guaranteed to turn her legs into jelly. His breath teased her skin, when he murmured, "So, sexy grandma, you wanna get it on with a dirty old man?"

"Always."

He clamped his hand on her behind as he brought their mouths together. His kiss was a drug that sparked her need. His kiss was a reminder that he could ignite that passion in both of them with barely a touch.

The man was a master at removing her clothes. One second she was kissing him and the next she was naked.

She undressed him slowly. Touching. Tasting. Burying her nose in his chest hair, hair that was now a mix of black and silver. The familiar scent of musk and man instantly readied her body for his. Her hands smoothed and stroked the strong muscles in his arms and shoulders. She let her fingers wander down the center of his torso. His waist was thicker these days, but she still loved the full weight of his formidable body on hers. She circled his cock at the root and dragged her fist up and down the shaft while she kissed his collarbones. His throat. That stubborn jaw.

"On the bed," he said huskily.

Carolyn playfully bounced on the mattress, throwing back her shoulders so her boobs didn't sag as much. Her middle was thicker too, as were her hips, butt and thighs, but the fierce and hungry look in her husband's eyes was pure lust and that was all she needed.

He crawled on top of her, taking her mouth in a possessive kiss. Then his lips trailed a wet path down her neck.

And speaking of wet...he had her so hot and bothered they'd be able to forego the lube this time.

"Carson, please."

"Never get tired of hearin' you beg for it, sugar."

She bit his shoulder.

He laughed. "Mmm. You know I like biting too."

She ran her hands down his back and dug her fingers into his firm butt cheeks. "Come on. Pin me down and pound into me."

"Huh-uh, no boring missionary for us." He planted sucking kisses across the tops of her breasts. "I'm gonna fuck you from behind. Hard. And while I'm ramming into this sweet little cunt that's been mine for thirty-three years, I'll be pulling your hair so I can suck on your neck until you're buckin' beneath me and cryin' out my name."

"Yes."

"Turn around."

The man eyed her butt shamelessly as she got into position.

She groaned when her body was caged beneath his—all hot, hard excited male. And the wild man did sink his teeth into the nape of her neck as he plowed inside her.

"Jesus, you're wet."

She angled her head and bit his biceps. "Language."

"Shit! Sorry. But damn. It feels good." He nuzzled her ear. "It always feels good but I love it when you're dripping for me, sugar."

Carson whispered raunchy things he wanted to do to her as he made her come undone twice, before he took his own pleasure.

It was glorious. The best celebration of new life and old love that she could've ever imagined.

As they were twined together on top of the sheets, she sighed.

"I'm feelin' it too."

Carolyn propped herself on his chest. "I want this with you again."

He raised an eyebrow. "I'm a grandpa now. I need a little time to recover."

She laughed. "Not *now*. I mean I want us to get back to this animal-type lust being part of who we are. That need brought us together. It's sustained us over some rough years. But it hasn't been a priority, at least not as much as it was. I realize me showing menopausal symptoms has a lot to do with it. It's been easier to focus on other things. I want to focus on us."

The kiss he bestowed on her brought tears to her eyes. The bone-deep sweetness in this man still got to her.

"I want that, Caro, more than anything. But you don't get to shoulder the blame. We've had major changes in the past six years. Cam joining the army, Cord leavin', Colby rodeoin' professionally, Carter goin' to college, the stuff that goes with runnin' a ranch this size that can occupy every wakin' minute of my day. That's not to say I didn't enjoy our time together, but I always enjoy nekkid time a helluva lot more." He kissed her forehead. "So let's plan on havin' more of it, okay?"

"Okay. Part of the reason I brought it up is I got invited to one of those 'private pleasures' parties this month."

He frowned. "What's that? Male strippers or something?"

"No. This party is about marital aids otherwise known as sex toys."

"No shit? Them kinda parties are popular in Wyoming?"

Carolyn rolled her eyes.

"So what kinda sex toys can you buy?"

"Dildos and vibrators and the like. Probably flavored body oils. Role-playing costumes. Naughty lingerie."

"How about some of that bondage stuff?"

"You're interested in bondage stuff?"

He shrugged. "Don't know unless we try. And you've liked it when I broke out the ropes."

"True. But I don't think I'm the whips and paddles type."

"You go ahead and buy whatever kinky stuff you want. Or you think I might want. Then we'll try it out."

"Even a strap on?"

His eyes narrowed. "Never. But I'm feelin' a little backdoor lovin' comin' your way with this new kinky streak."

She elbowed him.

"What? We've done it before."

"*Once* before, we were both drunk and it wasn't all that fun, if I recall, which is why we haven't done it again."

"That was what? Ten years ago? Maybe it's time to give it another shot."

"Maybe."

"This time we'll both be sober. And we've got plenty of lube."

She looked up at him. "If you wanted to poke me in the rear, why didn't you say something?"

"I dunno. Wasn't like our sex life was lacking. It took twenty-three years for you to want to try it at all so I didn't push it." He grinned. "I'm just glad it ain't gonna be twenty-three years before you wanna try it again. Maybe you oughta buy one of them gag things too so you can't argue with me."

"And with that, I'm calling it a night." Carolyn disentangled from his arms and went to the dresser for a nightie. As she was about to pull it over her head, she noticed Carson had a strange look on his face. "What?"

"How about you practice that wild streak and sleep nekkid?"

"Does that mean there's a chance you'll wake me up with your mouth between my legs?"

"I can pretty much guarantee it."

She threw the nightgown behind her.

He laughed.

They slipped beneath the sheets together and she admitted it'd be nice sleeping skin to skin with him all night.

Carson's lips brushed the top of her head. "I don't ever want you to think the passion between us is a thing of the past. It might not be as urgent as it once was, it may've grown and changed and ain't as frequent as either of us would like it to be, but sugar, it's still there. It always will be if I got anything to say about it."

"I remember you told me once that you'd still want me when you were a hundred-and-five-year-old man. At the time I thought that was sweet. As well as vaguely creepy."

"I meant it. I still mean it. There are folks who think a grandma and grandpa havin' a hot sex life is creepy, but I don't give a damn. Let them think we're whittlin' and knittin' in our spare time. Only we'll know that we're wearin' out the mattress and testin' out the sturdiness of all the furniture in this old house."

"Guess we'd better remember to start locking the door during the day."

She hated that the memory didn't fade to black like in the movies. Her head screamed as she pushed against the tide, her hands blindly reaching out to hold on to the moment only to spiral back down into that void again.

Chapter Twenty-Seven

Hospital, Day 5—afternoon

"Of course you're bringing him cookies," the nurse said. "That's pretty much been his diet. You're good to go in."

Carson watched as Chassie Glanzer came around the corner, holding a paper bag.

She smiled and passed it over. "I'm sure you heard what's in here."

"Yeah, it's pretty quiet up here." He peeked inside. "These are gigantic. What kind are they?"

"Rancher cookies. They're a mix of chocolate chip and oatmeal with butterscotch chips, peanuts and M&Ms. They're a favorite in our household."

"I can see why. Thanks, darlin', now supper is covered."

"I'll be honest; I wish I wasn't bringing them to you at all." She sat next to him. "Any news from the docs?"

"Nope. Still the same."

"I figured. India has kept me updated."

Usually Keely passed on news to her West relatives. "Indy stopped by. But she wasn't bearing cookies."

"Trust me, Uncle Carson, if she had you wouldn't want to eat them. I love her, and she has many talents, but cookin' ain't one of them."

"That description fits me too." He set the bag aside. "How're the kids?"

"Healthy, first off, or I wouldn't be here. Enjoying the summer. They're pretty involved in 4-H. It sucks we had to start our own club since no one wanted us in theirs. But with Colt and Indy's kids and ours, and now the Anderson triplets from up the road wanting to join, we're making inroads."

"It sucks that you gotta make inroads at all. People oughta mind their own business and not worry about what someone else is doin' behind closed doors." While he didn't understand two guys wanting to be together, he also didn't understand why half the damn couples in the county were together either.

Chassie leaned her head on his biceps—a very un-Chassie-like reaction. She'd always been a sweet and shy girl, thoughtful, kind, nothing at all like her asshole father. If she'd acted anything like

Harland West, Carson would've put his boot down and kept Chassie far away from Keely.

"I'm sorry," Chassie whispered. "Sorry this happened to Aunt Carolyn and sorry that you're goin' through hell."

"In the words your generation are so fond of, it sucks all around." She laughed softly and sniffled.

He couldn't deal with her tears—which he suspected were as rare as Keely's, so he changed the subject. "What're your men up to?"

"Getting ready to turn the bulls out. They've remodeled my goat pens into an actual barn and they're putting the finishing touches on it, and I gotta say, it is awesome. My men made sure everything is state of the art."

"I'll bet they did. Colt brags on you all the time, about how successful your products are."

"Colt is sweet and currently one of two of your kids who ain't on my shit list."

"Who's the other one?"

"Carter. Them two are the only ones..." She shook her head. "Not my business or my drama. Anyway, you and Aunt C oughta swing by our place sometime and check out my new goat grotto."

"I promise we'll do that when Carolyn is feelin' up to it."

"I love how optimistic you are about her recovery."

"I refuse to accept that she won't recover."

"In all the years my mom was sick, I never heard my dad say anything like that about her. I hated that he'd pretty much accepted she was gonna die."

"Behavior he learned from your grandfather Eli West," was all Carson said.

Chassie glommed onto that comment. "I know some of the backstory about why the Wests and McKays feuded all those years. But it was always more personal between you and my dad. Why?"

Carson met her serious gaze. "Harland was your father, so I won't say anything that'll disrespect him...except my issue with him was how he treated my wife—his sister. I never wished the man ill, but I never thought he'd done right by his family either. So darlin', I've always been happy that you ain't a chip off the old block."

"Me too. As I was driving here, thinkin' about all the times I spent with Aunt C, and how wonderful she's always been to me, from the time I was a kid, then after Dag died, and especially how accepting she was—you both are—after me'n Trevor and Edgard became a family..." Her chin wobbled and she looked away until she regained control. "Anyway, I remembered that last time me'n Keely and Ramona went to church camp. Keely ended up in a fight—no surprise, but the real surprise was learning that she hadn't gotten that fighting mentality just from you, but from her mother."

"Few people know how much of a scrapper Carolyn West McKay

really is beneath that sweet and proper church lady persona."

"I saw it firsthand and, man, was I ever impressed. I've never forgotten it. As a matter of fact, when we were dealin' with all that bullying a few years back with Westin, I remembered that incident at camp and how fierce she was and I'd promised myself I'd be exactly like that when it came to my kids. And now I am. Because of her."

Choked up, Carson patted Chassie's leg. "Girl, you'd better be tellin' your aunt that to her face because it'd mean a lot to her comin' from you."

"I will make a point of blubbering all over her while she's recovering." She lightly kissed his cheek. "Take care of yourself. You need anything, just call."

After she'd left, he helped himself to a cookie. He'd polished off two by the time the nurse informed him to suit up and head in.

As corny as it sounded—hell, as silly as it felt—for the last five days he always started those five minutes the same way, hoping the repetitive words would get through to her.

"Hey sugar. I'm sittin' here beside you. I know you can hear me. I *need* you to hear me. Come back to me. I need you to know that I'm right here, I ain't goin' anywhere."

He paused, but kept stroking her arm.

"I must look like a man with a sweet tooth, 'cause Lord Almighty, woman, everyone's bringing me cookies. So I ain't gonna lie, I've pretty much been existing on cookies and Dr. Pepper the past few days. I've gone to the cafeteria a few times, but the food is shit. I figured you let the grandkids eat as many cookies as they can shove in their greedy little mouths whenever they visit us, so no passin' judgment on me.

"The latest cookie fairy was your niece Chassie. That little gal has always had a tough row to hoe, so I'm happy to see she's doin' well and she's come into her own. She invited us over to see her new goat grotto. I reckon I might even try that goat cheese you all have been raving about. The funny thing? As thick as she and Keely have always been, she's ticked off at our daughter. Then she went on to remind me of that time Keely got kicked out of church camp. Do you remember that? After she left, I got to thinkin' that you never really told me what happened that day. As far as I know, you might've punched a nun. Or socked a priest. But I'd like to think you would've told me since you know how hot it makes me when you get your back up and come out swinging."

"Mr. McKay. Time's up."

"Come back to me. I'm right here. Where I've always been, where I'll always be. I love you. Please. Come back to me."

Punched a nun? Socked a priest? Really Carson?

Carolyn hadn't strayed far from the last time he'd visited—or maybe she had and she just didn't know it. But it seemed as if she'd been right there this time, hearing every word from the moment he started to speak. And she felt that pang of separation as acutely as he did.

I want out of here. Please. Let me go. Find a way to bring me back.

But whenever she fought against the darkness it enveloped her more quickly.

She batted aside the cobwebs in her mind, focusing on the memory until the thread appeared that led her straight to the phone call that started it all...

"Mrs. McKay?"

"Yes. Who is this?"

"This is Sister Grace from the Holy Rosary Church Camp in Grass Springs."

Her heart about stopped. "Has something happened to Keely?"

"No, she's fine, considering. She's..."

Carolyn waited for the nun to stutter out the issue.

"Directly to the point, your daughter has become a bit of a discipline problem."

Not exactly a newsflash. In the past two years, Keely resented going to church camp, even when she attended with her cousin Ramona, who she didn't get to see often. But Carolyn had warned her to suck it up; it was only fourteen days out of her summer. "Is Keely playing pranks again this year?"

"Not to my knowledge."

Carolyn didn't want to ask, but at age fifteen, Keely was already turning male heads. "Has she been visiting the boys' cabins? Because I'll remind you that she does have five older brothers and a dozen male cousins, so she tends to prefer the company of boys to girls."

"Mrs. McKay, that is not the problem either."

"Then please tell me what my daughter has done to earn the discipline problem phone call."

"She started a fight with not one, but two other girl campers. A fist fight," Sister Grace clarified.

"Good Lord." Carolyn bit her lip to stop from asking how bad the other girls' injuries were because Keely knew how to throw a punch, take a punch, and had no qualms about using her fists to get her point across.

Just like her father.

Or just like you.

It shouldn't have been a point of pride for Carolyn that her daughter never backed down from a fight—yet it was. Not that she'd ever admit that to anyone. "Was Keely injured?"

"Not as much as the other girls." She paused. "In light of this latest infraction...we're requesting that you come to camp and pick your daughter up."

She froze. "Excuse me? You're kicking Keely out of church camp?"

"Are you fuckin' serious?" Carson said behind her. "That girl is givin' me a goddamned ulcer."

Carolyn whirled around and glared at him.

"I'm sure you understand our decision. We cannot tolerate that type of behavior at a church camp where young people are supposed to be learning to exhibit Christian behavior and live lives of kindness and compassion."

"While I understand your reasoning, I'm just as interested to know what provoked my daughter into that type of reaction. Because she only comes out swinging when she's backed into a corner or if a member of her family is threatened."

Silence.

Which meant there was more to this incident than her hot-headed daughter just hauling off and slugging someone. "Sister Grace? What aren't you telling me?"

"We've gotten a statement from two other campers about how the situation started—but the statements are conflicting. And the parents of the girls your daughter attacked are demanding that Keely be removed from camp."

"I can drive up there today and get her," Carson offered. "I always thought makin' her go to church camp was punishment anyway."

"Hush," she hissed at him.

"Excuse me?" Sister Grace said.

"Sorry, Sister, I was talking to a yapping dog."

Carson grinned and let loose a howl.

Not funny, she mouthed at him. "Am I correct in assuming the other girls involved in the altercation are also being sent home?"

"No, since your daughter was the instigator—"

"Did Keely admit she started the fight?" Carolyn demanded.

"Well, no."

"So my daughter just got caught fighting with the other two girls. All you have is those girls' word that Keely started it, and I'll bet one of those conflicting reports you mentioned, backed Keely's version of events, didn't it?"

Silence.

"Sister Grace, I'll be more than happy to come to camp and discuss possible solutions to this predicament with you, the other camp counselors, my daughter, the girls involved and their parents. So please call me back when you've set up a time for that meeting to take place. God Bless." She hung up and tossed the phone aside. Bracing her hands on the counter, she closed her eyes, giving herself a mental pat for the foresight to end the conversation, rather than making it worse by tearing into a nun.

They'd call back. They had to. So she had some time to calm down or come up with a plan of attack.

Bad choice of words.

Carson moved in behind her. Those strong arms wrapped around her—just like she needed them to—and he placed a tender kiss on the back of her neck. "What can I do?"

"I don't know. I don't want to be one of those mothers who rushes in and defends her child, regardless if that child is in the right or the wrong, so the kid never learns to deal with the consequences. We've always made the boys deal with this stuff. I've never swooped in after one of their many, many, *many* fist fights." She took a breath. "I tell myself it's different with Keely, not because she's the baby, but because she's a girl. I tell myself that boys are boys, and McKay boys come by their need to solve problems by using their fists naturally."

"Evidently so do McKay girls."

"Carson—"

"Sugar, I'm not bein' flip." He turned her around. "When the boys were wronged, damn straight we made it our business to get to the bottom of it. Remember when Colt was in junior high and Mark Whaley tried to get him kicked off the basketball team by claiming Colt was beatin' on him in the locker room? Then Mark showed the coach the bruises to prove it? We backed our son, took the Whaley kid and his parents to task, and the truth came out in the end. Colt didn't have it in him to be a bully. We knew that." He lovingly tucked her hair behind her ear. "We've stood behind our sons, and this sorta thing has happened to each one of them at least once, partially because their last name is McKay. You know that's something I dealt with for years. As did my brothers all because our dad was the original instigator and folks around here have long memories."

"And short fuses," she murmured. "I remember I'd watch cowboys squaring off in the bars and then beat the tar out of each other. The next weekend they were best drinking buddies only to mix it up in the parking lot a few hours later. So I'd convinced myself it was a cowboy thing."

"That's part of it. Add alcohol and most guys think they're ten foot tall and bulletproof. But I also wanna point out that when Carter went after John Cagle and busted his nose and two teeth? We didn't defend his actions because Carter was in the wrong that time, fightin' over a girl. We made him deal with the consequences of his actions."

Carolyn slid her arms around her husband's waist and buried her face in his neck. "My man. Always the voice of reason. Thank you."

"Anytime, sugar." He kissed her forehead. "It's been important that me'n you are on the same page when it comes to disciplining our kids."

She looked at him. "So what do we do if these girls said something that ticked Keely off, and because she's a hormonal teenage girl she just decided to start throwing punches?"

"That girl has one trigger for her temper: when someone talks down her family. The level of crap that's said to her is proportional to whether she hurls verbal insults back at them, or if she punches them in the mouth to get them to shut it." He paused and his eyes slid away.

Her eyes narrowed. "What?"

"Or the other option is our sweet and sassy, but sly daughter decided she'd had enough of church camp and knew *exactly* what it'd take to get kicked out."

She sighed. "That thought had crossed my mind too."

"If that is the case...gonna be a long, shitty summer for her. And I do mean shitty, 'cause I'll have her scraping up cowshit, and horseshit and I'll even lend her to her Aunt Kimi to clean up chickenshit."

"Agreed. I wonder how long it'll be before they call back?"

The phone rang.

"Might not be them," Carson pointed out.

Carolyn sidestepped her husband to grab the phone but she kept her hand on his chest. "McKays."

"Mrs. McKay? This is Sister Grace again. We've set up the meeting for three hours from now. You'll be able to make it?"

Just barely. It was a two hour and forty-five minute drive to the camp. "Of course. Thank you, Sister Grace, for handling this so quickly. I'll see you soon."

Carson picked up her hand and kissed her palm. "Want me to come along?"

Yes. This man was her rock and she was his. But he'd worked himself to exhaustion the past week to the point he hadn't tried to get down and dirty with her—which was saying something. They needed that intimate connection even if it was just quick missionary position sex that was over too fast. She kissed him with more passion than their usual peck of affection. "Stay here and get some rest because no matter what happens I'll need something to take my mind off this later."

"That I can do."

Holy Rosary Church Camp was nestled in the foothills of the Bighorn Mountains. The setting was gorgeous—it'd always exuded a spiritual vibe, which was why she'd chosen it.

When she'd told Carson she thought two weeks at church camp would be good for Keely, he'd argued, reminding her that she hadn't had a choice but to attend Catholic school and he wanted his daughter to have a choice. But Carolyn had stood firm. The camp brought kids from all over the U.S. and their time was spent doing charitable works for the needy. As the baby of the family as well as the lone McKay girl, Keely could stand to learn some selflessness.

Carolyn parked in front of the chapel offices. She smoothed the wrinkles from her khaki pants, fluffed up her shoulder length hair—it seemed she kept cutting it shorter every year—and added a quick coat of peach lipstick before she exited her Toyota 4-Runner.

The nun manning the desk stood up and smiled, offering Carolyn her hand. "Welcome to Holy Rosary Church Camp. I'm Sister Beatrice. How may I help you?"

"I'm Carolyn McKay and I have a meeting scheduled with Sister Grace."

The nun's smile dried. "Of course. Follow me, please." Her black robes swished as she led Carolyn to a small conference room.

Keely sat in the corner, arms crossed over her chest, a mulish expression on her face. The wariness in her eyes disappeared when she saw her mother. Then her tough-talking cowgirl daughter threw herself into Carolyn's arms and squeezed her tight. "Mom. I'm so sorry."

"You want to tell me what happened?"

She shook her head. "I'm not allowed to tell my side of the story until the meeting. I wouldn't want to sway you into believing I'm tellin' the truth."

Sister Grace pointedly held the door open. "Ladies. We're meeting in Father Bartholomew's office."

They followed the nun single file; Keely in the lead, Carolyn in the rear. She froze in the doorway when she saw the woman sitting in the front row, next to a girl with a black eye.

Edie Knapp. Or whatever her last name was now after her second—or was it her third?—divorce. Edie's daughter—a carbon copy of her mother down to the tight-lipped sneer—gave Carolyn a critical once-over with the eye that wasn't swollen shut.

In that moment, Carolyn knew this situation—years in the making—was about to implode.

"Now that we're all here, I'll make introductions and ask that we can keep this civil," Old Father Bartholomew stated.

Good luck with that.

"Edie Shultz and her daughter Margo. Carolyn—"

"McKay, yeah, we've met. Can we get on with it?" Edie demanded.

The priest cleared his throat. "The allegations are that Keely has been harassing Margo since the first day of camp. The counselors have broken up shouting matches and near altercations several times. However, Margo says Keely attacked her this morning after chapel. When Amanda Peterson tried to step in, Miss McKay turned on her too."

That's when Carolyn craned her head and saw Tammy Peterson sitting in the second row. Tammy and Edie's daughters were thick as thieves? No surprise since those witches were in the same coven.

Tammy glared at her.

Carolyn had the oddest compulsion to wink and offer a finger wave because this whole thing was a farce.

"Keely has a different version of events," Father Bartholomew continued. "Keely claims Margo and Amanda have been saying inappropriate things to her and her cousins since the camp began. And she was only defending her family."

"Father Bartholomew," Edie began in a simpering tone, "the McKays and the Wests have reputations for being loudmouths and brawlers. Part of me feels sorry for Keely. Obviously being raised in a household of boys she wasn't taught the normal social graces and boundaries. Or how to act like a lady."

"Really, Edie? You going there?" Carolyn said. "Make sure you've grown thick enough skin to take it if you're gonna dish it out."

Edie seemed taken aback.

Good.

Carolyn patted Keely's shoulder. "Why don't you tell me what happened, sweetheart?"

Edie opened her mouth to object but the priest shushed her.

"This is the first year my cousin Chassie West has been at camp. Chassie's mom was Native American and since the first day Margo and Amanda have been makin' fun of her, callin' her squaw, Injun and chief. They've been tellin' everyone she's here as a charity case and too poor to even live on the rez. Today after chapel I heard Margo and Amanda brag they were gonna slice off a chunk of Chassie's hair to see how *she* liked bein' scalped like her ancestors did to the pioneers."

Margo leapt up. "That's a lie!"

Amanda leapt up too. "They're liars, and skanks, and they make fun of us for having solid morals!"

A snort echoed from the back of the room. "Oh please. You and Margo have been sneaking into the boys' dorms since last year and have the morals of an alley cat in heat."

Carolyn turned and looked at her niece Ramona, sitting next to Chassie.

"No one asked you," Margo snapped.

"Yeah, and you've got no way to prove it, either," Amanda shot back.

Ramona lifted a brow. "The guys you've been giving hand jobs to won't rat you out, but the guys who you sneer at and call losers who aren't getting the benefit of your slippery fists? They're more than ready to tell all. In fact, they've jotted down the dates and times you snuck in, and exactly what you received for your pole-polishing expertise—"

"Miss West! That is enough!" Sister Grace said.

"What? It's the truth."

"Keely was standing up for me," Chassie said softly. "She shouldn't be punished for doin' the right thing and callin' Margo and Amanda out on their very un-Christian-like behavior. I've turned the other cheek, as instructed in the Bible, when they've called me names. But when me'n Keely and Ramona all heard those girls talkin' about cutting me? I got scared."

"You have no way to prove we said anything like that," Margo said. "Keely will make up any kind of lie to justify using her fists because she likes hitting people. I heard her say that and so did a lot of others."

A beat of silence passed.

Edie spoke. "The fact of the matter is Keely caused physical harm to our daughters. She took matters into her own hands rather than discussing her concerns with the camp counselors. We want her removed from camp because of the threat she poses not only to our daughters, but to other campers."

"I did try to talk to my assigned camp counselor," Keely protested. "But it's the same one Margo has and she's on her knees before him all the time, but she sure as shootin' ain't prayin'."

"Miss McKay! That is completely inappropriate!" Sister Grace said.

"But it's entirely true," Ramona chimed in.

Edie leapt to her feet. "I cannot believe that you're not kicking these girls out right now for vulgar language! Not to mention the lies they're telling about lewd behavior that can't possibly be linked to my daughter."

"Why not? You know all about lewd behavior," Carolyn said. "And the apple doesn't fall far from the tree."

"I do not have to listen to this."

"I have to wonder how much of the nastiness directed at my daughter, from your daughter, has to do with our history, which I'm sure you wouldn't like me to detail in front of Sister Grace and Father Bartholomew. Then again, since you've been divorced twice and married three times, you are not exactly the best person to talk about moral behavior."

"Ladies. This has gotten completely out of hand. While the allegations of inappropriate physical contact are disturbing, they don't change the facts." He looked at Keely. "Remember where you are, child, when I ask you this question. Did you use physical violence against Margo and Amanda?"

"Yes, Father, I did."

"Then I'm afraid you have broken the rules. Even when defending a family member, violence isn't the answer."

"I disagree. Sometimes the only way you can get your point across *is* with a hard right cross. Followed by a left hook." Carolyn locked her gaze on Edie's. "Christ bled for us for our sins. I'm not opposed to making someone else bleed for lies and sins against my family. I've done it before, Edie, and you know I'll happily do it again. Am I making myself clear?"

Keely gaped at her, her jaw nearly hanging to the floor.

Edie crossed her arms over her chest. "I see you're still the dowdy housewife defending the violent and deplorable actions of the McKays and the Wests."

"I see you're still jealous about that."

Before Edie retorted, Carolyn walked to where Father Bartholomew sat. "I understand your reasons for Keely's expulsion. I disagree with them, but we will abide by camp rules. She'll be coming home with me. As will my nieces Ramona and Chassie West. Thank you for your time today. Don't bother sending camp registration next year because they won't be back."

All three girls followed her out of the room. Keely started to say something but Carolyn raised her hand. "Say your goodbyes to your other friends—quickly—get your stuff and meet me at the car."

They must've already been packed up because they piled in not ten minutes later.

Keely wasn't the first to speak, which was surprising. Ramona leaned over the seat. "Straight up, Aunt C, you are my hero."

Carolyn smiled.

"But how am I gonna explain to my parents that I got kicked out of church camp?"

"Good question. Because you know how my dad is, Aunt C. He won't be happy," Chassie added.

"Yeah, Daddy will lose his mind on me," Keely said.

"You don't have to tell them anything. There were only five days left. You girls can hang out at the ranch, watch movies, go horseback riding, bake cookies and do makeovers. Whatever you want. We'll call it the Wild West Ranch Camp for Wayward Women."

They started laughing, and giggling, and high-fiving each other. Finally Keely said, "But we're not really wayward, because we weren't in the wrong."

"I know, sweetie, but that has a nicer ring to it than Catholic Church Camp Castoffs."

Carolyn should be used to the ripping sensation by now, getting torn away from the fabric of her memory, but it jarred her, confused her and frightened her just the same as the image shimmered and she fell into the black hole of nothingness.

Chapter Twenty-Eight

Hospital, Day 6—mid-morning

Carson saw a flash of red out of the corner of his eye and looked up at his sister-in-law, Kimi, aka the blonde tornado.

He'd wondered when she'd show up. He'd actually made a side bet with Charlie as to which day. Looks like he owed Charlie fifty bucks— Carson figured Kimi wouldn't last two days without storming in.

They stared at each other, sizing one another up.

"Kimi. You're lookin' good."

"Wish I could say the same, but Carson McKay, you look like dog shit."

"So you're here to insult me?"

"Yes. No. Maybe." She sighed. "I'm just so frustrated with the situation that I need to yell at someone."

"Poor Cal's had enough of it and that's why you're here?"

"Got it on the first try. And before you ask, I haven't seen my grandkids since this ICU germ shit went down, so I ain't Typhoid Mary."

"Bet you're missin' those kids."

Kimi plopped into the chair next to him. "But that sacrifice ain't gonna get me in to see her, is it?"

"Nope."

"You are so damn stubborn."

"You expected less?"

"No. So I did some online research about this."

"Got your WebMD in the last couple days, did you?" he teased.

She nudged him with her shoulder. "Smartass. I just needed to know more information about her condition for myself. Of course they stressed that every case is different and to listen to your doctor."

"No. Really?"

"Knock it off. And if you get up and do an I-told-you-so dance, I'll trip you."

"Then I'll likely break my other hip."

Kimi leaned her head against his shoulder. "We used to crack sex jokes. Now we're cracking old people jokes. What happened to us?"

Carson put his arm around her. "Hate to break it to you, but we are old. The mind can fool us, but darlin', the body don't lie."

"I'll stick with the mental image I have of myself when I was twenty-five, thanks."

Silence settled between them, not uncomfortable, just...there.

"This sucks. I need a damn cigarette."

He smiled. "Got a pack in the truck if you're serious."

"You too, huh?"

"Yeah. It helped."

"You never were addicted to them like I was."

"True. Last time I bought a pack was after Keely's emergency C-section with the twins. Caro never said a word. In fact she rustled up a pack of matches for me."

"She's the best."

"No argument from me."

Kimi's voice was so soft he barely heard it. "I'm scared for her."

"So am I." Carson closed his eyes. "I'm scared for myself because I can't imagine..."

"Me neither. Besides Cal, she's everything to me. She's been there through it all. Watching over me at Catholic school, playing referee in our screwed up family situation, telling me that falling in love with Cal so fast wasn't a bad thing. Helping me through pregnancy even when she was pregnant herself. Showin' me how to be a good mother and bein' a second mother to my boys, lovin' them as if they were her own..." She sniffled. "Caro's been a daily part of my life for so long that even when I know she's here, I picked up the phone this mornin' to call her. As the line was ringing, I'm lookin' at my geraniums, thinking they never grow as good as hers and what is taking her so long to answer the damn phone...and then I remembered she wasn't there." She sniffled again and her voice turned hoarse. "Goddammit. I hate that she's not there. I just wanna talk to her."

"I do talk to her," Carson admitted. "From the moment I sit down in her room until the five minutes are up. In these last few days I've relived a lifetime of memories with her and it still ain't enough. I want more time. I tell her that too."

"Has she responded at all?"

"Like squeezed my hand or something?"

"Yeah."

"Nope. The faceguard forces me to talk real loud, and I'm sure the nurses think I'm just an old fool. But I'm talkin' to her as much for her as for me."

"In some of the articles I read online while I was getting my WebMD," Kimi said dryly, "it said patients who were in a coma remembered things that happened in the room that they shouldn't have been aware of. So you talkin' to her *is* the best thing you can do."

"I hope so. It's the only damn thing I can do."

Kimi lifted her head and looked at him. The fear in her eyes matched his own. "I'm sorry for bein' so difficult. Thank you for lookin' out for Carolyn above all else."

"Spent most of my life doin' it, I sure ain't gonna stop now."

"Cal's been extra attentive to me the past few days. It's helped. So I hope you're not pissy that he's been there for me and not for you."

"Nah. Only thing I'm pissy about is you didn't bring me food. What the hell woman? I'm starvin' here."

"Carolyn would kick my ass if I didn't feed you." Kimi reached into her oversized purse and pulled out a paper bag. "There's a PB and J sandwich and a baggie of carrots. Satisfied?"

"No cookies?"

She lightly punched his arm.

"Thanks, Kimi."

"You're welcome. Now that you and me ain't on the outs, can I come back another time and sit with you?"

"You gonna get all offended and shit if I tell you I hope I don't see you up here again? Because that'll mean Carolyn's awake and we're outta here."

"Fine. I hope I don't have to sit up here with your whiny ass either."

He laughed.

Neither spoke for a while. Then he said, "It's been so quiet."

"That's because your kids ain't been yappin' in your ear. And they made that choice to stay away. For what it's worth, they're regretting their decision."

Carson narrowed his eyes at her. "Been givin' our kids what for, have you?"

"Between me'n Vi we've got ya covered."

"I don't know what to say to that."

"You don't have to say anything. Because it's fun yelling at someone else's kids. But I do have to ask if one of your stubborn kids swallows their pride and shows up here...?"

"Would I turn them away?" He shook his head. "But the parameters haven't changed for seein' their mother."

"I'll pass that along." She stood. "Now get up here and give me a hug."

Carson held onto her for several long moments. "Thanks."

"You tell my sister I love her. You tell her not an hour goes by that she's not in my thoughts. You tell her I got no one else to gossip with or share secrets with and I need her to get better soon. You tell her I'm passing on information to the West family so we don't get accused of only caring about the McKays. You tell her—"

"Kimi, darlin', I only get five minutes with her."

Kimi laughed, stepped back and wiped her eyes. "Okay. I'm goin'. Take care of yourself."

"I will." He started to say something and then stopped.

"What?"

"You've been in my life longer than any woman besides Caro.

We've been through some great times together. Through some real shit storms too."

"This counts as one of them shit storm times. And I'll admit that it wasn't just me keepin' Cal away from here. Caro's been as much a part of his life as I've been of yours. The four of us are tied together on so many levels..." She blinked away more tears. "This is eating him alive, Carson. Knowin' he can't do nothin' to help you through it. Or me through it."

"What's he been doin'?"

"He's been over at Kade's, wrenching on that damn hot rod pickup Kade's been tinkering with for twenty years. Eliza, Shannie and Peyton have been helpin' him, getting greasy and loving every minute of it, although I don't think Skylar's too happy about it." She smirked. "I figured Eliza is buttering up Gramps to buy her first car sooner than Kade wants her drivin'."

"Can't blame Kade. When Keely turned eighteen and bought that Corvette with the money her Grandpa West had left her? I thought about takin' her car out and totaling it just so she couldn't drive it."

"You tellin' me Liesl isn't already scheming for a car?" Kimi demanded.

"Nope. She's got Anton to drive her where she needs to go. She's a bit gun shy on account of her peg leg. Hayden's not helpin' Cal?"

"He's splitting his time between early morning chores with Kane and workin' for Ginger at the law office in the afternoons. Maddie and Paul are at camp during the day for a week or so. Rumor has it that Hayden, Ky and Anton are out tearin' it up at night. Hard to believe I was Hayden's age when I met Cal."

"Doesn't seem possible. If Keely would've showed up at age eighteen and announced she was getting married like Caro did to Eli at that same age? I'd a..." *Lost my mind and threatened to cut her off like my dad did to me.*

"It's a different world now. Carolyn was young, but you both knew what you felt was real. Fifty years later you're still goin' strong."

"Cal said something like that to me the day I decided to propose." He studied her. "So if in a couple of years Eliza shows up wearing some guy's ring, you'd be okay with it?"

"Hell no. And if she got knocked up? I'd shoot the guy if Kade didn't get to him first."

Carson laughed.

"I know that makes me a hypocrite and I'm good with that." Kimi stopped before she turned the corner. "Is your truck unlocked?"

"Yep."

"I might bum a smoke or two."

"Go ahead. It'll be our secret."

For some reason that released a fresh flood of her tears before she disappeared.

He didn't have time to eat his sandwich before his hourly visitation. He washed up, suited up and scooted the rolling stool beside her bed.

"Hey sugar. I'm sittin' here beside you. I know you can hear me. I *need* you to hear me. Come back to me. I need you to know that I'm right here, I ain't goin' anywhere."

He paused and feathered his thumb over her knuckles.

"Your pesky little sister just visited. Kimi is missin' you like a limb. She didn't carry on as much as I expected, but I suspect she recognized how close I am to the edge and she didn't want to be the one to tip me over. Guess Cal's havin' a rough go of it too. The man is always on an even keel. But do you remember the time she and Cal had that epic fight right after Kade found out he was a daddy…?"

By the time Carolyn surfaced after hearing Kimi's name, she no longer heard Carson's voice.

Had Kimi been in here?

No.

She definitely would've made her presence known. Because her crazy little sister knew how to make an entrance…

Carolyn had spread out the ranch books on the dining room table, lost in numbers and contracts, knowing she had to get it all straight before she could start plugging the information into the computer.

The front door slammed and she didn't bother to look up, figuring it was Carson.

Footsteps—angry ones by the sounds of it—echoed and stopped.

Aha! There was that lease. She squinted even though she had her cheater eyeglasses on. Wait a minute. This document was supposed to have three pages, not just one. As she shuffled through another stack, she heard the liquor cabinet open.

"Sweetheart, you must be having an awful day if you're hitting the Jameson before noon."

"I feel a celebration is in order, but mostly I just need a fuckin' shot to calm my nerves."

Carolyn's head came up so fast her glasses slid off her nose and bounced against her chest, caught by the chain. "Kimi? Ah, why are you breaking into my liquor cabinet when I know there's booze at your place?"

Kimi scowled and knocked back a shot.

"Are you and Cal fighting?"

"You know Cal and I don't fight."

"Which would explain why you're so upset and why you're sucking down my whiskey."

She exhaled a long, slow breath. "Dammit, I need a cigarette."

"You quit smoking thirty-some years ago. Tell me what's going on."

"I'm a grandma."

Now she pinpointed the source of her sister's agitation: her son. "Did Kane just spring this 'you're gonna be a grandma' thing on you?"

Kimi shook her head. "That's where it's screwed up. It's not Kane. It's Kade. And it's not 'I'm gonna be a grandma'; it's I *am* a grandma. To a baby girl. I saw her today, Caro. A beautiful, perfect three-month-old girl with dark hair and the second I saw those blue eyes I knew she was a McKay."

"Where'd you see her?"

"In Sundance, but I guess they live outside of Moorcroft."

Confused, Carolyn said, "They? Who is the mama?"

"Skylar Ellison. She owns Sky Blue, that all-natural beauty product place. Her sister is that tattoo artist India from India's Ink. Anyway, Skylar is the one who broke Kade's heart last year and why he volunteered to leave. He had no idea she was pregnant. Since this is Kade, I believe him because no way would he walk away from a woman carryin' his child even if she stomped on his damn heart. No way. So I just stormed into the house and blew the whole thing about him bein' a daddy. Now he's on his way into town to deal with her and meet his baby girl."

"Kimi, that's a good thing. Kade will happily own up to his responsibilities. You know that." She squeezed her sister's hand. "A baby girl! How fun will that be?"

Kimi smiled. "Damn straight it'll be fun. We need to go shopping. Wait." She patted her face. "Do I look like a grandma? Lord, do I look as old as you?"

"Nice, Kimi, real nice. Trying to be supportive and you crack age jokes." She smirked. "Since Kade's baby mama makes wrinkle cream maybe she'll give you a good deal on it by the bucket."

"Oh, hush. You know you look good, way better than me. Which ain't fair. You should have ten times more frown lines and gray hair since you had three times as many kids as me."

"I feel it most days." She leaned back in her chair. "Does Cal know?"

She shook her head. "I came straight here. I figured after Kade talked to Skylar and saw his daughter, he'd call and let me know the details."

"Think Cal will be shocked?"

"Yeah. 'Cause like you said, I'd see Kane in this situation long before Kade."

Carolyn helped herself to a shot glass and filled hers and Kimi's with whiskey. Then she held her glass up for a toast. "Congrats."

They both knocked back their shots.

Kimi cocked her head. "And...?"

"And what?"

"I know you were gonna say something else."

Carolyn grinned. "Like father like son, huh?"

"Oh, piss off."

"But it's true," Carolyn said. "You and Cal went on what? Five dates and then you were pregnant?"

"Something like that. But there'd been a spark between us since the first time we met before you married Carson." She wagged her finger in Carolyn's face. "Although Cal swears he wasn't a monk pining for me, he claims he was waitin' for me to grow up and come back here."

After their mother's death, and after Kimi had graduated from St. Mary's, she'd sworn she wasn't returning to Wyoming. She worked in Alaska for a few years, until she finally got homesick. By that time Carolyn and Carson had two boys and no room for an extra houseguest so Kimi ended up staying with Cal. She'd pretty much moved in with him and had never left.

While at first Carolyn had been worried because Cal seemed to have a revolving door to his bedroom, she realized Cal really did worship her little sister. Oddly enough, so did Jed McKay. He had no issue with Cal and Kimi's hurry-up wedding. And after Jed's second heart attack, Kimi was the one who suggested he live with her and Cal and the twins.

Carolyn knew part of the reason Kimi had offered was because Carolyn had taken care of their mother the last year of her life. While Carson hadn't agreed with Carolyn's insistence on keeping Clara West's dire diagnosis from her children, he'd honored the request—only after having words with Eli that forced him to hire part-time health care to alleviate the stress on Carolyn.

"What're you thinkin' about, Caro?"

She looked at her sister. "Mom dying. Then getting pregnant with Cord and how lucky we are that neither of us inherited her health problems. And I'm thankful that our husbands have always had our backs when it comes to the West/McKay family crap."

"True. I'm glad that Dad didn't ignore his McKay grandkids."

"I think he did enjoy spending time with our boys." Carson had told her many times to wash her hands of her father. But after having her own children, she'd come to understand how far a parent would go to protect those children. Like most men of his generation, her father's communication skills were lacking; he just expected his word to be law with no discussion. She remembered one time her Aunt Hulda had told her that Eli West didn't act out of maliciousness, just ignorance. That didn't explain away his behavior, but it'd allowed Carolyn to forgive him and move on from the past.

"If it wasn't for Harland, Darren, Marshall and Stuart's wives agreeing with us the feud was stupid, I doubt our kids would know theirs at all," Kimi said.

Carolyn smiled. "That's because men act like the cock of the walk but women rule the roost." Her smile dried and sorrow washed over her. "Harland...was such a hard man. I hated that Dag couldn't be himself for fear of his father's reaction. Especially when Thomas and Susan were so accepting when Sebastian told them he was gay. Dag's was such a senseless death." She closed her eyes. God had been looking out for Colton. She said a prayer of thanks every day in the last year that her son had gotten the help he'd needed and he hadn't ended up like Dag. If not for Kade...

Kimi squeezed her hand. "I know. I'm thankful too. Colt will be all right. They say the first year is the hardest."

"I get that. It's hard that he's had to isolate himself from his family to keep the sobriety. But whatever works for him, right?"

"Right." Kimi sighed. "So damn many secrets in this family."

Carolyn shook her finger at her sister. "And quite a few that I wish you wouldn't have told me."

"So you've said. That's because I trust you and I kept them both for a long time. Think of my burden."

"I get that Jed loved you because you reminded him so much of Mom. But do you think he told you the truth about what happened to Jonas and Silas McKay because of our West lineage?"

Kimi jammed a hand through her hair. "Yes. I just wish I hadn't promised Jed not to tell McKay descendants the truth."

"I hated all the questions Keely asked when she did that genealogy paper and I had to lie to her and hide all Dinah McKay's journals up in the attic. Carson knew something was up."

"Well, our grandfather Zachariah West had a valid reason for his hatred toward the McKays: Silas McKay killed his brother Ezekiel and basically got away with it. Maybe it was self defense, but when Silas fled instead of letting a judge decide his fate...it sure made him look guilty," Kimi said.

"It didn't help that Jonas McKay paid Zachariah for the land he'd 'won' in the poker match—a few months after his twin escaped from jail. It did look like blood money."

"My opinion is Zachariah shouldn't have accepted the money. But he did and he agreed to keep his mouth shut about it. So like I said, his hatred of Jonas McKay was understandable, but Zachariah wasn't innocent either. In fact, he helped perpetrate the continuing hatred between the Wests and McKays—without telling anyone why the families were enemies."

Carolyn drummed her pen on the table. "It's sad the McKays and the Wests were just sucked into that mindset. When I first started dating Carson? Even my mother didn't know the issue between the McKays and Wests. At least that first generation. And I did not appreciate when Mom finally told me that she did sneak around with

Jed McKay for a month or so when she was dating our father. So yeah, Jed McKay deserved to get his ass kicked by Dad because we both know if the boot had been on the other foot and Eli West had been sneaking around with Jed McKay's girl? Jed would've come out swinging."

"True. Still, it's creepy to think that our mother slept with our husbands' father."

"Welcome to small-town Wyoming," Carolyn said wryly.

"Welcome to family confessions. Jesus. Neither one of us would've gone back through the boxes that Dad had kept or the ones we found in the attic upstairs on the McKay side if it wasn't for Jed spilling his guts to me."

"I hate the secrets and lies. Hate it."

"Me too. Especially that the McKays lied to everyone. I understand why, but it makes no sense on why Jonas, aka Silas, would make a deathbed confession to his son Jed, about who he really was, because he'd gotten away with impersonating his twin nearly all his life."

"Maybe the reason Jed told you about Silas and Jonas switching identities, before Jonas took off, and after he escaped from jail, is because you had identical McKay twins?" Carolyn suggested.

"Possibly. Jed told me that even though he was a grown man when his father told him the truth—that he was Silas, not Jonas—he had a hard time accepting that his father had killed a man."

"It was pretty ballsy of Silas, aka Jonas, to send a letter to his twin and Dinah a couple of years later telling them that he'd settled in Montana."

"I think our husbands would hire a private detective to track down the missing McKay descendants if they knew."

"Agreed."

Carolyn stared into space. "You think Charlie would search for the son Vi gave up for adoption if he knew the truth?"

"I don't know. I was pissed when Jed threw that whopper of a secret at me. How is it right that *we* know Charlie and Vi have another kid when Charlie doesn't have any idea?" Kimi shook her head. "That saying *confession is good for the soul* is a load of crap. I never wanted the burden of Jed's confessions. Especially when I'm keepin' those truths about the McKay family from my husband. Me'n Cal never fight, but if he found out that I know all this stuff? He'd really be hurt."

"So would Carson."

"Which is why I told you," Kimi said. "It was eatin' me alive."

"I just wish we could talk to Vi about it."

Kimi groaned. "Lord, she'll be fit to be tied when she hears I've got a grandchild before she does. I've heard her nag and bitch at Libby about when she's gonna make her a grandmother. The poor woman."

"Why some women see fit to meddle in their grown children's lives..." Carolyn looked at Kimi and they both burst out laughing.

"Lord. I couldn't even say that with a straight face."

"That's my cue to go." Kimi stood. "Thanks for the ear and the whiskey."

"Any time."

"Before I forget, are we doin' anything for the West reunion the weekend of the rodeo?"

"Just showing up with food, I guess, since Tracy is in charge."

"You gonna say anything to Stuart and Janet?"

Carolyn shook her head. "I know it's been a couple of years but I'm still mad at them. Chet and Remy know better to push me on this. At least they've stepped up."

"How could Stu and Janet just ignore that situation with Boone? He's their grandson—their only grandson. I mean, yeah, Dax screwed up years ago, but one strike and he's out of the family? That sounds like something Dad would've done."

"Which is why I don't want to go to the stupid reunion. Beings our boys are competing in the rodeo that day, I'm planning on having the McKays—and a few select Wests—over here the day after. Will that work?"

Kimi wrinkled her nose. "Can we selectively invite McKays too?"

"I wish. But I've already mentioned it to Joan. I'd like to make the event alcohol free—not just to keep Casper from getting stinking drunk." It'd be easier for Colt to be there, even when everything she'd read said the recovering alcoholic needed to decide the social limitations, not his family or friends. Just letting her son be was harder than she'd imagined.

"We've got time to figure out the menu. I'm just hopin' that Kade gets to bring his baby girl."

"How do you think Cal will react to the news he's a grandpa?"

"I'm about to find out." Kimi waved and she was gone.

Several hours later Kimi returned, livid about Cal chewing her out for telling her sister they were grandparents before she'd told him. So Kimi and Cal, the couple who never fought, had a huge row, right in front of Carolyn and Carson.

An infuriated Cal had chased after Kimi and stormed into the house. He'd cornered Kimi in the dining room. "Oh no you don't, you little brat. You don't get to tell me to fuck off and then run and hide."

Kimi swigged directly from the bottle of whiskey she'd lifted from the liquor cabinet. "Not running. Not hiding. You were a dick to me, Calvin McKay. So don't be so goddamned shocked that I don't wanna be around you."

He loomed over her. "Suck it up. You were in the wrong, and you know it."

"I was not. You weren't home!"

"I have a fuckin' cell phone for situations exactly like this one," he bellowed.

"Which you won't answer because you'll be too busy doin' some stupid cow thing."

"Stupid cow thing?" he repeated. "I'll remind you the stupid cow thing keeps you in hair dye and rhinestones."

Oh no. Cal did *not* go there. Carolyn heard Carson groan behind her.

"You are such a prick!" She whipped the bottle of whiskey at him.

Fortunately Kimi was a crappy shot and Cal had great reflexes. He caught the bottle. There wasn't much booze left. He drained the remainder and set it aside. "Apologize to me right now, Kimberly Jo West McKay."

He used her full name, knowing full well how much she hated it.

"Why should I? With that glug of booze you knocked back I see we won't kiss and make up since you'll have a case of whiskey dick."

Cal laughed. Hard. "Wild cat, I ain't ever had whiskey dick in my life and you damn well know it."

"Why are you being like this? You never give a damn what Caro and I talk about."

"This time is different. I always thought we'd hear about our first grandbaby together. How would you like it if I knew about that precious baby girl and told a buncha people before I told you?"

That gave Kimi pause. "Fine. I shoulda told you first."

"That ain't an apology. Try again."

At some point Cal had trapped Kimi against the wall. She put her hands on his hips to push him back. "I'm sorry."

Cal laughed—a little snidely. "That's one. You owe me more than one apology."

"For what?"

"For callin' me a dick. For callin' me a prick. For questioning my ability to perform. And wild cat, I've never left you wanting on that front, have I?"

"No."

"So apologize."

"Sorry."

"Huh-uh. Offer the proper apology to the injured party."

"What?"

"On your knees."

Kimi murmured something that caused Cal to growl and dip his head toward her chest.

That's when Carson grabbed Carolyn's hand and they hightailed it out of their own house.

They didn't stop moving until they reached the barn.

"Good Lord, I didn't need to witness that."

"No shit," Carson said. "That was about as awkward as the time Keely caught us playin' master and slave in the dining room."

Carolyn twined her arms around his neck. "Speaking of...been a

341

long time since we've horsed around like that."

He grinned. "No ball gag this time, slave, so on your knees."

"Right here in the barn?"

He quirked that sexy eyebrow in challenge. "You doin' something else right now?"

"No." She lowered to her knees and looked up at him. "But I'm still not ever calling you master."

For the first time she drifted away into the catacombs of her mind with a smile on her face and the taste of Carson on her tongue.

Chapter Twenty-Nine

"Today on *Maury*: I'm retired, I'm not raising your love child! We'll hear about one woman's struggle after she discovered her husband had fathered a child with their grandchildren's barely legal babysitter."

Seriously? There was such shit on daytime TV.

But Carson secretly loved this train-wreck show.

The talk show host came back on the screen. "How do you plan to spend your retirement? Eleanor Peabody imagined she and her husband of thirty-five years would travel the world together. But during the first few months of his retirement, Henry began an affair with their grandchildren's eighteen-year-old babysitter, Shania." Boos echoed from the audience. "Now Shania is pregnant and she expects Henry to take responsibility for his child. Where does this leave Eleanor? Stuck helping raise her husband's love child during her golden years? Henry is here too and he'll tell you why Eleanor needs to step up."

"Carson?"

He about shot out of his seat and turned to face his son-in-law. "Jesus, Jack. You scared the crap out of me."

"Sorry." He glanced up at the screen. "Am I interrupting?"

"No. I never watch this garbage. I was just bored." He stood and clicked off the TV.

"You seem surprised to see me."

Carson gave Jack Donohue a once-over. Dressed impeccably in a snappy suit and shined shoes. It no longer pained him to admit Keely had done well in her choice of husband. Jack was a smart, savvy businessman, who adored Keely but wasn't a pushover for their headstrong daughter. "I thought Keely might've put her foot down and said you couldn't break rank."

Jack lifted one dark brow. "You do know me, right? When have I ever let that sassy cowgirl dictate what I can and can't do?"

"Point taken."

They took seats opposite each other. "Since germs are an issue, I'll throw it out that Piper and Katie are as robustly healthy as their twin brothers."

"Happy to hear that. I know it was a rough winter."

"I had no idea kids got sick that much. I considered buying stock in the pharmaceutical company that manufactures amoxicillin. Summer weather seems to cure the nasty bugs, thank God."

"What is the wild bunch up to?"

"Piper has been holding princess school for Katie because she's been spending too much time playing with JJ and Liam."

Carson smiled. "What fun things are the Donohue twins doin' that's pullin' Katie away from her big sister?"

"That's the thing. Nothing. It's just Piper is so damn bossy. Katie gets sick of it."

"Cord and Colby had those same issues, as did Cam and Carter. Poor Colt got caught in the middle."

"Weird question, since you're a twin. Did you and Cal have your own...language?"

That was a weird question. "Not really. We've got nonverbal communication, which most folks find odd. But I'm not sure it's a twin thing as much as we've worked together since we were boys and we knew what needed done without havin' to say it out loud. Why? Are your twins speakin' in tongues or something?"

Jack shook his head. "Keely would swear they're speaking demon. They have that nonverbal thing too. We purposely don't dress them the same. At first when they were babies it was to tell them apart. We kept that ankle band on JJ for a year until the boys developed their own personalities."

"Kimi and Cal had to do the same thing with Kade and Kane. By the time they were three none of us had issues tellin' them apart. At least when they came over to our place."

"Why's that?"

"Because Kane immediately went lookin' for Colt. Them two were rough-housin' as soon as they could walk. Whereas Kade helped Caro with whatever kid of ours was a baby. Lots of experts about twins in this family." Carson swigged from his bottle of Dr. Pepper. "Are you here on Keely's behalf?"

"I told her I planned to stop by. She also knows I agreed with your decision to limit all access to your wife."

"Did that cause problems?"

"I wouldn't let it. Keely is acting like a spoiled brat and I told her so." Jack's eyes softened. "How are things with Carolyn?"

"No change. The docs are giving her another day. Then they'll bring her out of it."

"How are you holding up?"

"Been the worst six days of my life. Every goddamned minute feels like an hour." Or a lifetime.

"I can't imagine. You saw how much of a mess I was when Keely collapsed during her last pregnancy. And that was only a few hours I didn't know what was going on with her. I wouldn't have any hair left if it'd been longer."

"Your kids will turn it gray soon enough. What's new in the business world? Buy up any towns lately?"

"Working on it. I need some place to lock my daughters away when they turn fifteen."

Carson snorted. "If they take after Keely it'll start when they turn thirteen."

"You're kidding, right?"

"Nope. Carter caught Keely kissin' a friend of his behind the rodeo stands when she was only thirteen. I guess the poor kid about crapped his pants when Carter rounded up a bunch of McKays and warned him off his baby sister. Course, Keely took offense to bein' called a baby and punched Carter in the gut. When Colt stepped in, she kneed him in the nuts."

Jack mock shuddered. "She is one scary-ass woman when she's mad."

"She had to be or her brothers or cousins wouldn't take her seriously. At first they called her cute when she got mad. Then they realized she'd take an inch of skin offa them with that razor sharp tongue of hers. Then they also realized maybe they shouldn't have taught her how to punch so hard."

"Lettie at the Golden Boot told me that Keely gets a lot of her scrappiness from Carolyn. Is that true?"

"Let's just say Keely wasn't the first woman in our family to get a lifetime ban from a local bar."

Jack laughed. "I knew it."

"So with her Gran-gran's and her mom's DNA, I'm thinkin' Piper will be hell on wheels when she hits twenty-one." Or seventeen—not that he wanted to worry Jack ahead of time.

"Then I'll be pounding on your door, asking for advice. Or bail money."

Carson raised both eyebrows. "You're assuming I'll be around? I'll be damn near ninety-two."

"You'll be around," Jack assured him. "Medical technology already replaced one of your worn out body parts. You might end up being the first bionic McKay."

"Right. With just one part replaced there's still a bunch of stuff I can't do."

"Not back on a horse yet?"

"I'm wondering if I'll ever ride again." His eyes narrowed. "Don't you say nothin' to Keely. She'll get it in her head that I just need more damn therapy."

"Maybe the better question is do you *want* to ride again?"

"You're the first person who's asked me that."

"That's not an answer, Carson."

"I know. I've been ridin' my whole life. It's tough on a body. If I keep doin' it... What's next? Havin' my other hip replaced? Then my knees? Then havin' my spine fused together with metal rods? I ain't sure I wanna spend my life in the hospital. Especially after what happened with me during surgery."

"Can't say as I blame you. Besides you *are* retired. It's not like you *have* to ride a horse every day to make your living."

Carson shifted back in his chair. "Bein's we still live in the thick of things, the boys come over and ask for advice and help occasionally. I feel retired, but I'm not out of it completely."

"No plans to spend winters down south?"

"Maybe a week or two. Especially if Ky ends up goin' to ASU. But Caro won't ever want to stay away from here for long. Too many memories." Carson paused. "Too many grandkids."

Jack honed in on the ASU comment and they spent the next ten minutes discussing the activities various McKay offspring were involved in, which segued into a conversation about college sports, which led to a discussion about Carter's most recent commissions—metal sculptures depicting famous western athletes in action. Then the conversation came full circle as they talked about Jack's projects and the growth of Keely's physical therapy business.

"I want Keely to hire an employee, but she's dragging her feet," Jack said.

"Why? I thought she wanted to be home more."

"She does. But she doesn't think she'll find anyone who's qualified who only wants to work twenty hours a week. I've crunched the numbers for her and if she hires someone fulltime, she'll still be in the black the first year. With another therapist, if she increases the amount of clients by a third, she'll double her income in three years."

"And the girl ain't listening to you...why?"

"She's stubborn. She says I already have enough money—" he snorted as if that couldn't possibly be true, "—and *I* should retire and stay home with the kids."

"Retirement ain't all it's cracked up to be."

"I've heard that." Jack checked his watch. "Speaking of work... I have a phone conference to prepare for. Is there anything I can do for you before I take off?"

Carson shook his head. "It's a whole lot of waitin' around."

"If you think of something—anything at all—call me. I say that knowing full well that you won't."

"You've already done enough if you can keep my Keely girl on an even keel throughout this."

"She puts on a happy face for our kids but once they're down for the night, she does a whole lot of staring into space."

"I'm familiar with that. But I pace too, just to mix it up."

Jack smiled. Then he reached into his pocket and pulled out a flask. "For when you're missing your Irish and need a nip to get you through this last day."

"Thanks." Carson nestled it in the bag of magazines on the floor. "Comin' from Mr. Moneybags, I imagine it's higher quality stuff than Jameson."

"Of course. Once I get you used to drinking Laphroaig you'll never go back."

La-froyg. Even the name sounded fancy. "Unlikely, but I appreciate the gesture."

"Take care." Jack paused before he turned the corner. "Keely...*will* swallow her pride and come see you."

"I'd like that." Carson studied him. "So you *are* here on her behalf?"

"She's my wife, she's miserable and it's killing me that I can't fix it for her." He raked his hand through his hair. "So yeah, I have to at least try."

Yep, his baby girl had done very well in choosing the man to spend her life with.

As he watched Jack walk away, phone to his ear, he knew the man couldn't fathom retiring.

Funny how the years had crept up on him. One day he was a young, married man wondering how he'd support his growing family, then in the blink of an eye he was wondering how he'd spend his days because he had all this free time...

Carson, Cal and Charlie were at the Golden Boot discussing retirement after they'd handed over the reins of McKay Ranches. Casper hadn't been invited for a celebratory beer after the stink he'd raised about being forcibly retired. Carson was glad his boys got along well, for the most part, with each other and with their cousins.

"So it will sink in at some point, right?" Cal asked. "That we don't have to oversee what they're doin' on a daily basis?"

"I guess. None of us have been doin' as much as we used to. Seems like I've been semi-retired for a while anyway," Carson said.

"I hear ya." Charlie sipped his beer. "What did Dad do in retirement?"

"It wasn't like he officially retired. He couldn't do the daily work after the first heart attack. Mentally he was fine, but ain't a whole lot of ranch work that's mental. Menial?" Carson grinned. "Hell yes."

"After that last heart attack, he kept up with what his grandkids were doin' as long as he didn't have to venture too far from our place."

"I doubt Kimi kept him entertained," Charlie said. "So my question remains the same. What did he do all day?"

"He watched TV in his room."

"That's it?"

Cal shrugged. "I dunno. While Dad didn't have nothin' to do I sure did. I worked that section pretty much by myself. Then at night, I spent time with Kimi and the boys. After the twins went to bed if Dad was still up we'd bullshit about stuff. I never heard him say he was bored."

"I sure as fuck don't want my retirement to be sittin' around and watchin' goddamned TV," Carson said.

"I'm sure your kids would love to dump some of the two hundred grandkids you have off on you every day," Cal said.

"Piss off, Cal."

"Maybe you oughta tell Carolyn you're worried about bein' bored. She'll have you in the kitchen learnin' to cook in no time," Charlie added.

"You can piss off too, Charlie."

Cal and Charlie laughed and knocked their beer bottles together.

Carson's gaze traveled around the Golden Boot. "Maybe we oughta start a bar. This place needs some competition."

"It has competition: Ziggy's, Twin Pines, the Rusty Spur. Though I'll admit I liked that place better when it was the Silver Spur years ago," Cal said.

"Place was a fire hazard, which is why it burned to the ground. After the owners rebuilt it and renamed it the Rusty Spur, Carolyn made me take her there for a drink. She figured since the old place and old name was gone, then her lifetime ban oughta be lifted too."

"Was it?"

"Yep. I think the new manager was a little scared of her, to be honest."

"Any of your kids ever hear the story of their Mama's bar fight?" Charlie asked.

Carson shook his head. "I can't be sure someone else didn't tell them about it." He leaned back in the booth. "Charlie, you seem all het up about retirement."

"I am. I never had time for hobbies besides huntin'. Don't think I'm the sort to take up golf. Don't wanna be in Vi's hair all damn day."

Cal leaned forward. "I know what you can do. Start a senior citizens bull ridin' circuit. As the father of PBR World Finals contender Chase McKay, I'll bet you'd get lots of interest and sponsorships."

"Piss off, Cal," Charlie said. "I don't see *you* offerin' up any ideas on how you'll be spendin' your days."

"I'll be bangin' my wife."

"That'll kill three minutes," Carson said dryly, "then whatcha gonna do the rest of the day?"

"And you can piss off too," Cal said to Carson.

Another round of beers arrived. Carson looked at Lettie. "You a mind reader?"

"I'd be blushing for sure if I was reading your mind, Carson McKay," Lettie shot back. "I've known you since your brawling days. Not that I ever saw that trait passed on to your sons." She winked. "They flirt with me just as much as you do."

Carson snorted. "You've been flirtin' with *me* for forty-some years."

"And you love it." Lettie sighed. "We were hot stuff back in the day, weren't we?"

"Yes, we were. Hot tempered, hot bodied," he grinned at her, "hot to trot."

"Anyway, this round has been paid for. Enjoy."

They looked at each other and shrugged.

"Did either Kimi or Vi mention the urge to travel?" Carson asked.

"We get to several of Chase's PBR events during the year. Don't know if the boy will make it to Vegas this year. But besides that? Not really. Vi mentioned it'd be fun to take a family trip to Disney World with Quinn and Libby and the grandkids."

"That'd be my idea of hell," Carson grumbled. "God knows I love the grandkids, but there are so many of 'em we'd have to rent out the whole damn hotel."

"Kimi is content to stay home," Cal said. "Says she traveled enough after she graduated from the nunnery."

"What about Carolyn?" Charlie asked.

"That's the thing. I don't know. We've never really talked about it. Like Kimi she'd rather stay home. But I wouldn't mind hittin' the open road and seeing some sights."

Carson remembered that was the exact moment he decided to buy a RV. That way he and Carolyn could take off whenever they wanted and they'd still have the comforts of home.

In fact, he remembered thinking it was the most brilliant idea in the history of ideas. And since he was feeling more than a little smug, he decided he'd keep this fantastic idea to himself, lest one of his brothers take it and steal his thunder.

He'd make the purchase a surprise. He had a few months to research the best model. Next summer he'd just drive it on home. He couldn't wait to see the look on her face.

But five months later, when Carson pulled up in front of the house and honked the horn, he hadn't expected Carolyn's expression to border on horror as she walked down the porch steps.

After hopping out the driver's side door, he bounded up the sidewalk toward her. "Isn't she a beaut?"

"What in..." She closed her eyes and inhaled slowly. He recognized the posture as *Lord give me patience* but he'd seen it directed at the kids, not at him.

Maybe she was just stunned he'd done something so thoughtful.

"Sugar, come on and see the inside. You're gonna flip. It's got everything."

His ears must've been playing tricks on him because he swore he heard her mumble, "Including a maid?"

He pointed out the front area. "The seats are plush. Like sittin' in my easy chair drivin' down the road. And above us? We just slip a piece of padded wood across and it becomes an oversized bunk." He led her to the kitchen. "I figured you'd love the full sized stove and oven. And the table folds down so it can be a living area or an extra bed."

"Handy. I can make whoever is sleeping there breakfast in bed."

"Exactly." He paused. Wait a second. Was that...sarcasm?

Nah. He had to've misheard her.

"Down here you'll find the bathroom." He led her down the short hallway and pulled the folding door open. "With a corner shower it's bigger than standard. Same with the toilet." He gestured to the cabinet beside the door. "There's a compact washing machine and dryer in there."

She didn't seem too impressed.

"Check this out." Carson opened the door to the bedroom. "A king-sized bed. And look at all the storage."

"For laundry, cleaning and cooking supplies no doubt."

"No, I think it's mostly closet space. But you can put whatever you want back here." He perched on the edge of the bed and patted the mattress. "Shall we break it in?"

"Right now?"

He lifted an eyebrow. "You busy doin' something else?"

"Actually, yes. I was about to bake brownies and I'm starting supper. But maybe later?"

He stood and kissed her forehead. "Sure. But do you like it?"

"It's...something all right."

Later that night Carson convinced her to return to the camper, expecting she'd want to explore on her own. He was pretty damn proud of himself for figuring out how to hook up the satellite TV without pestering his kids for help.

After being married for so many years, he was all-pro at seducing his wife. But the whole time he was making love to her—or trying to—she didn't seem that into it.

He stopped moving and looked down at her. "Am I boring you or something?"

Carolyn opened her eyes. "No, it's fine."

Fine? That less than enthusiastic response made him more determined to feel her clinging to him and moaning in his ear as she came undone. He nuzzled her throat, scattering those little sucking love bites she loved so much down the arch of her neck. When even that didn't create the shivering and moaning effect, once again he stopped moving. "What's goin' on with you?"

"I can't relax."

"This is supposed to relax you."

"Well, it's not, it's just making me more tense so can we just get it over with please?"

"Over with?" That stung. He eased out of her body and pushed to the end of the bed, waiting for the soft caress of her hand assuring him she didn't mean it. Waiting for her to ask if they could start over. Because in all the years they'd been married, she'd only left him hanging like this a few times.

Carson felt the bed shift and glanced over to see her...grabbing her clothing.

What the hell?

Carolyn wouldn't meet his gaze as she slipped on her bra and hooked it behind her. "Look, I'll catch you later before we go to bed. I'm just really not in the mood right now."

No kidding.

She didn't stop and kiss him or touch him at all. She just breezed past him, leaving him nekkid and alone with a flagging erection and a sense of unease.

That night in their bed she'd kept to her word and more than made up for her odd behavior in the camper bedroom earlier.

Still, he knew something was going on with her.

A dose of the grandkids always cheered her up. He asked Colby and Channing if they could take their four boys to the lake for the weekend.

Gib, Braxton, Miles and Austin were highly impressed with the RV. Carolyn had just closed the garden gate when he pulled up and honked. Was she ever speechless when the grandsons spilled out, chattering a mile a minute about their surprise weekend camping adventure with Grandpa and Gran-gran.

Carolyn scooped Austin up and perched him on her hip, smooching his chubby cheek. "You boys ready to go camping?"

They all shouted, "Yes!"

Then his wife smiled at him—and it wasn't a nice smile. "Let's go."

"Right now?"

"You busy doin' something else?"

Why was she tossing his words from yesterday afternoon at him? "No."

"Good. I'll just grab my purse and lock the front door and we'll hit the road."

"But..."

She whirled on him. "But what? Isn't this the appeal of having a camper? We can just take off whenever the mood strikes us?"

"Yeah, but sugar, we don't have any food or supplies."

She flapped her hand at him. "Minor details."

Maybe she planned to stop at the grocery store on the way to the lake.

But she insisted they check into the campground to secure a good spot. Once they'd paid the fees and parked, everyone was hungry and there wasn't so much as a breath mint in the camper to feed four hungry boys and two adults. So they trekked to the marina convenience store and bought thirty bucks worth of food.

They roasted hot dogs and marshmallows over the campfire. The kids ate every bit of it.

When bedtime rolled around, Carolyn insisted he sleep with the boys in the bunk; she worried one of them would fall off in the middle of the night. She and Austin took the bedroom and they all slept in their clothes since no one had remembered to bring pajamas.

The next morning Carson returned to the marina convenience store and bought thirty bucks worth of donuts, milk and juice, which the boys devoured in one sitting. Since Carolyn didn't swim, she kept Austin in the camper with her.

The boys had brought swimming trunks, but no towels, so after they'd exited the water they'd had to dry off in the sun. Upon returning to the camper, once again the boys were starved.

Instead of traipsing back to the overpriced convenience store, Carson pulled up stakes and they drove into town for lunch. When neither their grandsons nor Carolyn seemed too keen on camping another night, they dropped the boys off and headed home.

Home. It was a pretty nice place to be. After polishing off a half a dozen cookies, Carson plopped in his easy chair to watch TV.

So the camping experiment hadn't gone too well the first time. Next time they'd be more prepared. He'd drifted into a mental road map of the places he'd like to visit when Carolyn snatched the remote out of his hand.

He looked up to see her planted in front of him, wearing her pissed-off face.

"How long have we been married?"

He opened his mouth to answer and she cut him off.

"In all those years have I *ever* told you it was my fondest dream to own an RV and travel the country?"

Shit.

"No, I haven't. You know why? Because that is my idea of hell. That is the single most asinine thing you've ever..." She made a huffing noise and leaned forward to jab her finger into his chest. "You don't cook, so who would be responsible for all the meals? Me. You don't clean, so who would be responsible for keeping the camper tidy? Me. You don't grocery shop, so who would be responsible for stocking the camper pantry? Me. How is that a fucking vacation for me, Carson McKay? It isn't. And it makes me think that you don't know me at all if you believe I'd want that nomadic life. Our life is here. Not with strangers at some senior citizens RV park playing bridge and comparing pictures of our grandkids. How the hell much did that camper cost?" She jabbed him in the chest again. "For that kind of money, we could fly wherever we wanted. We could stay at a five star hotel. We could eat at a different restaurant every night and still have money left over to do it again...ten or fifteen more times! *That* is a vacation. Dragging the whole damn house with us so I can cook and clean in an itty bitty space while you watch satellite TV in your plush captain's chair ain't gonna happen. Ever."

She stood and placed her hands on her hips. "Monday morning you *will* return that camper to the dealer. Tell them you changed your mind."

His mouth dropped open. "Do you know how much money we'll lose if I do that?"

"Do you know how much more money you'll lose if I divorce your stupid ass for expecting that's how I'd spend my retirement?"

Holy shit. She wasn't serious...was she? "Caro—"

She drilled that sharp index finger into his chest, punctuating every word. "I. Am. Not. Kidding. Me or the camper, Carson McKay. You choose."

After the camper was gone, they never spoke of it again.

Chapter Thirty

Hospital, Day 7—morning

Carson had overslept, and the nurses hadn't woken him so he'd missed three visits with Carolyn. By the time his visitation window arrived and he'd dragged himself into her room, he was a wreck.

"Hey sugar. I'm sittin' here beside you. I know you can hear me. I *need* you to hear me. Come back to me. I need you to know that I'm right here, I ain't goin' anywhere.

"I've tried to stay so positive every time I'm in here. But the closer it gets to them pullin' you out of this, the more I worry that you'll wake up in pain." He studied the rise and fall of her chest. "Every time you brought a child into this world, I hated the pain it caused you. Even when you swore it was worth it in the end, I wanted to shoulder that burden."

In his mind—maybe his crazy mind?—he heard her soft, *I know that.*

His phantom conversation with her seemed so much harder on the seventh day. He'd happily relived a lifetime of memories in the last six days. Why was he struggling now?

Because you've wanted it to be over and it almost is. And you're scared to find out what happens next.

So he kept babbling. "You've been so healthy over the years. You wouldn't get so much as a sniffle when it seemed at least one of the kids was always sick. Your blood pressure is good, so's your cholesterol. You didn't smoke, you didn't drink to excess. How's it fair that you're in here now..." *It should be me in that hospital bed. I should've been exercising my own damn horse. I asked too much of you. I always have.*

Stop with the guilt, Carson.

He really was losing it because he swore she'd whispered that in his ear.

Get it together.

Carson traced every bone in her hand. "I remember how worried you were that you'd inherited your mom's arthritis. I'd catch you starin' at your hands every once in a while, wondering if they'd turn on you like hers had. If you'd become frail like her. But again, you dodged that bullet. You are the strongest person I know, Caro."

Her sweet voice saying, *I know that too, sweetheart,* floated through him and his flesh became a mass of goose bumps.

Carson felt her. This time he knew she was listening to him.

"I was so damn disoriented when I woke up after surgery. Didn't remember nothin' about before. Nothin' during."

"Mr. McKay?" the nurse said from the doorway. "Time's up."

No. Don't make me leave her.

And for the first time in six days, Carson ignored the nurse and he kept on talking. "I don't want that for you, not remembering. In the past seven days I've remembered so much."

"Mr. McKay. You need to leave now."

"I gotta go. But I'll be here next hour. And the hour after that. And every hour until you open them pretty blue eyes and look at me. I love you, sugar. I can't live without you. Come back to me. Please."

After Carson ditched the protective suit, he told the nurses he was heading down to the cafeteria. But once he saw the long line, he cut out the side door and stepped into the sunshine.

Another hot, dry day. Be nice if they'd get some rain.

Typical rancher; weather is always the first topic of conversation.

Apparently that held true even when he talked to himself.

He meandered to his truck and snagged the pack of cigarettes and book of matches. After firing up a smoke, he dropped the tailgate, forcing himself to ease into a sitting position.

That'd been the hardest thing after his surgery, the lists of do's and don'ts. Even a movement as simple as crossing his legs wasn't allowed because of the pressure it'd put on the joint.

Now he could admit the surgery two months ago had helped. Every day had been a struggle before that...

Rain, shine, hot, cold, staying stationary or keeping active, nothing mattered.

The pain in his hip was getting worse.

And it was damn near excruciating when he was on horseback.

It wasn't his horse's fault that he'd become a crippled up old man. It wouldn't be so bad if the only time he was in pain was when he mounted and dismounted. But even a slow ride put him in agony. In trying to adjust his seat, he put extra pressure on his knee, which made that ache.

Getting old wasn't for pussies.

Carson managed to stay on for an hour, taking in the beauty of the early spring morning. The weather had been great this year for calving—no brutally cold temps and blizzard conditions that stretched out for weeks. He'd helped Colt with the midnight cattle check. But riding on the four-wheeler had caused pain—and Colt had noticed. Carson jokingly explained it as the cold settling in his brittle bones.

He'd been riding as long as he could remember—climbing on horseback had been a daily part of his life. But lately he'd only been able to ride once a week. His sons assumed he didn't ride much anymore because he'd retired.

His wife suspected something was up, but in typical Carolyn fashion, she hadn't said anything—yet.

He kept Sheridan at a canter as they headed for the barn. He was surprised to see Carolyn waiting by the fence for him.

Shit. He'd have to dismount in front of her. Or...maybe he could pretend he'd just swung by to see if she needed something before he continued his ride. He plastered on a grin. "Hey, sugar. What's goin' on?"

"Just getting some air. Wondered what you were up to. You've been out here a while."

"Enjoying the beautiful mornin'. Was there something you needed?"

"Actually, yes. I'm having a devil of the time with the back door to the kitchen sticking again."

"I'll take a look at it after I'm done with my ride."

"I thought you were done since I saw you heading toward the barn?"

"Nope. Saw you standing there, pretty as a picture and came over to say hey."

Her eyes turned shrewd. "Carson McKay, you are such a liar. Get off that horse right now."

He raised an eyebrow at her. "Feelin' a mite bossy this mornin'?"

"Don't pretend this has anything to do with me. I want to see you get off your horse."

"Caro—"

"I mean it. Then as soon as you dismount I want you to mount me." She paused and challenged, "But that seems to be a problem for you too, lately, doesn't it?"

"What are you—?"

"You haven't touched me for two months. *Two months.* The last time we went that long was after one of my pregnancies. So start explaining why you're suddenly acting like making love to me is repulsive."

That's what she thought?

Of course she would think that.

"Sugar, that ain't even close to the truth."

Her gaze narrowed further. "Are you gonna try and pass this problem off as you need Viagra because you can't get it up and that's why we haven't had sex, let alone even been sleeping close together at night?"

Dammit. He knew she wouldn't buy that either. The woman saw too much for her own good and she never made a move until she was sure. So he had no idea how long she'd been lying in wait to jump him about this so he glared at her.

"Huh-uh, cowboy. That squinty eyed stare won't work on me."

Carson snorted. "When has it ever worked on you?"

"Sweetheart. You don't have to glare at me to scare me. Why you're trying to hide the pain from me makes my fears ten times worse. Please. Tell me what's going on."

"Fine. You wanna see?" Embarrassed, because yeah, maybe he'd rather she thought he needed chemicals to get his dick hard rather than the truth; that he wasn't the agile man who could out-rope and out-ride everyone that he used to be.

Holding onto the saddle horn, he shifted his weight forward. Then he threw his right leg over the back of the horse, trying like hell to balance on his left side, knowing the instant his right foot touched the dirt would be the moment of agony and there was no way he could hide it from her.

His right boot heel hit the ground. Even with his left foot in the stirrup, he almost fell on his ass. The shooting pain was instantaneous. His vision went wonky even after he'd placed both feet on the dirt. He rested his forehead in the curve of his saddle.

Sheridan stayed still as Carson regained his balance. Sometimes the grinding fire in his joint forced him to double over and spew out every curse word he'd ever heard—if the torture hadn't caused him to stop breathing entirely.

The gate clanged behind him. Then Carolyn wrapped her arms around his middle and squeezed. "It's okay. I'm here. Please let me help you."

He breathed through the pain and held onto the reins when Sheridan tried to shift sideways. "Steady, girl."

"I'm sorry. But I've been worried and you won't tell me what's going on—"

"Sugar, I was talkin' to my horse."

"Oh." She laughed. "Of course you were."

"I'm better now."

"No, you're not. We can just stay like this until you settle."

Carson turned his head and nuzzled the side of her face. Feeling calmed by the words she'd so rarely had to say to him.

After a bit she murmured, "Better?"

"I'm always better when you're near."

"What can I do? You want me to unsaddle Sheridan and deal with the tack?"

"Nah. That's the easy part. I got it."

"I'll stick around and help you anyway."

"I'd like that."

After they'd dealt with his horse, they walked hand in hand back to the house in silence that wasn't uncomfortable, just resigned.

In the kitchen, Carson watched her busying herself getting them coffee and a slice of strudel cake. Then she watched him a little too closely for signs of pain as he took his usual chair in the dining room.

"It's your right hip, isn't it?"

Carson nodded.

"How long has it been bothering you?"

"Since Christmas."

Carolyn cocked her head as if she didn't believe him.

"Okay. Since Thanksgiving."

"And you didn't say anything because...?"

"At first I thought it might just be inflammation because I'd helped the boys more this fall than I'd done in a while. I figured it'd go away. When it didn't, I remembered my dad had a harder time with his joints hurtin' in the winter. But now that it's started warmin' up, it's getting worse, not better." He stared into his coffee cup. "I fuckin' hate that the last time I tried to make love to you it hurt so goddamned bad that I just wanted to get it over with."

She scooted closer, took his hand and curled it around her face. "Why did you hide that from me? We could've tried some way besides missionary—"

"It's embarrassing. Two things I've been good at—keepin' you satisfied in bed and ridin'—can't do either of them anymore." He sighed with pure frustration. "I ain't a young man, by any stretch. But Jesus, Caro. When did I get so damn old? I hate this constant aches and pains shit."

"I know. But it's not going away. So can we go to the doctor and see what can be done?"

We. Always *we.* "Yeah."

The relief in her eyes shamed him; she'd been prepared for a fight. "I think—"

"No more thinkin'. We'll get it taken care of. Soon. But right now, I'm takin' care of you." He helped her to her feet and slapped her butt hard enough she yelped. "Repulsive my ass. You are still the sexiest damn thing I've ever laid eyes on." He'd kissed her in the slow, patient, teasing way that drove her crazy. Then he spread her out on the dining room table and kissed her the same way between her legs.

And it hadn't hurt his hip at all.

"Daddy?"

Carson's head whipped up. Lost in the memory, he'd forgotten about the cigarette smoldering between his fingers.

But of course Keely noticed it right away. "Since when have you smoked?"

He lifted the butt to his lips, inhaled and slowly exhaled. "Since I was sixteen. It's a stress thing, not a regular habit."

"Does Mom know?" She paused. "Of course she does. You two keep each other's secrets."

Carson stared at his beautiful daughter. Sweet Jesus. She was doing a stellar zombie imitation. Dark circles hung under her eyes; her face was milky white. She wore no makeup; her hair looked like she'd stuck her head out the window zipping down the road at a hundred miles an hour. Even if Keely was only headed for the barn she took care with her appearance—a habit she'd learned from her mother. "Punkin, you look like hell."

"So do you."

"Yeah, well. I've been livin' there the last seven goddamned days." He sucked in another drag. Held the smoke in. Blew it out. "I ain't in the mood for you to chew my ass."

"Don't do that."

"Do what? Smoke?"

"No. Don't be a dick. I know you're hurtin', Daddy. I see it."

"You don't know the half of it, girlie." He slid off the tailgate, hiding a wince when the impact with the ground sent a sharp pain from his heel to his hip. He dropped the cigarette on the blacktop before he ground it out with his boot heel.

"I do know how bad you're hurtin', because I've seen the other half." Keely moved toward him, snaking her arms around his waist, burying her face on his chest, her shoulders heaving.

His response was automatic. Ingrained. He wrapped his arms around her and kissed the top of her head. His sweet baby. She'd always be his baby no matter how old she got.

"I'm sorry," she said through choked sobs.

And he'd forgive her no matter how bratty she acted. "I know you are."

Keely tilted her head back and met his gaze. In that moment she looked so much like her mother, his heart swelled even as it ached. "You deserved better from me. From all of us. I've never spoken for my brothers, and I ain't about to start now. I'm sorry I thought my connection to her should mean more than yours. I know better. I saw it that day of your surgery and it freaked me the hell out."

"That what you mean by you've seen the other half?"

She nodded. "You and Mom; you're two halves of a whole. She knew. Right away. I told her to calm down, it was routine surgery, the orthopedic surgeon performed that procedure ten times a week and it was nothing to worry about."

In seventy-four years of life Carson had never been put under. As they'd wheeled him in to pre-op, Carolyn promised she'd be waiting for him on the other side. She had no idea how true that statement had been at the time.

"The minute you coded on the operating table, she stood up in the waiting room and said, 'Come back to me. I'm right here. Where I've always been, where I'll always be. I love you. Please. Come back to me.'"

That jarred him; what did it mean that he'd been reciting those exact same words to Carolyn every time he'd left her side the last week?

That you are two halves of a whole.

Carolyn had never told him what she'd said to yank him back. He had a vague recollection of being in a black void and then a sensation of floating away. Not that he'd seen people or places or a bright light or anything that defined his idea of heaven. He'd just heard Carolyn's voice, pleading with him, and he'd battled his way back to find her.

Then later—minutes, hours, he hadn't been sure of the time elapse—he'd woken up in a hospital bed with his wife sitting beside him. One hand held his, her other hand rested on his heart. Carolyn's tears sliced through him until he realized they were tears of joy.

She'd whispered, "I thought I'd lost you."

"Sugar—"

"I can't... You died on that operating table, Carson. For two minutes you were gone. Gone. Away from me for good. Forever. You're here and I'm so blessed." She stood and kissed every inch of his face. The softness of her lips and the sweep of her breath on his skin, the scent of her shampoo and the occasional teardrop were a potent mix of love and fear and gratitude. So when her lips finally found his, when she looked in his eyes and said, "You are my life, Carson McKay, I'll never survive a world without you in it," his own tears fell without shame.

"You've kept me grounded every moment of every day for the last fifty years. Only you could fight god and nature for me and win."

"Because I know you'd do the same for me."

And I have. Sweet Jesus I'd fight the devil himself to have you back with me, whole, because I'm half of nothing without you.

"Daddy?"

He blinked and realized he was outside, in a parking lot, with his daughter. What did it say that this flashback stuff no longer spooked him? Because he feared if Carolyn didn't pull through that's all he would have of her? And he'd rather be lost in memories of his life with her and their past than face the reality of a future without her?

Don't think that way.

He refocused on Keely. "What, punkin?"

"I'm sorry for givin' you grief."

"You've been givin' me grief since the day you were born. But it ain't all your fault. I tend to be overprotective of the women in my life."

"Gee, ya think?"

Her gaze was so open and sweet that he couldn't help but reach out and stroke her cheek. "Smarty-pants."

"I knew from the time I was a little girl that you and Mom had the heart-body-and-soul kind of love everyone dreams of. As I grew up I knew I'd never settle for anything less."

"You didn't."

"I know." Her chin dropped to her chest and her hair hid her face.

"After all this shit happened with Mom, Jack told me what you said to him on our wedding day. That a husband's first priority is always his wife. Period. To love her, cherish her and protect her above all else. That you'd done that for your wife and you expected he'd do the same for me. Even if it went against what you and Mom wanted for me. The bond between parents and children was special. But a bond between husband and wife was sacred."

Keely looked up; those big blue eyes glistened with tears.

"Darlin' girl, I'm hangin' on by a thread here, and your tears do me in almost as quickly as your mother's, so can we talk about something else?"

"Sure." She blew out a long breath. "But it might make you mad."

Fuckin' fantastic. "What now?"

"We—all your kids—planned a huge surprise fiftieth wedding anniversary party for you and Mom next month. We rented out the Sundance community center, hired a band for the big dance. We came up with a killer menu with amazing food because we wanted to do something really special for Mom since she always makes such great meals for all of us."

"That she does."

"We compiled a list of two hundred of your closest family and friends to invite—" she grinned, "—plus we drafted an announcement to put in the paper the weekend before the party, opening the reception up to everyone in town. That's when we planned to tell you so you wouldn't have been caught totally off guard." Her eyes searched his. "Tell me the truth. Did you catch wind of any of this?"

"Hell no." He hated to burst her bubble, but a big damn party was the last thing they wanted to celebrate this milestone in their lives.

"Now, everything has changed. Who knows how long it will take Mom to recover, so we're cancelling it."

"It's disappointing after you put in so much work, but it's the right thing to do." He paused. "Tell you what, keep all them ideas and use 'em for our sixtieth anniversary celebration."

She smiled. "Good plan. Now that's out of the way, can we talk about the medical stuff?"

He nodded.

"When are the docs starting the coma reversal process?"

"I'm meetin' with them sometime today to hear their recommendation."

"You'll keep in touch with me so I can pass on the information?" Keely nudged him. "It'd be easier if you learned to text."

"No, missy, I surely do not need to learn that. If I need to tell you something I'll call ya."

"Stubborn."

"I have no idea what you're talkin' about."

She laughed and leaned over to kiss his cheek.

Carson slammed the tailgate shut. "Should I prepare myself for visits from your brothers?"

Her smile vanished. "Like I said, I don't speak for anyone besides myself. But they need to clear the air with you before you let them see Mom. Not as a stipulation for seeing her, but because they owe you an apology. And we both know Mom will pick up on any bad family vibes. She'll need to concentrate on getting herself better, not worry that her sons have redefined jackass in dealing with you. I'll tell them that if you'd like me to."

"Do what you have to, punkin. Your mom will want to see her sons regardless if they've been pissed off at me or not."

"You'll call? As soon as you know anything?"

"I promise. Give Pipsqueak and Katie-bug a hug from me. Same for JJ and LC." He was the only one who called Liam LC, but the boy was his namesake, so he was entitled.

"I will. Love you Daddy."

"Love you too, Keely girl."

His appetite had disappeared so he skipped the cafeteria and stepped into the elevator. He needed to shower and change his clothes but he couldn't get it done in the twenty minutes before he could visit Carolyn again.

He froze inside the ICU waiting room door, seeing Cord gazing out the window.

His son turned toward him. "This is a shitty view."

"Most of the time when I'm staring out I don't see nothin' anyway."

"Wish I coulda heard what you and Keely were talkin' about down there," Cord said.

Carson noticed Cord's hands were jammed in his pockets. An indication of his oldest son's nerves. "That wasn't a bait and switch? Keely talks to me while you sneak up here?"

"Keely don't know I'm here. I was surprised to see she'd shown up at the same damn time."

"She came to apologize."

"I came to apologize too." He blew out a breath. "Straight up, no excuses, Dad, I was an asshole. I don't know what the hell I was thinkin'. It's like I stood outside my body and watched myself reverting to that twenty-something kid who didn't like what you were tellin' me so you had to be wrong. The only reason you were actin' like that was because you had to show us that you still had power over us and weren't—"

"A retired rancher with nothin' better to do than deny my kids access to their mother when she's in a life or death situation?"

Been a long time since he'd seen his son blush, but he did.

"Sounds like we've got some things to talk about. Have a seat."

"Feels like I'm ten years old getting called into your office for some stupid stunt."

"You spent plenty of time on the bench over the years. Not as much as Cam and Carter." Carson lowered into the chair opposite Cord.

"How is Ma?"

"No change. I'm meetin' with the docs today. I imagine they'll start bringing her out of it in the next twenty-four hours."

"She's..." Cord closed his eyes. "Fuck. I can't imagine how you've held it together."

"Who says I have? I'm a fuckin' mess."

"Not that I've known since I haven't been around to offer any support. None of us have." Cord looked at him with anguished eyes. "The worst part is when I hear Mom's voice in my head: *I raised you better than this, Cord West McKay. Your father needs you.* Jesus. You've been there every goddamned time I've needed you. Even sometimes when I haven't wanted your help. And when you need me—you need us—you're forced to go it alone. How in the hell are you ever gonna forgive us?"

"I'da been alone in this even if you'd all been here. In some ways, this was my choice." He raked a hand through his hair. "Look. I ain't one for that psycho-babble crap, but I think there's more to how you reacted than you wanna admit. Yeah, I know you're scared for your mother. I know you're scared for your kid. Ky is bucking your authority, so the way you deal with it is by bucking mine."

"That's the definition of mature," he said dryly. "Ky said he talked to you. You told him that he needed to ask me about when I up and moved to Seattle. Did you really admit to him that you'd handled the situation wrong?"

"I told you I was in the wrong back then and I'm tellin' you now. You were right to go but it was hell when you left. I swore I'd never do to my kids what my dad done to me. But I did it to you. And because I'm a stubborn fool, I didn't learn my lesson, I did the same thing to Colt."

Cord rubbed the back of his neck. "What goes around, comes around, huh?"

"Yep. So I'm askin' you to be the bigger man and the better father. Don't make the same mistake with Ky that I made with you."

"What if he goes off to college and he doesn't ever come back here?"

There was the real fear and Carson remembered it clearly. "You'll survive. We did with Carter. I miss seeing him as often as I do you kids that live around here, but we keep in touch. Carter is doin' what he's meant to do. Ky will too. You'll find a way to deal with it. For now, let him decide where he wants to spend his college years. Your job is to enjoy the time you've got left with him here. And I will point out that you *did* come back."

Cord sighed. "When did you get so damn smart?"

"Learned it the hard way after years of bein' stupid."

He laughed. "I resemble that remark. You gonna tell Ma that I was a total dick to you?"

"I ain't gonna lie to her. She'll find out, but it won't be the first thing I tell her. And it shouldn't be the first thing none of you tell her neither."

"I ain't here only on my own behalf. Colby plans on comin' by in a few hours. As does Cam when he gets off shift. I don't know about Colt and Carter."

Probably wasn't the best time to tell Cord he'd talked to Colt and Carter the past two days. He'd never played favorites with his kids; there were just times when he had closer connections with some than others. This was one of those times.

"You will call us?" Cord prompted.

"As soon as she's awake."

Cord stood in front of him. "Give me a hug, old man."

They did the back slapping, man-hug thing and it was all good.

Chapter Thirty-One

Hospital, Day 7—late afternoon

The doctors approached Carson in the ICU waiting room twenty-four hours after he'd last spoken with them.

"I hope you're here with good news."

"Yes. The swelling is down and her EEG is within the normal range. The wound on the back of her head has healed quicker than we expected. We've determined it's time to bring her out."

Carson bowed his head and said a silent prayer of thanks.

"There are a few things you need to be aware of as she becomes conscious."

His head snapped up. "What?"

"She will be confused. Possibly agitated. She will have memory lapses."

"You told me this was the safest course of treatment for her and now you're tellin' me when she wakes up she might not remember..." Jesus. What if Carolyn opened her eyes and looked at him like he was a stranger?

His lunch threatened to come back up.

"Mr. McKay, this was the safest course of treatment. Any treatment has risks. But the memory lapse I'm speaking of is related to the day of the injury itself."

"So she won't look at me and not know who the hell I am?"

"Highly unlikely." Dr. McMillan leaned forward. "She will be very disoriented immediately upon waking. Some patients are angry, some are frustrated, some don't speak at all and remain in that dazed state for days. Other patients can't separate hallucinations from reality; unfortunately nightmares can sometimes be a side effect of being sedated with that particular cocktail of pharmaceuticals."

He froze. "You mean she might've been havin' nightmares the entire time she was under?"

Dr. Vincent nodded. "Before you start ripping into us, there is no way for us to accurately predict how this procedure will affect each individual."

"I've had follow up visits with patients who remember absolutely nothing of their time in the coma; they literally thought they'd been asleep for a few hours. And others who recall exactly what people said while speaking to them. And other patients who can recite specific medical progress and problems from physician's conversations."

"Which is why we're very careful to never speak negatively in front of the patient and never assume they cannot hear us," Dr. Vincent added.

"So she ain't outta the woods yet."

"Yes. And no. Yes, meaning we've successfully eliminated the swelling in her brain as intended. No, because your wife will have several days of recovery here at the hospital before she starts other forms of therapy. After a week of zero physical activity she will experience muscle weakness. Most likely she'll be hungry but eating might make her nauseous at first. We'll monitor her lung function very closely for signs of infection. She may be afraid to go to sleep. She may exhibit manic behavior. Happy one minute; crying or yelling the next. The most important thing you need to remember, Mr. McKay, is patience. But do not ignore or discount anything she tells you, even if it sounds bizarre. This has been a traumatic experience for you, but it's even more so for her."

Carson rubbed the back of his neck. "She'll need physical therapy?"

"It'll depend, but it's usually recommended. She might also need speech therapy. We can't be sure if she sustained any permanent damage in those cognitive areas due to the swelling until she's awake."

"How long will it take to wake her up?"

"Again, it depends. After we remove the ventilator and put her on oxygen, I've seen a person come out of it in as little as six hours."

Carson noticed he didn't give an estimate on a longer amount of time. "Can I be in the room with her?"

"Yes, as long as you understand that when she regains consciousness the medical team will have necessary assessment procedures to complete and you cannot interfere in any way."

"I ain't gonna get in anyone's way. I just...need to be there with her when she wakes up."

"Understood. We'll get this underway and the ICU nurse will keep you abreast of every step."

"I appreciate it."

Carson watched the doctors leave, conferring in low tones. He probably should let his kids know where they were in this process, but he couldn't deal with the questions he didn't have answers to until Carolyn actually woke up. And if she woke up confused and irritated... He didn't think their first interaction with their mother should be when she didn't have any idea what was going on.

The better plan was to wait to tell them.

He was fucking sick and tired of waiting. He wanted his wife—and his life back.

The staff had brought a chair into Carolyn's room. Like before, every hour he spoke to her, urging her to come back to him.

The first time she moved her hand, his heart leapt.

The first time her eyelids twitched, his entire body thrummed with anticipation.

Not long now.

Although the six hours he'd been sitting in the chair seemed like another six days.

At hour eight there was a flurry of activity, nurses coming into the room. They blocked the bed so he couldn't see. It took every ounce of control not to jump up and demand to know what the hell they were doing.

Then he heard it.

Carolyn's voice.

And nothing could've stopped him from going to her side.

Nothing.

He saw her eyes were open.

The nurse asked questions but Carolyn was too confused to answer. Agitated, she shook her head and winced.

When she noticed him, she blinked. The confusion remained in her eyes.

"Hey, sugar." He reached for her hand and kissed the tips of her fingers. "I've missed you like crazy."

Her hoarsely whispered, "Carson?" was the single most potent word he'd ever heard.

He let his tears fall, unable to make his vocal cords function, but also unable to stop smiling.

The nurses gently shunted him aside while still allowing him to hold her hand.

She asked for water. She asked to sit up.

He caught her wild-eyed gaze zipping around the room as she sipped from a straw. She lifted her other arm and tried to make a fist. When she could barely do it, she dropped her hand back in her lap. "How long have I been here?" she asked the nurse.

"Seven days."

"I've been lying in bed like a vegetable for a week?"

"You've been in a medically induced state of suspension while your body healed from your injury, ma'am."

That was PC.

"I need..." Carolyn became very frustrated when she couldn't verbalize her needs. She said, "I hate this," to no one in particular.

"It'll get better," the nurse assured her.

"I feel disgusting. I want a shower."

"The best I can offer you until you're more stable is a sponge bath."

Carolyn squeezed her eyes shut.

Carson saw her humiliation. As much as he didn't want to leave her side, he had to. She needed to feel like herself and have some control. "Sugar, if these ladies are bathing you, I'll step out for bit."

Her eyes flew open. "Don't go. Please."

He kissed her fingertips again. "I ain't goin' far. I brought a bag of your beauty stuff from home. I'll send it in with the nurses. It'll make you feel a little more you, okay?"

She didn't look convinced.

"I promise I'll be right outside." He spoke to the nurse. "It won't take you long to get her beautified, 'cause she's always beautiful, but how long do you expect you'll need?"

"An hour? If it goes quicker I'll track you down."

"I'll be in the waitin' room. Where I've been for the past seven days."

Walking out of the room was harder than he'd imagined. He needed a damn cigarette. Instead, he cleaned himself up. Although it was almost one in the morning, he started making phone calls. He could've just called Keely or Kimi and had them pass on the news, but after the tension of the last week, his kids needed to hear directly from him. The fairest way to do it was by birth order. He promised he'd call as soon as the doctors cleared her for visitation.

At the fifty-nine minute mark, Carson returned to her room.

The nurse was massaging Carolyn's calves. They'd changed her hospital gown. She was still on oxygen. She sipped from a mug and a tray with toast and Jell-O sat on her adjustable table.

She blinked at him, her face blank. Then something clicked and she offered him a soft smile. "You're back."

"I told ya I'd be."

"Man of your word," she murmured.

"Always."

The nurse adjusted the blanket over Carolyn's lower half. "If you need anything, please hit the call button. But you should be aware that we'll be coming in every thirty minutes to check on you."

"Thanks."

Then they were truly alone for the first time in a week.

Carson moved to the head of the bed. He framed Carolyn's face in his hands. Before he said a word, he kissed her. Softly at first since he wasn't sure if her mouth hurt from the ventilator tube. She tasted of toothpaste. She tasted like home.

She circled her hands around his wrists and held onto him.

More tears fell. His. Hers.

He kept the kiss easy and sweet. Then he rested his forehead to hers. "I love you. More than anything in this world."

"I know. I love you too."

"Thank you for comin' back to me." He kissed the corners of her mouth, tasting salty tears. "I was so goddamned scared you wouldn't." Shit. Should he have admitted that?

Carolyn pushed on his wrists so she could look into his eyes. "I heard you talking to me."

"You did?"

"Yes. Every time I heard your voice I surfaced from wherever my subconscious was. You talking about your memories of us kicked me into mine. But then..." Tears spilled out the corners of her eyes. "I wasn't sure if any of it was real."

"Any of what?"

"Our life together. If I'd imagined it. If I'd somehow died and found a level of hell where hearing your voice reminded me of what I wouldn't have again. I'd be lost forever floating in nothingness."

He kissed her palm. "I'm here. This is real. We're real. Been the real deal for fifty years."

"Thank God." She slumped back against the pillows. "Stay with me."

"Try and get me to leave."

After fifteen minutes of silence, it became apparent that not only was she highly uncomfortable, she was very agitated.

"Need something?" he asked casually.

"A different bed. This mattress is lumpy."

Nothing he could do about that.

"It's cold in here. I can see my breath."

"You want another blanket?"

"No. I want them to turn on the heat."

The logical part of his brain answered, "It's summer, heat isn't an option." But the part of him that wanted to soothe her responded with, "Maybe they'll bring you an electric blanket."

"Maybe they should just move me to a different room with a better bed, better ventilation and better food."

Carson leaned over and kissed her pouty mouth. "Have I told you how happy I am that you're complaining about everything?"

"I'm not complaining about everything," she said crossly.

"As long as it ain't me in your crosshairs, I don't care."

"The night is young," she warned. "You could still end up there."

The doctors had mentioned she might be out of sorts for several days and the best way to deal with it wasn't to ignore it. "Sugar. What's goin' on with you?"

"Why didn't you tell me that they'd sheared my head like a sheep's butt? I hate having half a head of hair. They should've shaved me bald." Her annoyance quickly morphed into tears. "I look hideous."

"No, you look beautiful and alive."

"I want it gone."

"What?"

More tears fell. "My hair. What's left of it."

"You sure?"

She nodded.

"I thought you might. I already talked to India about comin' in and helping you—"

"Absolutely not, Carson. No one can see me like this. Do you understand? No one." She cried harder.

Shit. "You want me to get the nurse?"

"No. You're the only one I trust to do it."

"Wait. You want *me* to trim your hair?"

"You used to give the boys haircuts." She closed her eyes again. "It's mortifying that I'm so weak I can't hold my head up."

"Good thing you've got me here to hold you up." He pushed the nurse's call button.

Nurse Lissa hustled into the room. "You rang?"

"Can you find a set of hair clippers? She'd like me to fix the chop job."

"I'm not sure what protocol is on that, so I'll check and get back to you."

"They'll say no," Carolyn said in a voice devoid of hope after the nurse left the room.

"You don't know that."

"Don't yell at me."

"I'm not." He counted to ten. "Why would I yell at you?"

"Because I'm acting crazy."

He chuckled. "Sugar, I survived six pregnancies with you. I remember them crazy times very well. So open them pretty blue eyes and gaze at me adoringly like you're prone to. That's how I'll know for sure you're you."

That earned him her first smile. "Cocky cowboy."

Nurse Lissa returned with an orderly pushing a wheelchair. "You're cleared to do this with my supervision but we can't do it in here. Brian and I will get you in the wheelchair."

Carson hung back.

They wheeled her into a small lab-looking room. After replacing the dressing on the back of her head, Nurse Lissa fastened a hair salon style cape around Carolyn's shoulders.

"Sugar, you sure this is what you want?"

"Positive."

He adjusted the guard on the clippers. "Ready?"

"Just do it."

He hoped she hadn't noticed how bad his hands shook as he gave her a buzz cut. He really hoped she hadn't seen his tears rolling down his cheeks as chunks of her beautiful blonde hair hit the floor. "There. Take a look."

She squinted in the hand mirror. "Mona at 'Hair It Is' doesn't need to worry that I've found a new stylist, but it looks better." Her fearful eyes met his. "Doesn't it?"

"You always look beautiful to me, Caro. You know that."

"But..."

"No buts."

"The kids—"

"Will be happy to see you. None of us loves you for your hair."

That and a few kisses quelled her tears and her fears.

Back in the room, Carolyn became subdued. Her voice sounded scratchy and he suspected it might be hurting her to talk after having a tube shoved down her throat for a week.

"What else is botherin' you?"

"My head hurts."

"Want me to get the nurse to give you some pain meds?"

She shook her head and winced. Then she closed her eyes. Two big tears rolled down her cheeks.

It would've hurt less if she'd punched him in the chest. Gently, he curled his hands around her face. "Caro. You're killin' me. How long's your head been hurtin'?"

"A while."

"You need to take something for the pain."

Another shake of her head. Another wince.

"Why in the hell..." He remembered the docs had said she might act unreasonable and he had to be the reasonable one. "It'll help you feel better."

"It'll knock me out. Then what if I go back to sleep and this time I don't wake up? I can't take that chance. Ever. I'll live with the pain."

He felt so goddamned helpless. This was another thing the doctors had warned him about: paranoia the coma would come back even when it was damn near medically impossible. He pressed his lips to her forehead. Then he kissed away her tears. "Sugar, look at me."

She opened her eyes.

"I'll ask if they can give you something that'll dull the pain but won't put you out. Okay?"

Her gaze searched his. "Promise me you won't trick me about this?"

"I promise. If they can't guarantee it won't put you under then I won't let you take it."

"Okay."

He brushed his lips over hers. "Be right back."

Five minutes later he trailed into the room behind Lissa. She piggy-backed a clear packet of liquid onto her IV. "This will help."

"Good. She needs it." Carson lowered the bedrail so he could move in closer. He stroked her head. Something about that stubble...he couldn't stop touching it. He couldn't stop touching her.

"That feels nice."

"Anything else I can do?"

"Since I'm pretty sure the meds will knock me out even when they swore they don't, I want your promise that you'll sleep with me."

"Much as I can't wait to get my hands on you, think about what you and me goin' at it does to your heart rate. You want the nurses to see that on the monitor and race in here and see my ass in the air as I'm bouncing on you?"

"Even when I'm decrepit in a hospital bed, with bad hair and a bad attitude, you're scheming to nail me." She smiled softly. "It's good to be me. But I'm serious. I want to sleep in your arms tonight, Carson. I'm never scared when I'm with you."

He stroked her cheek. "Did you have nightmares while you were under?"

"Only that I'd never find my way back to you."

"You did." He kissed her cheek. "Make room for me while I get undressed."

Lissa, the night nurse...

Lissa hadn't been in to check on Carolyn McKay for forty-five minutes. She'd gotten sidetracked but the monitor readings were normal so she wasn't worried. As she entered the room she was making a mental checklist of all the things she needed to accomplish before shift change so she didn't notice them at first.

But when she reached the foot of the bed she stopped and stared.

At some point in the last hour, Carson McKay had crawled into the hospital bed with his wife. The gruff rancher, always decked out in boots, jeans and a long sleeved western shirt, at all hours of the day or night, had donned a hospital gown and a pair of flannel pants. His bare feet stuck out the end of the bed, but she could see beneath the blanket his legs were entwined with Carolyn's.

Carolyn had curled into him, resting her head on his chest, her left hand clasped in his right. He'd draped his left arm across her back and palmed her butt. The posture couldn't have been more intimate even if they'd been naked.

Feeling intrusive, Lissa backed out of the room until her shoulders hit the wall. She couldn't stop the tears.

Justine, the other night nurse was right there. "Lissa? What's wrong?"

"Nothing. Everything is right."

"Then why are you crying?"

Lissa gestured to the room with her head. "I've been taking care of her for a week and watching him. It broke my heart because he was just so...lost without her. Now watching them together? That's the first time I've ever really seen the I-can't-live-without-you kind of love that everyone talks about. They have it. They've had it for half a century." She sniffled. "Now they're wrapped up in each other's arms, sleeping in that small bed, because they couldn't bear to spend another night apart. I can't imagine loving someone that much." She glanced through the doorway to the room. "I want that. I want a man who will be by my side for the next fifty years. I'm done settling for good enough."

"Good for you. But you know him sleeping in ICU is against the rules."

"Her vitals have improved in the last hour and that's all that matters, right?"

"Right."

"Let them be. After all they've been through they deserve this."

Chapter Thirty-Two

Carolyn didn't know why she was nervous to see her own kids. She'd birthed them, nursed them, raised them and cherished them. She'd let them go when they started families of their own.

Everything was so disjointed.

She still didn't feel like herself.

She'd lost a week of her life.

A week in which she'd relived her life-long love affair with Carson McKay.

Part of her feared this hospital scene was just another memory. That she was dying and this was her life flashing before her eyes.

Upon waking in Carson's arms in the small hospital bed, she'd been hit with the dizzying sensation of being plucked out of the void of her mind and shoved into a memory.

She'd panicked and fought against it.

No! I want to stay here, in this time.

Evidently her reaction had sent her heart rate soaring. The nurses burst into her room to see why their monitor screen had gone crazy.

That's when they'd kicked Carson out of her bed, but he'd refused to leave her room. He'd insisted the doctors check her out thoroughly. Immediately. The stubborn man made a real nuisance of himself until he got his way.

Speaking with her doctors didn't alleviate her anxiety. They'd performed a complete examination on her—physical and psychological—that took an eternity. Some of the questions they asked her didn't make sense. But she wondered if that was part of the test—if she could differentiate between gibberish and jabberish.

Was jabberish even a word? But that's what some of the tests they'd given her had looked like. Gibber-jabber.

She'd drifted in and out as they'd awaited the test results. Finally the doctors had declared her on track to recovery.

Except...the doctors had taken Carson out of the room and spoke to him out of earshot. She'd been a little pissy about that. It was her brain. If there were problems with it she deserved to know.

When the staff delivered her food, she managed to eat half of it, despite the fact it had zero flavor. She stared at the evening dinner menu choices, but again the words on the page were a jumbled mess. She'd have to ask Carson to find her reading glasses.

The therapist forced her to walk around. Moving about had buoyed her spirits even when she'd kept a snail's pace up and down the hallway.

Carson hadn't complained. He'd just hovered. Encouraged her. Held her up when her body and her will had started to falter.

Exhausted and sore from working her muscles after a week of no activity, she returned to her room. But her fear about getting lost in sleep kicked in again. She couldn't breathe, she couldn't think, she couldn't settle down until Carson climbed in bed with her.

Luckily she'd slept without dreams.

But again she woke in a panic.

Carson calmed her down before the nurses barreled in. "Hey, sugar. Listen to me. If something doesn't feel right, you need to tell someone. If you're havin' headaches or hallucinations or you're feelin' paranoid, some of that is a normal reaction as the drugs are getting washed out of your system. Don't be embarrassed. Don't try and hide it. The doctors can't help your recovery process if they don't know what they're dealin' with."

She closed her eyes and nestled her face in his neck. "I'm scared."

Carson didn't say anything; he just trailed his fingers up and down her spine.

After a bit she began to talk. Then it all spewed out, in a fragmented mess. Her emotions were all over the place.

"Did that help?"

"Just being with you helps."

"Mmm. I love the sweet talkin' side of you." He traced her jawline with his thumb. "You know you can tell me anything, but you oughta rethink your stance on talkin' to the lady psychologist because I think she can help you."

She frowned. "What stance?"

"You told her you didn't need her help."

"I don't remember." Another memory lapse. How many had she had since she came out of the coma? Two? Three? A dozen? "Was I rude to her?"

Carson shrugged. "I'm sure she's used to patients tellin' her to get the hell out of their rooms and to never come back."

Her stomach roiled. "I *said* that?"

"It wasn't like you made her cry or nothin'."

Carolyn wanted to cry. "Am I going through one of those personality changes? Where I was a nice woman and after bein' in a coma I become a total asshole?"

"Hey, it was one incident. You're entitled to a little bad behavior after what you've been through. Don't get yourself riled up."

"Too late."

"Sugar, just breathe, okay?"

"I can't. I'm suffocating."

He kissed her then, a sweet distraction. Soft smooches and the gentle brush of his lips across hers, the tease of his breath mingling with hers while his thumb continued to caress her face with utmost tenderness.

It settled her. It soothed her. She curled into him. His heart beat steadily beneath her ear. His outdoorsy scent filled her senses."What time are the kids coming?"

"Whenever you're feelin' up to it. No rush."

Carolyn lifted her head from his chest. "I thought they were all fired up to see me since you kept them out of ICU for the past week."

"They are very anxious to see you. But they were also warned you might have a setback the first couple of days, so they're on standby."

"Setback? I haven't had a setback."

The look in his eyes contradicted her statement. "Answer me this. How long have you been out of the coma?"

"Not even twenty-four hours."

He shook his head. "It's been forty-eight hours."

Time confusion in the first couple days is an aftereffect for coma patients, the doctors had assured her.

"You were agitated by the pain, so they had to sedate you and keep you in ICU."

"It's a blur."

"It'll get better."

"You're sure?"

"No, but whatever happens, Caro, we'll deal with it together."

"I hate that I put you through this."

"Just another bump in the road. We've had a few of 'em the past fifty years."

Later that day Carolyn felt a million times better after they let her shower. It was such a shock to see her hair buzzed almost to her scalp. Carson already said he was used to it and he liked it. Then he'd gone into great detail about all the places on his body he couldn't wait to feel her rubbing that short hair.

If the thought of that man's wicked mouth and skilled hands all over her didn't speed up her recovery process and her desire to go home, nothing would.

Carson had summoned their kids. She'd debated putting on makeup so as to not scare them, but nothing would hide the pallor of the last week so she opted to let her age show.

She was wired as she waited. Carson sat beside her on a tall chair, his hands in near constant motion. Seemed he had a case of nerves too.

The door opened and her children filed in, lined up by birth order like she used to demand whenever they were in trouble. No surprise they still knew how to do it.

Carson's hand tightened on hers. His mouth brushed her ear. "Any time this is too much, let me know and I'll kick 'em out."

"I always make you the bad guy, don't I?"

"No reason for us to change that now."

Her gaze started with Cord, who gripped a bouquet of flowers from her garden. Then she focused on Colby. His hair held more gray streaks than Cord's. Her gaze moved to Colt. Still the image of his handsome father, down to his dimpled grin. Cam, her burly boy, wept openly. He'd clamped his hand on Carter's shoulder, as if his little brother was holding him up. Then she noticed somber-eyed Carter also clasped Keely's hand. Tears streamed down her daughter's cheeks.

None of them said a word.

She cleared her throat. "What a fine looking bunch." And because she was feeling ornery, and because these hellions had played numerous pranks on her over the years, she kept a confused look on her face, and said, "Who are all of you again?"

The room, already silent, went deadly still. The kids exchanged bewildered looks with each other. Then they looked at Carson. And finally at her.

Just as Cord opened his mouth to speak, Carolyn smiled and said, "Just kidding."

"Jesus, Ma, that was mean," Cam complained.

"Really mean," Carter added.

She flapped her hand at them. "Oh pooh, you all deserved that and you damn well know it."

Colt grinned. "And you're swearing at us? Now I know you had a head injury."

Silence.

Then Colt said, "Ah, too soon?"

"Ya think, asshole?" Colby shoved him.

Cord elbowed Colby. "Knock it off, you two."

Carson sighed. "Some things never change."

"Thank God for that." Carolyn held her arms open. "Well, kids, come here and give me hugs. Then tell me everything I missed in the past week."

They gathered around, pushing each other out of the way to be the first in line.

Then they all started talking at once.

She turned her head and looked at Carson.

He gifted her with that dimpled grin and mouthed *I love you.*

That's when her topsy-turvy world righted itself.

This chaos was her life and she wouldn't have it any other way.

Epilogue

Ten years later...

"See that silver-haired fox over there?" Carson said to Cal. "She's comin' home with me tonight."

"You sure? That guy in the three-piece suit in the corner is eyeballin' her. Looks like he's gonna make a move soon." Cal chuckled. "Of course, he'd have to get up and outta that wheelchair first."

"Don't care if he's in a wheelchair. He puts a hand on her and I'll beat his wrinkled ass."

Cal snorted. "Good thing you're carryin' around a cane, old man. Your brawlin' days have been over for a long damn time."

"Piss off. That woman has been mine for sixty years. I ain't ever gonna be too old to fight for her."

Carolyn threw her head back and laughed at something Kyler said. She was holding someone's baby but there were so many kids around that he couldn't keep track of which ones belonged to whom.

"She is still something, all right," Carson said to Cal, never taking his eyes off his wife.

"Yep. Think she's got a sister?"

"I've heard that little whip of a thing is mouthy. Think you can handle her?"

"Been doin' my level best to handle that spitfire for the past fifty-three years," Cal said dryly. "Give me another ten years or so and I might have it figured out."

Carson grinned. "Been a helluva ride, bein' married to the West sisters."

"Got that right." Cal lifted his bottle for a toast. "Best thing I ever did was drag your ass to the dancehall that night."

He raised his bottle and touched it to his brother's. "Amen. And if I never said thank you..."

"You did. So how long is this party supposed to last?"

"Hell if I know. That's the good thing about bein' old; no one expects us to stay for the whole thing. They think we're goin' home early and goin' to bed." Which was partially true. He'd be taking his wife home to bed, but they sure wouldn't be sleeping.

Cal snorted and didn't say a word, but he knew what was on his brother's mind, probably because the same thing was on his. "The blonde tornado is givin' me the stink eye so I'd better see what's up."

Carson's gaze remained on Carolyn until she sensed him staring at her.

After passing the baby to Vi, she started toward him.

The background noise and the groups of people faded away and all he saw was her.

Carolyn moved slower now. She looked a little different. After her accident a decade ago, her hair follicles had sustained damage and her hair had never grown back the right way. He'd expected her vanity would force her into wearing a wig. But she refused and kept her hair in a military crew-cut style. Those once blonde tresses were completely silver. Now she was the very definition of a hot, sexy and hip grandma.

She stopped in front of him.

"You're still the most beautiful woman I've ever seen. How's about we run off together?"

"Does that line usually work for you, cowboy?"

He traced the edge of her jaw. "It did once. Got me what I wanted and it lasted for six glorious decades. So I wanna make sure you're onboard for the next six decades with me."

"Hmm. Well, I might have to think about it... There are pros and cons."

"Such as?"

"The cons? You are still too handsome for your own good. And you'd prefer to answer all challenges with your fists. You still sneak the occasional cigarette. You cuss like a sailor. You drive like an idiot." Carolyn placed her hand on his chest, over his heart. "The pros? You've got a full head of hair and your own teeth. You make me laugh. You set my blood on fire. You are still the best man I've ever known. So, I'll keep you around for a little while longer."

"Whew. I was worried there for a second you might want to upgrade this model for a newer one."

"The training period for a new model is far too long. Besides, they've replaced all your worn out parts."

In the last decade he'd had his other hip replaced and both knees. Most days he felt pretty good. He missed riding. He probably always would.

Carson leaned forward and kissed her. "How's my bride?"

"Been sixty years since I was a blushing bride."

"I can still getcha to blush though."

"That you can, wild man McKay." Carolyn fussed with the buttons on his shirt.

"Something on your mind?"

She looked up at him, worry in her eyes. "Liesl baked the anniversary cake. She used my Aunt Hulda's recipe for the traditional German chocolate butter cake we had at our wedding. She's hounding me to taste it to see if it's authentic. And I don't know what to say."

Another strange effect of Carolyn's accident; she'd lost all sense of taste. She could tell the difference between hot and cold; differentiate textures, but nothing else. After the six-month recovery period, when she attempted to return to daily cooking for them, she'd realized she couldn't cook at all. She had some sort of disconnect in her visual language skills which resulted in difficulty reading and she couldn't follow the most basic recipe.

So at age seventy-five he'd finally learned to cook. The only good thing about that? Since she couldn't taste, she couldn't tell the meals he prepared tasted like shit.

They ate out a lot.

And because cooking had been such a big part of what'd defined her, they'd kept her loss of skills to themselves. Carson told anyone who asked that after fifty years of kitchen duty she'd officially hung up her oven mitts and retired.

He curled his hand around her face. "Liesl is not lookin' for the truth, sugar. She's lookin' for validation from her Gran-gran because she respects the hell out of you. So tell her whatever she did surpassed the original recipe and you don't remember it ever tastin' that good."

"You always know just what to say, silver-tongued devil that you are," she murmured.

"How much longer do we have to stay?"

"Another hour or so. They're doing the whole cake-cutting thing and first dance thing, which is weird because we didn't have either of those things at our wedding. I doubt they're expecting us to stick around after that."

"Good. I have plans for us." He brushed an openmouthed kiss at the base of her neck. "Nekkid plans that include you, me, our hot tub and a bottle of bubbly."

She laughed. "You really believe that hot tub is the fountain of youth, don't you?"

"Yep. Makes me feel twenty years younger."

"Lord, crazy man, I love you. You really will be chasing me around when you're a hundred and five, won't you?"

Carson smiled. "Count on it."

About the Author

Lorelei James is the *New York Times* and *USA TODAY* bestselling author of contemporary erotic western romances set in the modern day Wild West and also contemporary erotic romances. Lorelei's books have been nominated for and won the *RT Book Reviews* Reviewer's Choice Award as well as the CAPA Award. Lorelei lives in western South Dakota with her family...and a whole closet full of cowgirl boots.

Connect with Lorelei James:

on Facebook: www.facebook.com/LoreleiJamesAuthor

on Twitter: @loreleijames

email: lorelei@loreleijames.com

website: www.loreleijames.com

When good, clean fun just isn't an option.

Dirty Deeds
© *2014 Lorelei James*

Just once, good girl Tate Cross wants to experience a red-hot, no-strings-attached affair. She's temporarily left her graphic artist position in Denver to settle her aunt's estate in Spearfish, South Dakota, but the city won't let her sell the property until the landscaping is up to snuff. The Native American landscape contractor her friend highly recommends looks like he can meet all her needs, in the flowerbed and out.

Nathan LeBeau believes few women look at the Native American man beneath the filthy work clothes and hard hat. When Tate offers to trade art lessons for dirt work, the tempting subtext is as plain as the lettering on the side of Nathan's truck. But in truth, he's tired of relationships based solely on sex. His goal of proving he's not completely hopeless in matters of the heart is second only to his dream of expanding his business.

It figures. Tate wants no-holds-barred sex right about the time the one-time Casanova wants a good old-fashioned romance. Bring on the battle of wills!

Warning: A reformed bad boy who wants a taste of real love, and a good girl who wants just one taste of the wild side—and she's willing to drive a *hard* bargain to get what she wants.

Available now in ebook and print from Samhain Publishing.

SAMHAIN
PUBLISHING

It's all about the story...

Romance

HORROR

Retro
ROMANCE

www.samhainpublishing.com

CPSIA information can be obtained at www.ICGtesting.com
Printed in the USA
BVOW07s1233250215

389225BV00001B/305/P